THE BEASTLY BEAUTY
The Enchanted Castle Archives Book 2

Michelle L. Levigne

www.YeOldeDragonBooks.com

Ye Olde Dragon Books
6909 Ackley Rd.
Parma, OH 44129

www.YeOldeDragonBooks.com

2OldeDragons@gmail.com

ISBN 13: 978-1-961129-30-6

Published in the United States of America
Publication Date: April 1, 2024

CHAPTER ONE

Ash went to bed her first night in Filby's home with her head spinning. Common sense said she couldn't take every opportunity the half-Fae woman offered her. She needed time to examine everything she and her hostess and the spirit ring had discussed that evening before she could even begin to start narrowing down her plans.

The next morning, the housekeeping breeze prepared her a bath scented with lemons. Ash took the bath, just because she had had to do without regular washing for so long. The utter luxury of all the hot water she wanted and scented soap and thick towels soothed something inside her that had given off little whimpers of resentment for years. She speculated it came from pretending to be a boy for so long.

A mirror floated into the bathing room and settled on a table that hadn't been there when she climbed into the tub. Ash approached it hesitantly. She wiped away steam with her towel, and sputtered laughter at her first glimpse of herself. Her dripping curls and thin face and big eyes reminded her of a kitten at Castle Fairhold that kept jumping into the mill pond to chase fish. She and Dunstan had spent quite a few days rescuing that kitten, in the glory days before he started growing and she no longer could pass as his double and decoy.

Ash stepped back, to really study herself. She wasn't going to need those breastbands she had found in the magical basket of clothes. Not for a few more months. Had her travels, her brushes with danger and going hungry for days slowed her blossoming?

She turned, trying to get a good look at her backside. The star on her bottom didn't seem any bigger than when she had first seen it years ago. She couldn't be sure if it was glowing, though it did have a pearly sheen. The star over her breastbone looked the same. What did that say about the magic that filled Filby's house?

Brisk toweling didn't do much to flatten her dark curls. Ash fussed with a brush for a short time, trying to arrange her hair instead of just raking it out of her eyes. She considered letting her hair grow until it was as long as Filby's thick, glossy silver mane, and braiding it with ribbons. A chuckle escaped her, when she realized how much time she had spent examining herself in the mirror.

"Ring, am I being vain? Silly?" She turned away from the mirror and reached for the clothes the housekeeping breeze had picked out for her.

Deep blue broadcloth trousers embroidered with silver vines along the seams and hems, a matching shirt, a pale lavender vest with several pockets on each side, embroidered in gryphons, unicorns, and dragons cavorting among trees loaded with jewel-toned fruit.

No, the spirit ring responded after a moment. *But you are wasting precious lesson time. You aren't being vain. You're slowly awakening to the person you can be.*

"I do hope she finds that spell to allow you to stay with me once I've completed the quest. What would I do without you, to speak common sense and teach me wisdom?"

Like any good parent, my lady, I look forward to the day you don't need me, but still want me around.

"Always!"

Filby looked like she had just sat down to breakfast, when Ash stepped out of the pocket of magic holding her bedroom, and into the sprawling living area at the back of the hostler's warehouse. She tipped her head to one side and smiled as Ash approached the low table with large pillows for seating.

"What do you think, Fang? Isn't our Ashlyn a lovely princess-to-be?"

Ash caught her breath, startled by Filby's words. They had to be teasing. Several discussions with Cecil on the subject raced up from her memories to slam into the front of her head. She would never want to be a princess. There were too many complications, too many evil or simply nastily insane people, and too many magical objects that targeted all royal blood for trouble and uncomfortable adventures.

The maniacal bunny came thumping around from the far end of the table, where he had been indulging in something very red and juicy for breakfast. He wiped at his face and his chest fur in between each hop, until he sat a dozen steps away from Ash, tipping his head from side to side, ears bobbing. A big grin brightened his face and he flung himself at her, to hug her knees.

Ash fought down a single flinch at the thought of all that red juice staining her new clothes.

"Thank you. Both of you. I've never ... well, I've never had a chance or even wanted to look nice before." Ash self-consciously raked a few curls out of her face and settled down on the thick pillow in front of the plate and cup and utensils set out for her, next to Filby.

This morning, breakfast filled a half-dozen platters and bowls and two pitchers, one of which steamed. Nothing like the amazing bounty last night that could have fed all of Castle Fairhold. Muffins, creamy butter, blackberry preserves, and a lovely concoction of sausages, eggs, and cheese were more than enough. One pitcher had a cold, tangy green juice, and the other held hot, spicy tea.

Ash served herself and ate while Filby laid out the proposed course of lessons for the day. First, riding and learning the various signals to communicate with the horses of the courier network. The signals ensured that no mounts could be stolen, simply because someone leaped into the saddle and dug their heels in and shouted, "Go." Ash needed to learn the proper care of the horses, and the various codes the couriers used to communicate the conditions in each country they traveled through, whenever they met up with each other. Sometimes, she would need to ride in disguise, because some kingdoms considered Filby's riders to be spies, and refused to accept their oath of honorable behavior.

"Unfortunately, the people least likely to trust others to act with honor are the ones who themselves have no honor." Filby reached for the pitcher of hot tea to refill her cup. "They live by a double standard, demanding total truth and honesty and scrupulous manners from strangers, while justifying cheating and lying to foreigners and strangers. Since they spy and steal and cheat, they expect foreigners to steal and cheat and spy. Three kingdoms hate my couriers because I refuse all errands for their kings, after the way my people were treated. As if I've committed a crime by refusing to put them in danger." Filby's eyes changed to a stormy gray. "I pay gladly for warding spells, so their messages never reach my people, requesting service."

"They still ask, even after you've told them no?" Ash didn't find that surprising, considering some of the officials she had encountered while serving Lady Charlotte.

"Asking isn't within their understanding." Filby's mouth twisted like she couldn't find the right words. Then a chuckle escaped her, as her eyes changed back to their normal violet hue. "When missions are so dire and time-sensitive that going through those kingdoms are unavoidable, I have found it worth the risk to send my people through the enchanted forest."

"But—" Ash shook her head, feeling dizzy with the weight of all the things she had learned about the enchanted forest.

The problem was that much of it was theory. What many people swore were facts contradicted each other. As if every person who went into the forest had a different experience.

"Ah, you've learned enough to think the place is a trap, pulling in the unwary and refusing to let them out again?" Filby gave her a crooked grin before raising her cup to drink.

"No, but making them wait days or even months before letting them out, and usually not to the same kingdom."

"True, but my people have a map of the portals. It would be entirely useless to use the enchanted forest to avoid troublesome kingdoms when time is off the essence if they couldn't get in and out quickly."

Ash couldn't remember reading anything about a map of the

enchanted forest. "But doesn't the forest keep changing, the geography, the landmarks, so it's nearly impossible to go to the same place twice?"

"Not exactly. The portals shift. Each portal out of the enchanted forest goes to multiple places in other kingdoms and changes to match those places. So a portal that looks like a gap in a massive, old tree will become a stone archway, then a waterfall curtain, then a cave or a tunnel. Depending on what place it opens into."

"Or a tunnel of roses in snow," Ash murmured.

"What was that?" Filby's eyes narrowed as she studied her.

Cecil the seer had several visions to warn her, before we were forced to move on, the ring said. *Whether she was to avoid the tunnel of roses in snow or go through it was unclear.*

"Hmm, yes, and I've felt for a long time that the guiding spirits have a nasty sense of humor when they send visions to prophets and seers."

"Very nasty," Ash agreed. "Why does it have to hurt seers so much to have visions?"

"To keep them from getting so proud that they are no longer any use to A'theosius." Filby sighed and put down her cup with a thump for punctuation. "Well, with that warning, we must add the enchanted forest and the map to your lessons. And we have very little time as it is. Certainly not as much as I had hoped. I would like to weave a few spells to guide you, but I fear that would be dangerous. Those advisory spells woven into you could be tricky. They're so deeply embedded, they could take offense if more spells are added. Maybe consider them invaders. Just like magic books that have grown so old and filled with magic that they become aware, long-established defensive and advisory spells become somewhat … hmm … proprietary. You belong to them."

"Wait." Ash didn't like the chill alertness that slapped her at Filby's words. "Why don't we have as much time as you hoped?"

I'm sorry, my lady, the ring said. *Circumstances require you to move on and move out as swiftly as possible. I fear part of that is my fault.*

"Not at all, my dear ring." Filby shook her head. The lines of her face sharpened, just for a moment, giving a hint of what she would be like when she was truly angry. "You are as much a victim as Ash of multiple layers of spells woven to disguise and hide and spy. I really must compose a letter of protest to the Enchanters Court, as soon as you two—"

Fang let out a squeal of protest from the far side of the long table.

"Sorry, as soon as the three of you are on the road again. Justiciar Camwell's dishonorable choices, how he has treated you … if I had any influence in Alfordia, I would request your King Ebrosion remove him from his office. In simple terms, he blinded the ring to several layers of spells, making him unaware of various traps I inadvertently triggered when I accessed the spell recording your adventures."

"Traps?" Ash caught her breath, chilled with apprehension and hotly furious at the same time. "Ring, what happened?"

First, Filby knows a great deal about you, even without talking to me and to Fang, because of a hitherto hidden branch of the spell that allows Camwell to keep track of your position and progress. I am rather disturbed to find that I have not after all been able to hide many of your actions, and details like names and faces and information you've learned. This hidden spell Lady Efilbiana tripped reports on your actions and reactions, your emotions, how you interact with people. No need to worry, my lady. I'm proud of you, and again, let me say I am delighted to have been assigned to you.

"Ring ..." She sighed, sensing he was delaying the revelation to soften the impact on her. Well, at least he wasn't saying he was sorry every other time he spoke.

One of the large flaws in this spell is that it broadcasts a report on you to anyone with even a touch of magic. It does somewhat explain the readiness of people to help you. They're being influenced by the report, which proclaims you are worthy of help, and trustworthy. It also explains some of the nastiness you've encountered, such as Magistrate Blosi in River's Edge. Such folk who use magic to cheat go on the offensive when they encounter people with silent reports such as yours. You make them look bad. They need to quash you. Put simply, you're polite and honest. When you are in need, you set out to earn food or shelter or help. You don't plot how to steal or cheat. You notice people in need of help, and you offer help when you can. Need I go on? I must confess I am rather flustered and irritated and incensed over all the nasty discoveries I've been making in the last few hours.

"Very understandable," Filby said. "But please do continue with Ash's answers."

While I believe you would be very happy as a courier, that might not be possible. Those reporting spells are so badly woven, enemies can use them to not only find you, but ensnare you. And you must be freed of them as quickly as possible. Meaning you must end the quest and yes, I fear, risk us being parted. Time is of the essence, for your safety. Lady Efilbiana cannot spend all the time she needs, awakening your magical potential and training it.

"Why can't she? Why can't you?" Ash blurted, turning to Filby. The woman smiled sadly and shook her head.

Well ... accessing that report on your character tripped another spell I wasn't aware of. An alarm, so to speak.

"This is worse than those hunters who came to Cecil's village, isn't it? The justiciar is sending more men after me? Armed with magic?"

Much worse. It appears Lathia and her rather unsavory magicians are convinced that she can't rid herself of her spirit ring until you and I have been separated. Or at least convince Camwell you are dead and the quest is over.

"Traveling all that distance to hunt me down is easier than fulfilling the quest? How hard can it be for those magicians to take her through a few caverns and over a few borders?"

It isn't enough to punish you for all the trouble Lathia believes you caused her. Winning the quest will prove she is in the right and you were wrong all along.

"Of course." Ash needed to wash the foul taste out of her mouth, but when she drank, she nearly choked. Coughing, she put the cup down and wiped her mouth. "I'm so sorry, Filby."

"You are the victim of injustice." Filby patted her shoulder. "Why should you apologize for being truthful and honorable and far more likeable than that arrogant, lying little snot?"

Her exasperated tone startled a gasping little chuckle from Ash. That helped.

It's worse, the ring said. *Time is of the essence, for more than just you, my lady. Lathia has made up quite a story with herself as the victim and you and many higher-ranking servants at Castle Fairhold attacking her out of jealousy.*

"Jealousy of what?" She winced when her voice rang off the plates and pitchers.

Well, now she believes she is the victim of love that never should have happened.

"Oh, ugh, that sounds like an especially sticky ballad, sung out of tune."

That earned a chuckle from Filby.

In rather a warped kind of justice, as Lathia adds to her lies, the magic woven around her by her spirit ring watcher and the spells the magicians are employing to try to free her grow more tangled, dark, and complex. The more she denies and resists the reports of the tattletale spells, the more her own nasty, selfish nature turns in on itself. Rather like distilling spirits, to be especially potent. I feel rather sorry for my friend, who is attached to her until one of you finishes the quest. For the sake of my friend, even if I didn't care quite a lot about you now, I must urge speed in ending the quest.

"Of course. But … will all those tangled spells you didn't know about interfere with … Filby, you said you'd try to find a way to keep the ring with me, after the quest ended. Can you do that, or is that one of those things we can't take care of, because I need to leave soon?"

"I'm working on it," Filby said, and patted her shoulder again.

Ashy had the awful feeling she was going to come to resent that encouraging, comforting touch, just as much has she resented the ring saying he was sorry.

Now, Lathia thoroughly believes she was in love with a handsome young servant, and was too shy and delicate to let him know. She didn't want to make him distraught over the obstacles to their happiness.

"Oh, ugh. There's that sticky ballad again," she muttered.

Indeed. The ring snorted in amusement. *You discovered her love for him through foul magical means, with the help of Hazel, the hedge witch. You, of course, were jealous because he rejected you. To embarrass her, you and several servants gave her love notes, supposedly from him, and promised to deliver her love notes to him. She was supposed to meet him in the library, to make plans to run off together. You went to the library to mock her, and she flung herself at you, believing you were her sweetheart.*

"She actually believes this, doesn't she?"

Worse. Her prince has put a bounty on your head, and on the servants involved. Especially the young man she secretly loved. Out of jealousy, as hard as that is to believe.

"And your friend has been able to tell you all this because Lathia still hasn't figured out that she's listening to everything she says and thinks. Even worse, those magicians haven't figured out what the ring can do, and haven't detected all those nasty extra spying spells, either. What use are they?" Ash wished she could laugh, but feared laughter would turn into hysterical tears. "This feels like a particularly wretched story that was a total waste of the paper and ink used to record it."

Indeed. The ring chuckled.

"So what do we do?" She shook her head. "I know what I need to do. Return to Fairhold to warn them. Which servants did Lathia accuse?"

"It's worse than that," Filby said. "She's implicated Lady Charlotte and Dunstan, several kitchen workers, your Granny Phlox, and Hazel the hedge witch. Lathia's prince has a magic mirror to communicate with the magicians and give them new information. And new pieces of Lathia's growing delusion of lies, to motivate them. They're a nasty group of self-righteous vigilantes, out to protect the world from the wrong kind of magic. They call themselves the Purple Sky."

"Why?"

They don't even know, the ring said with a snort of disgust.

"Some of my couriers have encountered them. They've tried to confiscate mirrors and defensive talismans, claiming A'theosious gave them authority to decide who is allowed to work magic." Filby shook her head. "That is neither here nor there. All you need to know is that if you see a purple tinge to the air, or a purple whirlwind coming toward you, run and pray A'theosious's protection."

Tell her the newest lie, the ring said. *This is why time is so vital.*

"Oh, yes." Again, the violet of Filby's eyes flickered into stormy gray, just for a moment. "Just this morning, Lathia pretended to be ill from a deluge of memories, freed from a spell that had blocked them. Now she insists she is a side victim of a terrible plot to keep her father from inheriting several large estates. The magicians are to ensure that those properties be turned over to Lord Winston before they return to Marcocia. Starting with Castle Fairhold."

Ash's insides seemed to congeal into ice. Lathia's father, Lord Winston, was a relative on Lady Charlotte's side of the family. She was lady of Castle Fairhold through marriage, not through inheritance. Winston had no legal claims whatsoever on any of the Fairhold properties. Obviously, that didn't matter to Lathia in what was clearly a plot to punish everyone who had ever criticized her or mocked her or told her no.

Common sense said to warn Castle Fairhold. Filby would send warnings by several couriers who would be passing by or passing through Alfordia, but they would only be a few days ahead of Ash, at best. She had tried to send warning through the mirror web, but the Purple Sky magicians had the help of several high-level mirrors at the main communication nodes in the web, searching for and reporting on any messages going to mirrors near Castle Fairhold. Filby had already spent some time before breakfast sending reports to the overseer mirrors, to try to resolve the problem, but that would take time. Mirrors were tangled in bureaucracy worse than most governments. She feared that the mirrors involved had already reported to the Purple Sky magicians, giving them more clues to track down Ash's location. Even more reason to get her out on the road as quickly as possible.

The ring could communicate with Justiciar Camwell directly if the information was vital to the quest. Lathia's plot did indeed have much to do with the quest, since the justiciar was near the top of her list of enemies and persecutors. However, when the ring tried to send the warning that morning, he found a message waiting for him. Camwell refused to listen to him about anything except the objects and goals of the quest.

The justiciar says I must learn discipline, to avoid falling victim to the blandishments of those with questionable ethical character.

"Oh, he did, did he?" Filby said. That glitter in her eyes wasn't humor. Ash shivered, getting a glimpse of the strength and resoluteness of her new patron. "Well, let his doom fall on his head. We will do what is right and continue to warn him, but we are guiltless if he is taken by surprise."

CHAPTER TWO

Forgive me, Lady Efilbiana, the ring began.

"Oh, please!" She chuckled. "I fully sympathize with Ash, when your insistence on formality becomes so irritating."

Lady Filby, he corrected. *If Lathia's minions reach the justiciar before they attack Castle Fairhold, they could confiscate quite a large number of magical items. Including more than a dozen spirit rings. They could then use the justiciar's spells that bind all the items together, and combine their strength and talents into a potent, potentially disastrous weapon.*

"I need to get to Castle Fairhold as quickly as possible," Ash said. "Once they're warned, they can call on others with magic to deal with and hopefully defend the justiciar. At least, I think so."

"You'll be racing into a trap." Filby clasped the girl's hands between her own, to emphasize her words. "You need preparation. I have the means to slow the flow of time to compress weeks of learning into a few days, but it will not be pleasant. Those who step into time pools become susceptible to falling into more such pools, until they become completely untethered from time's normal flow. Are you willing to face that risk?"

"Fairhold is my home, my friends, the only family I've ever had." Ash took a few deep breaths to still the shaking deep inside.

"May the Maker reward you for your loyalty." The woman leaned forward and kissed the girl's forehead.

The brief touch tingled sharply, just like the stars on her breastbone and buttocks did when she encountered strong magic. Ash flinched when those stars burned a moment later.

"Huh ..." Filby sat back, eyes narrowing. "That isn't ..."

It isn't good, the ring finished for her.

"Why? What?" Ash pressed her hand against the spot.

"We have been working on tracking all those spells wrapped around you since before you woke up, to unweave and untangle them," Filby said. "Multiple layers have been woven around you for so long, they've sunk into your flesh and your spirit. Many of them are good, beneficial, rooted in love. Protections granted by your parents. But that reaction ... do you have any odd birthmarks?"

Filby's frown deepened when Ash told her about the two stars, the one on her buttocks appearing just after she began living inside the castle, and the other starting to grow on her breastbone the previous winter.

"They're not birthmarks, are they?" Ash asked.

"Preventing birth, I fear. I am familiar with that spell. It warns of your inborn magic trying to manifest. A beacon, and a lock to keep your inborn magic bound. Yes, the stars react to strong magic that brushes up against you and the magic that should have begun manifesting in you for several years now. Someone wanted to ensure that didn't happen."

"Why?" She closed her eyes and pressed her hands over her face and shook her head a few times. "No, I can guess why. Enemies who don't want me to have magic."

"Not unless they can use that magic strength and potential for their own profit." Filby thumped her fist on the edge of the table, making their empty plates and cups bounce. "Curse them. Curse this wretched deadline ahead of us. The stars alone could take months to untangle, to free you properly. Without setting off alarms to warn your enemies that you are escaping. We are safe here, slightly outside of time," she added, gesturing around the massive room of luxury with its invisible doors to pocket dimensions. "They could conceivably follow the beacon to Willemsport, but it would take a great deal of magic to break the seals guarding us here. My faerie-kin relatives ensured that. But you can't just sit here for however long it takes to free you."

"Castle Fairhold doesn't have months," Ash murmured.

"We shall find a way. I promise you that. Protection and freedom. This can be of little comfort to you, Ash ..." Filby sighed and tried to smile. "So much magic woven around you indicates that you showed incredible potential, perhaps from birth. Thus, numerous forces arose against you, and for you. Magic woven around you to protect you. Magic woven around you to bind you, blind you, and prevent your potential from blossoming. And to warn your enemies that all their bindings are loosening, preparing to burst, and set you free."

That sounds rather uncomfortable, the ring offered.

Ash wished he had a body, so she could hug him, in gratitude for his dry sense of humor and his friendship.

They needed to choose a swift route to Castle Fairhold that would keep her safe from Lathia's magicians, who had latched onto Justiciar Camwell's tracking spells. Just as vital, she needed to go through that final cavern required by the quest. That should break the tracking spells, and free her from the Purple Sky's tracking spells, which were tangled with Camwell's.

"But what do we do if completing the quest triggers magic to take the ring away from me altogether?" Ash had to ask.

"That is the first magic I will weave," Filby said. "While I would feel more secure binding the ring to your hand, that gives enemy magic too many footholds to latch onto you. The ring will be able to detect if the tracking spells are broken or not. If not, and if you are able to remove the ring once the quest is complete, pin him to your coat with your courier badge. That will give you enough contact to still speak to each other, but without the skin contact, the tracking spell should break. That is the best I can do for now. Trust me. Trust A'theosius, who most certainly has been guiding your steps all this way."

It's all right, my lady, the ring assured her. *Once we have defeated our enemies, all their spells will unravel. Lady Filby is a powerful and skilled and clever spell weaver. She won't bungle and have to redo spells multiple times, and leave tangled and broken threads of magic, like those half-price magicians and low-rank wizards Camwell hired in the first place.*

Ash thanked him for his encouragement, and tried to find some humor in his scorn for the magic-users who had certainly bungled what should have been simple tasks.

Did those failures work for her and against Lathia's schemes, or the other way around?

Hiding from physical eyes was as important as hiding from magical senses. Ash would journey to Castle Fairhold as a courier. She would deliver messages in the relay system that covered nearly four-fifths of the known world. She would take shelter in the station houses and wayhouses along the way. That required her to take the courier's oath, to wear the identification of Filby's couriers and trigger their defensive magic.

After an intense morning of riding lessons and courier signals and signs, Ash was more than grateful to sit and study. She hurt in far more places than her bottom. The ring's constant corrections to her posture and how she gripped with her knees gave her a headache.

That didn't ease when she had washed up and reported to Filby, who would send her into another magic pocket room for her studies. The bracelet she needed to wear for entrance and exit tingled with magic. First a strong sting the moment it touched her wrist, then softening to a periodic surge, like the pulsing of a clock pendulum. Her stars both reacted with a quick, sharp stabbing sensation.

"That is your anchor to the flow of time here, in this place." Filby gestured around the sprawling central room of her home. "Pay attention to the rhythm, so you don't get distracted and drawn to other rooms that might brush up against the one you're going into. No," she hurried to say, when Ash opened her mouth to ask, "I do not have control over all the time pools that touch this place. We are stepping into the domain of the ancient ones who have far more experience, so we must be extremely careful to use good manners. Now, concentrate."

Filby then gave Ash a small disk that attached to the bracelet with a tugging sensation and click.

"Part of the attractive force is magnetism. The other part is magic. The disk is your key to the time pool that holds your study room. Our host has filled it with all the books you'll need, all the maps, and a journal, pen and ink pot to make all the notes you want. Journal and ink are both spelled to give you as much as you need, meaning you can't use up the ink or run out of pages." She laughed when Ash grinned at the thought. "I thought you might like that. Now, you are not permitted to bring either food or drink into the library wing we are borrowing, and I suggest you make use of the necessary before you go in. Once you come out, you can't return for three hours. You can only visit the time pool library three times. Entering will momentarily break the tracking spells. The more times you do that, even if seemingly only for a few heartbeats, the greater the chances the justiciar will notice and react with more spells. Stay as long as you can, until thirst, hunger, and weariness make studying difficult."

"Should I look for a way to keep the ring with me?" Ash asked, when she returned to the main room after using the necessary. Filby stood in front of an upright disk of swirling green mist, frowning into it.

"No. Leave that to me. You need to study the kingdoms you will be traveling through, the laws, the attitudes of the people, and the most recent courier run reports. And one more complication." She tapped Ash's breastbone, over the star. "You will ride too close to Tippessee for my taste. I agree, a trap waits for you, and any other children of magic-users who escaped the flood. Once you have warned Fairhold, hurry back here. We need to try to remove those stars. The longer your inborn magic is caged, the more painful it will be for you when it bursts forth."

Filby raised her hand and the swirling green disk became a doorway into a room full of lantern light and walls filled with books.

"I will be petitioning the Council of Enchanters and the Enchanters' Court for an advocate and mediator to judge whether Camwell has violated numerous laws of magic use. The problem with the Council and the Court is that they exist in constantly shifting time ... well, certainly not pools, more like oceans. So while their response to my petition is sure to be swift and courteous, what are mere hours to them will be months or even years to our perception. If you encounter any magical libraries or caches of magical books along the way, consult them to begin your own research. Exposure to this library will make you more sensitive to magical libraries. That should help."

Ash felt laughter bubbling deep inside. Just how much sensitivity would she need to find a magical library on her own? The more magic was concentrated in the books, the more alert and aware the books were. That meant stronger and more active spells protecting the libraries from discovery and abuse and misuse.

Filby stunned Ash by bending down and hugging her, then grasped her shoulders and turned her to face the green mist disk. "Take a deep breath, focus on the key in your bracelet, and ask for permission to enter."

Ash did so and took a step forward. Her knees folded and the room spun around her. She lunged forward to brace herself on the table directly in front of her. The dizzy sensation faded as quickly as it had come, but her two stars stung and burned, so she fought to stand upright instead of curling up and going to her knees.

Oh, dear, the ring said. *We were afraid that might happen. Your magic is struggling so hard to come out, it gave you a bad reaction from passing from one time stream to another.*

"You could have warned me!" Ash turned to ask Filby why she hadn't warned her. No doorway. No Filby. She took a few more breaths, forcing away that sting and burn by strength of will.

Yes, we could have, the ring said after a few moments. *However, a warning might have made you hesitate, and broken your focus on Filby's instructions. Even here, outside the normal stream of time, every second is precious.*

Ash reached for the chair and slid into it. The ring was right.

"Am I going to go through that every time I step in and out of here?"

I should hope not. Most of your pain is from the tracking spells.

Ash fought down another long sigh. "What do we do first? Where do we look?" She turned to survey the bookshelves filling all the walls of the room, with no door. She tipped her head back, looking for the lanterns or lamps, but found no source of the soft, warm, gold-tinted light. A shiver washed over her, but it was a good kind of shiver. Full of anticipation.

She paused to thank A'theosius for the blessings and gifts and all the help she had encountered so far on her journey. Perhaps as a reward for trying to live properly and according to holy writ? And yet, wasn't A'theosius the source of all magic and wonder and blessings and rules in the world? So yes, she should thank the Maker regularly, and far more than she had been doing.

The shelves were clearly marked. Each kingdom she would pass through on her way back to Alfordia had at least three shelves full of books and scrolls dealing with history, politics, the powerful families, current events in the kingdoms, and magical trends and traditions. How could she read everything on just one kingdom, let alone all of them?

The ring chuckled when she spoke that question aloud, after more than twenty minutes just studying the shelves, reading the labels, and figuring out how to move the clever ladder that ran on tracks at top and bottom, to allow her to climb up to any shelf.

Never you fear, my lady. I am gorging myself on all the information in those books. Thank A'theosius I am unable to suffer from indigestion. Certainly, I shall be a glutton here.

"Oh, believe me, I do thank A'theosius. Well, since you're absorbing all that kingdom-related information, what should I focus on? What is it important for me to know, instead of relying on you to remember it all for me?"

The library proved what others had told her about the tendency for magical books to become aware. As soon as she and the ring agreed on her course of study, the next section of the shelves changed over from kingdom information to a collection of courier reports and maps and information on the station houses, and the signals and codes she would need to know and use. Ash took those books to the table in the middle of the room and proceeded to copy everything over into the journal. She would study that information during rest stops and when she camped or stopped at a station house. This information needed to stay at the top of her mind, rather than depending on the ring to advise her. The slightest delay in responding as a courier ought could lead to trouble from suspicious and untrustworthy people.

Ash read and took notes until her hand cramped and her eyes ached. She put her head down on her crossed arms on the table and closed her eyes to rest them a few times, refusing to give up and leave the library so soon. She had no idea how long she spent in there, other than to calculate by the number of pages she had filled with notes. Her stomach ached, pinching her, then grew silent. Her eyes and mouth grew dry. There were no lamps to help calculate the time by how far the level of oil went down.

You need to take a rest, the ring said. Several times.

Ash ignored him until the words sent a throbbing ache through her head. Her eyes were dusty, dry, and sticky-gritty. Resting her head on the table and closing her eyes no longer brought her any temporary relief.

"There's so much we need to learn before we can leave, and time is running out," she countered.

Practically no time has passed in the real time stream, the ring said.

"It's not the amount of time we've saved, it's the limit on how many times we can come back here, remember?" A snort of laughter escaped her, struck by the irony of having to remind the ring for a change.

I do indeed. The ring sighed. *I must confess, there is a great deal of relief for me, stepping out of time into this place. I didn't realize the weight of the knotted and tangled spells, until I was temporarily freed of them. I shall have much to say in testimony against the justiciar, if we are ever called to testify.*

"You don't think we will?" Ash got up and twisted the bracelet around on her wrist until the disk was on top. She took a few breaths and braced herself for a repeat of that dizzy, wrung out sensation.

Much depends on who else has thought to register complaints against his misuse and rewriting of magical contracts in the past. There is a sad tendency in far too many kingdoms for victims to be taught to be ashamed that they were victimized, so the powerful and unethical grow more powerful and more callous when it comes to justice. They essentially believe they can do whatever they wish, because they have not been punished or even reprimanded. They are the most nastily self-righteous folk I have ever had the displeasure to encounter, because they feel themselves much abused when someone does call them to task for their cruelty and selfishness.

"Like Lord Winston, when he kept trying to justify what Lathia did." Ash pressed her fingertips against the disk and asked silently for the doorway to open. "I think I would be grateful to have magic that would bring people like them to justice and protect their victims."

Be careful what wishes you make, my lady. Especially wishes to make the world a better, kinder place. A'theosius and the guiding spirits hear and take you at your word. But even worse, the dark spirits hear you as well, and mark you as a potential opponent to be destroyed before you gain any strength.

"Now you tell me." She smiled, though, and stepped through the opening as soon as it was large enough to take her.

Ash stumbled under the weight of exhaustion, thirst, and hunger. Painful hunger. Filby wrapped an arm tight around her and guided her to the feasting table.

Fang was still curled up in a cushioned basket, right where he had been when Ash went into the library. In fact, she suspected he hadn't moved since she left.

"Is Fang all right?" she asked, keeping her voice down. A pang of guilt fought with the ache in her empty stomach. Had she been so involved in her own concerns that she had ignored Fang? Just because they were shielded inside Filby's home didn't mean he was safe from the complications of being only partially turned into a vampire.

"He's fine. You're the one we need to worry about." Filby waited until Ash had settled on the same thick floor pillow she had used at breakfast, then took a step back and studied her through narrowed eyes. "Water, first. Then we'll feed you. Bread and milk and honey, to coddle your stomach until it stops punishing you for going so long without food."

Pitchers and serving bowls and platters appeared across the table, woven out of the shadows, if Ash could believe her itchy-blurry-dry eyes. The first whiffs of aroma from the hot food made her feel nauseous. She almost refused the large mug Filby held out to her.

When she drank, there was more than water there. Something tangy. A hint of herbs.

"Slowly," Filby said, and pulled the mug from her hands before she could take a third gulp. "Ah, see?" she said, smiling, mischief and sympathy combined, when the cold water hit Ash's aching stomach like a quarterstaff that threatened to fold her in half.

We were in there the equivalent of two days, the ring offered. *You did an amazing amount of research, and I must confess I feel somewhat ... bloated, I suppose is the correct term. I've never been able to indulge so thoroughly before.*

Perhaps because there was never so much information available for me to absorb at one time.

"Two days?" Ash barely noticed when Filby put the mug back into her hands and guided it to her mouth. She sipped this time instead of gulping, as she wrapped her aching head around the concept. The ring was right. Her head was bloated with knowledge. She had often dreamed of being able to simply go from one book to another, free to fill her mind with no interruptions.

The wine Filby gave her next was almost gritty with herbs, and despite being watered went straight to her head. The floaty feeling was welcome after the stiffness and aches in her head and hands and back. Ash nibbled at the bread and honey and milk and let Filby and the ring discuss everything they had researched and discussed and noted. About halfway through a bowl of a savory stew of chicken and beans, Ash had revived enough to join the discussion, which had moved to the enchanted castle.

Every time she had tried to identify the possible location of a magical book with information to help free the ring from Camwell's control, the enchanted castle's library came up. Often, the chroniclers speculated that missing books had been collected in the enchanted castle's library to protect them. Far too many libraries over the last few decades had fallen into disrepair and neglect, or vanished altogether, because the heirs of the kings who built those libraries had little regard for the treasures of knowledge stored in books. Or those libraries had been sacked and pillaged by barbarians who thought books were abominations, that knowledge was corrupted when it was written down. Then there were the arrogant schemers like King Ruprick, who considered themselves entitled to steal from every accessible library to build up their own libraries. They hoped to start collegiums or attract enchanters into their service. Such depredations and loss of books, whether magical or dealing with magic or just plain volumes of facts and histories, made locating specific volumes with specific knowledge rather difficult. Rumors and folklore hinted or speculated that when books vanished, they were spirited away to the library in the enchanted castle, for safekeeping.

CHAPTER THREE

Filby and the ring had come to the conclusion that if Ash couldn't get justice from the Council of Enchanters and the Enchanters Court, and she couldn't find an enchanter with the information she needed to free herself and the ring from Camwell, she might need to go in search of the enchanted castle itself and search its library.

"How?" Ash asked. "From all I've heard, the smart thing to do is avoid it entirely. But since it seems to move around, won't that make it even harder to find?"

Perhaps, said the ring. He sounded rather smug. Or maybe that was what he sounded like when he suffered indigestion of knowledge? The richness and thickness to his voice worried her, just a little. Could the ring get sick?

"There is too much that isn't known about the enchanted forest and the enchanted castle." Filby lounged across several thick pillows, now that she no longer needed to ply Ash with food and make sure she ate slowly.

Tell her about the map, the ring said.

"A map of the forest?" Ash guessed.

"Yes and no." Filby held up a hand to halt the spill of questions poised on her tongue. "A theoretical map, connecting the portals scattered throughout the enchanted forest. Time passes differently there, so it is difficult to control how much time passes here on the outside, between the moment you enter and the moment you leave. The trick is to be certain where you are, and where you need to exit, and then know what the portal looks like when it opens to the kingdom where you want to go. Only couriers with strong guiding magic dare to go through the enchanted forest, and always after much prayer for A'theosius's leading."

"That's some trick," Ash muttered. She inhaled, as understanding seemed to stab through the middle of her forehead. "That's why I need to learn the characteristics of all those kingdoms, the plants native to them, their cycle of seasons, and what kingdoms have snow while others are in summer and even the position of the stars at different times of the year. So when I look through the portal, I'll know where and when I'm going ... but that means you expect me to go into the enchanted forest. Despite everything I've been warned about?"

"That vision of the snow and roses makes it a certainty you will stumble into the forest eventually. You can't avoid destiny or fate, so wisdom says to be prepared." She sighed and turned to put the goblet she had been sipping from on the edge of the table. "Many authorities, out of fear, work to suppress what little knowledge there is about the forest. Thinking of great, powerful, frightening, inexplicable things, especially those steeped in magic, has a tendency to draw them to you. Most people try not to think of the castle and the forest. They hide or destroy the books about them, and don't even warn their children about them. They fear that thinking about the portals will open them."

"Knowledge is power ... and power is dangerous," Ash murmured, recalling some things she had heard Lord Digory and Friar Ipswich and Captain Reginald discussing.

"*Can* be dangerous." Filby nodded. "Why do you think the proverbs about watching your heart and your tongue are so true? The things you think about, the things you fear, become true because you focus on them."

When Ash went to her room, she wobbled with exhaustion. She fumbled with her blankets as she crawled into her bed. Sleep wrapped around her as the housekeeping breeze pulled a quilt up to her chin.

"Thank you," she whispered. The breeze caressed hair off her forehead, and then Ash sank down into blessed darkness.

When she woke late in the evening, Filby had been busy. Several couriers had come into the station, and she dealt with the many faces of her business, providing horses, blacksmithing, and selling supplies. Filby found time to compose her letters to the Council and the Court. She and the ring had been in consultation for quite a while, compiling a list of the names, locations, and circumstances of other people who had worn the ring in the past, on quests or assignments for the justiciar. Looking at the thick sheaf of pages filled with names and details made Ash's hand ache in sympathy for Filby.

~~~~~

Three days after Ash arrived at Filby's headquarters, the protective wards alerted them that someone was tugging on the tracking spells woven around the ring to find Ash. Either Camwell or Lathia's magicians. The wards blurred details and directions on both sides of the barrier. Whoever was tracking Ash would come to Willemsport eventually, even if they couldn't narrow down the focus any further.

Ash, Fang, and the ring needed to leave. The spells tangled around the ring interfered with Filby's spells to ensure the ring would stay with Ash when the quest was completed. All they could do was pray for Atheosius's help, hope for the best, and keep trying to warn Camwell of what Lathia was doing.

Her head hurt from all the information crammed into it. Her hand ached after days of writing important information in the journal she now carried in her saddlebags. She proudly wore the uniform of a courier, and
~~~~~

the starburst pin on her collar identified her as a trainee to other couriers. Any courier she met would give her advice and guidance, and senior couriers would check her lessons along the way.

Ash carried more materials to study when she stopped to rest. She needed to understand her responsibilities and her options. Couriers sometimes took months or even years off, to attend to family needs, even to raise families, study, or spend time in spiritual contemplation. And deal with sensitive situations, such as warning Castle Fairhold.

"I think it would be wise for you to leave the road a good month in advance of your seventeenth birthday and stay off the road for a full month after," Filby had told her, when they were discussing Ash's future as a courier. "The seventeenth birthday is a tricky, delicate turning point in the life of anyone who has magic in their blood. You would be wise to find some place quiet and shielded to sit and be protected by friends." She had paused and tipped her head to one side, studying Ash's reaction to her pronouncement. "Is something wrong?"

"I don't know when exactly I was born. I have a birthday," Ash hurried on, "a date that Lady Charlotte gave me, when she brought the orphans to the castle, but nobody knows if that's my real birthday. I could be months older or younger than I've thought all these years."

"Well … that is a conundrum, isn't it?" Filby whispered.

"Maybe I should go to Tippessee after all?" Ash said. "Maybe someone there might have answers for me?"

Filby had grown even more somber. Her eyes seemed to take on shadows and she thought for several long moments.

"I agree with the ring, you could be opening yourself to danger. You need to learn discipline, to prepare to rein in and quiet your magic when it breaks free. It will break free, no matter how strong the binding spells attached to your stars. If you cannot touch your magic, it will be largely undisciplined and untrained, making you vulnerable when it breaks the binding. Your enemies could be waiting for that day, to harvest your magic. I'm sorry, but even if you could gain vital answers, I believe it best if you don't go to Tippessee until after you have been freed from all this unfriendly magic knotted around you."

The final step, before riding out of Filby's stable, was to repeat the courier's oath as Ash checked her horse's feet and legs, the fit of the saddle, not too tight or too loose, and then checked the gear attached to her saddle. She had memorized it and repeated it as she put on her uniform the first time, and now as she prepared to mount her horse.

Loyalty first to A'theosius, to peace, understanding, communication, truth, and justice. Let no one interfere with carrying out my mission. Turn my eyes outward and see and think about what happens in the world around me. Offer help whenever I see someone in need.

When she rode out of Willemsport, Fang was curled up in a basket attached to the back of Ash's saddle. Hanging from either side would be too rough a ride, thumping against the horse's constantly churning hindquarters. There was no other option, until he tired of being partially a vampire and wanted to be cured. Someone would eventually see the basket and assume it carried something valuable. Ash had to be ready to either flee or let Fang deal with hopeful thieves. A border crossing guard or village peacekeeper might feel his authority too much and insist on looking inside. She had to be ready to stop Fang from attacking.

Ash rode due east out of town and stayed on the wide road maintained by the kingdom. Each time she stopped at a station house, a senior courier would verify her credentials and share her likeness and identity with every courier who came through. Before winter slowed all travel, all the station houses and all the couriers on the entire continent would know who she was. Long before that, she would have completed Camwell's quest. And she would know if he had changed the conditions for his own entertainment.

Ash thought of the final cavern she would pass through, a magically shielded and sealed place maintained by the couriers because of the touchy nature of the kingdom where it was located. As soon as she left that cavern, she would know if Camwell had changed the conditions of the quest, and if the spell to keep the ring with her had worked.

~~~~~

That first night, Ash camped by the river, in the woods a short distance off the road. Fang gladly hopped out of the basket and into the shadows of the trees. She brushed down and watered and fed her horse, Garan, and checked his legs. She gathered wood for a fire, enough to last her all night, before twilight had fully fallen. With her flute, she threw up a shielding dome of magic around herself and Garan, to hide the firelight and prevent attracting unwanted visitors. She left a door in the dome that only Fang could find, when he returned before dawn. She was grateful to be able to stretch out on her blanket by the fire, with her saddle as a pillow, nibble on her bread, cheese, and dried fruit, and study the stars as they sparkled into life one by one high overhead. With the ring and the shield protecting her and Garan acting as sentinel, she didn't have to worry about keeping watch.

Magic certainly made life easier, now that she had learned some simple spells.

The ring laughed when she voiced her observation. They chatted about the book he had been reciting to her all day as she rode, until she grew sleepy. Then the ring let her sleep. His ability to pick up the entire text from all the books around him was handy. His powers of recall amazed her sometimes. He had been almost giddy when he told her about
~~~~~

the rooms and rooms full of books he had accessed via the invisible doorways in Filby's home. Ash would never be without a new book for him to share with her and to learn from.

Close to morning, she woke chilled and found the fire had died down. She built it up again and curled up next to it, staring into the flames, and looking ahead to exiting the cavern and finally having answers. She silently prayed to A'theosius that completing Justiciar Camwell's list wouldn't result in the ring disappearing, magically summoned back to his master. What legal standing did she and the ring have? Could she just stay away from Alfordia and keep the ring, or was she bound to return him to Camwell? Did the ring have any rights, any choice in his activities and locations? Could he request to stay with her? She hoped the ring could and would.

The following night, she stayed in a station house. Dolfus, the station master, greeted her and showed her where to find the supplies to groom, feed and water Garan. He also had half a side of venison waiting for Fang, in an outbuilding on the edge of the shield surrounding the station house. It was fresh and bloody, and the bunny's eyes seemed to spin as he contemplated the feast waiting for him. There were three older couriers already in for the night, relaxing in front of the massive fireplace, when Ash finished settling into her room, washed, and came downstairs to the main room.

The three all looked like they had many leagues and decades of travel under their belts. They nodded to Ash when she stepped into the room.

"New blood pays their way in stories," the one woman in the trio said, after Ash had picked up the bowl of stew and slab of bread dripping in butter and spices that Dolfus set out for her.

"What kind of stories?" Ash eyed the chairs, filled with blankets and cushions, the deep seats designed for comfortable lounging. Or should she take one of the tables, further back from the fire, where she could put her food down, and not worry about dropping something?

"Your stories." Dolfus stepped into the room with a tray full of steaming tankards that smelled of cider and spices. He gave Ash hers first and gestured with a jerk of his chin at a small table next to one of the chairs. "Start with how you came to have such an interesting traveling companion."

"Companion?" The one-eyed man of the three sat up and looked around. "Not to be unsociable, but station houses are sanctuaries for couriers alone, for a reason."

"A bunny with a taste for bloody meat. He's outside having his dinner." Dolfus took the seat next to Ash's. "Will he be joining us when he's done? And cleaned up?"

"No. Fang rides in a covered basket all day. He's halfway turned into a vampire, so he prefers to be active at night, and get some exercise." Ash saluted the other four with her tankard and took a testing sip.

"Half vampire?" The woman brightened and sat forward, resting her elbows on her knees. "I agree. That story first."

"Let the lass have her dinner while it's still hot. Then she can entertain us." The third courier didn't open his eyes, just stayed slouched back among the cushions, legs stretched out with his heels resting on the edge of the hearth.

Dolfus took over, introducing the three. The woman was Arli, the one-eyed man Ryfus, and the third Shyler. Each had come from a different country, bringing reports to the king of Ynderweil, about a king raiding the libraries of lower-level magical folk, to build up his own library.

"Do you mean Ruprick of Rathalshiffen?" Ash nearly choked on her mouthful of bread.

"Oh ho, a second story," Ryfus said with a grin. "Yes, that's the rotter. The word is that he's intending to build a collegium for wizards and enchanters and such, to persuade them to come settle in his kingdom and make their power available to him. He wants thousands of books to offer them. As if such folk won't have their own books already?" He made a sound like he would spit, but he glanced at Dolfus and gave a little shrug that was probably an apology.

"How do you know about him?" Arli said.

"His men raided the village where I was staying, trying to take the books belonging to the seer." Ash glanced down into her bowl. She could see her food would be cold by the time these folk let her finish talking.

"That kind of makes sense, taking them from a seer," Ryfus said. "He can't read them. How many did he have? I heard tell the king's bully boys used some kind of magic charm to lead them to large stashes of books."

"Don't matter if a seer can read with his eyes," Shyler said, still without moving. "The spirit of the books stays with him. And if he's smart, he has people nearby who can read for him, when he needs to remember the exact words. Isn't that right, lass?"

"Exactly." Ash took a gulp from her tankard and put it aside. "Fortunately, Cecil had a vision to warn him, so we were able to move most of his books into hiding."

The others made approving comments as she related all the trips to haul the books to the oak, and then rearranging the inside of Cecil's house so it didn't look like most of the library was missing. They laughed when she described the encounter with the raiders, and the fury of the people in the village. Then, because they wanted to know about Fang, she related how the bunny terrified the soldiers, then the warning that Justiciar Camwell was seeking her because she had been sitting still all summer, and the need to leave.

From there, she went backward, and related how Hazel had brought Fang to her, to look out for her and get him away from the bunny warren and their leadership, and the false accusations of murder. To protect his secrets, she gave the barest of details of entering Blaz's cavern home that was much bigger inside than outside, and how she had run afoul of the village in Nordwell, the accusations against Fang, and being sent into the vampire caverns.

Arli made her back up again and explain why she had to leave Fairhold. All four of her listeners laughed and made rude comments under their breaths about Lord Winston and Lathia. Ash considered relating what the ring had told her about Lathia and her prince, and the magicians sent to punish her and Castle Fairhold. No, she would save that story for later. She was tired, and she still hadn't told how Fang had become half-vampire, partially protected by his bunny magic. She would tell the story of the journey through the cavern with Morris and how Fang had taken the bite meant for her, then she would plead exhaustion and go to bed.

When she got to what she intended to be the end of the story, of seeing Fang's fur smoke in the daylight, Shyler moved for the first time. He sat up and brushed his shaggy mane of hair out of his face. It didn't change the impression of him as a mound of fur.

"Are you seeking a cure for Fang?"

"No. I wanted to," Ash hurried to add, "but he's happy as he is. He doesn't care about the murder charge. I think he likes being odd. He likes raw meat."

"Yon bunny was already twisted sideways before he was bitten." Arli grinned. "Can't think of how you could cure him, though. That would take powerful magic. Lots of it."

"Where could you find that much?" Dolfus said.

"Easy," Shyler said. "The enchanted castle." He looked at each of them in turn, his gaze going around the room. "You know? The enchanted castle that moves about the enchanted forest? The forest that is everywhere and nowhere, touching all kingdoms and all continents —"

"Not all kingdoms." Ryfus shook his head and stretched out further in his seat. "Just a few, and months apart. If you find a portal and fall into the enchanted forest, you had best get back out before sunrise, or it could be years before you find your way out again. If the castle doesn't eat you."

Arli made a rude noise. "Castles don't eat people."

"Then how do you explain all the princes and princesses and heroes who go to the castle on quests for magical swords and mirrors and spinning wheels and the lot, and never come out?"

"The castle is lonely. Castles aren't meant to be empty of people. And this one is as close to alive as a pile of stones can be. Because it's full of magical things. Dangerous and helpful and just plain tricky. Powerful things. Sorcerers and enchanters and the like have been using it for centuries as a dumping place to throw troublesome bits of magic, to store it, lock it away, keep it out of the hands of idiots who don't follow the rules. The kind who don't listen when you tell them that being greedy, keeping magic all to yourself, that's the surest way to turn it dark and sick and dangerous. All that magic, building up over the years, all the magic books hidden away there ... it's made the castle come to life."

"And that's why the lass should take the vampire bunny to the enchanted castle," Shyler said. "If there's enough magic knowledge and a trinket that can cure him, she'll find it there, if nowhere else in the world."

"But Fang doesn't want to be cured," Ash said.

Her head hurt a little, as if she had trouble adding all this new information about the castle and forest to what she had read in the time pool library and what Friar Ipswich and Cadswall had told her.

"He thinks he doesn't want to be cured," Arli said. "Vampires are tricksy creatures all in themselves. The magic to make other folk like them, it's tricksy. Twisted. It could be tricking your friend into thinking he likes being that way. I'll wager once you cure him, he'll be eternally grateful. Once his mind is cleared of the twisting and shadows."

Ash nodded and tried to look like she seriously considered the idea. Going to the enchanted castle was the last course of action to take when all other options had failed.

The others seemed satisfied with her response. Ash asked the ring if he agreed with what the other couriers said. The ring responded that much of this was new variations on theories that had been recorded in Cecil's and Filby's books. He recommended Ash listen carefully, because if she ignored such a discussion, she was guaranteeing fate would pick her up and throw her around and ensure she landed inside the enchanted castle before she could catch her breath.

So Ash listened to the senior couriers and their insight. All taken with a grain of salt, because if they didn't know about the theoretical map Filby had showed her, then they didn't have the inherent magic that made it possible for them to use the enchanted forest to avoid troublesome kingdoms. Everything they knew came from stories, not experience.

CHAPTER FOUR

Generations ago, a courier who asked politely when he entered the enchanted forest could be sure of riding across it and exiting to another kingdom in less than a day. Without any stretching or warping or massive loss of time. Before the enchanted castle was torn free of its roots and wandered the enchanted forest. Before the wandering got so bad that it tore the enchanted forest free of its moorings in time. Before there was no way out of the enchanted forest without months passing on the outside before the portal opened again. Before the portals opened and shut in an unpredictable schedule.

"Ah, but I know some who don't think they're unpredictable." Shyler winked at Ash.

"Oh, yes, the ones who spent years studying the reports of those who stumbled in and stumbled out again months, even years later." Dolfus shook his head, then drained his tankard. "How can you trust someone who went half-mad from exposure and avoiding the enchanted castle trying to take him prisoner, and never knowing where you are in the forest, because there's no sun and no moon?"

"How can there be no sun or moon?" Ash blurted. "Isn't there day or night in the forest?"

"Well," Arli said, "there is, and there isn't. There's light and there's darkness, and stars. But you're never sure where the light comes from in the day. It only makes sense, if you think about it. I was there when Filby was tending a man who vanished for eight years before he made his way back. To his reckoning, he was only gone seven months. He was being chased by bandits and went through a portal without realizing what he had done. He fell through at night, and didn't catch any landmarks, he had no way to know where the portal was anchored on the other side. He spent an entire month searching all the forest until he found all the portals, and then he wore out his horse racing from one to another, until he found the one that looked right. But it wasn't. He came out on the other side of the world. In Rashonal."

"And that's why he went mad," Ryfas said. This time he spat into the fire. "Those people are crazy. They spend their time studying things like philosophy and science when they should pay attention to magic. That's why they've lost most of the magic on the entire continent, not just that one kingdom. It's a disease of the mind and soul." He snorted. "They even deny they have a portal in Rashonal. Doesn't stop people from falling through."

"Daedrian, enchanter to King Dayon of Cartess, postulates that science and magic are two different kinds of energy, complete opposites," Shyler said. "They cancel each other out."

"No, no," Arli said. "He didn't go mad from visiting Rashonal. He found someone with a map to get to the portal in Festra. There are only two on that entire insane continent. He waited until it opened, to get back into the forest. He repeated what he did the first time, and kept trying portals, jumping out into other kingdoms, figuring out where he was and jumping back through before it closed. Finally, he came out a portal in Cammerlang, and decided to go overland back to Ynderweil. When he learned he had been gone more than eight years, he broke inside and fell ill, and other couriers found him and brought him to Filby."

Arli shuddered. "The enchanted forest is a dangerous place, even for those of us who know the right words and are polite and careful."

"How many portals are there?" Ash asked. "How far apart are they? How quickly do they open and close again?"

"You're not planning on going there and exploring, are you?" Dolfus asked. Ryfus and Shyler chuckled.

"No, not me." Ash wrapped her arms around herself. The shivering from deep inside wasn't entirely from cold. A sense of excitement gripped her, and she couldn't understand why. "I just think it would be helpful if more was known about the place, so people could avoid trouble. Couriers get chased by bandits constantly, don't we?"

"Or kings' soldiers and spies, disguised as bandits," Ryfus said.

The other couriers offered bits of information they had heard in stories from those who had either been chased into the enchanted forest or stumbled through a portal by accident. They confirmed what she had read: no two portals looked alike. In one kingdom a portal was a tunnel in a sheer wall of craggy rock, covered with ivy. In another kingdom, it was an archway formed by fallen trees, with sunlight slanting through from the wrong direction. Or just a shimmer like water in the air.

Shyler scowled into the fire. "The forest used to be friendlier. It kept you out sometimes, and it liked to change the paths, so you got lost and wasted time you couldn't spare, but it never tried to keep you there once you were in and you wanted to get out. It got angry when the castle broke loose of its anchors and knocked the forest loose. So now the forest doesn't play nice with anyone."

"What kind of anchors?" Ash asked.

"No one knows," Dolfus said with a shrug. "Lots of stories, but no one can be sure of anything, because you have to get into the castle to anchor it, and no one has ever gone in and come out again. There's a song my granny used to sing to us when we were wee bitty ones, about a blade that was broken and needing another blade, and a long jump, and holding the castle fast. Like when the thief Fairgas stole the casket with the queen's laughter, and the hero Balthar pinned him in place with knives through his sleeves and the toes of his boots."

"Take an awfully big knife blade to pin the enchanted castle," Arli said.

Shyler snorted. "The only thing anyone needs to know about the enchanted castle is to never go in. The only thing you need to know about the enchanted forest is that if you get in, get back out as fast as you can."

~~~~~

Though she rode swiftly, time seemed to drag until Ash neared the border of Machpellan, the last kingdom between her and Alfordia. She had gone far east and then north, to avoid the kingdoms she had passed through before. There was a particularly nasty tracking spell that awoke if the prey retraced its steps. The Purple Sky magicians had a reputation for using the nastiest spells possible. Once over the border of Cammerlang into Machpellan, she had a short ride, maybe four miles, until she entered the final cavern on Justiciar Camwell's list.

The four miles, however, could be tricky. Machpellan was a problematic kingdom. Far too willing to rewrite situations and events to suit whatever their current need or complaint might be. The current proverb was that a kingdom's reasonableness was in converse proportion to its size. Machpellan seemed resolved to make up for its size by causing as much diplomatic turmoil as possible, as often as possible. The faerie-kin had stopped being amused by the hereditary insanity of Machpellan's rulers, and gave Filby and her couriers a dimensional passage to cross the kingdom quickly. However, the doorway to that passage lay in a cavern four miles inside the border.

To complicate matters, when Ash stopped at the station house in Cammerlang, Station Master Yolli had asked her to carry a message from King Marcos to King Ebrosian of Alfordia. Cammerlang wasn't an enemy of Machpellan, but it wasn't a friend, either. There was no predicting how the border guards would react to seeing the king's emblem on a sealed letter, if they chose to search Ash's courier pouch. Then again, they might not search her at all. Again, there was no predicting. The king's insanity affected the entire kingdom.

Fang thinks you're being foolish, the ring reported as they approached the border crossing.

"How?" Ash smiled when Garan's ears twitched at the sound of her voice. Did he wonder if she was talking to him?

He thinks you should simply change your clothes. Don't wear your uniform.

"If the border guards or one of the random patrols looking for a fight
~~~~~

search me and find my uniform, I'd be considered a spy."

I tried to explain that to him. He thinks clothes in general are ridiculous.

"He's right," she admitted with a chuckle. Yet, would she have been able to do the things she had done, growing up, if she hadn't been able to disguise herself as a boy?

She had no more time to consider such things. The border crossing station lay ahead of her. If she could see the wall stretching out from either side of the road, until it vanished into the trees, then the guards could see her. She prayed for a peaceful kingdom, and no special orders regarding the wealthy or powerful or couriers.

"Please tell Fang not to do anything unless I yell his name," she murmured, and kept her gaze on the guard in a dark green uniform who stepped out from the shelter and raised a hand, signaling her to stop.

As if she wouldn't stop? That gate was too high for her horse to jump, even if she had sent Garan into a full gallop.

"Ring?" Ash nearly pulled up on the reins, startled by his silence. Now was not the time for him to get distracted.

I'm sorry. Yes, I know you hate hearing me say that constantly. I don't say it that often, you know.

"What's—" She scolded herself to keep their conversation in her mind. She didn't need those border guards seeing her lips moving and wondering if a madwoman approached them. Or worse, preparing a spell to use against them. *What's wrong?*

I fear Lathia's hired brigands are near. There's a seeking spell at work. Tuned to me, of course. Using my link with her ring. We really must do something to free my friend from that deplorable child. Did no one ever tell her that nobles have far more responsibilities than privileges?

Ring, you're nattering. How close are they? Can you tell if they're on Machpellan's side of the border, or Cammerlang's?

Huh … you're right. I'm nattering. I should have considered … Just a moment, Lady Ashlyn.

She grinned. That teasing address meant he was calming down.

Then she was fifty paces from the border and those guards with their hands on the swords at their hips. Was this standard practice for these guards, more posturing than preparation for attack?

Or had Lathia's magicians traveled this far, and convinced the officials of Cammerlang that everyone approaching the border, whether entering or leaving, was a threat? And how could they know what kingdom's borders she was approaching on her roundabout route back home to Alfordia and Castle Fairhold?

Now you're mentally nattering, the ring said. *And no, the magic doesn't allow them to identify you at the distance I sense. They are merely seeking. Right now. However, the closer they get to us, the easier it is for them to identify you.*

Especially if there are few people nearby. We need to lose ourselves in a crowd.

Problem. Ash nodded to the guard who gestured for her to guide her horse to the left of the gate. A second guard stepped up to take the reins of her horse. *There are no towns between here and the cavern entrance. If they're on the same road we're traveling, how many people do we need to have around us to confuse them?*

One thing at a time. I will go silent in case they have a simple sensing spell attached to the communication link between spirit rings.

Ash nodded, to him and to the guard who gestured for her to step away from her horse. He pointed to a table out in the open just a few paces away, with a chair on either side. He sat down and studied the badge on her shoulder before gesturing for her to take the chair facing him.

"Well, Lady Filby hires younger and younger." He smiled, looking a little too weary for so early in the day. "Congratulations."

"Thank you, sir." Ash took encouragement from him saying "Lady Filby," and his tone of respect.

It took all her self-control not to turn to look at her horse directly behind her. Now for the tricky part. She and the ring and Fang had agreed on this approach for handling all border crossings. So far, no one had reacted with anger or disbelief. There was always a first time, though.

"I should warn you that the basket behind my saddle holds an extremely cranky bunny. He bites if you wake him from his nap."

"A bunny, you say? Do they really have magic?" He leaned forward, resting his elbows on the table. Was he actually interested?

"This is the only one I've met, but yes, he does have magic. And a foul temper. He won't attack if I open the basket, if you want to verify my words."

"Are you delivering him to someone? To take part in some sort of ritual? Some spell requiring ..." The guard shook his head. "No, forget I asked. I've been reading all sorts of warnings and speculative reports. All sorts of uprisings and rebellions in other kingdoms, idiots trying to commandeer magic that doesn't belong to them, steal it from those who earned it. We've learned to trust Lady Filby and her people. No sense in keeping you here any longer than necessary." He half-rose from his seat and gestured to the men behind Ash.

When the guard finished asking what had become a routine, standard list of questions, he escorted her to the gate, officially letting her into Machpellan, and handed her over to the guards on the other side of the border. They merely had her sign a paper listing what she brought with her. No searching of her horse or bags, and especially not the basket where Fang slept and whistle-snored slightly. Ash was relieved he did sleep soundly enough to make those noises. It meant his magically enhanced sense for trouble hadn't awakened.

She hoped Fang snored and whistled and slept all the way to the cavern.

Less than twenty minutes after she dismounted at the Cammerlang side of the border, she climbed back into the saddle in Machpellan, nodded her thanks to the guards, turned her horse, and trotted away.

Now, she needed to pray for a crowded road ahead of her, so if the Purple Sky detected the ring, they couldn't find her in the crowd. The ring was sure that before they were close enough to focus on her, he would sense them and warn her in time to flee. Hopefully the courier uniform would deflect their interest, so they would focus on someone more likely to be a girl disguised as a boy.

The road ahead disappointed her with its emptiness. Ash resisted the temptation to move from the energy-saving trot of long-distance travel to a ground-devouring, mad-dash gallop. She would tire her horse, and likely just before she needed most to run for her life. That was always how it happened in poems and stories with a blatant moral of "Don't be an idiot, plan ahead." Besides, racing like she had fire demons on her tail would just attract attention she didn't need. Any innocent travelers on the road ahead would be immediately suspicious, even fearful, if she suddenly slowed to ride with them. They would rightly assume she was using them to hide from trouble, and they wouldn't welcome her.

Riding at a sensible pace was the hardest thing she had done since letting Filby pierce her ears and insert her first pair of earrings. She thought she had felt naked when she put on her first skirt since the flood that swept her to Tippessee. This was harder, more exposed than that.

One mile behind us, the ring announced.

Ash nearly yanked on the reins. She pulled herself out of her tangled thoughts in time to see the marker post before Garan trotted past it.

"One down, three to go."

Fang thumped hard on the basket, jolting against her back. She laughed, recognizing the difference in the force. He wasn't complaining that she had awakened him, but teasing her about her obliviousness.

"You're right. You're both right," she hurried to add, sensing what the ring would add in another moment. "I haven't been paying attention. That's foolish. I shouldn't put all our defensive work on you."

Several softer thumps against her back. Considering Fang's strength, those were reassuring pats. Soon, he would resume whistle-snoring. They rode on in silence, until she wondered why the ring hadn't teased her, or started a lesson of some kind. Or at least a philosophical discussion about ignoring the landscape to indulge in speculations.

It might be useful to use your flute and call up a hazing spell around us, the ring said.

Is someone watching us from hiding? Ash pulled up the hood of her cloak, to hide the movements of her head as she looked from side to side.

They passed another marker, another half mile behind them. She brought out her flute, but now she had to decide between several hazing tunes. Just the magical senses? Or eyes and magical senses combined?

I sense seeking, but whoever is hunting hasn't found us yet, the ring said after another thoughtful pause.

If they sense us, they might see us as well?

Ah ... good point.

Ring? Are you all right? She winced. Speaking inside her head hurt, just a little, pulse points of needle-like stabs at her temples.

No, I fear not. The ring's voice seemed to wobble in her head. *I fear I am betraying you.*

"I don't understand," she whispered. "Why is talking in my head hurting now?"

Silence. She feared to ask him again, either in her mind or aloud.

I do betray you, he said, when they had passed the post showing they had put two miles behind them. They were halfway to the cavern.

"How?"

The power tracking us is linked to me. It's working around the blinding magic Lady Filby wove around me. As we feared, it is using the bond between all spirit rings, and between magical items in the service of a particular individual. What terrifies me is that I can feel the presence of more powerful, far older magical items. They have a taste and a scent from a realm that only the most ancient, knowledgeable magical folk dare approach. Where magical items are so old and powerful, they come very near to having minds and souls.

"But ... isn't that what you are? What you have done?"

Oh, my dear Lady ... The ring's voice vibrated like it tried to laugh. *Spirit rings are indeed alert, sentient beings, but whether we lost our souls or never had them doesn't matter now. Let's save such discussions for more leisurely times. What matters is that we have been granted an opportunity by A'theosius to ... well, to be rather simplistic, we have the opportunity to earn souls, or perhaps purify and redeem our damaged souls, through service. Through humility. By harnessing our magical power and potential to A'theosius's plan and purpose. The magical traditions of other lands speak of all sorts of powerful beings who, as a condition, let us say, of their limitless power, are ... limited. They can only employ that power in the service of another, never for their own purpose and profit. I fear someone has found ancient magical items, taken them from the place where they were put away, locked away to protect the world from their power. They are being used to latch onto the magic binding me, getting my taste and scent ... to find you.*

"What do we do?" Ash snorted and nearly slapped her own forehead. "I know what we do. I haze us. What tune?"

Follow your instincts. Trust the guarding and guiding magic woven into you.

Ash would have preferred a specific tune. She tied the reins to the front loops of her saddle, where she tied the bundles of courier pouches. She raised the flute to her lips, inhaled slowly and deeply, and held still. Or as still as she could riding at a gently rocking trot. She wanted to snatch the reins into her hands and race the last two miles to the safety of the cavern. Now that someone had caught their magical scent, that was the worst, most attention-catching thing she could do.

A large patch of forest lay ahead, with the road wrapping around it going to the right, so she couldn't see very far. That was the most likely place to run into other travelers. A good place for an ambush.

She needed that hazing spell to start working before people saw her. Vanishing or turning into a blur would just draw curiosity, maybe prompt people with minor magical gifts to employ them to discern what had happened. Such magical activity would draw the attention of whoever was seeking her.

There's no way to win this battle, is there? Another stab in her temples. Now irritation turned to anger. The dangerous kind that could prompt her to react without thinking.

Trust A'theosius and prepare. Ah, good. Look ahead.

Ash raised her head and exhaled in relief. They had come around the bend in the road, and the way ahead was fairly straight for some distance, with forest on only one side. Another road met hers. Several wagons and a number of mounted people slowly trundled down the road in the direction she was headed. She would soon pass them.

Play, the ring said.

She had to decide on the hazing tune quickly, before someone in that group ahead heard her horse's hoofbeats and looked back. And saw her fade out of sight.

Can you make Fang sleep more soundly?

"I don't … know …" She tried not to force the niggling, glimmering little idea out of the shadows at the edges of her spinning thoughts. That would only make it crumple and die before she could see it clearly.

You thought of something?

CHAPTER FIVE

"There's a song. I used to hum it, when I was trying to hide from the bullies among the servant children, or I had to tend some of the very little ones, and … I made them sleep. I always believed I was invisible, and … what if I wasn't an especially good hider, but I *was* making myself invisible? They couldn't hear me humming it, either, now that I think of it. Children are so perceptive, but so blind at the same time!" She nearly slapped herself with the hand holding the flute.

Where did the tune come from?

"I don't know. Maybe before I came to Fairhold?"

Play, my lady.

Ash remembered more fragments of those odd times in her childhood. What if she had had magic despite the blocking spells woven into those stars, and used it, but didn't realize it? She tried to remember, as her horse drew closer to the travelers ahead. She thought about how she had focused on each child when she tried to will the smallest ones to fall asleep, or she had focused on visible openings in hedges and stone walls and willed her tormenters not to see those gaps that led into her hiding places. She played the simple tune, just six or seven measures, and thought about what she wanted.

She needed to still the hum of magical energy emanating from the ring. And after several repeats, she added herself to the list.

Fang asleep.

The ring invisible on her hand.

She repeated the tune until she was within a dozen horse lengths of the travelers. Several looked back at her. She put the flute back into her belt pouch and hummed the tune. Nobody should have heard through the noise of wheels and wagons creaking and hooves stomping down the road covered with gravel or puddles.

Several travelers nodded to her but said nothing. She nodded to them, kept humming, and let her horse choose where it wanted to slide in among the wagons and carts and saddled horses. The groupings of travelers on the road changed depending on the speed of the horses or oxen pulling their vehicles or being ridden. One wagon had a lopsided canopy across the back, and several small children slept in the shade. Ash smiled, guessing they had run alongside the wagon until they were too tired to keep up, or they were exhausted from having to sit all day.

She stopped humming for a few moments as that thought struck her. How did she know that? Had she done that, traveling with her parents, when she was very small? Before the flood and being caught up in the net with other half-drowned orphans at Tippessee?

Keep humming, the ring said.

Ash swallowed and returned to the beginning of the tune. She glanced back once as she left the wagon behind, noting the weary-looking women sitting with their backs to the two men driving the wagon. Were they the mothers of the children who slept in the shade?

What had her mother looked like? Ash shoved that thought away before she got distracted and stopped humming again. Such questions should wait.

Her focus was reaching the cavern before the hunters caught up with her. That meant humming and moving along and blending in with this knot of travelers. Ash let Garan pick the pace. Couriers had to trust their mounts. She was grateful to have one less thing to think about and distract her from holding up the haze to keep the hunters from noticing her.

Twelve more repeats of the song, and her throat felt dry enough she feared she might cough if she didn't get a drink. Could she afford to pause for a sip of water? Ash reached for the water skin hanging from one of the loops on the side of her saddle. Garan picked up the pace to get around a wagon pulled by four oxen. The woman driving the wagon glanced over at her and cocked an eyebrow at her. Ash nodded to her and kept her expression pleasant as a chill trickled down her back. Something in the way the woman looked at her. Could she be one of the hunters, disguised as an innocent traveler? Ash pretended to have trouble with the loop of the water skin and bowed her head, turning it slightly, to avoid looking at the woman.

Three miles behind us, the ring said, just as she passed the front set of oxen.

Thank you, A'theosius.

"In a hurry, are you?" a man said as Ash drew even with his group of four riders.

They all rode matching chestnut horses, with black-dyed gear. All wore unrelieved black. Ash wouldn't have been surprised to learn their matching, short-trimmed haircuts and beards were dyed black. Each had a silver crescent moon pin holding their cloaks closed.

That emblem explained everything. They were the Alsharp, a sect the seer Cecil had disliked discussing. Bad enough they believed in earning their way into A'theosius's Halls by their righteous acts, but they granted themselves the authority to determine what righteousness was, and to assign a value and a price. Meaning forgiveness and redemption could be earned or purchased without any repentance or remorse. They also vilified anyone who taught that A'theosius offered forgiveness and redemption as a gift, rather than insisting his followers earn their way.

"They believe the more miserable and constricted their lives, the bigger their reward," Cecil had said, while he and Ash had been butchering a hog one of the villagers had given him. "Unfortunately, they believe they gain even more rewards from A'theosius if they inflict their misery on others."

Now, in answer to the man's question, Ash turned enough to show him her courier pin. She hoped he didn't know the differences in the colors, and that she was in training.

"Time is a precious gift and must never be wasted, sir," she said, deciding to safeguard herself by quoting from Holy Writ. Even an Alsharp couldn't criticize that.

"What are you supposed to be?" the third man over in the row of riders asked.

Ash sighed. She had hoped she could keep moving and get ahead of them. It never profited anyone to be rude to the critical and self-righteous. That just gave them justification for whatever selfish, interfering actions they took.

"I'm a courier, sir." She nodded to them and nudged her horse, just enough to get it moving faster, but not enough for these men to see.

"Clearly, but are you a man or a woman?" His upper lip curled up as if he smelled something foul. "That's something that needs to be rectified immediately, if not sooner."

"The laws of the highways here won't be changed to suit you," the oldest man in the group said, without turning to look at either him or Ash.

"Right is right." The third man spat. "I despise all those kingdoms that consider themselves enlightened and allow women to dress up and pretend to be men."

Ash choked back the retort that burned her lips: She had never pretended to be a man. She had pretended to be a boy, yes, but there was a large difference. Her clothes now very clearly marked her as a woman. The cut between men's and women's clothes, even if both wore trousers, was obvious and evident to her. Didn't this man have any experience with such things? She muffled a chuckle. She hadn't had any experience, until she left Alfordia and went to kingdoms where women wore trousers every day, not just for messy, demanding physical work.

"Excuse me, but I must not be late," she said, nodding to the four, and this time nudged her horse enough to be seen.

"Just you watch and see," the third man called as she put distance between her and them. "We'll get the laws of this vile kingdom changed, and abominations like you won't be allowed to travel the king's highways."

Ash passed two wagons loaded with crates of unhappy, noisy chickens, then an enclosed carriage. The passengers peered through gauzy curtains at her. A small troop of soldiers rode ahead of the carriage, in two columns, five soldiers long. Plenty of room to go around them, but should she? That depended on who rode in the carriage, and what they feared. When she drew even with the closest row of soldiers, the one closest to her was a woman. The soldier glanced at her, just a shifting of her eyes instead of turning her head. Her gaze searched Ash from head to foot and back again.

"Huh, so you're what that sour crow was yelling about?" She winked at Ash.

Ash grinned back at her.

"We've managed to stay ahead of them, but our lady wants very much to confound them with a puzzle. If she must be guarded by women, to protect her virtue, then how can we be soldiers if that violates their sour prophet's laws?"

"Our lady wants to see their teeny tiny heads explode," the soldier ahead of them called, looking over her shoulder at them. Ash muffled a chuckle, seeing now all of the soldiers were women. Maybe the difference in clothes wasn't that obvious after all?

"You'd better be far away when she confronts them," the first soldier said. "Their kind have a nasty tendency to take their embarrassment out on those who can't defend themselves."

"Thank you." Ash nodded salute to the soldiers and nudged her horse to move a little faster.

She realized she had stopped humming. Her stomach went cold and heavy.

How long have I been silent?

No response from her companion.

She passed the troop of soldiers and slid into a wide gap between traveling companies, maybe twenty paces long.

Ring?

They're coming, the ring said. *The crossroads ahead of us. Can you see it?*

Ash stood up in her stirrups and saw the crossroads, maybe one hundred paces ahead of them. And coming from the right, a cloud of dust and movement.

You need to be past the crossroads before they reach it, or they'll stop you.

She dropped into her saddle and pulled her feet up to the second level of loops, for faster riding. Garan needed no other signal. He leaped into a gallop. Behind her, Fang snorted and twisted in his basket, kicking her. Now was not the time for him to have a temper tantrum. Or worse, stick his head up and get jolted out of the basket.

The bunny went still again. She hoped that meant he understood why they were racing now, and he hadn't fallen out. How long could Fang bounce down the road in daylight, before the smoking and the pain crippled him? Slowing Garan to let him catch up would just draw more attention. As if a smoking bunny wouldn't?

Ash hunched low, reducing wind resistance, and clung to the horse. She refused to look at the crossroads ahead of her. Seeing the enemy coming would do her no good. Why did they have to be on a wide open plain right at this point? The enemy could see her.

Ring, will it help to hum now, or just let them know I'm here?

Hum, by all means. His tone was tight. She wondered if he was being sarcastic. *When we catch up with the company ahead of us. Every little bit will help confuse and slow them.*

She wanted to ask how much distance lay between them and the cavern mouth. Ash saw where the plain abruptly ended, and the mountains thrust upward like bulky swords piercing a lumpy quilt. The map was burned into her mind. At the first turn, once she had gone between the sentinel pillars of jagged rock, the cavern mouth would open for her, reacting to the magic signal in her courier pin. No one else could see the cavern mouth, or step through what appeared to be solid stone.

From the corner of her left eye, she saw the streak of road cutting through the dull, dark grass of the plain. They had reached the crossroads. Ash focused on humming and tried not to listen for the sounds of hooves crashing down on her from the right.

I was right, the ring said. *I'm sorry, I wish I was wrong!*

About what?

There is more pulling on me than the bond between spirit rings. The feel, the smell, the taste of ancient magic, bound in artifacts ... it's strong enough to choke me. This magic isn't Lathia's hunters. Something stronger and darker moves them. Reach the cavern, Ashlyn! Get in and get through. Finish the quest. Free yourself of me as soon as you can. I'm the only anchor to find you. Lose me!

She wanted to scream no, she didn't want to lose him, there had to be another way. Terror and fury clogged her throat. She closed her eyes and breathed through her nose and fought to keep humming. The song seemed a ridiculously pitiful, weak weapon. Not even a weapon, but a shield, as thin as mist. She begged A'theosius for help, raised her voice, and sang the notes.

Through the song, she heard hooves behind her. People called out. Someone shouted to stop. Someone else shouted curses in response. Were they refusing to stop? Had the hunters, who had been nothing but a dark cloud surrounded by dust, tried to stop that armed company of merchants she had just passed? Was it possible they didn't see her?

Fire scorched her ear. A crossbow bolt slammed into the ground ahead of her.

No, they saw her. She sang louder. Had she missed notes? Enough to break the hazing spell and let them clearly see her?

Shadows swallowed her. Ash raised her head as the road dipped down, entering the maze of canyons and ravines ahead of her, and saw the sentinel pillars. She nearly laughed aloud. As wide as a palace at the bottom, they rose up, sheer and jagged and black, streaked with silver and brown, taller than any tower she had ever seen. Ash leaned low over Garan's neck. The horse's heart banged against her legs, in time with the bellows roar of his lungs. How much longer could he run all out like this?

The courier pin at her throat warmed, startling her, shattering the song. Blue-green light flared ahead, around the bend in the road. Ash howled triumph. The road curved around the base of the sheer cliff face and there it was, a low oval, softly pulsing with blue light.

The horse let out a defiant shriek and plunged down the ramp, into the underground shelter. Across a shallow stream. Lights flared to life around her, pushing aside the blackness, and Garan stumbled to a trot. Up out of the stream, he slowed more. Up a gradual incline, another thirty steps, and finally he stopped. Ash looked back.

The cliff face had closed up behind her. She was safe inside the cavern.

"Ring?"

We made it. He sounded weak.

Ash wanted nothing more than to slide out of the saddle and collapse in a puddle of aching on the ground. But she couldn't do that. The first rule for all couriers was to see to the needs of their mounts. Stable boxes and supplies to feed and water and curry the horses waited on the other side of the cavern, by the other entrance, with the station master, Callun. There she would find hot food and clean clothes, hot water for washing, and a bed. When she left would depend on Callun and what the magic hiding this cavern told him about the people hunting her.

Trying not to groan aloud, she slid out of her saddle and stayed upright on her feet, took Garan's reins, and followed the path illuminated for her by the floating blobs of magic light. Fang chirped happily as he leaped out of his basket and bounced off into the darkness. Ash couldn't have called him back if she wanted to. She let him go and trusted him to stay out of trouble, or at least, out of large trouble, while he explored the darkness.

"Can this ancient artifact magic reach through the protective walls and find us?"

The rock faces all around her threw back reflections of the light and echoed her voice, so she dropped to a whisper by the time she finished asking her question.

I ... don't ... know, the ring said. His voice had a hollow tone inside her head. As if he spoke from a far distance.

Ash hoped Callun would know. Each station master was bound to the station house with magic ties. Surely he could sense if magic tried to pierce the shelter and find those who had vanished inside.

The journey through the darkness, led by floating lights, seemed to take several hours. Ash blamed her weariness. She knew, because Filby had told her, magic folded distances so she could cross in less than an hour what would normally take a day to travel. When Callun met her and offered an arm for her to hold herself upright, she nearly wept from gratitude.

Callun assured her the defensive web of magic around the cavern made them invisible to the seeking magic of the enemy. He said he had sensed something trying to penetrate, but it failed. The cavern's magic defended by sitting quietly and pretending to be solid rock, rather than striking back and confirming something there needed defending.

When Ash had tended her horse and could finally change her clothes and wash, she collapsed into her bed. Fang was curled up next to her when she woke half a day later. Two couriers had come through while she slept, and both reported a band of brigands searching up and down the road, using a magic mirror to communicate with their partners on another road.

Ash stayed in the cavern station house for two days, until couriers coming from both directions reported no one used questing magic on the roads leading to the cavern. Callun reported the probing spells had ceased digging at the cavern. The enemy with their odd, ancient magic, had moved on and were likely harassing travelers on other roads.

That was little comfort, as she packed her saddle bags and saddled her horse.

Fang was eager to leave. The cavern was disappointingly empty of any kind of life worth hunting or terrifying. Still, he had enjoyed the constant darkness, once he persuaded the magic lights not to follow him and illuminate his every bouncing step. He wanted to move on and find better hunting. If Ash correctly read the signs made with his ears, he had plans to persuade a tribe of vampires to let him join them. The thought of losing her maniacal, bloodthirsty companion hurt more than she would have thought possible just a few months ago.

"Ready?" she whispered, after she and the ring and Fang had said goodbye to the other couriers and thanked Callun. Garan trotted up the ramp of stone to the barrier over the exit.

Always, the ring responded.

The days of rest and safety had been good for him, as well. Something made her want to cry, just a little bit, when Ash sensed the difference in the sound of his voice in her mind. She heard an echo of her own mixed apprehension and fear and teeth-gritted hope as they approached the way out of the cavern.

Justiciar Camwell had been rather selfish and self-serving and utterly unfair when he imposed the quest on her and Lathia. Ash still felt some resentment, despite admitting some benefits she enjoyed now. Her months of travel and adventure and danger had changed her. She had discovered things and remembered things about herself that she might never have found if she had stayed at Castle Fairhold. Gratitude didn't wipe out what the selfish, fat old man had done. Especially now that she faced losing the spirit ring. How could she learn about her inborn magic, and discover the truth about her parents' deaths and her own identity, without his help?

The stone face of the cavern mouth evaporated in front of her. She bent low in the saddle, even though the arch of the doorway was twice her height. She had to resist the sensation of a massive mouth about to close down on top of her. Ash glanced back once, before the stone returned to block the doorway. Then she nudged her horse's sides with her heels.

The ring sparked hot, burning, drawing a surprised cry of pain from Ash's throat. The sound of her voice echoed off the rock faces of the passageway around her. Fire bit her finger. Gritting her teeth to hold back curses, she yanked her glove off.

She nearly yanked the ring off with it.

The ring rotated around her finger, clearly too big for it now.

Just the size it had been when she first put it on.

It didn't gleam with promises of magic. No sparks traveled around the three strands of its braid. The metal looked dull, as if scratched repeatedly, or coated by a thick layer of skin oil and dirt.

"Ring?"

Silence.

"Please? Ring? Talk to me?"

Silence.

CHAPTER SIX

Ash shivered, looking up and all around, feeling as if the rock faces stared down at her. Disapproving. Poised to pounce. She needed to move.

She considered for a moment. The ring was large enough to be uncomfortable, sliding around inside her glove, getting in the way when she grasped the reins. She unfastened her courier pin and slid the ring onto the bar, then refastened it to her cloak. Now it was safe. She hoped.

Part of her wanted to fling the ring away, a taunting reminder of the friend she had lost. But what if she hadn't truly lost him? What if he was there, but perhaps through the pique of Justiciar Camwell, or the attacks from those ancient magical artifacts, he had been silenced?

How could she get him back? Go to Cecil for answers, hidden in one of his many books? Go to Justiciar Camwell and … and do what? Threaten him until he restored the spirit of the ring?

She needed answers. Sitting here and dithering wouldn't do her any good. She slid her glove back on her hand, clucked to the horse, and tugged on the reins. In moments the horse headed down the road, through the maze of ravines, and out to the highway again.

Ash gnawed on her problem, on the options to find answers, the possibilities of forcing Camwell to give the ring's spirit back to her. What if he hadn't taken or silenced the spirit? What rights did she have to make such a demand? The moment she crossed the border into Alfordia, if Lord Digory hadn't received Filby's request to release Ash to join the couriers, she would be a servant bound to Castle Fairhold. Then there was the threat from Lathia and her prince and the Purple Sky magicians.

First, she had to warn Castle Fairhold of Lathia's intentions. Then find Justiciar Camwell and warn him. Would he listen now, without the ring to support her story?

What would she do once she warned Fairhold? Return to Cecil, or try to find the Enchanters Council? Or seek magical libraries, on the thin chance an ancient book of magic would restore the ring to her?

Far too many questions and avenues that could lead to disaster.

If Ash's ring had gone silent and was too large to wear, logic said the same had happened to the ring Lathia wore, because the quest had ended. Knowing Lathia, Ash had no hope she would call off the hunt and give up her quest for revenge.

The sound of approaching hooves broke into her thoughts. Ash mentally slapped herself for being distracted. Yet again. She looked around. No options for escape, other than turning and running. The sides of the ravine leading back to the highway were too steep for her horse to climb. Turning and running would just warn the oncoming riders that she had something to fear, and something to protect, worth stealing.

"Fang, are you ready?"

Two thumps against the basket and her back. She smiled and felt for the knives tucked into the saddle, the knife at her waist, the knives tucked into the high tops of her riding boots. How many riders were there? The best option was to depend on Garan's speed and agility to get her out of their reach.

"A'theosius, please guide me, guard me ... save me from blood," she whispered.

Thirty paces, and the riders were close enough to see details. Four men, all dressed in leathers and chain mail, with crossbows strapped to the sides of their saddles in easy reach, and swords at their waists. They were coated with dust. Their horses were the big, sturdy kind better suited to long journeys rather than racing into battle. Were they heavily armed to defend themselves as they traveled through many lands? If so, what were they seeking? Or did they flee some stronger power and authority?

A dark blotch dropped from the sky, resolving into a hawk that glided along after the man in the lead. When the travelers drew closer, Ash saw the harness on the hawk's leg. It either hunted for the man it followed, or it carried messages.

Callun hadn't detected the hunters, but he had admitted that didn't mean they had gone away. They could have simply stopped all use of magic, going silent and undetected. Without the ring's guidance and his senses, she had no way of knowing if they were using magic right this moment and targeting her.

Without the ring ... maybe they couldn't sense her? They had no proof she was different from any other courier?

Ten paces away, the leader raised his hand and called to her to stop. Ash complied because she had no other options. There was no room to slide past them to flee. Her only options were to fight, lead them back to the cavern and hide there until they went away, or comply and hope they weren't hunting for her. Had she changed enough that she didn't match the scrawny servant girl pretending to be a boy Lathia would have described to them?

"Show us your hands," the leader called, once he moved his horse forward so there were only four paces between their horses' noses.

Ash hesitated, wagering that an innocent person would do so. She slowly raised her gloves hands. The man on the right of the leader swung down out of his saddle and stomped up to her.

"Gloves off," he snapped.

"Sir, why?"

He raised a hand as if to strike her. His leader called something in a foreign language. Just a few words. It stopped him. The man, now standing by her stirrup on her right side, bared his teeth in a fierce, challenging smile. He produced a long, thin blade from nowhere. Ash caught her breath and braced for him to flick that knife at her face, or her throat. She held up her hands to show she was complying.

The leader chuckled. It sounded friendly, but the fierce light in his eyes gave it an entirely different feel. Ash pulled off both gloves and tucked them into her belt. She held out her hands, palms facing them.

Too late, she wondered if wearing the ring all this time had left a dent in her finger, or worse, a lighter patch of skin. She didn't dare risk a single glance at her finger. That would give away far too much. At the very least, it would reveal she knew what they were looking for.

The man caught hold of one hand, turning it over several times. Then he caught hold of the other, also examining it. Ash tried not to resist, but an itchy sort of hum spilled through her at the touch of his gloved hands. She feared the sensation would be far worse if his skin was bare as well. Was she sensing magic, or something else working in and through him?

He called out a string of words in that foreign language. The anger in his voice turned the sound harsh. Ash braced for him to turn and strike, slash her with the knife, maybe reach up and pull her from the saddle. She hoped Fang was awake, although she hated asking him to go into the bright sunlight spilling down straight into this ravine. How much blood could he coat himself with to stave off the smoking in his fur?

Then the man stomped away from her, back to his horse. The hawk swooped down and landed on the leader's shoulder. Finally, the leader spoke, again in that foreign language. The four men turned as one, like in a dance, and headed down the road the way they had come. Without another word to her.

She smiled, shaky, suddenly dripping with sweat. Holding out her bare hands, she wasn't surprised to see them shake. Just a little.

So, the ring was right, and they couldn't sense her without it.

Was that final proof that the spirit was no longer in the ring? What were her chances for restoring him?

Yes, Fang was a handy surprise weapon to have on hand, but she needed the ring's guidance and memory and his sense for magic if she was going to get any answers for herself.

"That's what we'll do," she said, speaking more to herself than to Fang. She turned as far as she could and reached under the loose top of the basket, to pat him. "We need the ring back. Tomorrow we'll be out of Machpellan and in Alfordia. Two days to reach Castle Fairhold. Hopefully by then I'll have some idea how to persuade the justiciar to restore the ring."

Fang made a doubtful purr, ending on a high, inquisitive note.

"What do I do if he can't restore the ring, if what just happened here was caused by magic out of his control?" Ash shook her head. "We go to Cecil. If Cecil can't find me an answer …" She shuddered and thought of the enchanted castle again. To get the ring back, would she risk getting caught in the castle or the forest?

Yes, she thought she just might.

Ash took a deep breath, whispered a short prayer for help, and clucked at Garan to get moving. They had a long road ahead of them.

~~~~~

Ash's head ached from the storm of thoughts, speculations and trying to interpret every odd sound, every inquisitive look as she passed various groups of travelers by the end of that first day without the ring's guidance.

She could almost have laughed at the sense of being alone inside her own head, and the ringing silence just beyond the nattering of her own thoughts. She scolded herself multiple times through the day for having grown so dependent on the ring to warn her when trouble approached, so she didn't trust her own instincts. What had happened to her alertness and instincts to determine if someone were friend or foe, and what to say or do? That sensitivity had helped her avoid trouble and stay somewhat invisible in the busy world of Castle Fairhold.

"Face the ugly truth, Ash," she whispered, as she approached the station house through growing darkness. "You've grown lazy." She pressed her hand against the pin with the ring hidden behind it. "Ring, if you can still hear me, if this is just a nasty reprisal spell from the justiciar keeping me from hearing you … I hope you have some advice waiting when we can talk again, to help me avoid this problem in the future. Of course, I hope we can cure this and I never need to go without your help again." A shaky chuckle escaped her. "I certainly miss all your lessons, as we ride along."

She flinched when the star on her breastbone hummed softly, followed a few seconds later by the one on her buttocks. Magic was at work. Likely the defensive spells of the station house.

She smiled at the irony that what her parents' enemies intended for evil, either to keep her from realizing her magical potential or help them to track and trap her, had turned out to be somewhat useful for her. Ash reminded herself not to grow dependent on the stars. She wanted and needed to get rid of them as soon as possible. Ash made a note in her mind to talk with Hazel when she returned to Castle Fairhold. Now was the time to learn everything the hedge witch hadn't been able to teach her
~~~~~

before she and Fang had fled.

"Oh, Fang ..." She nearly yanked on Garan's reins to stop him just a few steps away from the gate of the fence around the station house. "Are you going to be in trouble once we're back within Fairhold Downs?"

A few chirps came from her passenger, who had fortunately slept most of the day without any restless shifting. Ash had no idea how to interpret those sounds. She was getting better interpreting Fang's ear movements. Another place where she had been somewhat lazy, depending on the ring to speak for Fang, to hear his thoughts when she couldn't see him.

"We'll figure it out. Maybe I should leave you somewhere half a day's ride from Fairhold?"

A hard thump of the basket against her back was a clear enough negative answer. She grinned at Fang's refusal to be separated from her. Then the horse stepped through the gate. The star on her buttocks flared like a stab from a very large needle. She needed to get rid of the stars.

"You're just in time," a woman called as the door of the station house creaked open. "I'm about to take the bread out of the oven. Hurry and settle your horse. I hope you have some good stories to tell." She leaned out, a tangle of bright red curls framing her cheerful, sharp-boned face, and gestured at the stables attached to the building on the left side. "It's been deathly quiet around here the last month or so."

"Quiet sounds wonderful," Ash responded, and slid out of her saddle.

She watched from the corner of her eye as she led Garan around to the side entrance of the small stable of five stalls. The woman shut the door. Before she reached for the loop of leather holding the lid of the basket, Fang popped up and out. He turned three somersaults before he hit the ground.

"Have fun. Don't get into trouble," she called as he leaped out into the thickening shadows.

Fang made a rude sound, somewhere between an explosion of gas and clicks, waggled his ears at her, and vanished.

The station master was Leticia, and the aromas of cooking that reached out to Ash when she opened the door were just as welcoming as the woman's smile. Leticia handed her a short rod of green crystal and pointed at a blank spot on the wall opposite the massive hearth. "That's the key to your room."

Before Ash could ask, a dimensional doorway opened up, just like at Filby's home. The stars didn't react. Ash made a note of that in her journal as soon as she could get her satchel open, to discuss later with Filby. There was so much that was tangled and knotted in the magic woven around her, making it difficult to predict or even understand how the different spells worked with and against each other.

She hurried to wash, because as Leticia had said, the bread was fresh from the oven. Ash slid the rod into her belt pouch and stepped out into the main room, which took up most of the station house. She reflected that the dimensional pocket magic allowed the station house to look small to outsiders while housing many people. She supposed that was necessary in a kingdom that could turn unfriendly toward all outsiders without warning. When she asked about the stables, and hiding large numbers of horses, Leticia confirmed dimensional magic worked there also.

The station master was a good hostess, doing most of the talking at the beginning of the meal, to allow Ash to eat while the food was hot. Then, once the berry tarts came out of the oven and she drenched them with cream and poured mugs of hot honey and lemon tea, it was Ash's turn to talk. She reported what she had seen and heard, the types of people she had passed on the road, the conditions of the villages she had ridden through or past. The road agents had left her alone, mostly nodding and waving her to keep going, when she got close enough for them to see her courier pin.

"Filby warned me when I asked to retire here, I would face months of boredom, speckled with weeks of tension and frustration with hide-bound bureaucrats." She chuckled and tugged down the collar of her dress, to reveal a necklace of a soft, pastel rainbow of crystal beads. Several glowed. "I keep watch on the surrounding crossroads. Have the mates to these lovelies embedded in trees or mile markers. That's how I knew you were close enough for me to put the bread in and make sure it was fresh." She winked, then stroked a larger, oval crystal. "This one lets me speak with Filby every once in a while. We're cousins on our maternal grandmothers' side." One corner of her mouth twitched, mischief sparkling in her eyes, as she tugged up her mane of curly red hair to reveal a delicately pointed ear. "I always considered Filby's side of the family the lucky ones, fewer obligations to the Fae Court. Retirement in the human realms is much more enjoyable. Do you have any messages to pass on to her when we talk?"

Ash thought for several moments, while she let the berry tart melt in her mouth. Her instincts didn't clang and buzz, warning her to be cautious. She considered that Letica wouldn't have revealed her Fae blood except to prove herself. Unless they were representatives of the Fae Court to the local government, Fae usually kept their identities hidden because of the general cold feelings toward their race, lingering generations after the Outbreak and several other magical incursions from other dimensions.

"Did she mention my ... birthmarks?" she finally said.

"That's a lovely little frustrating puzzle, indeed." The station master cradled her mug in both hands as she sipped, eyes sparkling. "Have they done anything odd since you left Filby?"

"What do you think they are?" One more test. The woman's answers were vague enough they could be covering a lack of knowledge.

"Besides not being birthmarks at all?" Leticia put the mug down with a soft thump for punctuation. "You were marked, and quite unfairly." She tapped her breastbone, then shifted to one side, as if she sat on something uncomfortable.

Ash grinned, and the woman chuckled. That was clear enough proof she knew, and delicately didn't mention the locations.

"You're wise to be cautious, girl. I agree with Filby, those are tags, a beacon to lead your enemies to you when the time is right for them and wrong for you. The sooner you can free yourself of that trouble, the better." The humor faded slowly from her eyes, and she turned the mug around between her hands several times before looking up again. "Filby chose your route so we could meet. I had a good friend who died in the battle to stop that cursed wave that made Tippessee a coastal town."

Ash fumbled the mug, then clutched it in both hands and swallowed hard, her mouth suddenly dry. She flinched when Leticia reached across the table and put two fingers under the mug, to raise it, and resisted a moment before taking a sip. That helped, but only a little.

"Do you know—do I look like—no, you probably didn't know my parents," she finally said, when she untangled the incoherent questions swirling through her head.

"No, I'm sorry, I never met anyone in the troop who went to fight the Dalwanga. That's the name of the greedy, arrogant brutes who conjured up that wave. And their leader. They believe, most wrongly, that because they come from long lines of enchanters, that gives them the authority to reshape the world to suit them. They used to claim they were favored of A'theosius, until they grew so twisted in their minds and souls they declared themselves wiser than the Maker, and proclaimed they would free all the worlds and dimensions of his rule." Leticia sighed and looked into her mug again. She frowned, as if surprised to find it empty, and got up to fetch the iron pot where more tea steeped.

"My friend told me about everyone in the troop, where they came from, some of their training, their loves," she said, once she had refilled their mugs and settled at the table again. She sighed. "Their families. Nine children among them, all under the age of six years. Five girls, between the ages of two and four. Yes, Filby asked me to dredge up everything I could remember. I put it in a little book somewhere ..." She glanced around, frowning slightly. "I'll find it before you leave. I hope it helps you. Plenty of room to write down what you find as you search. You do plan to search, don't you? But don't go back to Tippessee until you're free of those wretched stars, hear me?"

"Yes." Ash made a face. "I've been warned enough times, I'd be an utter fool to cast aside all that good advice."

Leticia chuckled. "Filby said you were smart. Now, what have those nasty tricks been doing to you lately? What sort of magic do they react to? And not react to. That could be more revealing in finding a way to unweave them."

Before Ash went to bed, she and Leticia talked through everything she could remember of the stars. When they first started to appear, how they had reacted to spells in use and proximity to magical objects.

"It's a sad, cruel trick that pompous fool of a justiciar played on you," Leticia said.

They had talked themselves dry. Ash had showed her the journal where she had been writing down everything she could remember about the stars and any encounters with seers and visionaries through her short life.

"Taking your friend away from you when you need him most." She snorted and reached to gather up their empty mugs. "Of course, he had no obligation to show you any mercy or kindness, and he likely didn't intend for you to make friends with your overseer. Still, to lose him just when his wisdom could have helped us. Why, what's wrong, girl?" She put down one mug and reached to put two fingers under Ash's chin and tip her head up, to look in her face.

"I didn't exactly lose the ring," Ash whispered, when she couldn't be sure a sudden, aching surge of sorrow that squeezed her throat wouldn't emerge as an undignified sob. "He's silent, and he came off my finger. I was hoping it was just me, that I wasn't allowed to hear him anymore, but maybe he could ..." She held up a finger, gesturing for Leticia to wait, and hurried to her room, where she had hung up her jacket to air. She brought it out, freeing the courier pin from her jacket, to let the ring slide off the bar. Bracing for some negative reaction, she held the ring out to Leticia.

"Huh. That's interesting." The station master took the ring between two fingers and held it out at arm's length, studying it with narrowed eyes. "At first glance, it's nothing more than a nice little bauble."

"He's completely gone?" Her voice cracked. This was worse than she had feared. She wished she hadn't even asked.

CHAPTER SEVEN

"Not exactly," Leticia said. "I can feel a nasty little silence spell, and a darkness spell, if I don't miss my guess. I'm greatly out of practice with some of the finer, more delicate methods of peering between the threads of magic. It would take me several hours of reading, brushing up on the theory, and then more hours of study to sharpen my eyes. I'd guess, however, that someone slapped a spell on the ring itself, to keep him from seeing out and hearing and speaking."

"But he's still in there?" Breathing grew a little easier, just for a few seconds, before the full implications hit Ash. "He's trapped. He can't reach out, nothing can get in. That's cruel!"

"If it's any comfort, this is a sophisticated bit of weaving. From what Filby told me about the justiciar, this is beyond the kinds of spells he would employ, and most likely far too expensive for his tastes and means. This is from someone truly nasty, who doesn't care how much effort and energy is expended in the spell's creation. The suffering of the victim matters more."

"Lathia." Ash shuddered. "We never thought to check the magic woven around the ring, just all the tangles and knots affecting me."

"Either she hates all spirit rings, because of the one inflicted on her, or she's out to hurt the ring because she knows he's your friend."

"She's out to hurt anyone and everyone who ever stood against her." Another shudder. "And that reminds me. I need to get to Fairhold and warn everyone, as swiftly as I can."

"Then you'd best say your prayers, girl, and get as much rest as you can." Leticia gestured with a lift of her chin. "To bed with you. I'll wake you before dawn, and the housekeeping breezes will have your horse ready."

Leticia did more than that. When she woke Ash at dawn, she handed her a small book the size of her hand, bound in creamy blue leather, filled with the promised information on the magical troop who had faced the Dalwanga's wave of devastation. Ash hurried through washing and dressing and stepped out into the main room. She found Fang finishing a very red breakfast of strawberries and tomatoes, chattering with wild flips and twists and flaps of his ears. Leticia laughed, her wet eyes and red cheeks indicating she had been laughing at whatever the bunny said for some time now. It made perfect sense that Leticia would understand the bunny language.

"Breakfast to eat in the saddle." Leticia pointed at a cloth pouch and a small drinking skin that bulged. "That's food for the day and tomorrow, and I've put a feedbag of magic-fortified grain on the front loop of your saddle. You'll still need to water your horse, but you'll be able to ride him two days straight before he'll need to stop and rest for a night. That should chop some hours off your journey. At the very least, get you over the border into Alfordia, and into more friendly territory."

"Thank you. That's … I don't understand how I am so lucky —"

"Blessed, girl, not lucky. A'theosius is watching out for you, guiding you to friendly hearts and minds. Most likely because you have a strange and wondrous destiny, some heavy duty ahead of you, some task only you can do. You need training, and you'll come against enough enemies and blocks and barriers to test you and make you strong. Friends like Filby and me, we're here to provide refreshment and support, and make sure you never feel alone. And remind you to say your prayers."

"Blessed." Ash nodded and swallowed hard, then let her heart lead and reached out to hug the woman. Leticia startled, then she laughed and wrapped her arms tight around her, just for two heartbeats. "Thank you. For so much. I can't even begin …"

"Don't waste time." She gave a friendly cuff to the back of Ash's head, like Myrtle used to do when Ash worked in the kitchens at Fairhold. "Get on with you. And you," she pointed to Fang, who was sitting up and starting to groom away the signs of his messy breakfast. "Watch out for her and keep your head down. I've heard enough rumblings through the whispers, the bunny council is irritated with you. Catch them at the wrong phase of the moon, they'll be accusing you of more than totally false murder charges."

Ash thought about those words as she hurried out to her waiting horse, checked the feedbag, tied her packs into place, and lifted Fang into his basket. Garan trotted down the road, his footsteps sounding oddly muffled in the dawn quiet, as if the melting shadows somehow thickened the very air. Finally, when the sparkle of dew wasn't quite so bright, but the road ahead and behind them was still empty, she spoke.

"Fang, will you be in trouble with the bunny council? I mean, yes, you were in trouble when you fled. That's why you had to leave Alfordia with me. Will you be in more trouble when you return? Because you fled? Maybe you should stay back, when we reach Fairhold? Don't step foot onto the downs?"

Fang thumped hard four times against the basket, thudding against her back. His chittering and grumbling reinforced what she took to be an emphatic no to her suggestion.

"What will they do if they catch you? Can they sense when you get near? Maybe you should stay in the basket until we leave Fairhold?"

This time, there was a long delay, and the two thumps from inside the basket had only half the force of the first ones.

"We'll figure something out to keep you safe." She sighed. "Please, A'theosius, help me keep Fang safe."

When she met up with traffic heading down the road, going the same direction, and she didn't have to be quite as string-snapping alert, Ash opened the little blue journal. Leticia had warned her there wasn't as much information in there as she could have wished, but it was a starting point. She listed the numbers of people in the magical troop, eighteen men and twelve women. Eight married couples. Four had children. Leticia knew the names of the couples and the villages they came from, the towers where they had studied and trained and the names of their mentors. She knew which ones had children, and their numbers, but not the names or ages of the children with each couple. Ash could have been an only child, or had one or two siblings. That bit of information did help her narrow down which couples and their home villages and families she could search out. Someday. When other concerns were resolved. She wondered if she looked like her mother or her father, or perhaps she didn't look like either, but someone else in their families, a grandparent or aunt or uncle, or even cousins.

Speculating on such things put an odd little ache in her head and chest. She laughed at herself a few times, when she realized that she really hadn't wondered that much about her family, her origins, and any relatives who had given her up for dead. All orphans at one time or another wondered about such things, but she knew from talking with the boys who had been given into Granny Phlox's care, most let such questions die, because they had so little hope of finding answers. After all, Tippessee was three days away by horse from Castle Fairhold, and no one had protested when the twelve orphans were gathered up and given into Lady Charlotte's custody. Perhaps no one really noticed, in all the fuss and loss and devastation.

Perhaps one of those boys was her brother. Ash tried to remember the faces of the boys she had grown up with, but her memory failed her. The older boys had been adopted out or sent to apprenticeships when she was so young, she hadn't really paid attention to them. They were all so young. Life was cruel to orphans, but Lady Charlotte and Granny Phlox had done their best to give them good childhoods despite that.

Ash resolved to make removing the stars her next task once she had warned Castle Fairhold. The sooner she could return to Tippessee in safety and start asking questions, the better.

She was careful to stop every four hours to water Garan and let him rest for half an hour at a time. She studied the map of the territory the king's highway would take her through as she headed for the border with Alfordia, and tried to calculate where she would be riding at night. She could depend on the horse to take care of her, staying on the highway and warning her of approaching dangers. Ash doubted she would be able to sleep in the saddle. Curiosity drove her to taste the grain Leticia had given her. She took a pinch of the grain and sniffed it. Whatever herbs had been added to the grain, she couldn't detect them. Just the same dusty, rich smell of grain she expected. Her throat closed at the thought of trying to eat some of it. She wondered if a human eating food meant for a horse would do her any harm, or just make her sick. Maybe the magic to help the horse was so specialized, it wouldn't work for a human?

There was so very much she didn't know about magic, despite all the studying she had done with Cecil. She had depended on the ring to teach her along the way, from all those books he had accessed and devoured. Another strike against Justiciar Camwell for wrapping that spell around the ring to take him away from her when the quest was fulfilled. And a larger strike against Lathia for the magic her minions had added to the spell, to silence and blind him.

~~~~~

Ash tried again to persuade Fang to stay behind when she reached the borders of Castle Fairhold's territory. He squealed at her and hit the basket hard enough to slam into her back and likely leave a bruise. She had to laugh and thanked him for his loyalty. Even if he was rather painfully adamant about it.

Then she had more important things to think about. How should she approach the residents of Fairhold? Should she look for Hazel and Granny Phlox, first? Would anyone recognize her, with her longer hair and different clothes, riding a horse, dressed as a woman instead of a servant boy? Would they let her talk to Lady Charlotte if they didn't recognize her?

That dilemma was taken out of her hands when a shout arose from a field ahead of her, as she crested a rise in the landscape. A crossroads lay ahead of her, and two men on horseback came down the intersecting road, apparently intending to meet up with her. Ash let Garan slow so the two men, now visible in Fairhold livery, reached the crossroads first.

They stopped and turned their horses, not blocking the road, but clearly waiting for her. Ash said a silent prayer. Fang thumped gently against the basket.

"It's all right." She hoped that would be true. Then a yelp caught in her throat when the square, ruddy features of one of the men snagged her attention. She knew him. Aron. The oldest of Granny Phlox's pups. Could this be a gift, some encouragement from A'theosius?

"Courier, what word?" the other man called, when Ash was maybe
~~~~~

five horse lengths from them. She recognized him now, Randall, Captain Reginald's nephew and second-in-command.

Of course, they recognized her uniform jacket, the badge, the colored braids on the horse's tack, to identify couriers across all kingdoms. She tried to remember if any trouble was stirring for Fairhold, maybe for Alfordia in general, from all the gossip she had overheard along the way. She didn't dare lie and claim to have a message for Lady Charlotte. The mission she had come on was too important to taint it with lies, even if well-intentioned.

"I'm here—" She stopped herself from saying "personal reasons," because that wouldn't sound any better than lying. "I don't carry an official message from any kings or nobles, but I do have ... grave news, for Castle Fairhold, its family and many of its servants."

Randall leaned forward and he frowned as he stared at her. Ash stopped her horse with two lengths between them.

"My pardon, courier. What grave news is this?"

"I'm sorry, but Lady Charlotte and Lord Digory would not appreciate my talking about family business that could be embarrassing, if not painful. Not out where someone might overhear."

"Painful in what way?" Randall's expression cooled, along with his tone.

"Not out here." She gestured at the field to their left, where several dozen people surrounded four or five wagons, busy gathering up sheaves of wheat to haul them into the barns and likely the threshing floors. "Voices carry too well in the cooling air."

"Aye, they do." He glanced at Aron, gesturing with his chin, then beckoned for Ash to follow.

As she expected, Aron turned his horse to follow behind her, as she followed Randall. Neither man said anything to her on the ride of nearly an hour to Castle Fairhold. Ash rehearsed the possible speeches she had prepared, to get in to speak to Lady Charlotte. Perhaps she should have asked for Dunstan? Why hadn't she used any of the rehearsed words she had been working on since she left Willemsport? How she wished the ring was here to advise her, or at the very least, tease her out of her nerves.

Ash's swirling thoughts led back to her questions about the other orphans gathered up from Tippessee. Was it possible Aron was her brother? Did Aron look anything like her? Turning to look at him now would only make Randall suspicious.

Would she help or make things worse, by introducing herself now? Randall had been friendly to the servant boys, giving them opportunities to try their hand with the wooden practice swords and shields and blunted arrows and crossbow bolts. He hadn't been present during the inquiries, and he hadn't come to say goodbye to her and wish her well during the last two days at Castle Fairhold before she fled. Maybe he was one of those who had been offended to learn the boy, Ash, was a girl in disguise?

Stop nattering yourself into knots and a headache and twitchy innards, she scolded herself.

"Have you been a courier long?" Randall said, turning to speak over his shoulder.

"No." Ash tried to smile.

He slowed his horse, so it fell back to walk beside hers.

"How long?" His gaze traveled over her briefly, then studied the pouches, the bags strapped to the saddle, and lingered especially long on the basket holding Fang.

"I'm still in training. I came to Lady Filby just over a month ago."

"Ah, that explains ..." Randall rubbed his eye with a knuckle. "You seem over-young for a courier."

"I'm nearly sixteen." *In the spring,* Ash silently added.

"Where are you from?"

"I don't really know. I'm an orphan." She listened to the tiny thrill that shot through her, like an echo of a whisper of laughter, encouraging her. Did she dare hope that was the ring, somehow breaking through the spells silencing him? "I was separated from my family in the great flood that hit Tippessee and raised with other orphans."

"Huh. Interesting." He glanced sideways, as if barely stopping himself in time from looking over his shoulder at Aron, riding behind them.

"You're older than me, Aron," she said, and turned to look at him.

Aron showed his good training by not gasping or swearing or sitting up straight or yanking on his horse's reins. His eyes widened, but he did nothing else.

"Do you remember anything from before the flood hit, and before Lady Charlotte gathered us up and gave us to Granny Phlox?"

"Why would you ask ..." Randall reached out, his arm swift and his grip tight around her wrist. "I know you." He gripped harder, until she flinched and hissed. He loosened his hold but didn't let go. "But I don't know you."

"Ash," Aron said on a groan.

Randall cursed. He yanked the reins to stop his horse and let go of her wrist to catch the reins out of her hands. When her horse stopped, he turned his so he faced her now, and caught her chin in his palm. His eyes widened and narrowed several times as he studied her face. He leaned back, shook his head twice, then abruptly released her and tipped his head back and laughed, three great barks.

"Hazel warned me to be on the lookout for you," he said on a growl, punctuated with a few muttered words that were probably curses.

"My quest is over, and I have news of Lathia. If anyone cares," she added.

That got a grin from Randall. He looked her over again. "Are you supposed to be a girl now?"

"I've always been a girl. Boy clothes really are more comfortable and sensible, especially for a servant with all sorts of chores."

"You would have had different chores if you let us know you were a girl," Aron said, finally bringing his horse up alongside her, so she was bracketed between them.

"Why are you disguised as a courier?" Randal said.

"I'm not. I'm serving with Filby's couriers. For now. Her letter asking Lord Digory to release me to her service should have gotten here already."

"Not that they'd tell us lower ranks ..." He nodded and gestured with a jerk of his chin toward the castle, then finally let go of the reins. "What took you so long getting back here?"

"I was on foot. Do you know how long it takes to get through all the caverns and cross all the borders the justiciar required, when you're walking?"

That got laughter from both men. Randall nudged his horse faster, moving ahead of them. Ash caught Aron giving her sideways glances as they followed close behind. He had always been one of the nicer older brothers when they were living in Granny Phlox's cottage, protecting the younger ones from the boys who had to prove they were stronger and faster than someone. She hoped he wasn't going to get silly, now that he knew she was a girl. If Aron decided to get protective, older brother to younger sister, or worse, show interest in her as a girl with nothing brotherly about it, she didn't want to have to hurt him. In either his heart or his stomach, with a good right hook to double him over and knock some sense into him.

Several people along the road to the castle were close enough to see and recognize the courier markings, and the cry went ahead of them. Ash studied the sun, sitting a handspan above the horizon, and willed it to drop faster. She didn't want to take Fang through the gates. Getting him out of the basket and outside where he could roam during the night would be difficult, at best. On the other hand, the shadows within the castle's walls would be strong enough to protect him if he had to move about before full night fell. If she asked that nobody touch the basket, that would just attract attention and questions. Someone would get curious enough to look, or when they knew who she was, they would get irritated and investigate simply because she said not to. Then there would be trouble.

On the other hand ... she grinned as she imagined how Fang would deal with the servants who hadn't been pleasant to work with, the self-righteous and sour-mouthed who spent their days trying to prove they were smarter and better than everyone around them.

A buzz settled into the star on her breastbone when Ash was two horse lengths from the main castle gates. She braced herself. The buzz turned into a dull stab, in both stars, then faded away before she took a breath. That was new. Had someone felt the need to set warning spells or some other kind of magic on the gates or the castle walls since she left? Or had she simply grown more sensitive to magic at work?

Randall stopped his horse in the second courtyard, leading to the stables, and gestured at one of the rails for tethering the horses outside. He dismounted after Ash stopped her horse next to his and held out his hands for her reins. She didn't know how to take it when he tied Garan to the rail, beckoned with a turn of his head, and turned and headed for the door into the castle.

There was no remedy for it. She glanced once at Aron, then tugged loose the loop for the basket closure and raised the lid slightly.

"I'm going inside, but I don't plan to stay long. I hope nobody will bother you, but try not to make a mess if you have to come look for me." She lowered the lid before Fang thumped his response, making the basket shake a little.

"What's that?" Aron asked, as she slid down from the saddle.

"My traveling companion. A very cranky bunny. Did you know bunnies have magic?" She didn't wait for him to catch up with her. She almost hoped he would stay behind to guard her horse. Not that she expected anyone to steal within Castle Fairhold, but there were always a few curious souls who thought privacy and secrets were crimes against humanity.

"Don't talk to us about bunnies." Aron shuddered as he fell into step with her.

CHAPTER EIGHT

"Trouble?" Ash asked.

"We were overrun with a herd of bunnies back in …" Aron caught hold of her elbow and nearly stopped her, but Randall was waiting, just inside the doorway, watching them. "Just after you left. What did you do to rile bunnies? Who most of us didn't know until then had magic," he added with a grin.

"I didn't do anything. My friend was falsely accused of bunny crimes and had to run for his life. Hazel sent him with me. She thought we might help each other."

"And did you?" Randall said. He led the way into the castle and turned right, to go up a narrow flight of stone steps.

"He saved my life, and now I look after him." She snorted. "And try to keep him out of trouble."

They came out onto the landing on the next floor. He led the way to the right, to Lord Digory's study. Ash fought down the sense of impending doom. When had Lord Digory ever been unreasonable or unjust? Then again, she had been gone more than two-thirds of the year. There was no telling what changes had occurred, what damages might have resulted from the whole Lathia incident. She hoped Winston had listened to Justiciar Camwell and stayed away from Fairhold, although she couldn't imagine the other distant relatives were at all pleased to have him spend even more time in their homes.

Dunstan trotted down the corridor from the other direction, his face bright with anticipation. Ash stumbled, startled to see the changes in him. She hadn't been gone that long, but Dunstan seemed older, certainly taller, hardened in some way. Had he spent the summer and early fall going on adventures, preparing for his time of travel next year? Or had something awful happened to age and toughen him?

Their gazes met, he nodded politely, and hurried into his father's study ahead of Randall. Ash snorted, both amused and a little hurt that Dunstan hadn't recognized her. Ridiculous. Why should he? It wasn't like they had spent much time together over the last handful of years, so he would know her no matter what changes she had made in her clothes and hair.

"Father, the courier is here," Dunstan said, as Ash followed Randall into Lord Digory's office.

"Well, so soon?" Lord Digory turned from the small window that faced the farmlands sprawling out behind the castle to the west. He looked Ash over once, then strode around behind his worktable full of papers and wax tablets and ledgers and pens and ink pots. A gusting sigh escaped him as he settled down into his wide chair. One corner of his mouth quirked up as he swept his gaze over her again. "Welcome home, Ashlyn."

Dunstan's muffled exclamation and his wide eyes were most gratifying. Ash returned Lord Digory's grin, feeling as if she had done something that pleased him greatly. She was nearly breathless for a few seconds with relief that he wasn't angry on seeing her.

"Thank you, my lord."

"Ash?" Dunstan settled on a clear corner of the table and shook his head, looking her over. "You ... you look different."

"I look like a girl now?" She flinched when Randall clapped a hand on her shoulder, then relaxed when he grinned at her, nodded, and turned to leave the study, taking Aron with him. "Sir, I assume Lady Filby's letter reached you?"

"And saying you were bringing details of the danger facing our family, information she couldn't include in the letter because the story was too long." Lord Digory settled back in his chair and crossed his hands over his stomach. "Should we include my mother?"

"This concerns the whole family, my lord, and many of the servants. Lathia—Lady Lathia," she corrected herself, "has fallen into some power and authority, and she is essentially setting out to punish everyone who ever crossed her."

"That sounds like her," Dunstan said with a snort.

"We also need to send warning to Justiciar Camwell. The spirit rings he gave us were able to not just hear and watch everything we did, but could look into our thoughts when necessary. Her ring told my ring what Lathia has planned. Or at least what the magicians in her service intend to do."

"Magicians in her service, is it?" Lord Digory nodded, his expression darkening with seriousness. "Dunstan, fetch your mother. Ash and I will be in your grandmother's study. That is the most secure place to hold a war council."

Dunstan slid off the corner of the table and hurried out of the study. Lord Digory's smile was weary as he levered himself out of his chair. He led Ash back down the stairs, to cross the entryway and the outer hall, to the tower stairs leading up to Lady Charlotte's study. They were both silent, and Ash caught him watching the various servants they passed. No one showed any recognition in those few seconds when their gazes landed on her and then she passed them. If they recognized her, they didn't react where she could see or hear. Ash wondered if Lord Digory would have recognized her if he hadn't been warned by Filby.

A tickle of coolness touched the star on her bottom when she was halfway up the final turn of the stairs to reach the tower room. Ash braced herself for a stronger reaction, expecting some sort of guarding ward on Lady Charlotte's door.

"Sir, have you been preparing for attack of some kind? Are there defensive spells through the castle now?"

"Hmm? No. Why do you ask? Should we gather defensive spells?" He paused a moment to look over his shoulder at her.

"I'm not really sure. Perhaps we should call in Hazel, and she can send for magicians or wizards more experienced in these things. I asked because I felt some magic at work."

"Did you now?" He paused with his hand on the latch of Lady Charlotte's partially open door. "What amazing things have you done since you were forced to flee, Ashlyn?"

"She's awakening to her inborn magic, I daresay," Hazel said, as she pulled the door open. "I thought I felt a disturbance … and yes, I heard you asking, and yes, I have woven a few spells around the castle. Mostly as sentinels, to give us some warning." She stepped aside as Lord Digory came into the room and held out her arms to embrace Ash as she came into the doorway. "How the child has grown. Didn't I tell you she would come into her own?" she added, turning Ash to face Lady Charlotte at her worktable.

"Welcome home, dear girl," Lady Charlotte murmured. She smiled, her pleasure evident, but the happy flush couldn't disguise her pallor.

Lady Charlotte looked much thinner, more frail than she had been when Ash left in the early spring. She didn't get up from her chair, which was filled with cushions that seemed to envelope her.

"My lady." Ash swallowed down a cry of apology. All she could think was that Lathia's minions had somehow sent some nasty spells ahead of them, already attacking Lady Charlotte.

"Sentinel spells?" Lord Digory tugged two chairs away from the far wall and brought them up next to Lady Charlotte's table. "Why?"

"Lathia was breathing out threats with every other sentence out of her nasty mouth when she finally left," Lady Charlotte said. "It only made sense that someone sent out on a quest with a magical overseer and required to investigate magic would stumble into something magical, one way or another. Even if it was just a magic mirror to give her advice or let her spy on people from hundreds of miles away. Being Winston's daughter, Lathia would naturally choose some kind of nasty, petty revenge on people who didn't toady to her every whim."

"That sounds far too much like her," Lady Beatrice said on entering the room. A delighted smile lit her face. "Oh, very well done, Ashlyn. You have thrived, despite that odious quest."

"Thank you, my lady." Ash bobbed the abbreviated curtsy Filby had taught her, that didn't look at all ridiculous in trousers.

Seneschal Gilbert followed Lady Beatrice and Dunstan in and stopped in the doorway. "My lord? My lady thought that perhaps you would prefer to take dinner here, in private? May I remind you there are no guests at the table ..." He trailed off as his gaze landed on Ash and he clearly did not recognize her.

"No, my lady is right. This is too important to risk gossipy ears hearing. You don't mind, Mother?" Lord Digory added, turning to Lady Charlotte.

"How grave is your news, Ash?" she asked after only a moment of thought.

"I can't be sure, my lady. You all know Lady Lathia better than I do."

"Wish we didn't," Dunstan muttered. He winked at Ash.

"But the telling of the tale could take some time," Ash added, and deliberately didn't look at Gilbert. He made not a sound, but she didn't want to see his expression.

"Gilbert, we will need more chairs." Lady Charlotte settled back in her chair, wriggling a little to adjust the pillows enfolding her, rested her elbows on the arms of the chair and her chin on her interlaced fingers. "Now, what sort of trouble has that simpering little brat gotten into now?"

Ash wished, as she went through the tale, that the ring could break through the binding and silencing spells and tell the story himself. Not just as proof and verification of what she had to say, but because his droll tone of voice added so much to the telling. She had been practicing what to say and in what order to deliver the information, and tried to imagine what she would want to know first if she was hearing the story new.

She started by explaining about the spirit rings, how she had made friends with her ring immediately and how Lathia even now likely didn't know that her spirit ring could hear and see and share with others what went on around her, and even what Lathia was thinking. The family verified what the ring had told her about Lathia's last day at the castle. How she had raged and insisted that Ash be forced to serve her on the quest. How she kept insisting that she had done nothing wrong, that the justiciar was being unfair. And the threats she made against the entire family for lying about her. She begged Petroc and Aron and several other older servant boys, the most handsome and strong ones, to accompany her. She insisted they were in love with her and accused several of them of trying to seduce her. She insisted that they all had magic rings that let them walk through walls or turn invisible, when her father, aghast, pointed out that any visitors in the night would have to go through his bedroom to reach Lathia and Leena's bedroom. And besides, he always locked his daughters into their room at night.

Hearing that, Lathia had shrieked and accused her father of being as cruel to her as everyone else at the castle, only twice as much.

"Yes, logic and mathematics aren't her strong suit, are they?" Lady Charlotte muttered, when Dunstan finished relaying that last bit of idiocy.

Lathia had ridden out of the castle with her two servants, with only her father to see her off. He left when her parting shot was to declare she hated him and she would make him suffer for being so unfair to her. She had pouted and kicked her horse until the poor creature tried to throw her. Hazel showed mercy on the horse by blowing a sleeping powder into Lathia's face. She had to be tied to her saddle, for an ignominious exit.

"She threatened her own father? What about Lady Leena?" Ash asked, shuddering as all sorts of new, horrified thoughts came to her.

"Oh, she hates her sister because Leena wouldn't ride with her or call on the maiden warriors to attack Justiciar Camwell and make him set her free," Dunstan reported. "Leena just laughed at her and walked away. She stayed here only a few days after Cousin Winston left, and as far as we know, she's staying permanently with the maiden warriors at the chapter house in the capitol."

"We need to warn both of them." She wondered if Winston would finally believe the warnings about his daughter's vindictiveness. It was the right thing to do, even if she didn't like the idea of protecting him from what he had certainly brought on himself.

Lord Digory promised they would send warnings. Lady Charlotte remarked that several other relatives had reported that Winston had gotten into arguments with nearly everyone whose homes he visited throughout the year. Quite a few servants, of all ages, at nearly every estate, had finally had the courage to make complaints about Lathia's treatment of them over the last several years. Quite a few relatives notified Winston that he would no longer be a welcome guest in their homes.

"There are always a few, however, who are even worse, backward-minded arrogant boobies," Lady Charlotte mused, punctuated with a delicate sniff of disgust. "They have rallied around Winston, insisting he was entirely in the right to support his daughter against the accusations of a servant. However, the hypocrites don't want him in their homes either. They granted him a cottage to live in and limited him to three servants. One of whom is an overseer to ensure he lives within the means of the small allowance he receives from the family estate. I wonder if he's learned anything yet."

Ash made a quick prayer that she wouldn't be required to go to that cottage to give Winston warning face-to-face.

Finally, she was free to relate what the ring had told her about Lathia's adventures. Tripping the curse that freed her servants. Becoming a servant of an ogre, and so unsatisfactory she had been thrown out. Then falling victim to the people she had accidentally freed through her own greedy actions. Dunstan made sounds of disgust when she related how Lathia had been found by a prince. He laughed when the prince delegated the rescuing work to others.

By that time, Gilbert and Myrtle and several serving boys had brought in a trestle table and set up dinner for them. She found it far easier to sit at the table with the family than she had anticipated. She supposed her travels and experiences had broken her of the fear the castle would crumble around them if she, a mere servant, sat in the presence of her superiors.

Lord Digory asked Gilbert to have Scholar Malchus and Friar Ipswich join them after dinner. He wanted to dictate letters to Winston and Justiciar Camwell. He needed to gather information about Marcocia and the kingdom where Lathia was now a princess, to determine just how much power her prince had. He asked Hazel who she could contact to learn about the styles and strengths of magic employed by the Purple Sky, and what defenses they needed to prepare.

"Now that I think about it," he said, when Gilbert had left on his errands, "Camwell should be here in another fortnight, riding his regular circuit. How long can you stay before your duties take you away, Ashlyn? It might be good to tell him everything you've told us, face to face."

"No, Father," Dunstan said, pausing in lifting his cup to his mouth. "I can't imagine the justiciar would want to hear any of that directly from her. And honestly, it isn't kind to Ash to make her face him again. He knew Lathia was lying from the beginning, but he pretended he was being fair to both of them, just to have his fun."

"True," Lady Beatrice said. "But this is an opportunity to teach him some badly needed humility."

"I need to face him." Ash held out her hand with the ring on her thumb, made to fit securely by means of yarn wrapped around the band, courtesy of Hazel. "His badly done magic is at least partly responsible for the spells that have silenced my friend. I need him restored. I need him entirely freed from the justiciar's service."

"You don't know if he'll be given back his voice," Hazel said. "All those knotted and tangled spells are beyond me and my experience and sight, but I can detect several different signatures or scents or what have you of magic. Removing one set of knots might not loosen the others."

"I have to try. The ring befriended me. He gave me the warnings I gave you."

"You're right. And we shall stand with you when you face the justiciar," Lord Digory said.

<p style="text-align:center">~~~~~</p>

Ash and Hazel went to visit Granny Phlox once dinner was over. Partly that was to get Fang out of the castle, so he could escape for his night's roaming. Ash needed to escape the curious and critical and gawking former fellow servants. More important than those two reasons to flee, she needed to talk with the two women about the boys rescued from Tippessee, to share with them what she had learned about the wave, the league of magic-users who had sacrificed themselves, and their lost children.

"And you'll be staying with me, of course," Hazel added, after Fang had saluted them and bounced away into the darkness. They walked down the long pathway that wound around and through the various holdings and meadows and crofter's farms belonging to Castle Fairhold. They couldn't cut across the fields and through the orchards at night, and certainly not leading Ash's horse.

"Thank you. I was hoping to stay with either you or Granny Phlox. I had the awful feeling Lady Beatrice would feel compelled to put me into one of those guest rooms and that's just … not me. I wouldn't be able to sleep there."

"No one would leave you alone, for one thing." Hazel patted Ash's shoulder. "You've done very well. I'm proud of you. And I hope in return, I can help loosen some of those knots. It's a mercy you can even breathe, they're woven so tight around you."

"You can sense the magic on me? Did you sense it before?"

"Something. Waiting. Sleeping. Vague to the point that anyone would think I was going a little mad if I had mentioned it. You've blossomed, girl. In many different ways," she added with a chuckle.

"I was cursed."

"How's that?" Hazel turned to frown at her through the moonlight-streaked shadows cast by the orchard on the right side of the path.

"It's a long story, but two stars have appeared on me. They were put there by enemies of my parents, to block the blooming of my magic, and to help them find me when my magic awoke. Filby thinks they want to either drain my magic or turn me to serve them."

"Hmm … makes too much sense." Another pat on Ash's shoulder. "I'm sorry I didn't sense that. I could have tried to do something while the curse was weak."

"Do you think you can try to do something about it now?"

"I'll try. Can't promise I'll succeed."

The two boys still living with Granny Phlox were already in bed, but Ash doubted they were asleep. She thought she heard creaks and whispers coming from the loft as she and Granny and Hazel talked long into the night, but she didn't grudge the listeners. If they were also children of the league of magic-users who had stood against the great wave of destruction, then they had a right to know. She shared her adventures, the things she had learned from Blaz and Cecil and Filby.

Messages would have to be sent to the boys who had been apprenticed out, and Granny would send for the boys who were still living in or near the castle, to have them come and be examined. What they would do if any of the other orphans showed signs of blocked and bound magic would be guided by what they found, how much, and how many were affected. Ash thought about traveling with a handful of boys and young men, some of whom might be brothers or cousins to her. She couldn't interpret the queasy, excited feeling churning through her. Was it good or bad, excitement or fear?

Ash went home with Hazel for the night. The hedge witch proposed making an herbal infusion to help both of them sleep. Ash had just slipped into her nightshirt when a thudding started on the cottage door. Hazel came from the kitchen, which took up half of the cottage, to answer the door. She muttered something and Ash's stars twinged, indicating she had just activated some spell. Then she pulled the door open.

Fang tumbled through the door, grumbling and hissing. He skidded to a stop on the flagstone floor and spun around three times before launching himself at Ash to wrap himself around her legs. His ears gestured wildly, but when he tipped his head back to look up at her, she saw something like triumph, maybe mischief, sparkling in actual gleams of green magic among the reddish tint in his eyes.

That reddish tint was new. His vampiric side had strengthened. Had something happened during his roaming that had brought it out?

"He's excited and angry, but he did something nasty in exchange for whatever happened to him out there," she guessed. Ash silently scolded herself for not working harder to learn to interpret Fang's ear signals. She had relied on the ring far too much.

"The question is," Hazel said, as she shut the door with a thud, "whether he accidentally ran into someone who reported him to the bunny council, or he deliberately sought out their attention."

CHAPTER NINE

Fang squealed what certainly sounded like injured innocence to Ash. He let go of her legs and gesticulated even more wildly with his ears.

"Oh, so you think that terrifying those bullies into confessing what they did will exonerate you?" Hazel rolled her eyes and turned to go back into the kitchen. She gestured for Ash and Fang to follow her. "What makes you think that revealing your vampire side will make the warren welcome you back with open … paws?"

"At least his name has been cleared. From murder at least," Ash hurried to add.

Hazel muttered something and picked up a large wooden spoon to stir the copper pot hanging over the fire. A tantalizing swirl of aromas arose from it. Spicy and sweet and bitter. She gestured for Ash to come closer.

"Inhale deeply. Slowly. Hold it as long as you can, then take another deep breath." She turned back to Fang. "So, Ash tells me you don't want to be freed. You like turning the tables on anything bigger than you, scaring the fewmets out of them. Didn't you consider the consequences if you let that foreign nature dig its roots deeper into you?"

The third deep breath of the aromatic steam made Ash a little dizzy. She could have sworn the stone paving undulated under her feet, just enough to make her wobble. Eyes closed, she didn't see Fang's side of the conversation. Hazel mostly responded with, "Oh, really?" and "I'll wager they didn't see that coming." With each breath she took, Hazel's voice grew more muted and distant. The woman's hands on her arms, guiding her away from the fireplace, barely cut through the hazy, thick feeling muffling all her senses.

"There now, that's enough. I've done something, but time will tell if I did any good." Hazel settled Ash on a bench next to the window, where chilly, leaf-scented air filtered through the ajar shutters.

"What did you do?" Ash shook her head and muffled a giggle when it felt like everything inside her sloshed around a little. "Try to do?"

"Well, something's been loosened a little. Whether any knots have come undone, that will take time." Hazel hmm'ed a few times, tracing her fingers over Ash's face, her arms, turned her hands over and studied her palms. "Open your shirt, let me see that star?"

"Star?" Ash opened her eyes and took a couple deeper breaths, which dispelled some of the muffling. She wondered if she were dreaming as she looked at her hands.

They glowed softly. A pale luminescence shifting between blue and green, with swirls of silver through them.

"What did you do to me?"

"That, my girl, is your magic finding weak spots in the barriers woven around you, leaking out and working on those knots. You were so tightly bound, there was no wiggling space inside, but your magic has fresh air and room to move, and it's finally breaking free to start defending you. Which makes me think that binding was inflicted on you while the seeds of magic were still too small, too young, too much asleep, to even feel the change. I have to wonder if your lack of memories from before the wave are a result of that nasty spell, as well."

"That's me?" Ash whispered, slightly mesmerized by the movement of color across her skin. Then she remembered what else Hazel had said and fumbled with the laces of her nightshirt.

The star was still there, but looked more gray than the milky silver she was used to. It didn't glow. It looked rather uneven around the edges.

"Well, it's a start, at least." Hazel nodded. "I'll dose the boys with that, whether they have any markings or not. And I'll give you some flasks of the mixture, concentrated, to take in regular doses to continue the loosening effect."

"Thank you," Ash whispered, trembling. Fang leaned against her, his forepaws on her knees, looking up at her with very evident concern in his big eyes. That disturbing hint of red was gone. He patted her thighs with his ears. "Yes, I think I'm all right now. Thank you for asking."

~~~~~

Three days later, Ash needed to return to her travels. Lingering any longer wouldn't be wise.

Granny Phlox and Hazel examined and questioned all the boys who had grown up with Ash. Only the youngest, Timoteo, had any reaction to Hazel's potion. A star glowed on his forehead. He yelped and claimed it burned. Hazel splashed the potion on the star. It fell off his forehead and disintegrated in a shower of evil-smelling sparks before it hit the table where he had been sitting. Hazel declared she would make the boy her apprentice and keep a watchful eye on him. Hopefully, catching the star before it reacted to his awakening magic meant the enemy who had inflicted it on him wouldn't know it had been destroyed. Timoteo seemed rather pleased, if a little dazed, at the news that he had inborn magic.

Ash wondered what had happened to the other children of the magic-users. Leticia had said there were nine, after all. Had the rest died in the flood? Or had the enemy found them before Lady Charlotte swept in and gathered up the orphans? Were Ash's possible sisters or brothers
~~~~~

even now in the service of the evil conclave of magicians and wizards? Perhaps dead, drained of their magic long ago?

Lady Charlotte promised she would write to officials and their successors who had been involved in the rescue after the flood, to learn what had happened to all the children found in the wake of the damage.

Justiciar Camwell was missing. How such a large, pompous, loud man could just vanish without a sound, without a bit of disturbance, boggled the imagination. He had been in good spirits six days ago. As far as anyone knew, nothing happened to frighten or anger him, no messages that created any reaction, good or bad. His household servants had overheard him talking to the magic mirror in his study, sending messages to fellow justiciars requesting a convocation a month earlier than normally scheduled.

Then, when the housekeeper came to summon him to dinner, he wasn't there. No one had seen him walk out of his study. He was too enormous to fit through the windows. No one had been in to visit him all day. His magic mirror, Diatribe, had been busy in the mirror network, delivering messages and catching up on legal matters chatter, and didn't hear any outcry. There was no sign of struggle or disturbance in the study, nothing out of place. The justiciar's three clerks had been busy running errands and delivering messages and filing documents in the territorial courthouse, so they hadn't seen Camwell for the last two days.

"What are the possibilities he got the warning from Father and just packed up and fled?" Dunstan said, when he and Ash discussed the news a few hours later.

Lord Digory had asked the same question before he got to the end of the report. The justiciar's lead clerk didn't know if Camwell had read the message from Castle Fairhold, but it had arrived that morning.

Ash knew then she needed to leave, if only to attract the attention of Lathia's magicians and keep them moving. If they were busy trying to find her, they wouldn't have time or malevolent magic to employ against the residents of Castle Fairhold. She made her farewells and took Garan from the stable to go to Hazel's cottage to retrieve her bags and Fang. She had bundled Fang into the basket under cover of a cloak to protect him from the late afternoon sunshine, when Dunstan came running with more news. Lord Winston had responded to the warning from Lord Digory.

Typical of him, Winston ignored the bitter fight he had with Lathia before she left the castle. He mocked Lord Digory and scorned his concern and warnings. He declared Lathia would at long last get justice and fulfill his righteous claims to an estate.

"Righteous claims?" Dunstan snorted and spat, which surprised Ash, because usually he had such lovely manners. "Grandmother laughed at that part. She said Cousin Winston's grandmother was the shame of the family, producing five children and unable to identify which men sired them. Her brother was extremely charitable to raise those children, and not send her to a cloister, to control her promiscuity."

"I wish I could see him when Lathia's men find him and he finds out how wrong he is," she said. "I know it's wrong of me, but I want to laugh in his face."

A rapid thumping resounded from Fang's basket, making her flinch. "What's that?" Dunstan reached for the lid of the basket.

"Don't. It's not safe. For Fang, and maybe not for you," Ash added, ending on a chuckle. "He's … he has a bad reaction to sunlight. I only let him out at night. Have Hazel tell you about Fang when I'm gone. That's a part of my story I just didn't feel safe to share."

"I wish I had gone with you. I wish I could go with you now."

"When you leave on your adventure next spring, send a message to me through Filby, and I'll try to meet you on the road." She caught her breath at a sudden pang in her chest that had nothing to do with the fading star. "If it's safe."

"A'theosius guide and guard you," he murmured, and reached out to clasp her forearm. She returned the gesture, like two warriors making a vow before riding into battle.

Dunstan walked with her to the main road, and for a short time they could talk like the young friends they had been, making plans for his travels, the places he would go, the things he would see, the adventures he hoped to face. They grew silent when they crested the last rise in the landscape and the graveled road came within sight. They gripped each other's forearms once again when they reached the side of the road. Ash climbed into the saddle and rode away in silence. She looked back three times, and each time, until the rolling landscape came between them, Dunstan was still there, watching her go.

~~~~~

Ash headed north at the first crossroads. She refused to lead the Purple Sky to Cecil. There was still that tracking spell to deal with. The more times she retraced her steps, the stronger the beacon to lead the enemy to her. She hoped that traveling quickly would leave a fainter trail that faded easily and lost the hunters.

She crossed the northern border of Alfordia into Dagomar, then headed west, down through Berengrave. Ash stopped at three courier station houses along the way, checking for messages from Filby, and picking up courier packets waiting to be dropped at the next station house or to be delivered to an official.

Two weeks after leaving Fairhold, she crossed into Cammerlang, and the weather changed rapidly. From chilly mornings and pleasantly warm afternoons, the temperature dropped so frost covered the ground in the
~~~~~

mornings. Just as spring had come early at Castle Fairhold, now fall had passed in a few breaths, and winter approached. That made no sense because the leaves still held a large amount of green. They should be entirely gold and scarlet, starting to shrivel to dull brown as they dripped from the trees before the cold settled in like this.

Why was the weather colder when she was traveling south?

Was this maybe a sign of Lathia's magicians chasing her?

"Ring, I need you. Please, if you can at least hear me now ..." Ash shuddered at the break in her voice.

What was wrong with her? Besides feeling utterly alone again, and hating it? Maybe it was the helplessness, the sense of having no recourse, no ideas what to do.

She had used up the last dose of Hazel's loosening potion three days ago. She drank a few swallows every three days, but the wretched star on her breastbone was still visible.

"What I need is a library full of magic books, some guidance. I didn't read the right books when I had the chance, didn't write down the right information." She imagined the book full of her notes from the time pool library vibrated a little in the saddlebag pressed against her leg. "Please, A'theosius ... what do I do? Guide me? Lead me to someone who can help me?"

Later, Ash wondered if she had prayed foolishly. Perhaps she had irritated the Maker with her whining? Or perhaps, as Cecil had remarked several times, A'theosius sometimes had a nasty sense of humor.

Midway through the afternoon, she came to a fork in the road that shouldn't have been there, according to the map she had consulted at the last station house. She took the fork that looked more traveled, less covered with the first of the falling leaves. The trees seemed to move closer with every few steps Garan took. The shadows thickened, and the breeze chilled. Ash's breath turned to gusts of fog in front of her. She looked back, and though she was sure she had only been riding maybe a quarter mile, she couldn't see the massive boulder she had passed at the fork in the road. The trees seemed even closer to the road behind her than ahead of her.

Snowflakes swirled in front of her eyes. One landed on her nose. She crossed her eyes to stare at the bit of crystal, but it melted before she could focus. Ash turned forward again. Garan kept moving, and she chose to take comfort in that. Courier horses were chosen for their intelligence and sensitivity to danger. The moment Garan showed signs of uneasiness, sensing trouble ahead, she would turn right around and head back the way she came.

No more snowflakes danced through the air. Maybe she had imagined it?

Fang thumped on the basket, startling a muffled yelp from her. Ash looked around, assessing the sunlight. Between the hints of darkening clouds she glimpsed in the gaps between the trees, and the leaves still thick overhead, she judged there were enough shadows to risk opening the basket. Fang rose up high on his hind legs, resting his forepaws on the edge of the basket, and turned his head in all directions, sniffing loudly.

"What do you smell? Danger?" Ash murmured. She took deep, slow breaths.

All she could smell was the crisp, tangy perfume of leaves that had turned color far too soon in the season. The breeze seemed to grow more chilly with every other heartbeat, and she wished for a big, hot fire to sit by, and warmed cider. The next station house on her route was more than a day away, and she had been planning to spend the night in the forest. She thought she had enough to keep her warm between her jacket and cloak and two blankets in her bedroll.

"Should we turn back?" she asked when Fang settled down into the basket again.

He tipped his head to the right, studying her just long enough to make her feel twitchy. Then he twisted his ears around to point back the way they had come.

Ash tugged on the reins to turn Garan, who resisted for a moment. Always a bad sign, Filby had told her. Yet how could the horse sense something that she and Fang had missed, that made him want to keep going down the road?

Fang squeaked and slapped her back with his ears

"What?" Her voice sounded dead, as if it had hit something massive and soft, so the sound didn't bounce back at her. Fang sniffed, and so did Ash.

She smelled something sweet-sour. Like wine, but with a greenish quality, like something alive.

Flowers? She sniffed again. What kind of flowers could be blooming at this time of year?

Roses. Ash took another sniff. Yes, she smelled roses. She opened her mouth to ask Fang if that was what he smelled.

Snow swirled around them, flakes filling her eyes. Whirls and streaks of snow danced through the air in a way that snow shouldn't. Not without a massive wind blowing it upward and around in billows and spirals. Yet Ash felt practically no wind at all.

"Snow ... and roses." Her mind blanked as she grappled to understand. Ash knew that was a danger sign, the scent of roses amid snow, but she couldn't remember why!

Garan leaped forward. Into a gallop.

The tunnel through the trees turned white ... dotted with red and pink and yellow.

Roses?

Before she could yank on the reins to stop the horse, they had plunged into the tunnel of roses amid the snow.

Buzzing whispered along her skin. The marrow of her bones itched. The world tipped sideways underneath her, threatening to spill her off. She tightened her legs around the horse's sides. Nausea twisted through her guts.

Just like the sensation when she entered the time pools library.

A change in flow of time? Where was she going? Ash yanked harder on the reins to stop the horse, turn him in mid-flight, go back.

Fire stabbed her, like a red-hot poker piercing her breastbone. Her saddle turned to fire underneath her. Ash screamed. The sound echoed off the thick walls of the tunnel.

Then it died, along with the cold and snow and shadows, as the horse stumbled out into daylight from among thick, luxuriant trees bright with spring buds, jeweled with dew. The air was warm, heavy with the scents of new life bursting out of the prison of winter.

The horse stumbled to a stop and Ash threw herself out of the saddle. She tugged open her jacket and vest and shirt, expecting to find a scar and smoking flesh where the fire had touched.

Flakes of silver sparkling ash blew away on the warm breeze.

The star on her breastbone had vanished.

She gingerly touched her bottom, expecting residual pain. Had that dratted glowing star been burned away, just like the one on her breastbone?

Fang squealed and thudded the basket lid closed on himself. Ash inhaled to shout and ask him what was wrong, but that was a stupid question, wasn't it? She smelled scorched fur. Of course, all that sunlight after the soothing shadows.

"Sorry, Fang." Her voice cracked. "Please, A'theosius ... what happened?"

She knew what happened, but she didn't want to even think the words.

Cecil's vision had caught up with her. She had entered the enchanted forest.

She looked back, and maybe twenty paces away, she saw the tunnel of snow and roses, and at the far end she saw the scarlet and amber streaked with green of the forest she had been riding through. Not just a tunnel, but a portal.

"Stupid, stupid, stupid," she scolded herself, and vaulted into the saddle, yanking on the reins to turn Garan and go back before the doorway closed.

He snorted and shook his head, fighting her, turning reluctantly.

In those few seconds, the portal faded away, so all she saw was shadows, hints of snow and roses, like a painted screen, with the springtime forest bleeding through. In another breath, even that had vanished.

Ash stared at the spot and let Garan keep going. She couldn't think. What was she supposed to do? How could she get back to where she had been? The portals opened again. Filby had told her that. Why couldn't she remember all the things they had discussed, all the things she and Cecil had discussed, the many fables about the enchanted forest?

Garan nickered, yanking her out of her spinning thoughts and she yanked on the reins to stop him.

The trees warped and seemed to melt a few steps in front of his nose. The gray-streaked bark smoothed and turned soft brown streaked with white. The leaves vanished. Before her stood an archway through stone, into shadows, with flickers of light at the far end that made her think of sunshine sparkling through leaves dancing in a high wind. A smell like salt and hot stone seeped up through the darkness. Ash shuddered and listened to that sense of guidance that had been with her all her life. Filby and Cecil had both said she had been wrapped with guarding and guiding spells. Why hadn't those spells warned her away from the tunnel of roses and snow?

Unless ... the magic guarding and guiding her ... wanted her here?

She turned the horse, moving back away from that archway.

It was another portal, opening into a new land. Somewhere else on this same continent, or halfway around the world? Several of the books she had read, and the stories from other couriers, agreed that the portals in the enchanted forest took turns becoming doors to different places.

When would the tunnel of snow through roses return?

Ash clutched her stomach, feeling dizzy and queasy at a new thought. *When* was an important question. Far too many stories she had read and heard about the enchanted forest insisted that time passed differently. While she might sit here and wait a day, maybe two, maybe three until the tunnel of snow and roses opened again, she had no promise that when she came out the other end that the same amount of time had passed in the place she had left behind.

CHAPTER TEN

"Think, you idiot," she whispered, and her voice cracked again.

Fang thumped against the basket and her back, accompanied by a plaintive crooning. She understood. He wanted out, and he wanted answers.

"In a few minutes, Fang. I need to find a nice shady place to hide, then I'll let you out. We're in trouble."

The crooning rose, higher in pitch and louder, with a few clicks and chirps. She grinned shakily, know his response was the equivalent of a sarcastic, "Oh, do you really think so?" She imagined Cecil giving her his narrow-eyed, pursed-lip look of teasing disappointment. It had always helped her relax when she had tied her brain into knots of frustration over a problem she couldn't resolve.

"A'theosius ... help me? Clear my mind?" she whispered, as she turned the horse and put the stone arch behind her.

The forest in front of her looked so warm and bright and inviting. The perfumes of dozens of flowers and the rich sunshine-on-leaves smell urged her to relax, take off her cloak, let the horse wander as he pleased. Maybe find a shady spot to spread a blanket and take a nap.

The welcome of the forest could be a trap. What if she gave in and let herself wander, and never found her way back to this spot again?

"Help," she whispered, half-prayer and half-scolding. "I need to get back to this spot. If the portals take turns in an orderly fashion, as Filby said, then this is the only way to get back to where I was. Even if it isn't the same *when* that I was."

First task: mark this place so she could find it again. Yet far enough away from the area affected by the magic that changed the portal so the marker itself was unaffected. She based her plans on what Filby had told her about the enchanted forest. Ash chose to believe there was some order, some rhythm and pattern to the forest. Even if it had been knocked off balance and loose of its moorings by whatever knocked the enchanted castle loose. This portal would always take her to the same place. She simply needed to wait long enough for it to come around again to that section of forest in Cammerlang.

"Simply," she muttered, punctuated with a snort.

The important thing was to stay close by so she could watch and learn the rhythm and patterns. Not go chasing through the forest, looking for every opening that gave a hint, most likely false, of taking her back to where she started. That was always how people in the accounts she had read had lost their minds, visited kingdoms around the world, and lost the people they loved and the lives they had left behind.

Several fallen trees a short distance away, partially covered with vines and forest debris, provided what she needed. Ash dismounted and got to work hauling the larger limbs over to the spot ten steps away from the stone archway. She set up rough pillars on either side of the opening. The ground was soft enough to dig down more than a foot, to set the limbs in. She tied them together at the top with the tough cord from the traveling kit Filby referred to as "possibly useful trash." Ash made a note to let the woman know that yes, the trash was indeed useful. She spread red ink on the limbs in each bundle, from the small pot included in the kit. Ash wiped her fingers clean on fallen leaves and considered the other items in the kit, wondering when they would prove useful as well.

Fang thumped on the basket and chittered impatiently at her. She sighed.

"Sorry. We'll get into shade soon."

She could have created a temporary shady spot for him by spreading her cloak over some bushes and at least let him out of the basket while she worked. Then Ash looked up at the sky. The task had taken her more than an hour, but the angle of the light through the leaves hadn't changed. Now that she considered her surroundings, there really was no "angle" of light, was there? She sensed how much had passed because she had a good inner time sense. Yet judging by the light of the forest, no time had passed. A shiver crawled down her sweaty back. Someone had told her there was no sun or moon in the enchanted forest.

How could she tell direction without watching the sun's journey across the sky? How could she navigate away from this spot to explore, to find food and shelter, if she couldn't be sure of finding her way back?

Ash's hands shook slightly as she tugged on the lid of the compartment in the front of her saddle and pulled out the compass in its padded box embedded in the frame. She had half-expected to find the needle spinning wildly, reacting to inimical magic. What else could be affecting the forest, but inimical magic?

The tiny star in the tip of the longer, wider end of the needle pointed into the forest. Testing, she pulled the compass out of its box and walked across the clearing she had disturbed with her work, shifting her gaze between the needle and the spot it pointed to. Relief slid cool through her innards as the needle adjusted to keep pointing at the same spot. Good, at least she had a sense of north. That was a starting place.

With the pillars marking the portal, no matter how much it changed, she had an anchor spot. Now to find a place where Fang could get out of the basket. Even if this place had no sun, the light still burned him. Then she needed to set up a camp, or at the very least make a defensible place, and then forage for food. There was no telling how long she would be here until the portal opened again.

Back in the saddle, the height let her detect several trails through the forest, most likely created by animals as they went to either feeding grounds or to water. Ash said a silent prayer for water and guided Garan down the widest and straightest trail. The sounds of bird song and the rustling of tree creatures filtered through the whisper of the breeze among the branches and leaves. It made a comforting music at the back of her mind, assuring her nothing large and dangerous was nearby. Silence suddenly falling around her meant danger approaching.

The trees parted ahead of her, with a sparkle of what had to be sunlight on water. Then the sound of water flowing over rocks reached her ears. The horse's ears flicked forward and he picked up the pace. The underbrush grew thinner and the trees sparser with every few steps down the trail, until they emerged into a clearing that crossed a shallow stream.

Not too shallow for fish to live in it. Dark shapes wriggled through the soft light and shadows dappling the water. The smallest was as long as her hand, the largest the length of her arm. Fresh fish, cooked over a campfire, would be a welcome break from salted and dried provisions, washed down with weak wine or the always-fresh water from that miraculous water skin Blaz had given her.

Dismounting, Ash looked back the way she had come. The animal trail was nearly straight, which sent a prickle of unease up her back. Animals simply didn't walk in straight lines. Had this perhaps been made by people at one time, and the animals simply kept it open because it was easy to follow? What mattered was that she could see all the way to that arch of stone, and even some of the red ink she had smeared on the markers she had created. Good. She could keep an eye on the portal and note how long it remained in that form.

Fang thumped on the basket, hard enough to make it rock against the leather straps holding it in place. Loud sighs and groans followed.

"As soon as I have a shelter put together, you can come out," she promised him. "How good are you at fishing?"

That got a few curious chirps from him. Ash laughed Nothing like a challenge and fresh food to get Fang's interest and raise his spirits.

She studied the clear space between the underbrush and the stream, trying to pick a good camping spot without having to leave the line of sight of the portal. The grass gave way to mossy growth in an almost clear line. Suspicious, she dug with the heel of her boot and found a layer of what looked like sand over smoothed rock. Following the line of the slope down to the stream with her eyes, Ash guessed that at one time, this had been a river, much wider, and higher. She hoped she was right, that the moss covering the ground for more than two horse lengths meant chances of sudden floods were small, and she could camp safely here. At least, until there was a torrential downpour. Did it rain in the enchanted forest?

The ring would know. She couldn't ask him though, could she? Ash mentally slapped herself for that bit of laziness, assuming she would always have the ring to fill in the information she needed. She had written notes about the enchanted forest in that wondrous journal that let her write as much as she wanted, without running out of blank pages. The question was if she had written enough of the right information.

"Well, if I manage to make a fire, that's what I'll be doing before I go to sleep. Reading. Learning. A'theosius ... help me? Give me wisdom? Keep us safe?" she ended on a whisper.

She saw a clump of what she hoped were berry bushes, hanging over the stream where the bank seemed to rise up higher than her head. A dozen steps took her close enough to see the bank of the stream curved out a little ways and her angle changed.

That wasn't entirely a massive clump of bushes, full of jewel-like clusters of blue-black berries. They grew over a hunched outcropping of rock, and a dark space underneath was where the river, when it was three horse-lengths wider, had carved out the bank. Ash's heart skipped a few beats as she envisioned a snug camp, tucked up under that rock, giving her a place to put her back to if danger approached. And plenty of shade for Fang to stretch out in.

She looked back to where she had left Garan. That was a short enough walk back to where she could see the portal, wasn't it? Common sense said not to walk down that trail to the portal in the dark, anyway. If it ever got dark.

"Please, A'theosius, some darkness, just so Fang can hunt and explore? And I'll need sleep eventually, but it's hard to sleep in daylight ..." She sighed and looked upward at the perfect sky, that pale blue with only a few streaks of clouds that could never turn to rain, and far-off dots of what she hoped were birds. Ordinary birds. If birds that lived in the enchanted forest could ever be ordinary.

Complaining and whining were bad for the beginning of however long she stayed here. Ash told herself to be grateful for what she had. She needed to set up camp and get to work studying.

Fang chirped his thanks when she set the basket down in the shade of the overhang and opened the lid. He jumped out, nearly hitting his head, and crouched at the edge of the shadow. Ash tried to understand how, with no visible sun, there could be shadows. It made her head hurt after only a few minutes, so she gave up. Something she could do, though—she hung her cloak on the berry bushes hanging off one side of the outcropping, creating more shadow, widening the space where Fang was safe. He crooned and moved to the new edge of shadow, and leaned out, studying the stream and the length of the bank. Until faint steam rose from the tips of his ears. Ash was busy unsaddling Garan and figuring out how to picket him. The moss and sand were too shallow to drive a stake into the ground. She shoved her saddlebags into the shade with her foot and resorted to tangling the reins with the berry bush dripping over the front lip of the overhang.

She pulled the altered shirt out of the bottom of her saddle bag and held it up, silently asking Fang if he wanted to resort to it. He studied it for a moment, then seemed to wilt a little, sighed loudly, and hopped over to where she sat. In a moment, he was covered, with the tail of the shirt dragging on the moss and sand. His ears twitched as she slipped the sleeves over them. Ash pitied Fang and his mangled dignity, having to resort to her old shirt to protect him from the light. Until night fell, if it ever fell, he either had to hide in the shade of the rock or suffer some indignity to be able to move freely.

His injured pride made him a zealous fisherman, although he seemed to do ten times as much splashing as he did catching. By the time Ash had found a stick long enough and thick enough to serve as a fishing spear, Fang had caught two fish, snapping their spines with one bite of his massive teeth and shaking them back and forth in his mouth as he hopped up to their campsite to deposit them.

She waded out, barefoot, her trousers rolled up above her knees, to what seemed like the middle of the stream. It rose barely to her knees. Then she stood still, as the older servant boys had taught the younger children at Fairhold, until the fish grew used to the presence of her legs in the water and swam near again. The water was pleasantly cold, the air pleasantly warm, and Ash played with the idea of staying here indefinitely. Not because the portal never opened again to that tunnel of roses in snow, but because she chose to. She would be safe from Lathia's magicians, wouldn't she? But how would she find help to regain the ring, free him from whatever kept him silent, and perhaps blind and deaf? Cecil and Filby might have answers in their books, or at least know where to look, where to go to find those answers. She hoped they wouldn't have to depend on the Enchanters Council or even the Court for help.

Ash grew busy with considering her options, scolding herself for giving in to the longing to just find some place safe to rest. She nearly didn't see the fish that circled her legs. She waited until the longest, fattest fish came close enough to brush its tail against her ankles, three times. Then she plunged the spear down. She was as startled as the fish when she succeeded on the first try. Wading back to the bank would mean wading back out and waiting again until the water calmed and the fish returned. Could she throw the fish that far, to reach the bank? More important, could she trust Fang not to eat that fish while she waited to spear another?

She resorted to tucking the dying fish into her belt, though it dripped down her trousers and wriggled uncomfortably against her ribs. Next time, Ash promised herself, she would have a bag, or maybe a basket that floated on the water, to put her catch in until she had caught enough. She glanced back at the camp. Fang was down at the water's edge now, splashing in the water. She saw no sign of the fish he had caught. And again, nearly missed the fish that circled her ankles in curiosity. This one wasn't quite as large as the first, but they would make dinner and a satisfying breakfast. If Fang didn't get hungry in the night and take the leftovers.

This fish took three stabs, but she got him, and waded back to the bank with the spear raised high, the fish wriggling, and the one in her belt giving feeble writhing death throes.

She wisely wrapped the fish in her saddle blanket to protect them. Fang was sniffing at them when she came back with an armload of branches to make a fire. She glared at him and he didn't even try to look guilty as he hopped away, back to the water's edge to resume fishing.

The first tenuous flames of the fire drew her attention to the sky. Ash sat back on her heels and caught her breath in wonder at the streaks of purple and pink and gold that seemed to push the blue from the sky. So this was what sunset looked like when there was no sun.

"Night does come here," she whispered, and grinned. "Thank you, A'theosius. Thank you I didn't waste time. Thank you for shelter and food. Please … help me find my way out of here? Soon?"

Then she got to work building up the fire and cleaning the fish to cook.. A splash and then the sounds of struggle showed Fang's success. She had her fish on a long green stick, bobbing slightly over the fire, when he returned to sit in the growing shadows and nibble at his catch.

When the first star twinkled to life in the deepest purple of the night sky, directly overhead, Fang hopped over to Ash and pawed at his covered ears. She put aside the half-eaten fish on a platter of enormous leaves and helped him remove the shirt. Then he vanished like a shot into the darkness, the sounds of his feet splatting on the moss fading in mere heartbeats.

She read until the last of her sticks went on the fire, then made a torch and walked up to the edge of the underbrush to gather more firewood. This time she made three trips, to hopefully get through the night without having to leave the fire again. Garan was calm, and she trusted him to act as her sentinel. Ash tried not to grumble, even if silently, about the lack of the ring to help her, as guard and as provider of light, and most importantly, as teacher. How was she going to deal with this unwanted stay in the enchanted forest?

Visit, she corrected herself a moment later. She did not want to stay, she refused to stay. This was a visit. A short one. Nothing more.

Ash read through her journal full of notes until her eyes blurred. She realized that making the fire bright enough for reading meant burning the wood quickly. Meaning more trips to the forest to gather wood. She put her journal away and spread her blankets beside the fire, and lay where she could look beyond the fire, up at the sky. She had made notes on navigating by the stars, and tried to determine where the forest might be in its wandering by looking for familiar constellations.

After another hour, Ash couldn't find anything familiar in the sky above her. She was ready to close her eyes and try to sleep when a new thought struck her. Had those stars moved at all since night fell? Stars were supposed to move in the night sky, just like the moon moved and the sun moved. Even if there were no sun and moon here in the enchanted forest, shouldn't the stars move?

"I'm going to think myself into headaches worse than Cecil had with visions," she whispered. The horse snorted in response and she sighed laughter.

She was still awake, feeling the first tendrils of drowsiness, when Fang returned to the camp. He had something clutched to his chest, and for a moment she feared he had been wounded. He had something clutched in his teeth, as well. He spread his arms, and the dark spots resolved into four apples, a deep ruby shade, small enough for perhaps four bites each. He opened his mouth and dropped a small knife next to the fire. It glinted gold, with blue and green sparkles. Ash's fingertips tingled when she picked it up. Were those chips of jewels in the hilt?

"Well, and where did you come from? Fang, please tell me you didn't steal this from some other trapped traveler."

No, he rescued me, a sweet, metallic voice whispered in her head. *I was stolen from my home and dropped when the thief fled. Please, take me home, and there will be great rewards.*

Ash put the little knife down on one of the rocks that ringed her fire, when she wanted to fling it away. The reaction was ridiculous, she knew, because she hadn't been afraid when the ring first spoke to her. Then again, she knew the ring was magic before she picked it up. She didn't expect a pretty gold knife dusted with sapphire and emerald chips to talk to her.

The knife seesawed twice on the uneven rock where she had put it. Not wise to irritate magical objects.

"Where is your home?" Ash knew from far too many stories that asking about a reward was the wrong question. She would look greedy.

And besides, in several stories the rewards were never promised to the hapless hero or the fool who happened to find the magical talking beast or object. The rewards were for the lost or stolen creature or item that lured another victim into a trap.

No answer.

"Fang, did the knife talk to you?"

He nodded.

"Knife, why won't you speak to me?" She swallowed. "Did I hurt your feelings?" Logic provided the answer. Sighing, she picked up the knife. "I'm sorry, knife, do I have to touch you to hear you?"

That's quite all right, the knife said, sounding a little too cheerful for Ash's tastes. *You don't understand much about magic, do you? We can help with that!*

"Who are 'we,' and where is your home?" Ash caught herself hunching her shoulders in anticipation of the answer.

The castle. And we are all the many lost and escaped magical treasures and tools that have gathered there over the decades.

Ash fought down a whimper. That confirmed what she had tried not to admit, tried not to even think about for the last few hours. If she was in the enchanted forest, then the enchanted castle was somewhere nearby. After all the warnings she had received, all the things she had read about the castle, whether they were mere fables or truth, she knew better than to blithely walk through the main gates of the castle and expect to walk out again without any trouble or struggle.

She also knew better than to deny the knife's request for help getting home. Even if this was a trap. Or more accurately, *especially* if this was a trap. She needed to be as kind and generous and honorable and clever as all the heroes she had read about.

CHAPTER ELEVEN

"Why are you gathered there?" she asked, to gain time to think.

Lost. Stolen. Abused. Worn out. Hidden. So much magic has seeped into the air and soil and stone, it grows and we are alive. You will take me home, won't you? I'm so lonely for my friends. A magpie found me and tried to take me to his nest, but I was too heavy. He left me in the crotch of a tree and I've been sitting there in the rain and wind and sunshine, waiting. I miss my family. I despaired when the tree branch broke in a storm, but then the bunny found me and agreed to bring me to you.

"I'll see what I can do. I'm trying to find my way home, too. I'm waiting until the portal back to my home opens again."

Oh, Eyesallova knows all about portals, the knife chirped, sounding eager and delighted. *You can take me home and she'll help you.*

"Who is Eyesallova?"

The mirror.

Ash knew she was tired, because her mind snagged on the way the knife said "the mirror," as if there was only one magic mirror in the enchanted castle. No, if magical items were being collected in the castle, logic said there would be more than one magic mirror. Maybe she was the leader of the mirrors? Maybe she was the node for the magic mirror communication web? Magic mirrors weren't exactly rare, but they weren't common, either. Kings and enchanters and the heads of collegiums had them, to share news and give information and advice. Sometimes war leaders carried smaller magic mirrors into battle, to communicate with their scattered troops and battalions, and with the country's leaders, safely back home behind high stone walls.

"Please," she said on a sigh. Her head ached and she felt a little dizzy from the effort of thinking. "I'm so very tired. Would you mind if we discuss this in the morning? I don't want to travel in the darkness, anyway."

Very wise. Yes. Thank you. You're very kind to take me home. I know everyone will want to help you.

"In the morning," Ash said, and put the knife down where it glinted in the firelight. She had a sudden fear that her head was so fuzzy, she would agree to something that would get her into trouble. "Fang, can you check on the portal? Wake me if it changes?"

He bobbed his head and hopped over next to her blankets to pat her shoulder. As she closed her eyes, she saw him bend down, pick up the knife, and hop out of the firelight. Ash's last thought before the softly swirling darkness pulled her down into sleep was to hope he lost the knife during his rambles in the darkness.

~~~~~

Ash woke three times, and each time rolled over onto her back to wriggle out from under the overhang of the rock and study the stars. They never changed. She wondered if they were still there in the same positions during the day, but invisible because of the stronger light. She fell asleep the third time contemplating how she could use the stars to navigate if she was forced to stay longer than a few days in the enchanted forest. She would eventually run out of food, meaning she had to set out to forage.

Fang woke her when the sky had faded from deep purple shot with silver and pale blue stars to a silvery gray shot with pink and lavender stripes. He gestured toward the trail with ears and paws and hopped away. Ash snatched up her boots and followed, hopping several steps on each foot to put them on. She didn't bother tying the laces and feared tripping and falling flat on her face as she raced after him.

The portal had changed. She was relieved to see the bundles of tree limbs hadn't moved during the night. She had half-feared the magic that changed the portal would reach out far enough to affect them. That was the only good news.

Now the portal was a pool inside a shadowy cave. Light glimmered at the bottom. Tiny wavelets disturbed the image, so she couldn't get a clear idea of how far away it was, how large or small it was, and how deep the pool was. Ash considered diving down, just once, to get an idea, but she had read too many stories about nasty creatures hiding in seemingly harmless, lovely, peaceful pools. Besides, until she knew where that pool would take her, what kingdom, why should she risk getting trapped somewhere far away from her horse and supplies?

"Thank you, Fang." She stepped back, past the tree limb markers, and considered her sense of time's passage. "I think maybe twelve hours passed since the last change. Maybe a little more. The question is, do we wait here, watching, until the next change, and hope it's back to the roses? Or do we go exploring? Find the other portals?" She caught her breath as another thought came to her. "Maybe there are only a few portals, but the openings move around, like the hands of a clock, going to different places here in the forest. Filby's map had ten spots … so if I sat here, waiting, I'd have to wait five days for the roses to appear here again … when I might be able to find them somewhere else, sooner."

Ash gnawed on that thought as she headed back to her camp and brought out some trail bread and cheese for breakfast. She would save the cold cooked fish for another meal. Garan whickered and nudged her shoulder when she loosed his halter from the brambles and led him up the
~~~~~

bank to where grass and tender plants offered good eating. Ash imagined he was thanking her.

"It would be convenient if you could talk to me," she murmured.

I know ten rings and five crowns and three necklaces and sixteen belts that can do that for you, a chiming voice called.

Ash turned around twice, looking for the speaker. Did the sound come from somewhere on her? Memory returned as she patted herself, feeling a little panicky, and found the little gold knife tucked in one of the inner pockets of her vest. How it got in there, she couldn't imagine. Could the knife crawl, or had Fang helped it? She decided she didn't want to know.

"It's not polite to climb up on people and ride them without being invited," she said, after tossing aside a handful of other things that weren't exactly polite.

I'm sorry. The knife did sound rather contrite. *But the air was cold and you are so nice and warm. I like being around people. Touched by people. My sort like to be put to use.*

"Oh, really? And just how well does a knife made of gold cut anything? I wouldn't want to bend you or scratch you." Ash fought a choking sensation that might be laughter. She couldn't believe she was having this conversation with a knife.

Oh, I don't cut things. Solid things, the knife hurried to add. *I'm to be used in magic, and for ceremonies.* He sighed. *And mostly for decoration. I miss my family. We're made to be a set, you know. Will you take me home today? Please?*

"Let me have my breakfast and neaten up the camp for the day, will you? Then we'll … figure out where we are and what we should do. I want to keep an eye on that portal, so when it changes back to the one I came through, I can go home."

Oh, the mirror knows all about the portals. She knows everything. You can ask her, instead of sitting around and waiting. The knife wriggled a little in her grasp, like an excited, eager child. Ash nearly dropped him. Well, that answered that question of how he got into her pocket.

"Oh … that's … good to know. Thank you." She started to put him back into her pocket, then decided she didn't want to feel him moving around there and kept him in her hand as she went back down the bank to her camp.

She ended up putting him on one of the flat rocks that surrounded her dying fire, and tried not to look at him as she settled down to eat. Fang curled up in the shade cast by her cloak and went to sleep. She felt somewhat abandoned. She didn't like the idea of exploring the forest in the dark, but she couldn't ask Fang to hop around for very long in the daylight, even with the sloppy shelter of the shirt she had altered to cover him. She didn't want to stay here by the stream, waiting for the roses tunnel to reappear. Especially if that knife kept asking her to take it home.

Not that the knife kept asking her. It waited politely, silently, as she ate and then shook out her blankets and folded them neatly and arranged her belongings in the shelter of the rock. Ash pulled out her socks and underthings and swished them through the water and wrung them out several times, and then hung them on the brambles that streamed down one side of the rock overhang, to dry in the sunshine. The longer the silence from the knife lasted, the more guilty she felt for making him wait.

Then she remembered: she couldn't hear him unless she was touching him. Her face warmed and she hoped she wasn't too red. She picked him up, even though she didn't want to pick him up. The sooner she got him home, the better.

At least, she hoped so.

"I'm sorry for leaving you alone so long," she began.

Oh, my lady, don't be! The knife trilled laughter that made his blade twinkle and his handle vibrate, tickling her hand. *The last person I talked to was so frightened, he threw me into the bushes. I was there for a very long time. It's just lucky that it doesn't snow here in the enchanted forest. At least, outside the reach of the portals, it doesn't snow. Whatever weather is on the other end of the portal, that's the weather that touches the forest for a few paces on this side of the portal. I did have to wait through months of rain and animals stepping on me, and several magpies trying to carry me home to their stashes.*

"Well, that doesn't sound very comfortable." She took a breath, trying to phrase what she said next so she wouldn't get herself trapped into some kind of bargain that would work against her.

How many stories had she read about people making rash promises without realizing what those simple words implied, until it was too late to free themselves? She and Cecil had had several fascinating discussions of the perils of unwise wishes, not being specific when asking for something or speaking hopes and dreams that opened doors better left shut.

"So, knife ... do you have a name? I feel rather rude, just calling you knife. The ring preferred being called 'ring,' just because his name was hard to pronounce by flesh and blood." She sighed, with a brief, sharp ache of longing for her friend and mentor. Ash hoped he was at least able to listen and share her adventures, if not speak with her.

How funny! I've never thought about having a name. It's only been us in my set. I'm the butter knife. There is the big knife and the big fork and little fork and stirring spoon and porridge spoon. You don't have to worry about a name for me. I'll be with my family soon and you don't want to have to pick us up constantly and talk to us, so ... I suppose it doesn't really matter.

"Oh. All right. If you don't mind then ..." Ash shrugged. "As I was going to say, knife, how exactly do I get you home? How far into the castle do I need to take you? It seems to me you can move on your own. In a fashion. Do I just take you in through the door and you can find your way to your family from there? I don't want to be rude and go intruding on someone else's home without being invited. Is there someone there who can take you and put you with your family when we get there?"

I don't really know. It depends on what happened after the thieves got frightened and fled the castle, and what kind of a mess they left behind.

That didn't really answer her questions. Ash wanted to go into the enchanted castle even less than before.

"Is there anyone in the castle to help you? I mean, people? Like me? With hands and feet?"

Oh. No. But there are several suits of armor that can walk around when there is need. To defend the castle. Or close doors. Or put new magical refugees in the storage rooms. You could put me on a table in the welcoming hall and one of them could put me away. If the rest of my family is still there.

"No one else who can move?" She wondered how quickly those suits of armor could move. She didn't have to go inside at night, so maybe that wouldn't be a problem.

Some of the furniture, but they can't pick up things. Most things. Oh, and the books. They're very good at jumping off shelves and tumbling around. And they can fly and hit intruders when they need to. My family spent quite a lot of time in the library, and the books would make up dances, flying through the air and tumbling around the floor, and jumping from shelves and tables.

"A library." Ash caught her breath and nearly laughed aloud. How had she forgotten? Friar Ipswich and Cecil and so many books had mentioned the library in the enchanted castle. Books about magic and books that were magic. How had she forgotten her hopes of finding answers to her many dilemmas in a library large enough to contain those answers? If any place in the world could have the magic, the right spell to free the ring from his bonds of silence and give him back to her, and protect them from the Purple Sky magicians, certainly that place would be the enchanted castle's library.

Just as quickly as that thought came, she remembered all the warnings to avoid the castle.

Perhaps she could earn some goodwill, returning the knife to his home and family? Enough to protect her from whatever traps might fill the castle? Maybe with the knife as her guide, she could avoid those traps?

Ash looked at Fang, curled up, contentedly sleeping in the shadows. He wasn't deeply enough asleep yet to snort and snore.

"Fang? Would you mind going exploring with me? I might need you to protect me, if there's trouble."

The bunny opened one eye, then the other. A slow, greedy, eager sort of smile lit his face and he sat up.

"Thank you." She thought for a moment, then held out the knife to him. "Keep our friend company while I pull out your shirt. Ask him how to get to the castle?"

Fang didn't hesitate to hop up to her and hold out both paws to take the knife. He chirped with what she hoped was eagerness and clasped the gold blade to his chest.

~~~~~

Ash tucked the knife in the top pocket of her vest, on the outside. She had to have some sort of contact with him to hear him, and have him direct her through the forest.

Can you hear the song now? the knife asked, after they had walked for nearly half an hour.

"No. What song?" She slowed her pace and turned her head, trying to locate whatever the knife was hearing. Fang stopped several paces ahead of her and looked back. "Fang, do you hear a song?"

He nodded and pointed slightly to the right off the animal trail they had been following.

"Can you get us back to camp?"

Another nod, and several gestures with his ears that made her think he was a little offended by her question. Maybe he thought she doubted his tracking abilities?

"What song?" she asked again. "How far off is the castle?" When Fang hopped forward again, she followed, even as something tightened inside her, warning her not to leave the trail.

Close. The knife wriggled a little, making her glad again she had put him in an outside pocket. *Now can you hear it?*

"What song?"

The castle sings, calling me home.

Ash supposed that made sense. She wondered just what it was that allowed Fang to hear the song, but not her. The stars on breastbone and buttocks were gone, so did that mean whatever blocked her magic had been removed by entering the enchanted forest? Yet if that was true, did that mean her inborn magic would finally start to bloom? Did it mean she was hobbled now by reduced sensitivity to magic at work? Temporarily deafened? If she lingered in the forest, would she eventually start to hear the castle sing?

Was it safe to hear the castle sing?

Then she stepped around a cluster of vines wrapping around something tall that she had an awful suspicion wasn't a tree, and all her questions died before they were clear in her head.

Her first impression was of seeing through water, studying something sitting in the bottom of one of the rare glass goblets Lady
~~~~~

Beatrice prized. The air around the castle seemed to curve and the trees and even small lumps of upturned soil were flattened and pressed aside.

No, she decided after another twenty or so steps closer. There was no *seemed* about it. She had wondered how the castle could move without leaving a trail of destruction in its wake, but now she understood, though she didn't want to twist her brain around the concepts too closely. Everything around the castle, in the place where they had been, was pressed outward and compressed to make room. How quickly did the trees and ground and perhaps even animals resume their normal shapes and positions after the castle had passed?

She didn't want to see, afraid she might be sick. For all she knew, the castle left permanently flattened and compressed plants and animals in its wake. If it had a dungeon, was there a deep trench in its wake, like the trail of slime left by an enormous, poisonous kind of snail?

More important, how deep was that layer of compression directly in front of her, between her and the front gates of the castle? How hard would it be to go through it, to get inside the castle? Did she want to walk through? Would she be compressed?

Maybe this was a bad idea? If she just threw the knife toward what certainly looked like a curtain of faintly shimmering water, would he eventually get home?

Oh, but there were books inside the castle. All the books she might ever need. Answers. Information. Guidance, perhaps, as her inborn magic finally awoke.

"Fang? What do you think?" She kept her voice soft, afraid of catching the attention of something that might be watching and listening, perched among the shadows behind those crenelated walls, four stories high. The towers on all the corners. How many corners did this massive castle have? Eight? Ten? Enough to give an impression of roundness.

Oh, don't be afraid. The knife wriggled again, and Ash could have sworn he muffled a giggle. *You're welcome here. Can't you hear the song now? The castle likes you.*

Ash bit back her retort of, "How do you know?"

With a sighing sound, the drawbridge lowered. Beyond them, massive double doors at the top of a short flight of stairs swung open. Darkness inside for a few heartbeats, until torches flickered into life. They reminded her of the lanterns in Cecil's cottage that lit when they were needed. That similarity wasn't comforting. The drawbridge made her look a little closer. Yes, there was a moat. How did the moat travel with the castle? Did the water slosh as it moved? Her head ached from all the questions swirling through her mind. She supposed the massive, strange magic that allowed the castle to move through the enchanted forest was complex enough to handle the moat without any trouble.

Yet what good was the moat? Hadn't the knife said he was stolen by thieves? So people could get into the castle, and apparently leave easily enough to take their plunder. What did that say about the castle's defenses?

Ash had the awful feeling she hadn't asked the right questions, or enough questions.

"What do you think, Fang?"

The bunny turned to look up at her, then back to the castle, then back to her. His ears twisted rapidly, so they were almost a blur. She had grown to understand his expressions well enough, even in the shadows of the hood that protected him from the light. Fang wanted to go in. Of course, he was slightly insane to begin with, so could she really trust his judgment?

Did she have a choice?

When Fang bounced forward, Ash followed, muffling a sigh.

Please, A'theosius, if this is foolish, if this is dangerous, give me a warning sign before I go any further?

She held her breath, ears straining for a voice calling not to go in, a flash of lightning, maybe even for the drawbridge to creak upward and the massive double doors of the castle to slam closed.

None of that happened. On the positive side, she felt nothing as she passed through that wall of magic that wavered and wobbled like the surface of a pond. Ash had to consciously keep her eyes open and not hold her breath as she stepped up to and into and through it. Nothing. No sting of magic at work. No sensation of resistance, perhaps floating for a moment like a speck of dust or lint on the surface of the water before it sank.

CHAPTER TWELVE

Birds still sang softly in the distance and the breeze gently swirled around her, bringing the scents of ripening apples and cherries and plums and berries and blooming flowers. To the left, Ash saw gates that hung open in the wall, and a glimpse of what looked like a formal garden. Were those people?

No. She shuddered as she realized those people were too pale, and too still. Statues. What had she read about the statues in the castle? They were once people who had been enchanted. They had been caught in spells in the castle or enchanted elsewhere and brought here to make rescue difficult. Or, some chroniclers speculated, the enchanters who cursed them ran out of room to store them and brought them here to get them out of their way.

Ash stepped onto the drawbridge. Something swirled through the water of the moat but didn't appear. She didn't look.

No one came to the doors as she crossed the inner courtyard. Birds sang, the breeze whispered across the pavement stones and the decorative flags high on the walls rustled. Ash looked around, trying to see everything. No grass grew between the paving stones. No moss spotted the walls. No dust. No horse droppings. No signs of plunder dropped along the way as terrified thieves fled for their lives. She wondered if the stolen things had crawled or wriggled back to their proper places. Perhaps this place had housekeeping breezes like Filby's home, and they picked up the mess that intruders made. Certainly they wouldn't have much to do in a place like this. Did housekeeping breezes get bored?

Then she was at the bottom of the stairs. Fang leaped all five of them, landing in front of the open doors. He looked back at her, waggling his ears in his sign for, "Come on, what are you waiting for?"

"A'theosius, keep us safe," Ash whispered, took a deep breath, and put her foot on the first step.

More torches flickered to life the moment she leaned in through the open doors and looked in all directions. The entryway of the castle was massive, reaching up three stories, with a wide stairway that stopped at landings halfway up to each floor and turned back on itself. The entryway itself was wider than the formal dining and meeting room at Castle Fairhold, and she imagined it could hold a table twice as wide and long as Filby's table. The wall opposite the main doors was broken by four sets of double doors, easily twenty paces apart, with long tapestries depicting forest and battle and pastoral scenes hanging between them. None of the doors opened.

Up, the knife said. *Go up. The mirror will want to see you. Of course, she can already see you, but she can't talk to you yet.* He giggled, a tinkling sound that made Ash wonder if magical items had birth and growth, and the knife was very, very young.

She suspected she considered such ridiculous questions to keep her mind from latching onto more troubling thoughts that might have her flee in another moment, perhaps shrieking in a quite undignified manner.

With Fang leading the way, giving the impression he knew where he was going, they climbed the stairs to the third floor. Utter silence all around them. Ash didn't like those suits of armor standing at attention on either side of the stairs, on each floor. Though they didn't move, she had the impression they were watching her. What would she find if she opened one of those visors? No, she wouldn't take the risk, no matter how painful her curiosity grew.

What she wouldn't give to have the ring commenting on everything around them, testing the magical streams or breezes, warning her from making foolish mistakes that someone would mock, when reading the account of her adventures in another fifty or hundred years. Would someone read of her adventures? Would she live long enough to tell them to someone who would write them down? Or even live long enough to record them herself?

Stop it, she scolded herself. *Pay attention. No daydreaming allowed.* A crooked smile caught one corner of her mouth, as she realized she was indeed planning to have her story told many generations in the future. Was she a hero like the ones she had always dreamed of meeting? This was certainly an adventure, even if one she would not have chosen for herself.

On the third floor, the knife directed her to the glass doors full of light, in the direction of the gardens Ash had glimpsed earlier. Would they be going out onto a balcony? What was a mirror doing outside? Granted, being part of the enchanted castle, the mirror was protected by magic, but why waste the effort and energy when it made more sense to keep something so valuable indoors?

Before she reached to push the doors open, Ash saw she had been wrong. Outside didn't lie beyond those doors, but a room roofed with glass. She felt the chiming and shimmering when she touched the metal frame of the door to push it open. The sound filled her ears and whispered across her skin and gently pulled her into the room.

Mirrors hung on the two long walls. All different sizes and styles of frames. The wall opposite where Ash had come in had more glass doors, and through them she saw the balustrade of a balcony and greenery, indicating a garden.

The floor was paved in a maze pattern, in blue and green and white tiles. Benches and stools and thick cushioned chairs were scattered across it, arranged in sloppy circles around a tall, ornate, gilded frame holding the largest mirror Ash had ever seen in her life. It was twice as tall as her, and wider than her outstretched arms.

"Welcome!" The mirror turned, with small wheels on its multiple legs. Blue and green and gold sparkles swirled across her surface as she spoke. A rich, alto, female voice. "How lovely that you brought Butter home. Your family has missed you greatly, dear boy."

"Butter?" Ash said, echoed by a chirping snort from Fang. She knew better than to laugh. "That seems a very appropriate name. Butter is highly prized," she offered, as she took the knife out of her front pocket.

You would think so, wouldn't you? The little knife sounded just slightly disgruntled, or perhaps embarrassed.

Something banged on the glass doors. Ash turned as they swung open, hard enough to thud against the walls. Two suits of armor strode in, clomping softly on the stone flooring, holding out their arms.

"What did I do? I didn't mean to do anything wrong. Whatever I did, I'm sorry!"

"Oh, no, no, nothing wrong at all! They're here to welcome you home," the mirror said.

"This isn't my home. Please, I just wanted to help the knife, and I was hoping you could help me understand the portals, figure out their patterns, so I can go home, back the way I came."

"Yes, that's very sensible. Oh, but you can't talk suits of armor out of something once they've made up their minds. This could be your home. There's quite strong magic in you … or rather, the possibility, the potential for incredible, clever, healing magic in you. They sense it, so they want you to make this your home."

Ash remembered what Cecil had said. Warned her about, if she really thought about it. How castles, especially ones with magic in them, needed a princess. She supposed if the magic of the castle was strong enough, no matter how much she wasn't a princess, it would succeed and change her to suit its needs.

She backed toward the mirror, hoping for refuge. She had an image in her head of going behind the mirror, trying to hide from the armor. But that wouldn't work, would it? There were two of them. They could split up and come at her from each side.

The armor carried crowns. At least three on each arm. Every princess needed a crown. Common sense said some of those crowns were magic, perhaps all of them. Common sense also said that not all magic was good.

The odds were strong that at least one crown was cursed. Hadn't numerous people and books told her the castle was used to store magic of all kinds? Worn out magic, rogue magic, dangerous magic, crazy magic, injured magic. Curses.

"Please, I just want to get some information. I can't stay. I have to make sure my friends are safe. There's this nasty, spoiled brat of a princess who wants to hurt them. I need to break whatever spell is on my friend, the spirit ring, so he can talk to me, so we can protect my friends. Will you help me?"

All the while, the suits of armor got closer. She backed up until she was only two steps away from the mirror. Ash considered the open spaces between the benches and chairs. The suits didn't move very quickly. She thought she could outrun them, maybe knock some benches over to get in their way.

"Please, mirror? You're the heart of the castle, aren't you? Can't you tell them to leave me alone?"

"Well, I am temporarily the heart of the castle, the guide, the one who tries to look after all the others. There is little else I can do while I am cut off from the magic mirror web ..." The mirror sighed, a soft shimmer of crystalline sound. "Only until we find a princess to lead us, to give us purpose, to organize the storerooms and break the curse that sends the castle floating every which way. We need stability. The broken magical things down in the lower levels need someone to soothe them and help them sleep. And especially we need someone here to keep the doors closed against thieves. The nasty kind who want to steal all the magic they can get their hands on, to give them power over the innocent and defenseless. Won't you consider the task? You seem like a sensible, responsible person who cares about others."

"I'm not a princess!"

"Oh, but you could be. I see so very much potential in you."

"Mirror—"

"I'm sorry, dear, but we haven't been properly introduced. I'm Eyesallova. And you are?"

"Ash."

Fang chirped, and bounced out in front of her, coming between her and the suits of armor, which split up to go around a long bench.

"Lady Ashlyn. What a lovely name."

"I'm not—" She sighed. "Please, can't you at least tell them to stop?"

"Oh, suits of armor have a mind of their own. Their primary purpose is to guard the princess of the castle, do her bidding. Thus, they need to find a princess to serve. Once we have a princess again, then they can step back and focus on other things, such as protecting the castle. There's that nasty king who keeps finding his way in here, constantly throwing all sorts of magic against us, trying to get at the books. The books are half the reason the castle keeps moving, when it should by all rights sit still. They're so afraid, so upset at being separated."

"Wait a moment. King? A king who tries to steal books? Not Ruprick of Rathelshiffen?"

"I don't know his name, but he and then his son and grandson and great-grandson keep coming every year or so, when they can find the open portal, with more magic, nastier magic. They ravage the forest, hunting all the animals, whether they can talk or not, riling up the kispies, making the Snarl River knot up and rise out of its bed, always trying to chase down the castle and pry the doors open so they can get at the libraries."

"Libraries? You have more than one?" Ash shook her head, exasperated at how she could get so easily sidetracked. Still, the thought of so many books there was more than one library ... it boggled her mind.

And still those suits of armor came closer. Fang snarled and leaped up and bounced off them, each in turn. They turned aside, detouring around the magic bunny and the benches he knocked in their path. They never swung at him. Maybe they didn't even see him there. They just kept getting closer.

"How can I stop them?"

"If you accept one of those crowns, they'll be satisfied. What would it hurt?"

"That's all?" Ash shuddered. Her imagination and all the reading she had done answered that question. Depending on the crown, she could be cursing herself, or accepting the title and duties of princess of the enchanted castle. Which amounted to a curse, as far as she was concerned. "Which one won't make me a princess? Which one has the least amount of magic?"

"What's the fun in that?" Eyesallova sounded genuinely confused, not upset or offended or even amused.

"Please, Eyesallova, help me? I can't afford to be trapped here. I have friends I need to help. If I've earned any grace by helping the knife, won't you help me? Which crown doesn't have magic, or at least as little as possible?"

The mirror sighed. "No magic at all is impossible. That's the nature of this place. Everything is touched with magic of some kind. Even if something came here without any magic, eventually some soaks in. You can't imagine the traffic through here sometimes, all the princes on quests, seeking an enchanted sword or ring or crown or something to help them win a kingdom or drive away an evil enchanter or a monster. We get our unfair share of wicked princes and selfish princesses and sorcerers' apprentices, seeking something to give them power." Another sigh. "But what does that have to do with you, yes? You want advice? Accept a crown. That will let the armor go back to their places. For a while. Wear the crown for as short a time as you can manage. Every time you take it off, they'll wake up and come after you, to make you put it on again, or make you put on a different one. Once you accept the crown, it's yours for life, so choose wisely."

"For life," Ash muttered, and took a step toward the suits of armor.

To her surprise, they stopped. Was that all it took to stop them chasing her? Stop running away?

She took another step. No movement. Whatever was inside those suits of armor, she felt the weight of their regard. Studying her. Judging her?

The crowns glittered and gleamed, overwhelming with gold and silver and a rainbow of gems. Some were gaudy, studded with multiple colors of gems in no discernible pattern. Others stuck to specific colors, one all gold and emeralds, from tiny chips like dust to stones the size of hens' eggs. Another was all silver and diamonds, multiple spiky points, making her think she would turn to ice if she put it on. Others had velvet caps inside the circlets of braided gold and arches made of sapphires and rubies.

Then she saw a crown that stood out by its very simplicity. Five strands of silver wire, braided, with sapphire chips every few twists. Small enough to hide under a cap, or among the growing curls of her hair.

"What about this one? What magic is attached to it?" Ash dared to touch it with one finger. She half-expected the suit of armor to grab her wrist with its other hand.

"Oh, very wise choice, dear," Eyesallova said. "That says something about you that you could see it at all. That crown is more powerful in what it symbolizes. Acceptance of duty and responsibility. Common sense, if you really think about it. Something that won't get in the way, that won't require lots of extra care from you."

"Is it safe to wear?"

"Dear girl, no crown is ever safe to wear. Not even straw crowns given to children for games or dramas. Crowns make you a target of something, sooner or later. But yes, it's the safest of any crown in the entire castle. Wear it to protect you whenever you're inside. You will come back, won't you? The crown will help you find your way, no matter where you are in the forest. And eventually, even if you've left the forest, it will help you come back."

"Will it help me find the library?"

"Why do you want to find the library?" Eyesallova's tone sharpened a little.

"My friend." Ash turned back to the mirror, making sure she didn't move away from the armor and give it reason to act. Such as grab her and slap a crown on her head. She unfastened her courier badge, to show the spirit ring. "He's being kept from talking to me. I don't know if he's entirely blind and deaf, or he just can't talk to me. Maybe he's been separated from the ring that's his body. I don't know. I just know I miss him and we both want to be free of the justiciar who sent me on this idiotic quest in the first place."

"Interesting ..." the mirror whispered. "To be befriended by a spirit ring says much about you. And hints even more. Tell me about this justiciar and the quest. Oh, if only I weren't cut off from the mirror web. It's been ages since the castle and the forest were yanked out of the stream of time. I would ask among my friends in the web, to see what we could do about your problem, if I could talk to them. But I promise you, my dear, I will help you as much as I am permitted."

Ash took a step toward the bench facing the mirror. An iron hand gripped her elbow. She ducked and yelped and twisted, trying to get free. But couldn't. The iron gauntlet of the suit of armor didn't hold on tight enough to bruise, but she couldn't get free.

"Oh, dear, they really are single-minded," Eyesallova said. "Do take the crown, dear, and let them go on their way."

Sighing, Ash turned back to the suit of armor. It let go. She reached for the braided silver circlet. Naturally, it wasn't the front one of the three hanging on that arm of the armor. She didn't want to touch the other crowns, to move them out of the way. With her luck, the armor would assume she had chosen the first crown she touched.

"Ask it to give you the crown," the mirror said.

Ash licked her lips, considering how to do that. Sometimes the simplest tasks were the ones most fraught with peril. She had learned that from the books she had devoured in her hunger for adventure. Maybe all the reading she had done hadn't been quite as beneficial as she thought? How many times had she hesitated to think, consider all the possible pitfalls and complications, when she would have been wiser to just react?

"Please, would you let me have this one?" She touched the simple crown with one finger.

A pause. Then, creaking slightly, the suit of armor slid the first two crowns on its arm onto the other arm, then let her choice slide down to catch on its bent fingers.

"Thank you."

An image flashed into her mind as she slipped the crown off its fingers. Of a suite of rooms, one leading into another, full of dresses and shoes and scarves and shawls and jewelry. All pretty, fluffy, glittery, and delicate. Worthy of a princess. And rooms full of delicate furniture, with bright tapestries on the walls, where they weren't filled with books. All waiting to be used.

Waiting for her.

Would it be so bad, staying here? All the books she could ever read, all the silence and solitude she could ever want, and no one ordering her about, chasing her.

"Be sure of what you want," Eyesallova said.

"Hmm?" Ash shook her head, feeling as if she pushed up through water that made her thoughts heavy and slow.

The suit of armor still stood there, holding its hand out now, palm flat. The second suit was already heading across the mirror room to the doors that opened on the gallery and staircase.

"Give Butter to him, dear, so he can go back to his family."

"Oh. Right. Yes. Thank you for your help," she said, pulling the knife out of her pocket.

Much obliged. I hope you stay with us, princess, the knife called as she put him on the palm of the armor's iron hand.

Ash swallowed down the retort that she wasn't a princess. Sometimes, as Cecil had warned her, the more something was resisted, the stronger it grew. She needed to simply ignore the attempts to get her to accept being a princess. She held her breath as both suits of armor walked away. The doors closed behind them without anyone touching them.

"Thank you." She turned back to Eyesallova and remembered what else the mirror had said. "Right. Justiciar Camwell and the quest."

"Camwell? Oh, my. I do know about him. I can't talk to my friends in the mirror web, but I am able to catch echoes of the others talking. His mirror doesn't like him. Too self-righteous." Eyesallova seemed to shake a little in her frame. Like a woman seeing a big, ugly rat staring up at her. Just before she braced herself to kick it aside. "Tell me what he did to you."

Ash quelled a sigh. This would have been easier, taken much less time, if the ring was here to pass on all that information. She settled down on the bench and opened her mouth to begin the tale. First, Eyesallova reminded her to put on the crown. Otherwise, the suits of armor would return far too soon, and they would choose a crown for her. One that would cast an enchantment over her so she would comply with the castle's desires.

CHAPTER THIRTEEN

"The more freedom of choice you have, dear," the mirror told her, "the better for everyone. Thanks to all the tangled magic mucking up everything, all the attempts by would-be sorcerers to tame the castle, the purpose and vision have been twisted, dimmed, I suppose you could say. The idea of a proper princess has been covered in all sorts of ridiculous images from centuries of silly stories, all the wrong sorts of ideas. You need to be careful, or the castle will impose that on you. We don't need that, any of us here. The more of a little puppet princess you are, the less effective you will be in protecting the castle. You started very wisely with that simple duty crown. Sort of a practice crown, to start things off slowly. Don't ruin it, please?"

Ash put that bit of information aside for later. Especially since the immediate implication was that she had indeed agreed, if only vaguely, distantly, to be the castle's princess.

She couldn't do that. She couldn't stay. She had responsibilities. Starting with protecting Castle Fairhold and her fellow servants from Lathia.

But … she could come back, couldn't she? If she was the castle's princess, if the castle at least wanted her as a princess, then she could come back? And use the library?

Definitely something to consider later. After she had fulfilled her promises to her friends and made sure they were safe.

Telling the tale of the inquiry and quest and Lathia's nasty tricks and false accusations didn't take much time. Eyesallova didn't ask many questions. She made small comments, often just murmuring along the lines of, "Oh, yes, I see that now. Despicable."

Finally, Ash could ask her questions.

"It's very simple, dear. From the inside, at least," Eyesallova said. "Oh, where has your little friend — there he is. Bunny, dear, do be careful. The garden is friendly, but some of the statues in there aren't."

Ash turned to look where the mirror now faced and saw the doors to the balcony and the garden beyond were open. Some time during the tale, once Fang had finished making comments in chirps and growls that Eyesallova certainly seemed to understand with no trouble, he had wandered away.

"Some fool prince came through here a few months ago," Eyesallova continued, when Fang settled down on the balcony, facing back into the mirror room. "He had enough magic in his blood, great-grandson of a Fae enchanter, he interfered with quite a few sleeping spells. He went around, kissing every statue he could find, trying to free a princess he had only known through correspondence. There was some real affection involved, fortunately, so when he kissed the right statue, he woke up the right girl.

"Unfortunately, interfering with the curses and such on the other statues woke some of them partially. You know how grumpy and oblivious or single-minded some people can be when they're only half-awake? What makes things worse is that he didn't kiss just the girl statues. He kissed every statue he found, because he couldn't be sure his princess still looked like a girl. It turns out he was right, she was disguised as a deer, but still ... some of the statues were rather touchy, didn't take well to how they were awakened.

"Well, now we have quite a few statues wandering around out there. They'll walk over anything and anyone who gets in their way, and never even know it. Most of them, anyway. Some are statues that entirely deserved to be cursed and turned into statues forever." She sighed. "Now ... the portals. You were asking about using them. Very easy. Unless you're a stickler for exact timetables. Then it gets tricky. When the forest got knocked out of the time stream, everything got twisted sideways. The forest and the portals used to be so orderly and reliable until that whole ugly mess with the castle and the sword and the anchors and ..." Eyesallova shuddered and the swirls of color across her surface dimmed.

"Where was I? Generally, the portals shift every twelve hours. There are ten anchor spots for the portals in and out of the forest. Each one has between four and six different locations they open onto, and the anchor locations generally change every hour or so in sequence. Sometimes a few minutes short of an hour, sometimes a few minutes longer than an hour. Which is where the exact and predictable timetables can drive you insane if you depend on them. Or if you lost track of time and forget when and where you came through. It all evens out when you get back to the starting point. However, to make things even more tricky, they don't shift in exact sequence like moving around the sundial or the clock. They skip, they take turns shifting."

"That's what the map Filby gave me means!" Ash could have laughed aloud as insight shot through her mind. She dug into her belt pouch and brought out the carefully folded and protected parchment with the starburst design on it. There were indeed ten points marked on the star, with lines connecting the points. She showed it to Eyesallova.

Starting at one, the connecting line went to four, then to seven, ten, three, six, nine, two, five, eight, and back to one.

"Can you get from one portal anchor spot to another within the hour time frame, if you knew the place the portal opened onto, and in what sequence?"

"In theory. The fact that the portals don't open to the same number of places throws off the sequence. Or rather, you need to remember a much larger pattern."

"That helps some. I've already seen two new openings, at the portal where I came through. So conceivably in ..." Ash sat back and searched her sense of time. "Another seven hours, my particular portal will change, to a third location, and then in twelve hours at the earliest, change to the one I came through."

"In theory, dear. But keep this in mind. Every hour here in the enchanted forest is equal to thirty hours in the outside world. Give or take a few minutes."

"Thirty ..." Ash caught her breath. "So if it takes two days for my portal to re-open, when I cross back through ... more than two months will have passed. It will be the dead of winter. Who knows what Lathia and her magicians could have done to Fairhold by then?"

"The thought of how much time they have lost with their friends and families is often the undoing of those who stumble through the portals, or who try to use the portals and the narrow paths through the enchanted forest for their own profit," the mirror warned her. "And another drawback is that the portals are rather like the tides. They don't always let you leave when you want to leave or return when you want to return. Say you walk out, back to the place you left, without any resistance. Well, depending on the churning of the magic in the forest, sometimes you can't turn around and walk back through right away. You have to wait for the tide to change. It might not change before the portal closes."

Yes, Ash could see how some people could lose their minds, trying to navigate through the portals, to find their lost lives or go to other lands.

The thought of all that effort made her tired. She thought of that lovely suite of rooms she had seen in the vision when she touched the crown. The impression underneath had been that those rooms belonged to her now. Would it be so bad to go up to that room and take a nap? Rest. Taste a bit of luxury. She had time until the next portal change. If it didn't open to the tunnel of roses in snow, then she had twelve hours to come back here and ...

What had she been planning to do again? Besides explore the pretty room and relax. What she wouldn't give to sleep in a real bed again, on a soft, thick mattress.

"Dear, you might want to take off that crown. Just for a little while. Until you get used to fighting the allure," Eyesallova said.

"Hmm?"

Fang raised up on his hind legs and thumped Ash's knees. She started. When had he come inside? She pressed her hand to her chest, laughing a little at the sudden racing of her heart.

"Take off the crown. Just for a little while. You have maybe forty minutes, maybe an hour, depending on how alert the armor is, until they come chasing you down to make you put on another." Eyesallova's sparkles were slightly darker now, tending toward more indigo and purple than green and sky blue.

"All right." Ash reached up and lifted the braided silver. Her fingers tingled like they had started to fall asleep. The feeling whispered through her body and she inhaled deeply, as if waking. "How odd."

"You'll grow stronger the more you resist," the mirror said.

"Resist?"

"You wanted to investigate the library, didn't you?"

"Yes, the library." Ash got to her feet, pressing her hand over the badge to make sure she had pinned it and the ring back into place. She had the awful feeling she had forgotten something important.

"Visit the library for maybe two hours, then you need to go back out and watch the portal, to see where it opens."

"Yes, thank you." Ash moved toward the door, with Fang hopping ahead of her. She stopped halfway there. "Can you guide me to a useful book? Where exactly should I look in the library?"

"Oh, if only I could tell you." The mirror's laughter sounded slightly strained. "Most thieves come looking for gold and jewels and magical weapons, but they always find it necessary to trample through the libraries and knock books off shelves. What do they think they'll find? Bags of gold inside the pages?" She made a rude sound that would have been a combination of a snort and clearing her throat in someone with an actual mouth. "The libraries are somewhat messy. If you could do a little bit of cleaning and organizing while you're looking, the books will be your friends forever. They'll protect you against other forces in the castle, if necessary. Pick up the books lying on the floor, remove the worst of the dust. They'll love you so much, they might not let you leave!" She laughed.

Ash tried to laugh, but the thought of being held prisoner by books needing her to endlessly organize and dust them was not that amusing. Even if, as a child, she had often dreamed of living in the library at Castle Fairhold.

"There are ever so many books, and several rooms to the library, I don't doubt you'll need several trips, dear, to find what you want. But take a word of advice. Don't be here at night. Don't fall asleep here. Not unless you intend to stay. Quite a lot of the furniture and clothes can be quite nasty if you stay for a little while, and then leave just when they get used to you."

"Thank you," Ash said as she pulled the door open. "Fang, keep watch, will you? Don't let furniture and clothes and especially the suits of armor sneak up on me?"

Fang bounced in place several times, crossing his heart with his ears. Then he leaped out through the doors ahead of her.

"Good luck, dear," Eyesallova called. "Do let me know if you have any success."

"Thank you. I will."

She listened for sounds of movement and life in the castle as she went down the staircase. Especially the sounds of armor coming after her with more crowns to try on.

On the ground floor, those closed doors caught her attention. The great hall and other rooms for entertaining guests and dispensing justice and whatever other business the castle oversaw would take place in rooms directly off the main doors and entryway. But there was no telling how long the castle had been without occupants, and some of the books she had read about the enchanted castle did say that it was mostly a storage place now. Wouldn't it make sense, with all the magic books and books about magic the castle protected, that large rooms would be turned into libraries, and additional library rooms?

Silently praying that she wouldn't have to go searching through the castle and lose precious time she couldn't afford to waste, Ash went to the nearest set of double doors and gently turned the knob. She half-expected the door to be locked, since there was a keyhole next to the knob, but no key. It clicked softly and the door whispered open. No groaning, no creaking. As if someone took care of the castle and oiled hinges. Well, the lack of dust and debris from the last time it had been robbed and raided indicated something or someone had cleaned up. Eyesallova had somewhat implied that the furniture took care of itself.

Shadows filled the room. Her first impression was of vastness. Some light did get in, and Ash stepped further into the shadows and partially closed the door, to block out the light behind her and let her eyes adjust. Streaks of light across the floor came from spots on either side of her, indicating the other doors she had seen on this side of the entryway led into this room. A whispering sound and a hint of movement drew her attention upward. Ash blinked, muffling a gasp as dust filtered into her eyes. She rubbed it away and stared, her mouth falling open, as light spilled down from overhead. Through teary eyes, she watched panels move aside in the ceiling, revealing long panels of glass.

Then she lowered her gaze to the room, to take in its vastness, and let out a sigh of wonder. Ending on a chuckle of glee.

Bookshelves, as far as she could see. Shelves built into the walls, rising three stories high, with galleries and balconies in some places, and long ladders on wheels and rails, like she had seen in the time pool library in other places. Bookshelves as high as her shoulders filled the floor to the right and left for a good hundred yards. Then more bookshelves, rising above her head, extended beyond them in both directions, until they met the walls. Aisles extended out from the spot where she stood, in a starburst pattern, with tables every eight or so shelves. And books everywhere.

Literally everywhere. On the shelves, piled on the tables, under the tables, piled on top of the shorter shelves. Spilled on the floor. Tumbled into piles. Books lying twisted among themselves, lying bent open, pages rumpled and bent, even torn. And dust covering everything.

Fang leaned against Ash's left leg. She looked down at him. He twisted his ears, pointing around the room, clearly asking what she was going to do.

"I don't know. It's such a dreadful mess. I would like to find whoever did this to these books and ..." She shuddered, in anger this time. "I would like to do the same to them, toss them around and leave them upside down and tear some of their pages and bend them and ... It's just not right! I'll wager they couldn't even read, the brutes who did this."

Sighing in disgust, she stepped over to the closest pile of discarded, abused books, and picked up one that lay pages down. She turned it over and caught her breath at the mess of bent pages and others nearly torn from the spine. Ash went to the nearest table, piled some of the books neatly to create a clear space, and smoothed out the pages of the book the best she could. A whispery sound like a tired sigh tickled her ears. She gently closed it and bent to pick up another fallen book. This one wasn't quite so bad. She closed it and set it next to the first and reached for another.

Fang nudged her, chirping several times. Ash caught her breath as she looked around and found a clear area around the table where there had been books literally carpeting the floor just a moment ago. The table was now covered with neat piles of books, all dust-free. Her hands stung slightly and she muffled a chuckle as she turned them palms up and found numerous paper cuts across her fingers. Her hands were clean, despite all the dusty books she must have been touching for ... how long? The angle of light coming from the glass ceiling hadn't changed, so how could she know? Ash looked down at herself and found the explanation for her clean hands. Long streaks of dust smudged the sides of her trousers where she had wiped her hands.

"How long have we been in here?" she whispered. Of course, Fang couldn't tell her. Ash shivered when her sense of time failed her. She could have been in here for half an hour, half a day, maybe longer.

The silence, the unchanged light, the sense of something sleeping and waiting, was affecting her mind. Just how had she let herself get so distracted? She should be looking for books about spirit rings, not doing a librarian's job of mending and cleaning. Although from the state of things, this library hadn't had a librarian in a dragon's age.

"I need an index, a directory to show me where books on specific subjects are stored. Otherwise, it could take me years to look through all these books." She turned around, surveying the shelves reaching to the ceiling three floors above her. Maybe a lifetime of searching? If there was no librarian here, what were her chances anyone had ever tried to organize these books?

Did the books organize themselves? Yet if the books were aware, as Cecil had taught her, as the rules of magic indicated should be happening here ... how had they gotten in such a mess? How or why had they sat still for so long, bent and torn and dusty? Why had the mess from the last raid been cleaned up elsewhere in the castle, but not here?

Unless the raiders had worked some magic on the books when they fled?

Ash wished her stars hadn't been burned away, or maybe just put to sleep, when she passed through the portal to the enchanted forest. She could use some help in detecting magic at work right now. Something was keeping these books asleep, maybe even keeping the other occupants of the castle from entering and cleaning up the mess.

"Fang ... can you see anything that doesn't belong here?"

The bunny responded with a cranky-sounding chirp.

"I mean, anything that doesn't look like books?"

He hopped away, leaping over piles of books, stopping to sniff at other piles, perching on bookshelves, then leaping down, constantly changing direction as he went through the library. Since he went right, she went left. Ash picked up books as she went, smoothing out pages, closing open books, setting them in the shelves, but sternly reminding herself she didn't have time to waste every time she wanted to linger and read a page here, a page there, smooth out the wrinkles and close open books. She wiped off the thicker clots of dust with her hands, then wiped them on her legs and her seat. A chuckle escaped her when she wondered how long she could keep doing that before she was too dirty to do any good.

What had Cecil said about magic books getting extremely cranky when they were left unread for too long, and allowed to go to dust?

So why weren't these books cranky and attacking from the moment she opened the door? Common sense said some nasty spell was at work, making the books sleep. But where was it? What was it?

And what exactly would be the reaction of the books the moment she found the spell and removed it? Could she remove it?

"A'theosius ... please, give me some wisdom and insight? Help me help these books? I need their help to free the ring. He doesn't deserve whatever has been done to him. It's not a crime to be my friend, is it?" Ash started rubbing her eyes, then realized how dusty dry her hands were, and stopped herself before she made things worse. She felt literally coated, inside and out, with dust.

She lowered her hands and paused. Something gleamed dully on the handle of the door two doors down from where she had entered. Yet the angle of the light coming from overhead didn't seem right, to cause that gleam right there. Ash held her breath as she hurried to the door. Strings wrapped around both knobs, with little disks of some metal on the strings. Ash caught her breath as she recognized the ancient emblems for books and silence and sleep and obedience. Cecil had taught her the emblems, even as he sniffed in disdain for the branch of magic spellwork he called "arrogance personified." The ancient practitioners had believed that finding the true name and true emblem granted power over that thing and forced it to share its life energy with the one who commanded the name. Cecil had taught her the emblems because of a much older, deeper magic, which was that the power of belief made things possible. The fact that the misguided practitioners of emblem magic and name magic *believed* it would work *made* it work, and Ash needed to understand how their minds worked to counteract that magic.

Someone very arrogant and selfish had believed this simple trick gave them power over the library. By binding the doors, had they thought to bind the books in sleep and silence? Maybe make the ones they stole obey them?

Well, Cecil had taught her an even older, stronger magic than that. Ash closed her eyes and reached for silence inside herself.

"A'theosius, make me your instrument of freedom and healing."

Then, eyes still closed, she reached for the knobs of the door. Her fingers tingled and itched, as if some energy guided her. Or perhaps tried to ward away her hands. She found the knobs and took a deep breath and pulled, as hard as she could.

CHAPTER FOURTEEN

The strings snapped with a sound like tight wires breaking. A smell like burned hair and sour herbs stung her nose. Ash staggered back, letting go of the doorknobs and opening her eyes. Light from the entryway spilled through the door, along with a gust of air that stirred clouds of dust from the closest piles of books.

Nothing else happened.

Ash thought for a moment, then gathered up the broken, scorched strings and the little metal emblems, which felt hot, the markings partially melted. She grinned and tried not to feel some sense of pride. After all, she hadn't done that. Not in her own power and strength.

She went to the next door. The same arrangement of strings and little metal disks. Again, she prayed. This time she held her breath so she wouldn't smell the stink of destroyed magic.

Again, no change in the library.

There were five sets of double doors into the library. The one she had entered through hadn't had that reaction. Ash supposed that made sense. The raiders wouldn't have been able to leave if they bound that set of doors closed. She repeated herself at the next doors. Fang returned from searching the library as she approached the last set of doors. He chirped, sounding interested, and backed away. What did he sense that she didn't?

Ash waited several moments longer before praying and yanking on the doorknobs. This time the strings resisted her. She gritted her teeth and pulled harder. Fang hopped up next to her and dug his teeth into one of the strings.

A shriek echoed through the library, light erupting from the strings and sending Ash and Fang stumbling backward. The doors burst open. Wind gushed through the library, stirring up massive clouds of dust. Thin, high, whispery voices cried out in a chorus. Ash covered her eyes with her arm, lying on her back, as dust rained down on her. Fang tapped her ankle. Then her arm. Then her calf on her other side. Then the sole of her boot. Then several taps in all those places at the same time.

Ash sat up, nearly leaping to her feet as she blinked away the dust and found herself surrounded by books. Standing up, closed books, pivoting back and forth on their spines, and tapping her. Rubbing against her. Rather like the dogs at Castle Fairhold after she had played with them or brushed out their tangled coats.

"Hello," she said, her voice just as dusty as the rest of her. Movement from the corners of her eyes had her turning, to find more books pivoting their way across the floor toward her, books wriggling themselves off of piles. "So, you're awake now?"

That was an idiot's question. Too bad Cecil had never taught her how to talk to magic books.

A rustling and dragging sound had her turning around, half-expecting something to leap at her from a shelf overhead. Two books dragged a third that was in two pieces, torn right down the spine. Ash guessed they wanted her to fix the book.

"I wish I could help, but I'll need glue and needle and thread and … I don't know what else."

A rustling sound of hundreds of pages turning at once swirled through the air. The two books pushed the pieces of the torn book onto the toes of her boots and hopped backward. Ash caught her breath as the books in front of her moved aside, some pushing the others, to clear the tile floor. At an intersection of aisles, the path that cleared before her turned right. She guessed the books wanted her to go that direction. She considered just for a moment that they weren't asking for help but blamed her for the damage done to the torn book. What if they were leading her into a trap, to a place where she couldn't escape, and they would proceed to … what? Bludgeon her to death? Bury her under books until she smothered?

Ash took a deep breath, regretting it when all that dust still swirling through the air coated her throat. Muffling her coughs, she picked up the broken book and followed the clear path through the books, turned right, continued down the aisle, until she saw a door into a small room built into a corner of the library. She nearly turned and ran at this affirmation of her fearful imagination.

"Fang? What do you think?"

The bunny hopped down the cleared space after her. He looked right and left, as if he didn't trust the books that piled themselves up on either side with a definite impression of watching and waiting. He passed Ash and paused in the open doorway, to look inside. There was no door, just an opening. All right, that wasn't quite as bad as she had feared.

Fang hopped into the room and went to the left and vanished from sight. Ash hurried to follow him and took two steps into the room before she saw him. He hopped around the room, sniffing at the shelves full of pieces of wood and leather, spools of thread, papers, knives, all sorts of tools that looked like a combination of carpentry shop and leather worker's shop. Ash lifted the lid on a large pot and the pungent, familiar smell of glue reached up to tweak her nose.

"It's a bindery," she whispered.

Friar Ipswich had given her basic lessons in repairing books, when he discovered how much she loved to read. In return for more time in the library, she gladly helped with repairs and reclaiming some volumes that had been set aside for years because they were simply too fragile for use.

"All right, I'll try to repair your friend," she told the books that had now filled in the clear space on the floor and clustered before the door of the room. "I can't promise I'll do a very good job, but I'll try. Understand?"

She could have laughed at herself for expecting to hear some sort of response from the books, but her throat was too dry. Ash set the book down on the long table running down the center of the room and searched the shelves for what she would need. Fang crouched in the doorway and chirped at her. When she looked at him, he gestured with his ears out into the library.

"I know. Just this one. I told them I'd try. If they know I'm a friend, maybe they'll let me read." She wondered now if she had made the wise choice of waking up the books. On the one hand, the spell putting them to sleep had been cruel, and they deserved their freedom and the ability to move about, if they truly were aware, as Cecil had theorized and taught her. On the other hand, what if the books decided she had to stay and fix all of them? What if they got offended when she tried to read some of them?

Ash chewed on that problem as she smoothed out wrinkled and bent pages and repaired the individual bundles of pages. Then glued them into the binding. Then sewed the ripped leather of the cover. Every time she looked up, she found books leaning in through the doorway, apparently watching her. How they could watch when they had no eyes, she had no idea.

When she stepped out of the bindery room, carrying the repaired book, Ash stumbled two steps in shock. Nearly all the books were off the floor. Piles of books had arranged themselves at the foot of bookshelves. Feather dusters flew through the air, dislodging curdles and clots and clouds of dust from everywhere. Swirls of dust gathered themselves together and spun out the five sets of open doors. So, the books could take care of themselves. To a point.

Piles of books still covered the tables. They shifted and slid around over and under each other as Ash watched. She wondered if there was a system they used to arrange themselves, some kind of order, or if this was a kind of game that books played. She imagined books rearranging themselves, out of the order the librarian had left them in, at night when the doors were closed and the librarian was asleep.

Then all the movement went still. Ash had the distinct impression that suddenly every book in the library was looking at her.

"Hello." She held out the repaired book. "I did the best I could. He needs to rest a while, let the glue dry and set. Could I ask a favor?" she hurried on, frightened by an image of a dozen more wounded books needing repair surrounding her. "I'm looking for information on spirit rings. My friend has been silenced. I don't know if he's been imprisoned inside the ring, or he simply isn't allowed to talk to me. Maybe not allowed to talk to anyone. I'd like to find a way to free him. That's why I came in here. I would have helped you even if I didn't need help," she hurried to add. "But do any of you have information like that?"

That sound like hundreds of rustling pages, just on the edge of hearing, flowed through the library. Ash walked over to the closest table and put the repaired book down. She stroked the cover, her fingers lingering over the place where she had stitched the torn leather together.

"You did hear me, didn't you? You need to rest and let the glue set and dry." Then she yanked her hand back and fought the urge to look around and make sure no one had heard her. Was she really talking to books, and expecting them to understand?

Several feather dusters flew down from the top shelves, leaving a trail of dust in the air as they zoomed to the far reaches of the library. Ash watched them for a moment, then aimed herself at a podium she had seen earlier, set against the far wall. Perhaps that podium held the index or map of the library that she needed. She stepped out into an open area, with neatly arranged seats in a half-circle facing the podium. At one time, someone had stood there and read aloud to people sitting in those chairs. She wondered how long ago people had lived here. What had this castle been like before some evil deed, some nasty, powerful magic, had yanked it free of its anchors and sent it traveling through the enchanted forest?

Fang had gone exploring while she repaired the book. Now he chirped and came bouncing back to her, sometimes leaping over bookshelves and tables, sometimes bouncing off them to turn a corner. His ears pointed at her as he approached.

Something bumped against her right foot. Ash jumped sideways, half-expecting to find a rat. A giggle pressed at her lips as she imagined hundreds of books throwing themselves at rats to drive them out of the library before their pages were nibbled.

Not a rat, but pretty green and blue dancing slippers. They were covered with faceted beads that caught the soft light and shimmered. They bumped their toes against Ash's boot.

"What are you doing in here?" She bent down to get a closer look. "There is no dancing in the library, because there's no music." Ash chuckled when the slippers wriggled themselves around to rest their toes on her toes. She had a distinct impression of ... begging.

Fang chirped and clicked and slid to stop at Ash's feet, pushing the slippers away. She muffled a scolding rising up in her throat. Movement in the doorway had her turning, to see a pretty dress, all flowing lines and gossamer panels, the same blues and greens of the slippers. The dress flew toward her. Ash felt the stirring of a breeze, and guessed the castle had housekeeping breezes, just like in Filby's home. Why hadn't the housekeeping breezes cleaned up the mess of the library? Why had they let the dust settle for so long? Had those spells she broke kept out everything and everyone? Even other magic?

Ash blinked and found herself holding the dress up to her shoulders, as if guessing the fit. When had she accepted it from the breezes?

It would look pretty on her, wouldn't it? She had gone far too long, hiding under dirt and boy clothes. Hadn't she earned the right to be pretty, to have pretty clothes, to feel like a girl even if there was no one but a manic bunny to see her?

What would it hurt to try on the clothes?

Ash blinked and shook her head. What was she thinking?

The slippers nudged her feet, tapping on her toes. She looked down and laughed. They reminded her of puppies, somehow. Her feet did feel rather hot and heavy in her boots. As long as she was going to be here for a while, why not try on the slippers?

A cluster of feather dusters flew out of the far reaches of the library and slid to a landing on the table in front of Ash. One duster flipped upward, turning a somersault, and tickled her nose when she didn't look at them. Ash sneezed and reached to brush the duster away.

Two books sat on the long handles and bunches of feathers. Intrigued, she hung the dress over her elbow and reached with her free hand to open one of the books. The title page declared it dealt with history of spirit rings. That was interesting. Ash wondered why the feather dusters had brought her a book about spirit rings. She turned and caught the dress with both hands again and held it up to her shoulders. If only there was a looking glass in here, so she could get an idea of how she would look in it.

Fang chattered at her and leaped, hitting her square in the chest. She fell backward, stumbling against a short bookshelf, then sliding down to sit on the pile of books in front of it. Fang chirped and clicked and climbed up into her lap, pawing at the dress, yanking it out of her hands, then clawing the dress with his hind feet, shoving it away, so it slid down to the floor.

"What did you do that for?" Ash yelped as Fang put a hind foot into her belly, slightly knocking the breath out of her, and leaped up onto the bookshelf behind her. He pawed at her hair, and a moment later the braided silver crown clattered to the floor.

She caught her breath, feeling as if she had been slapped with a cold cloth. Ash rubbed at her face, taking more deep breaths, fighting the sensation that she had been slowly, softly, sliding down into sticky shadows. The housekeeping breeze swirled down to pick up the dress again and held it up, offering it to her. The slippers again bumped at her toes. Ash frowned, wondering why she had thought that was cute. It was annoying. She was likely to trip over them.

Wait. Weren't there books? Flying down to her on a raft of feather dusters?

She got up and stepped over to the table, and nearly stepped on the slippers. Yes, a book on spirit rings. The second book also dealt with spirit rings. One covered the history of spirit rings, who had used them, what help they had given or trouble they had caused. The other book discussed theories of their origins and their purpose and possible future, depending on the reasons why they had been made in the first place.

Fang shrieked, a scolding sound, and leaped at the dress, yanking it out of the air. He bounced up and down on it, and for good measure kicked away the crown that lay next to it.

Eyesallova had said something about the furniture and clothes ...

A clanking and creaking and the sound of metal scraping on stone approached through the central doors. The suit of armor she had seen next to the door walked into the library. Ash backed up two steps, then reached and picked up the two books, cradling them against her chest. If she was going to get chased out of the library now, she was taking those books with her.

How long had she been in here? Why was her sense of time so muddled?

The slippers flung themselves at Fang, hitting him in the face, driving him back several steps until he got off the dress. The housekeeping breeze swooped in and picked up the dress and the slippers. They approached Ash, twitching aside as Fang leaped at them.

Four books jumped from the piles sitting on top of the short shelves, hit the dress and the slippers, and pinned them to the floor. Ash laughed.

The armor stopped and bent down. It picked up the crown. Fang jumped up, trying to snatch the crown. The iron-clad arm swept him aside so he flew over four bookshelves with a shriek that made Ash gasp. Then the armor held out the crown to her.

"No, no, no," she whispered, suddenly understanding what was going on, what Eyesallova had warned her about. What Cecil had talked about.

The castle wanted a princess. It was trying to turn her into a princess. What would have happened if she had, just for fun, tried on those slippers? Would she have put on the dress next, and completely forgotten what she was doing here in the library? Would she have stayed? Would she have gone into the living quarters and found that suite of rooms she had glimpsed in a vision, waiting for her?

The crown was a trap. She had worn it because Eyesallova had advised her to, so the castle would accept her, so the armor would leave her alone. Yet what if the crown was trying to change her, take over her mind, bend her will to the purpose of the castle?

"Fang, we have to get out of here." Ash dodged the armor and that crown that had seemed so harmless such a short time ago. She ran for the door.

Where was Fang? Had the armor killed him?

Screaming fury, Fang bounced off the bookshelves, catching up with her in two leaps. He bounced through the door, out into the entryway. Ash clutched the books to her chest and ran.

Books tumbled in a sideways avalanche from both sides of the room, blocking the door. The armor clanked and scraped across the floor, holding out the crown to her. Ash tried to climb, but the books piled up higher, creating a smooth, angled surface that sent her sliding back to the floor. The books she clutched wriggled out of her arms.

"Please! I need to learn—" Ash stopped, arms stretched out after the books, as the armor shoved the crown against her fingertips.

It did no good to argue with anything here. The magical items wanted what they wanted, and she was the stranger, the intruder. The outsider they were trying to change and bend to their purpose. She couldn't reason with them.

She had to reason her way around them. Ash swallowed hard and wished for the ring to wake up and advise her.

Stop wasting time, she scolded herself. *Think. Give them what they want without getting trapped.*

Holding her breath, she reached a little further, spreading her fingers to take the crown. She drew it back to herself, watching the armor, wishing there was something like a face, something to give her a clue what it was thinking, feeling. If a suit of armor could feel.

Ash exhaled, lips trembling in a grin, as the armor stepped back. Apparently, just taking the crown satisfied it. She waited until it was far enough away it couldn't touch her, then stood up. She slipped on a few more books, and moved sideways, so she could watch armor and the barricade of books at the same time.

"I need to go out and check on my horse and my camp and see if the portal to go back to my own country has opened. I will come back in the morning." She swallowed. Took a deep breath. Braced herself. She feared this was going to be a huge mistake, but she had no alternative. "I promise I will come back in the morning. I need to find out what the books have to say about spirit rings. I will come back and repair five more books. I promise. If you will help me, and keep the clothes from trying to trap me, all right?"

Of course, the books couldn't talk to her. She might shriek and not stop for some time, if the books talked now.

Slowly, the avalanche of books slid aside, wriggling and bouncing and tumbling out of the way, to clear a path through the doorway. Fang came barreling through the door, panting, and flung his forelegs around her knees. Ash nearly choked on the need to laugh. She bent and patted him, then gently pried him loose, so she could walk.

"Thank you. I promise I'll come back tomorrow."

Walking slightly sideways, she stepped through the door, keeping an eye on the suit of armor. It didn't follow her. She hoped she could get away with just holding the crown, rather than wearing it.

"Fang, I'm going to need your help. You have to keep checking on me, make sure I'm not … changed, when I come back here tomorrow."

Fang chirped, punctuated with a few rasping sounds that she suspected were the equivalent of bunny cursing. From the angry twisting and bending of his ears, she guessed he was telling her she was being stupid.

"I promised. It was the only way I could get out. You don't dare make promises to magical things, especially something as full of magic as this entire castle, and then break those promises. I need you to protect me, wake me up, keep this place from making me a princess."

Ash was out the main doors and halfway across the drawbridge before her words seemed to echo in her head. She had told Eyesallova she would come back and tell her what happened. Breaking that promise would be foolish. Yet how could she go back to the mirror room, knowing the mirror had essentially set her up to be trapped, changed, made an occupant of the castle?

Or had she? Ash paused, turned around facing the main doors, and tried to remember what the mirror had said. Eyesallova had warned her, hadn't she? Maybe not as clearly as Ash would have liked, but then, magic or the will of the castle might have restrained the mirror as well.

CHAPTER FIFTEEN

"Stop making excuses," Ash snarled at herself, when she realized she had been standing on that drawbridge, thinking until her temples throbbed. "I made a promise, I have to keep it. I just don't dare trust anything, for however long I stay here."

She looked behind herself, at the trail through the forest.

The landscape outside the castle had changed. The trail she had followed was gone. When she went into the castle, apple trees filled the air with soft, tangy perfume. Now the ruby gleam of cherries almost overwhelmed the green of the leaves. The castle had kept moving.

"Fang, can you find the way back to our camp?" she whispered, even though it was probably useless to do so.

He rose up on his hind legs, resting one paw against her thigh, and nodded solemnly.

"All right then. We're going up to the mirror room, then we're out of here as fast as we can move and going straight back to the camp."

Pulling her shoulders back, taking a couple deep breaths, Ash turned around and headed back across the drawbridge and through the gates and up the steps into the castle.

The mirror room doors swung open before Ash put her foot on the top step of the stairs. She clenched her fists, and feared the silver braid of the crown bent, just slightly. Fang hopped ahead of her, paused on the threshold, then looked back at her and chirped, and continued inside.

"Oh, well done, dear," Eyesallova greeted her. "I was worried for you, but since I haven't been able to see inside the libraries since those brutes invaded, I had no idea what was done, nor how to break that nasty bit of spellwork. The books adore you."

"Yes, I can see that. To the point of wanting to make me a prisoner."

"They'll protect you now. Ask them to keep the rest of the castle from playing tricks on you, and they will."

"Yes, playing tricks. How can I trust you? You didn't warn me."

"Yes …" The mirror's swirls of green and blue darkened slightly. "You can see it that way, can't you? I'm affected and influenced just as much by the spirit of the castle as everything in it. Over the years, I've tried to warn so many adventurers and princesses and noble youths. The more I warn them, the more mistakes they make. I've managed to keep some from being trapped by not giving clear warnings. So much depends on the cleverness of the heroes who make it up the stairs to consult with me. You can spend as much time here in safety as you want, as long as you leave before nightfall and you don't sleep here, you don't eat here, you don't take anything out of the castle. I'm sorry. I know you need those books, but you'll just have to study and make notes. Knowledge you can take. Things you can hold in your hand, you must leave behind."

"That makes sense ... I suppose." Ash sighed, and with that breath went so much of the angry energy that had made her tremble. Weight pressed on her shoulders and dragged on her legs, and her sense of time returned, like a slap against the back of her head. She had gone all day without eating. How much time had she lost in the library? "Thank you for your help." She turned to leave, then felt the crown slide across her leg. She turned back and held it out. "What do I do with this? I don't have to wear it, do I?"

"Yes, unfortunately. There are two more suits of armor coming up the stairs right now, with more crowns to offer you. I suggest you wear it to get out through the doors, then put it in a safe place where you can find it when you come back. That crown will be your safe pass, in and out. The books will protect you from the rest of the castle's inhabitants, so you can wear the crown safely when you're in the library. Just be sure you do come back. You don't want the suits of armor or the larger pieces of furniture, and especially not the carriages or wagons to come hunting for you."

Ash nodded. She wished she could find the mental image of being chased by wagons and carriages without horses amusing, but she was too tired. She thanked Eyesallova, tamping down a small surge of resentment and the fear she was still being tricked, and headed out the doors.

The suits of armor were on the landing between the first and second floors. She glared at them and slapped the crown back on her head. They turned to watch her as she descended the stairs, and moved aside when she reached them. They stayed on the landing as she reached the main doors and stepped outside.

Ash nearly forgot to find a safe place to leave the crown, on castle grounds and yet outside. She found several decorative ledges of stone all around the doorway and stood on her toes to reach as high as possible. The ledge was wide enough for the crown to hang from it, catching securely so it couldn't be knocked off by breezes during the night. Then Ash crossed the drawbridge. She wanted dearly to run, but she was too tired. And too stubborn to display just how uneasy the castle made her.

Fang hopped ahead of her, no need to ask him to lead the way. She studied the sky, trying to determine how much time she had until the next change. Eyesallova had said the changes were sometimes short of twelve hours, sometimes more than twelve. Sometimes the portals opened to four places in sequence, sometimes five. Ash had the awful feeling she hadn't asked several important questions. Starting with if the portals opened in the same sequence all the time, or they changed order.

"Not that I plan on staying here that long to find out such details," she muttered as she followed Fang down an animal trail that seemed to wobble drunkenly. She couldn't see more than a dozen paces down the trail before it curved to the right or left. Definitely not the path she had followed before.

Then to her relief they came out on the stream. At least, she hoped this was the same stream where she had camped. If so, had the castle moved closer to her camp while she was inside? Should she be worried about that?

Something crashed among the trees behind her. Was that the sound a suit of armor made when it tripped over roots or ran into low-hanging branches? A snort escaped her at the mental image of one of those persistent suits of armor knocking a helmet off and having to fumble about, trying to find it and put it back on. Or maybe tripping and banging into a trunk and knocking an arm loose. If there was nothing inside the iron casing. What if there was something inside, even if just a magical mist, that made it move?

That thought made her shiver. She tried to shove it out of her mind. Fang chirped happily and bounced back to meet her. His ears pointed back and to the right at such a tight angle, her own ears ached for him. Just how did he do that without breaking his ears off at the root?

She found Garan, placidly grazing on the grass at the edge of the slope covered over by moss. Ash breathed her thanks and stumbled a few steps, feeling a little weak with relief. First thing she wanted was a long drink of water. All that dust she had been breathing and wiping off her face and hands made her dry, inside and out.

No. First thing was to check the portal.

Fang hopped toward the overhang and their camp and squeaked, sounding a little worried when she didn't follow him.

"We need to see if the portal changed," she told him.

He let out a gusting sigh, sounding so much like Justiciar Camwell, Ash wondered if he was teasing her. He leaped high, getting ahead of her in just a few bounds.

The portal still showed the pool and that spot of underwater light. Ash shook her head, refusing to even contemplate trying to dive that deep and swim to that light. There was no indication of what she would find when she came up out of the water on the other side. That was too much danger. Plus, how could she carry her gear, or bring her horse? Fang certainly wouldn't go through that particular portal with her. He had hated water any deeper than his head, ever since that plunge through the waterfall to escape Morris.

"How long do you—" Ash flinched as sparks danced along her fingertips.

She took two steps back as more sparks swirled around the edges of the pool. The rock stretched upward, turning into a massive tree, and the portal became a bulging sort of slit in the center of the trunk. The sides of the passageway were smooth, streaked with moss in a few places.

On the other side was darkness, with starlight at the top. A warm breeze scented with something sweetly fruity reached through to tickle her nose. Then a stronger swirling of breeze followed, damp, scented with salt. Had this portal opened somewhere near the sea as well? Where did it open? Could she go through and explore for a few days and come back here? How long would it take her to map all the places the portals opened out to from the enchanted forest?

Ash took several more steps back, stunned by the thought. Why would she want to spend her time doing that?

Someone had already figured out how to use the portals scattered through the enchanted forest to travel around the world. If a selfish, illiterate boor like King Ruprick had figured it out—granted, with the help of those half-baked magicians Cecil had so despised—then others could as well. And use the portals to do more than steal books.

Understanding the pathways of the enchanted forest was knowledge. Filby lived for knowledge. People with the power to defend the innocent and defenseless, who accepted that responsibility, could use the knowledge of the pathways for good purposes, not for selfish ones.

"One thing at a time," Ash muttered, and turned her back on the portal that opened onto some place that was currently night. She wondered how long it would stay night there, since as Eyesallova had told her, the difference between the enchanted forest and the outside world was a factor of thirty. She couldn't and quite frankly didn't want to waste time sitting and watching the light change. She was thirsty, she was hungry, and she needed to write down everything she had learned and done today in her journal before she forgot a single detail.

~~~~~

Fang woke Ash when dawn was merely a faint hint of chilly silver streaks across the sky. She took time to splash water on her face. She still felt the dusty dry effects of yesterday's explorations. Then she followed him back to the portal, stumbling a few times on the laces of her boots, which she hadn't taken the time to tie. The scent of roses touched her nose before she saw the pale golden light of a winter afternoon coming through the tunnel. Ash went to her knees, grinning and blinking away totally ridiculous tears. Winter, when she had come through in late fall. Two months had passed in Cammerlang, but only two days here. What had happened at Castle Fairhold? Had Lathia struck? Had Justiciar Camwell
~~~~~

reappeared?

"Ready to go home, Fang?"

He chirped and bounced up and down in place, and she laughed. She wiped the damp from her eyes and struggled to her feet. Then stopped and bent down to tie her bootlaces before heading back to camp.

Her journal still sat out, the page held down with her ivory pen, to allow the last lines she had written to dry. She had written until her hand cramped and her eyes blurred with sticky weariness last night. Ash leaned over to read it as she chewed on a dried apricot. A pang shot through her at the words she had written, to remind herself.

"I did promise to go back, didn't I?" she whispered, more to herself than Fang. Instinct and common sense told her not to break any promises made in the enchanted castle. She sighed. "I need to find out what those books say about spirit rings."

She packed her journal in her satchel, along with two pens, the pot of ink, trail bread and several spiced meat sticks, and a packet of raisins. Ash picketed Garan on a long lead so he could reach the water and the grass. She took a dozen steps away from the camp, then remembered the water flask. How could she have forgotten it, after that long, dry, dusty day?

The drawbridge was down, but the main doors into the castle stayed shut when Ash approached. She stretched her senses, waiting for the first sound of approaching iron feet, trying to detect the sensation of magical eyes watching her. All was silent, as if the castle were sleeping, or perhaps empty of all life and awareness.

She took the crown down from the stone ledge. Ash paused, hand raised, shivering at the sensation that someone, many someones, had inhaled sharply in anticipation. She looked down at Fang, who stayed by her side, close enough he threatened to interfere with her steps. He flipped his ears, looking unconcerned.

Was she wrong to depend on Fang to sense trouble before it approached? He was sometimes more prone to make trouble than help her avoid it.

With another deep breath, Ash rested the crown as lightly as she could on her head.

Dozens of someones exhaled. Sighing. Relief, if not happiness.

The main doors swung open. Well, Eyesallova had told her the crown was her pass inside. Would it keep away those insistent suits of armor?

Inside the entry hallway, the doors to the library were all closed. Had they closed on their own, or had the books closed the doors? Or had the clothes or housekeeping breezes or whatever had been competing with the books for her attention closed the doors in pique? Ash walked slowly, listening, waiting for some further reaction from the castle. She thought the central doors to the library rattled a little, in preparation for opening.

Then she thought of something. A sound like a sigh, maybe a whimper from dusty, papery throats, filtered up the stairs after her as she raced up, two steps at a time, to the mirror room.

"Good morning, Eyesallova," she called as the doors swung open before her.

"Welcome back, dear! Ready for another day of exploring and adventure?" the magic mirror greeted her.

"As much as I can learn," Ash said, after a pause to choose her words carefully. Just like unwise wishes, unwise words, even if they weren't promises, could trap her. "You warned me not to eat anything the castle offers me. Is it safe for me to eat what I bring in with me, or should I just not eat or drink anything inside the castle?"

"Ah, and the child learns swiftly," she murmured, ending on a bubbling sigh of laughter. "Your food is safe today, but bring fresh food tomorrow, if you have anything left over today. The longer something stays in the castle, the stronger the tendency for it to become part of the castle."

Ash nearly asked, "And does that include me?" but she shuddered at the certainty that merely speaking the words would make them true. Silence was wisdom.

"Thank you." She turned to leave, then thought of something. "Have you heard anything about Justiciar Camwell? He vanished, when Lord Digory tried to warn him that Lathia was a danger."

"I will listen. There may be chatter. I can only listen, not ask. Check back this evening, before you go back to your camp."

"Thank you."

Ash promised herself she would be gone long before evening threw shadows across the forest and through the castle's windows.

A suit of armor waited next to the library doors, both arms stretched out, with four crowns strung on each arm. Beautiful crowns, glittering with jewels like ice, intricate swirls of engraving in the silver and gold, the cloth encrusted with diamond dust. Ash felt those watchful eyes from inside the helmet and had to swallow hard to get enough moisture in her mouth to speak. Politeness, as Lady Charlotte had always maintained, covered over many perilous situations.

"Thank you, but I have work to do, and those crowns are so heavy and so beautiful, I'd be afraid of them falling off my head and breaking." She reached for the doorknob.

The doors into the library slammed open, and a tidal wave of books moved back, opening a clear pathway across the gleaming tile floor to the table in the center aisle of the room. Ash stepped into the room quickly, half-expecting the suit of armor to try to grab her and stop her, maybe force a crown onto her head.

"Good morning, my friends," she said, mouth still dry. "I've come to study. Will you help me?"

A thousand pages rustled. To her relief, the air stayed clear, no clouds of dust gushing outward.

"Would you mind closing the doors, so nobody can interrupt me?"

A muffled roar of movement behind her had her spinning around on her heel, to see that pile of books moving like a wave, pushing the doors closed and then piling up against them. Ash smiled, but found it hard to hold onto her smile when she had a sudden image of those books staying there, refusing to move when she tried to leave in mid-afternoon. She couldn't afford to be late returning to the portal and have the tunnel of roses and snow close, keeping her here two more days. Two more months.

"Thank you. That's perfect." She glanced down at Fang, who chirped at her and flipped his ears in his signal she interpreted as meaning, "I'm off to explore, don't get into any trouble while I'm gone." Then he bounced away. "Would it be too much trouble for the books on spirit rings to come back? I especially need to learn from them."

At the table, two books popped upright, waggling to get her attention. Ash grinned as she headed down the aisle to the table. She wondered how long it would take until she grew so used to this magical help, she took it for granted.

She stumbled on her third step. Grow used to this? The idea of growing used to this implied she planned on staying here for some time. A long time. Perhaps living here.

"Help me," she whispered, to A'theosius and to the ring. She reached up and pressed on her courier badge, and the ring hidden behind it.

Then she thought of something. Would it help? Would it bring more cooperation, and hopefully protection, from the books? Or make them resentful and unwilling to help her?

There was no way of knowing until she tried. Ash unpinned her badge as she settled at the table. She slid the ring off the back and put it on the table in the clear spot in the center.

"This is my friend. He's a spirit ring. Some awful magic has silenced him. I don't know if he can hear or see me, if he's been cut off from all the other spirit rings who are his friends. This research is to help him. He would love to meet all of you and learn from you. We've talked often about the library here in the enchanted castle, and all the treasures of knowledge you contain. Will you help me awaken him, give him his ears and voice back?"

Another rustling of thousands of pages, then the book on the history of spirit rings flopped down flat on the table and snapped its cover open.

Ash read until her eyes felt dusty dry again. Disappointingly, she found very little that she and the ring hadn't already discussed.

Everything was theory, repetition of folk tales and speculations, rather than actual factual history of spirit rings. When she sat up and arched her back and tried to straighten her shoulders after being bent for more than an hour of reading, a touch on her ankle startled a squeak out of her. She looked down, half-expecting those dancing slippers from yesterday, some other magical piece of clothing, or perhaps a rat after all.

A bedraggled little book wobbled on its end and tapped her foot. Its leather cover had worn away in spots so the wooden base of its cover showed through. She bent down and picked it up and found it small enough to fit in her hand. It flipped open, showing her where the threads of the binding had been torn out of the pages. Clearly, it wanted mending.

"Well, it would do me some good to get up and move, wouldn't it?" she murmured. "But I have so very much studying to do. Please don't bring me all the injured books. Not all at once." Her voice seemed to echo hollowly at her, and she felt rather ungrateful. She didn't want to refuse to help, because she felt as Friar Ipswich did, that books were sacred and deserved protecting and decent care and respect. "I'll try to mend one book every time I come in here to study, how about that?"

She flinched, wishing she had stopped to think a little longer before she made that promise. She hadn't promised to come back, had she? If she never came back, the books couldn't accuse her of breaking her promise. Could they?

A few stitches with sturdy thread and a few swipes of glue solved the problem for the little book. Ash spread it open flat and told it to lie still and let the glue set before it moved again. She hurried back to her study table and reached for the water flask. Silently thanking Blaz for his gift of nearly endless fresh water, she took a long drink. Before she finished the final swallow, a bang-clang of metal on metal sounded from some distance, and cool air spiraled around her. Movement from the corner of her eye had her looking up. A shawl in a peacock's feather pattern floated down slowly toward her, the edges flapping like wings.

Ash swallowed down the first dozen things she thought of saying, some of them angry, some of them frightened, some of them irritated.

CHAPTER SIXTEEN

"Thank you," she called to the housekeeping breeze carrying the shawl, "but that doesn't go with any of my clothes."

The shawl folded up in midair and fell straight down, to sprawl across a low set of bookshelves a dozen or so steps away from her table. Ash looked up and saw where a large panel in the glass ceiling had opened up like a trap door. So, if the books wouldn't let any furniture or clothes in through the doors, the castle found another way to tempt and trap her. She considered how difficult it would be for the books to reach up that high and close the panel and keep others from opening. Very difficult. The image of a fountain of books, floating up high and knocking invading shoes and dresses and stockings and shirts back out through the opening was ridiculous enough to get a chuckle from her. Ash took one last sip from the flask, closed it, and settled down to read more.

Gloves floated down and landed across her wrist as she reached to dip her pen in the inkwell. Ash picked them up and put them on the stack of books on the far end of the table, rather than shaking them off, preferably across the room. Politeness would protect her, she reminded herself, with an echo of Lady Charlotte's voice in her head. She longed for the elderly lady to be right here with her. She didn't doubt the woman would thoroughly enjoy the riches of books, and the challenge of navigating the temptation traps the castle offered.

A scarf landed so softly across Ash's shoulder, she didn't notice until a book jumped up from the floor to her lap, and from her lap to her shoulder, apparently trying to dislodge the scarf. Ash's fingers tangled around it, reveling in the whispery softness, the shimmering colors like a swirl of rainbows that changed as the light from far overhead danced across it. With a little regret, she folded up the scarf and put it aside with the gloves. She thought about giving that scarf to Lady Charlotte, knowing the woman would be delighted with it.

The scarf was followed by a delicate chain shaped like flowers, the petals of topaz thin enough to see through. Ash didn't know the necklace was there until it slid down off the stack of books it had landed on. A matching bracelet and earrings appeared on the table, just out of her sight until she lifted her gaze from the book to dip the pen again to make a few more notes. Lady Beatrice would look lovely, the delicate streaks of gold and orange and yellow contrasting with her dark hair and eyes and olive complexion. Ash lingered over the jewelry, contemplating how she could persuade the castle to let her take it with her.

The book she was reading snapped closed, startling her. She dropped an earring.

What was she doing?

Ash put the bracelet and earrings with the necklace and got up, reasoning she needed to take a break, move around, breathe deeply, stretch her legs. She ate a few bites of trail bread, but it tasted rather bland. As if it had been dampened and lost its saltiness and then allowed to dry and go stale. She dug in her satchel and took out one slice each of dried apple and apricot, and then a meat stick to cut the sweetness. Then back to work.

She had two pages of notes when she finished going through the book on the history of spirit rings. To celebrate, she dipped into her satchel again and found a handful of dried cherries. The taste exploded across her tongue and she closed her eyes, savoring the richness. In just a few bites, she had eaten them all, and dug in her satchel for more. No, all gone. Why hadn't she put more cherries in this morning? She loved cherries. Sighing, she reached for her water flask and dislodged a circlet sitting across it. This one sparkled softly, spirals of sapphire and emerald chips on the simple band of cool ebony.

Wait a moment. She didn't pack cherries this morning. She didn't have cherries in her supplies.

The sparkle of the jewels against the black background caught her attention and she grinned, feeling a little guilty, a little mischievous, as she raised the circlet to put on her head. What would it hurt to try it on? Just for a moment. She needed a break. She needed to celebrate all the work she had done that morning.

Ash blinked. She knew she had been working at something, but for the life of her, she couldn't remember what it was. Certainly, her hand ached a little from clutching the pen. Frowning, she sat back and looked around the library. What had she come in here for? A luscious aroma tickled her nose. Apples and cinnamon and fresh bread. Her mouth watered.

She followed her nose. The books moved aside when she approached the doors. Something squealed and chittered behind her, but the aroma was too alluring to let her pause. She stepped out into the main entryway. A hungry rumbling rose from her stomach. Ash laughed at herself as she approached the table, large enough for six people, set with delicate glass plates rimmed in silver, with silver utensils and a dainty lace tablecloth and matching napkins, embroidered with tiny blue and green and gold peacocks. A huge loaf of fresh, steaming bread and a pot of butter sat next to the place setting at the end of the table, where a chair lined with blue and green peacock patterned cushions waited for her to sit down.

Thumping approached from behind her, and more squeals.

Ash reached for the arm of the chair to sit down. Her gaze landed on a bowl of stewed cherries. She did love cherries, but something struck her as odd …

What had she been thinking before, about cherries?

Oh, that was right. She had found cherries in her satchel, but she knew she didn't have any in her supplies. How had the cherries gotten in there?

Fang chattered and squeaked, leaping onto the table in front of her, sending the plate and utensils and napkin skidding aside. His eyes were red and huge with furious alarm. Ash shook her head, positive in another moment she would understand what he was saying, and just as positive she wouldn't like it.

Shrieking, Fang lunged at her. She leaned back and ducked down, trying to avoid him. He landed on her head and yanked off the ebony circlet. A flash of violet light burst from the circlet. Fang hit the floor and slammed the circlet down. Another flash, brilliant enough to make her wince and press her hands to her eyes. A bitter smell like dried blood clashed with the aromas of butter and cinnamon and bread and cherries.

"Cherries," Ash murmured.

Panicking, she fumbled to get to her feet and away from that chair. Fury made her stumble as she staggered back, holding her arms out to block that table if it tried to follow her. There was no telling what would move, here in the castle.

"Sneaky," she growled, and reached back blindly with one hand, trying to find the door back into the library.

The castle had caught her attention with the jewelry, perhaps opening up her defenses and weakening her resolve, and somehow had snuck those dried cherries into her satchel without her noticing. She had eaten them and weakened herself even more, so she put the new crown on, giving the castle more power over her.

What would have happened if she had eaten that bread?

"Thank you, Fang," she said, and backed through the door into the library. "Please, friends … close the door?"

The tidal wave of books swept up and pushed the doors closed. Fang barely squeezed through in time. Ash went back to her study table. She picked up her books and other supplies and moved to another table. Better that than risk being weakened and influenced again by being near, let alone touching that jewelry and the gloves to move them. She checked her satchel for more food she hadn't packed.

The aroma of almonds gushed out when she lifted the flap, and she found four delicate strawberries, glistening with a sweet coating.

Marzipan. Lady Charlotte had given her a piece of marzipan last year for her birthday. Ash thought she had never tasted anything so incredible and luxurious.

"You overreached yourself," she said, dumping the sweets out on the table at the far end from where she had now settled. "I didn't notice the cherries, but I would have noticed the marzipan and known something was wrong." She sighed, wishing she dared to take even a tiny bite. What would happen if she took the marzipan with her when she left at the end of the day?

No, better not to take the risk and find out the hard way.

Fang stayed with her, napping on a seat tucked under the table. From time to time, he hopped away, loudly, in pursuit of something. Ash refused to take her gaze off the text for one moment. This book was all stories of people who had been guided or enslaved by spirit rings and detailed how the various enchantments that attached to them had been a blessing or curse, and how they had been shattered. Many stories reinforced the general teaching that spirit rings were rare. So how had Justiciar Camwell come to be in possession of so many that he could use them to keep watch on multiple people at the same time, and give spirit rings to his servants? Apparently, he kept watch over them all with a master ring. Was the master ring more than a spirit ring? Did it serve him willingly, enslaving the other spirit rings?

Ash lost what little pity and concern she had for Camwell in the face of Lathia's vengeance. Wherever he had fled, she hoped he was miserable and quaking in fear. Just as long as in the end Lathia didn't gain control over not just the ring she wore, but the master ring.

She remembered what Hazel had asked the ring, the night she fled Castle Fairhold with Fang. Would he like to come to a place where he would be surrounded by other magical items like himself, able to rest from his duties and socialize and share stories? And now, be safe from arrogant, self-righteous creatures like Camwell and Lathia?

"Would you like that, someday?" she whispered, raising her gaze from the book to look at the ring, lying on the table next to her inkwell. "Retire here, free to do what you wish, talk with all the books, rest with the other magical things hidden and stored here?"

Ash couldn't decide if she hoped the ring could hear her, even if he couldn't speak. Wouldn't he have an awful lot to say to her, answering all the questions she had asked him, correcting all her misconceptions, when he could finally speak again?

Again, the library muted her sense of time passing. Ash measured it by how many stories she read, how many times she drank from the water flask, and when she ran out of the food she had brought. She smiled wryly when the castle didn't try to slip anything else into her satchel. So, it learned from its mistakes. She would also learn from her mistakes and be even more watchful.

Or perhaps she would be wiser simply never to return?

An ache settled into her chest at the thought of never coming back, never sitting here in the library, surrounded by more books than she could read in three lifetimes. The thought of all those damaged books, waiting for mending, added to that ache.

Munching on the last bite of trail bread, Ash got up to step out of the library and get a sense of the time of day. Books slid across the floor and added themselves to the barricade in front of the doors.

"Thank you for protecting me," she said, and managed to smile. She clasped her hands so they wouldn't shake. Now was not the time to be trapped here. When would the books change from protecting her to holding her prisoner? "I just want to step outside and check the time, see how late in the day it is. I promised Eyesallova I would report to her on what I had found. You don't want me to break my promise, do you?"

That seemed to do the trick. The wave of books shifted aside. Numerous books small enough to hide in her fist made chains, and wrapped around the doorknobs to pull the doors open. Ash shivered at the cleverness of the books and their ability to work together. Cecil had indeed been right to warn her about magic books. Best to keep them as her friends and never lose their good will.

She took deep breaths of air that didn't smell of paper, leather, glue, and ink, and crossed the entryway toward the main doors. They hung open. Whether they had just opened now, or they had remained open since she entered the castle this morning, Ash couldn't be sure. She took it as a good sign that they weren't closed, intending to keep her prisoner. Just to be safe, she stopped a good five paces away from the threshold and raised her arms to the ceiling and stretched and arched her back, loosening muscles that had tightened from being bent over books all day. She grinned at this proof that her dream of spending entire days in study wasn't as glorious as she had imagined.

Her sense of time returned. Even without shadows slanting from west to east, she knew now this was late afternoon. She had been busy in her studies for nearly eight hours. She needed to go back to her camp and the portal. Ash couldn't afford to miscalculate. Bracing herself, she turned to look at the place where the table had been set and Fang had smashed the ebony crown.

Not a scratch in the paving stones, not a piece of furniture, not a whiff of aroma from the fresh bread. She regretted that fresh bread more than anything else.

Ash went back into the library and closed the book, stoppered her inkwell, and made a mental note that she needed to replenish her supply at the next station house. She put her pen back into its protective sleeve, blew on the last page in her journal where she had written, and touched the final period with her fingertip, testing if it had dried. It had. She closed the journal and slid it into her satchel.

Behind her, books slid and rustled and thumped, reforming the barricade across the doors. She sternly told herself not to be afraid. Morris had taught her, after all, that emotions affected her scent. Who knew if the books could smell that trepidation chilling her now?

"Thank you, but I need to go upstairs and report to Eyesallova," she called. "Please let me out?" Ash walked down the aisle to the doors, silently pleading with the books to listen. She didn't know what she would do if they got stubborn. When would they team up with the clothes and furniture to trap her here?

Books moved aside, lowering the barricade. Slowly. There was more noise than the last time they had parted to allow her out. Did they suspect something?

The small books formed a chain again, and darted up like a snake striking, to loop around the strap of her satchel, nearly yanking it off her shoulder. Ash pulled, her heart skipping a few beats at how strong that chain was.

The books suspected she was leaving the castle, not just going to Eyesallova. Just like that village in Nordwell had nearly kept Fang prisoner with them, to ensure she didn't run away, the books wanted to keep her satchel.

"I need my journal, to remember what I wrote down, what I learned," she said, after several minutes of tangled thoughts. Ash hoped that wasn't too much prevarication. She wasn't lying, was she? Even by implication? Did the books think she meant she needed the journal to report to Eyesallova?

What was she doing, arguing with books and worrying about whether they trusted her or thought she lied to them?

She needed to get out of the enchanted castle, and out of the enchanted forest, before she lost her mind.

"Please, let me go upstairs?" She waited, trying to smile, afraid to look at some shiny surface and see how false her expression might be.

The little books finally let go. Fang chirped and bounded up the stairs ahead of her. Ash fought not to run, leaping two or even three steps at a time. She couldn't show any fear, couldn't give the slightest hint she needed to flee this place.

A rustling, rumbling sort of sound caught her attention as she reached the landing between the second and third floors. Ash looked down and saw the tidal wave of books reaching out of the library, across the entryway, pushing the big double doors of the castle closed.

That answered that question.

She kept her steps slow, pretending she had no worries, no suspicions, as she crossed the gallery to the doors of the mirror room. Fang waited in the open doorway, ears sticking straight up, swiveling, listening. Ash knew better than to look behind herself, though she imagined every sound was books climbing the stairs to chase her, or perhaps suits of armor coming with more crowns to replace the one Fang had smashed.

"I am losing my mind," she announced, and startled herself because she hadn't meant to say that aloud.

"In what way, dear?" Eyesallova's voice had a rich tone, as if she found some amusement, but was polite enough not to laugh.

"This place terrifies me, but I want to stay. Am I going mad? I want to stay and organize the library and mend all the damaged books. I have a vision of a suite of rooms, and I know it's mine, and I want to stay there. I don't want to wear any crowns, but this one feels so right." She yanked the braided silver circlet off her head and strung it on her arm. "What is wrong with me?"

"Perhaps the better question is to ask what has been wrong that is being mended."

"That doesn't help me at all."

"No, questions often seem to confuse for quite a while, before they start making sense, and you start finding the right answers."

"I have to leave. Will you help me?" Ash gestured behind herself. "The books are barricading the doors out of the castle, but I need to get back to the portal before it changes again and I've lost my chance to go home."

Eyesallova was silent so long, Ash feared the mirror was calling the books, the armor, all the furniture in the castle, to come capture her.

"This could be your home, dear," the mirror finally said, her voice soft and soothing and sympathetic.

"Not yet." Ash caught her breath. Why had she said that? Why did it make sense, make something seem to ring inside her chest, like when the right piece in a puzzle box slid into place and it unlocked? "Not yet," she said again. Yes, she would like to come back. But later, much later. "I have things I have to do, promises to friends. I want to find out who I am. I want to … I don't know, do something to avenge my parents and all the other magicians and enchanters who fought that wave that … I just need to leave now. I promised the books I would mend some, every time I came back, so I guess I do need to come back, don't I?"

"Oh, indeed. Even if you didn't intend to make that promise." The mirror sighed. "Very well. You are right. Promises are vital, and broken promises can taint your magic and your destiny." The doors to the balcony swung open. "There are stairs down to the garden. You can see the gates out of the garden to the right. Go straight through. Don't let any of the statues stop you, no matter how pitiful they sound."

"Statues?" Ash squeaked, as she hurried around the cluster of benches and chairs surrounding the magic mirror. Fang chirped and bounced ahead of her.

"Yes, all those statues that idiot prince kissed and halfway woke. Some are friendly. The intelligent ones, who have learned their lesson and repented of their foolishness. The others are even more selfish and featherheaded than before they were enchanted. And then there are some truly nasty ones. They'll never learn their lesson even if they're broken into a thousand pieces and spend the next several centuries as nothing but gravel. Get out as quickly as you can. Oh, dear. Here they come. Go!"

Ash fled out the doors. Fang avoided the steps and bounced over the balcony railing into the garden. She darted down the stairs and smothered a groan when she had to detour around a fountain and couldn't see the gates. Eyesallova had said the gates were to the right, hadn't she? Ash imagined she heard the scraping and clattering of suits of armor, bursting into the mirror room.

There! The gates swung open as Fang approached, taking shallow, short leaps, looking back at her with every other bounce.

Movements at the edges of her vision tried to snag her attention. Ash hunched her shoulders and ran, refusing to see the statue arms waving at her, the pleading expressions on stone faces. Half the garden seemed to be gray figures of people and animals, haphazardly littering the open spaces between fountains and decorative paths and little gazebos and bridges over tiny silver streams. Just how large were these gardens? How did the castle drag the gardens along with it?

Magic, Ash decided in those frantic moments as she fled, dodging and ducking, made absolutely no sense sometimes.

The gates were closing! Her lungs and thighs burned and strained as she put on desperate speed and darted between them. One side brushed her arm and she twisted, stunned by the zing through her sleeve and flesh. Ash stumbled, off balance for a moment, and looked back. The gates swung closed, clanging softly.

CHAPTER SEVENTEEN

Gasping, she bent, bracing her hands on her knees. Just a few seconds to catch her breath. That was all she needed.

Her legs and her straining lungs disagreed as she straightened and stumbled forward, running again. Where was Fang? He hadn't left her behind, had he?

A blur of white and chattering to her right. She leaped over a mound of something covered in trailing vines and went off the path. She held her breath as she approached the watery barrier where the castle's magic pushed aside and warped the forest around it. Then she was through.

Up a rise in the landscape, through a cluster of trees, and she was out on the stream. She saw her camp on the opposite bank. Ash splashed through the water, struggling to get enough breath, enough moisture in her mouth to whistle for Garan. Ahead of her, Fang chattered, his voice going shrill, as whisps of steam rose from his fur.

Too much sunlight for him at this time of day. She groaned, silently apologizing for not putting the shirt on him, to protect from the sun. Ash promised herself, on her next visit to the castle, she would ask the books for a magic spell to reverse Fang's partial change to vampire. It was simply too inconvenient.

She snatched up her bags, grateful she had packed everything that morning before she left camp. The saddle and blanket and bridle were waiting next to where she had picketed her horse. Ash considered leaving the saddle and riding bareback, but that would be uncomfortable and simply irresponsible. Did she have time to saddle Garan?

She would have to make the time. But first—

"Fang, here!" She pulled her cloak out of the top of the bag and threw it to him. He chattered and ducked down as the cloak settled to the ground. "I'm sorry. I'm so sorry!" She let her bags drop to the ground and stumbled as she bent to snatch up the blanket. She tossed it over Garan and quite frankly didn't care if it was smooth or straight. Yanking on the bridle, she brought him back over to where the saddle waited and bent to heave it up into place.

The jangling of tack sounded like armor stumbling through the forest, catching up with her. Ash refused to waste the time to turn and look. She yanked on the straps and untied the ties holding the stirrups out of the way and slung her bags onto the hooks and hoped they would hold until she could securely tie them down. On the other side of the portal.

"Please, please, please," she gasped, still out of breath, as she slapped Fang's basket into place and attached only two of the five straps that attached it to the saddle. "Please, A'theosius, let it still be open. Let it still be roses and snow." She bent down and gathered up Fang, cloak and all, and slammed him into the basket. He didn't squeal or chatter in protest. Either he was in too much pain, or he was frightened.

Ash looked back. Were shadows gathering? Had she been wrong, and night was coming sooner than she thought?

Or were those shadows suits of armor, struggling through the forest, following her?

She slung the bridle over her shoulder and clambered up into the saddle. She would exchange halter for bridle on the other side. Garan leaped forward, down the straight trail, before she could dig her heels into his sides.

Ahead of her, she saw darkness within the arch of the portal. She couldn't discern colors. Were there still snow and roses, or had the other side of the portal already changed to something else? Right now, she didn't care where she ended up, as long as it was away.

The horse galloped, his mane whipping her face. Ash held on tight, muffling a yelp when the saddle slid to the right a little. Not tight enough. No time to adjust it.

There! Starlight in the darkness ahead.

Even better — starlight on snow.

A whiff of roses and an icy breeze reached out to wrap around her, a dozen paces from the opening. Ash grinned into the mane slashing her face and held her breath as Garan raced into the portal, and through, and out into a crusty layer of snow that crackled under his hooves. Ash sat up, gasping, pressing a hand over her heart, while yanking on the bridle to slow him. They were through.

But were they safe?

She looked back at the glimpse of sunlight on the other side. Shadows danced across the opening. Was that a breeze moving leaves, or pursuers?

Best not to take any chances. She clucked to Garan and sat up, adjusting her seat in the saddle. It shifted to the right a little more. She judged she could ride until she put this stand of trees out of sight behind her, before stopping to tighten the saddle. And pull out her cloak. Wind damp with ice curled around her, biting through her jacket. Ash rubbed her arms and tried to remember which bag she had stashed her gloves in. Another problem with travel to the enchanted forest: the shock of sudden changes in weather.

She had lost two months in the two days she spent in the enchanted forest. Winter had come to Cammerlang. What had happened to everyone at Castle Fairhold in those two months? The station house was a little more than half a day away, once she got out onto the highway again. She would find out then.

"How are you, Fang? Feeling better?"

He answered with chittering muffled by the cloak wrapped around him. She choked on the need to laugh. He wouldn't take it kindly.

"Would you feel better if you could roll in the snow?"

That stopped his chittering. Ash reached back, trying to tug on the cloak enough to let Fang emerge. It was night here, after all. Her efforts made the saddle slip a little more to the right. She sighed and scolded herself to sit still, until they were a little further away from the portal. Could the suits of armor leave the enchanted forest to chase her? When would the portal shift to another opening?

The only way to be sure was to go back and chart the shifts between portal openings down to the minute. Ash couldn't imagine having the patience to do that.

"Too much to think about, too much to worry about," she muttered, and raked her fingers through her hair. It shocked her, being sweaty from her exertions.

And her fingers caught on the braided silver crown.

She had forgotten to leave the crown behind at the castle.

Take it back or keep it with her? Definitely she could not just toss it away and put as much distance between her and it as possible. Any of those choices would be trouble.

~~~~~

By the time she reached the crossroads, Ash had heard no sounds of pursuit. Maybe she had gone slightly mad from her time in the castle and the forest because she found some humor in the image of those suits of armor, lumbering slowly through the forest and down the road behind her, as slowly as they had moved in the castle. She dared to hope the magic of the forest, the difference in time, kept the armor from stepping through a portal to follow her. Although, in the case of those who pillaged the castle, such as King Ruprick, she would welcome the ability to chase thieves through the portals to take back what was stolen.

Then again, maybe something had followed her out, and was even now aiming at her, guided by the crown. She needed to get to that station house and send a message to Filby and ask what to do. Then she needed to ride to Cecil. If A'theosius had blessed her, the old seer had had a vision of this dilemma already, and he would have advice for her. Not that she wanted him to ever suffer on her behalf that awful pain that came with having a vision.

Ash let out a long, deep breath of relief at the sight of the stone marker at the crossroads. She had been riding for nearly an hour now. All
~~~~~

was quiet, the air icy and the night sky clear, the light sharp, and enough snow on the ground to muffle sounds. The rasping of her breath, as if she had been running instead of riding all this time, was still too loud for her comfort. That was her fear talking.

And her guilt. She hadn't like deceiving the books. The rest of the castle, fine. The clothes and the housekeeping breezes had certainly treated her in an underhanded fashion. The books, however, were depending on her to return. She had promised to repair them.

"There's no remedy for it, is there?" she asked Fang, when she had stopped her horse and could turn around and unbundle him from the cloak jammed into the basket. She was glad to wrap that cloak around herself because winter had finally soaked into her flesh, now that she had calmed down from the panic of the escape.

Fang looked up at her, eyes big and solemn. No twisting and flapping of his ears, no quivering of eagerness or frustration. He settled into his basket with the lid hanging down the back, rested his forelegs on the edge of the basket, and looked at her. Then he shook his head.

"We have to go back. I just need a plan, so I don't get trapped. I wonder if there are any charms in the castle that can protect me from the castle. Although yes, it would be lovely to live there and just indulge in all those books, and be taken care of and ..." A sigh escaped her. "Did you like living in the forest?"

Fang gave her a grin, much like the manic grins he had worn when they first started on their journey. Before Morris bit him.

"Are there huge, magical creatures for you to hunt and fight?" she mused.

Fang's grin got bigger. Ash laughed and scratched between his ears and down his back. He purred and settled down in the basket again. She turned around, settled in her saddle, and was about to nudge the horse to get moving again when she remembered an unanswered question.

She tugged open her jacket and shirt. The moonlight was bright enough, she could see her chest.

The star was still gone. If it had come back, it would be glowing in the moonlight, but it wasn't and hadn't.

"Thank you, A'theosius," she whispered, and considered her bottom. Could she hope that star was gone, too? She would need to find a mirror in the station house to get a good look at her backside and make sure.

So, did that mean she was now safe from the enemy who had killed her parents at Tippessee?

If the stars were gone, would her inborn magic begin to awaken? Most definitely, she needed to send news of this development to Filby, and then race to Cecil for his guidance.

~~~~~
~~~~~

Ash reached the station house just before dawn. Kuper, the station master, stood at the gate in the high wall around the house, a ball of faerie light bobbing over his head, shifting between green and blue and purple. He moved back from the gate, gesturing for her to come in, and said nothing until he had closed the gate and reached for the reins of her horse.

"Well, you've got an adventure to tell our lady, don't you?" he said as he led her to the stables on the right side of the station house. His narrow-eyed look relaxed as he glanced back over his shoulder at her. "What's that in your saddlebag? It's glowing through the leather." He laughed when Ash looked back at the bag on her right side. "Not the kind of light our eyes can see, lass. Here now, get into the house. The mirror's name is Teedle. She's waiting to call on Filby. I told her you were coming."

"Mirror?" Ash paused in sliding out of the saddle.

"Some of us have magic mirrors for speaking. Those of us with stronger ties to the faerie-kin. We got an interesting report from the mirror web more than a month back. A mirror none of us have heard from in years—"

"Eyesallova told you I was all right?" Ash nearly laughed, shocked at her relief that the mirror was indeed on her side. Just how powerful was Eyesallova, that she could act against the castle and its wishes?

"She reported you were exploring the enchanted castle and you had the sense to ask the right questions. Gave us quite a shock. Yes, Filby was worried about you, but the reverberations through the mirror web nearly drowned that out. Most people believed Eyesallova had been destroyed during some huge cataclysmic battle between enchanter enclaves. It never occurred to anyone that she would end up in the castle."

"She helped me escape."

"But I've got the feeling you didn't listen to her advice entirely." He pointed at the saddlebag she unhooked.

"It was an accident." She yanked open the bag and pulled out the crown. "I forgot to take it off when I ran. I had to get through the portal before it changed." She sighed. "I have to take it back. I made promises ..."

"Ah, been learning about the rules of magic now, have you?" His stern look softened into a sympathetic smile. "Get on into the house, I'll settle your horse. Here, you." He slapped the side of the basket, rousing Fang, who was half-asleep. "There's a fresh side of beef out in that shed, and a cozy dark nest for your day's sleep." He laughed when Fang sat up, blinking and rubbing his eyes, and chirped at him. "And you're very welcome."

"You speak bunny?" Ash asked, as Fang bounced off the horse's rump and bounded away in the direction of the outbuilding Kuper had indicated.

"This station is quiet enough, I have plenty of time for studies. There comes a time when a man has enough years behind him, he wants to sit still and fill his mind with all the things he didn't have time for when he was young and busy and trying to be a hero." He winked and tugged up the cap pulled down low on his head. Enough to reveal the pointed tip of one ear. Then he gestured at the station house. "Filby is waiting."

Ash got her feet moving, and grinned as she shouldered her bags and hurried into the house. The mirror was small, the size of her head, but easy enough to find, sitting on a stand on the long table in the center of the room. It glowed, the shimmering light shifting yellow to green to blue and back to green again. Her steps slowed as she approached the table. It was one thing to talk to a magic mirror. It was another to talk through a magic mirror. What exactly were the proper manners?

"Hello, Teedle. I'm Ash—"

"Ash?" Filby's voice came through the mirror, and then her face appeared, replacing the green glow. "Two months late." She tried to smile, but concern gleamed in her eyes. "I hope you have a good story to make up for worrying us."

"I don't know how good it is." Ash pulled out the bench and set her bags on the floor next to her, then held up the crown as she settled in front of the mirror. "The castle tried to make me into a princess."

"You need to return that." Filby's smile faded.

"I know. And I intend to go back. After I make sure everyone is safe. Or as safe as they can be. Filby, my stars are gone. When I went through the portal, they were burned off me. And I found books about spirit rings in the library of the castle. I need to do more reading. That's why I have to go back. I need to be prepared better when I go back, because if I eat anything the castle gives me—"

"Stop!" Filby leaned back from the mirror on her side and raised her hands. "Tell the story in the order that things happened, in the order that you learned. Have Kuper wake his oak pen. It will write down all the things you say, to save you time. So I suggest you think and plan before you begin telling your tale."

"Good idea," Kuper called from the doorway. "I'm intrigued enough already to want to hear the whole thing. Filby, the lass chimes of magic. I heard her coming from more than a mile away."

"That isn't good. Ash, you need to stay where you are until Kuper can give you some discipline lessons on quieting your magic. I would hazard a guess it's been bottled up for so long, it's gushing forth, like a geyser rather than the tiny spring it should be."

"Or maybe I soaked up some magic when I was in the castle," Ash offered, more than half-joking.

"That could be as well," Kuper said. He went to a cabinet and opened it, retrieving a stack of paper, a glass inkwell three-quarters full of green ink, and a pen carved of wood. He directed Ash to hold it between both her hands for a moment, press the thickest part of the barrel to her lips, then put the silver tip into the open inkwell. "When you're ready to begin, simply say so."

The wood tingled against her lips. Ash settled back and closed her eyes, composing her thoughts. Tell the events in the order they happened, and the things she learned, the things she thought, as they happened. She thought she could do that. Certainly, she hadn't had time to write down what had happened since she finished her reading in the library and realized she needed to flee the castle and forest.

"I'm ready to start."

The pen tapped the tip against the side of the well and floated over to the top sheet of paper and poised, ready to begin. Ash closed her eyes again, going back in her memory to that ride through the forest, when she realized there was something odd happening in the shadows.

Kuper brought her hot spiced cider and porridge, which she ate and drank in quick sips that refreshed her voice and made it easy to keep talking for more than two hours. He had to go back to the cupboard and bring out two more stacks of paper before Ash finished. The ink in the well never went down.

Then, while Kuper cooked sausages and onions in a massive iron skillet, Filby told Ash the news. She had heard from Hazel, who reported several attempts to get past the wards she had spread around Castle Fairhold. The wards weren't strong enough to keep out someone determined to enter, but the intruder had chosen to back away. Either they were discouraged by the signs that someone expected them, or they had discovered their chosen target wasn't inside the wards.

Filby chose that theory, because four days later, Winston's cottage had been attacked. The walls were punched full of holes and the rooms filled with rags and other refuse. All the food rotted and the dishes shattered. Winston had vanished for two days. He was found cowering in a barn, gibbering and terrified by the slightest noise. So far, he hadn't said an intelligible word.

Ash shuddered, and clutched her mug of cider so her hands wouldn't shake. She knew Lathia was vindictive, but this went beyond the petty nastiness the girl had displayed during her visits to Castle Fairhold. She had gone entirely dark and vicious. Attacking her own father, who had supported her and encouraged her to believe she was the center of the world?

Justiciar Camwell had been found, alive and starving, a good three stone lighter than he had been in years. While he was missing, his home had been pillaged. Every magical item in his possession had either been broken, and drained of magic, or taken. The inventory of what he had once possessed was staggering. Filby was especially worried by the loss of the master ring, and five other spirit rings.

"The justiciar has sworn out a warrant for your capture and arrest. He grudgingly admitted that you were not with the people who tortured and robbed him, but he insists all the same that you have to be involved. Only a powerful, evil sorcerer could suborn a spirit ring." Filby shook her head. "The man entirely lives down to all the distressing things I've heard about him. Your King Ebrosion needs a lesson on choosing his officials more wisely, with more investigation into their minds and hearts."

"So I can't go home to Fairhold." That news didn't really hurt. Maybe she was just too tired to feel anything.

"You can't go back to Alfordia, and I would stay far away from the borders, if I were you," Kuper said.

"Winston's daughter, Leena, has contacted me several times, asking after you, offering her help," Filby said. "She has suggested that you take shelter in a chapter house of the maiden warriors in Inderweil or even cross the ocean to Sandovar, until this whole ugly mess has been dealt with and your good name cleared."

"Or I could just go back through the portal and stay a month or two at the castle, which would be years here. Until Justiciar Camwell has either given up or been shamed, so all his orders are rescinded. Or he dies." Definitely, she was too tired to feel anything.

Did she truly want to go back to the forest and let time speed by, until she was safe? Or was it the lure of all those books, so she was willing to give up the life she had known? She didn't want to lose Cecil or Filby or Lady Charlotte or Dunstan or Hazel or Granny Phlox, true, but …

Her head ached with weariness. She wasn't thinking clearly. That was the problem.

Filby agreed with her plan to go to Cecil and consult with him, maybe settle down for the remainder of the winter and learn some discipline over her blooming magic. Then she was to come straight to Willemsport, so Filby's magic could hide her from the Purple Sky magicians.

CHAPTER EIGHTEEN

Ash slept most of the day away. Kuper said much of her exhaustion was of a magical nature, because of the eruption of her inborn magic. He taught her how to sit quietly and hear the counterpoint music of the magic running in her blood, under her pulse and breathing. When she could hear it, she could slide into unity with it, flow with it, and lose the noise that resulted when she unconsciously worked against it. He speculated that the stars had been put on her not just to alert her parents' enemy that her magic was awakening, but to cause such a loud noise in the magical atmosphere that the enemy could find her from kingdoms away.

"You were lucky the rupture happened in the enchanted forest," Kuper said, over dinner on the second day of Ash's stay. "No one heard, and the forest soaked up much of what gushed out of you." He shrugged. "Luck, or A'theosius's hand on you in protection."

Ash much preferred the second option. She would rather be grateful to A'theosius than the unpredictable, unreliable vagaries of luck.

In between her lessons, she wrote long letters to Lady Charlotte and to Dunstan, Hazel, and Friar Ipswich, telling them about her adventures, the things she had discovered, about magic and about herself. She depended on Lady Charlotte and Hazel to pass on her greetings and her story to Granny Phlox. She asked Hazel to send her news through Filby of the charges against Fang, if the bunny council had discovered the real murderer yet. She made a map of her travels for Dunstan and sent a copy of the starburst map of connections between the portals in the enchanted forest to Friar Ipswich. She told him her idea for how to chart the times of the changes in the portals, the kingdoms each one opened into, and using those portals for travel over long distances. She spent much of her letter to the friar describing the library in the enchanted castle. She thought a long time about the possible outcomes if she gave Friar Ipswich a map to the portal of snow and roses. She thought he might have the courage to enter the forest and brave the magic in pursuit of knowledge. At the very least, the castle's library would adore him. He could be very happy spending his life mending and arranging and tending to the books.

Filby reported that several collegiums of enchanters were outraged at the news that the library at the castle had been raided. They were enacting spells to try to locate the stolen books. Most likely they were upset the books were in the hands of thieves and raiders, rather than that the books had been stolen from a magical library. Filby confided in Ash that if those books were rescued, she doubted anyone would make any effort to return them to the library. They would end up in either the collegiums' libraries or divided up among the wizards and enchanters who tracked down the thieves. She reported that the news had shaken loose some disturbing information, about abandoned castles and wizards' retreats that had been broken into and the libraries ransacked. Many such places were discovered when the spells of invisibility had failed, or physical damage had occurred to the buildings.

There was some uproar spreading slowly through the magical learning communities over how little value even nobles placed on libraries nowadays, and how printers were abandoning the trade because of the dropping profits. Centers of learning for entirely non-magical studies were being neglected and abandoned, the books left on shelves and buildings allowed to fall into disrepair. Men such as King Ruprick, hoping to control all learning and information, were taking advantage of this neglect. Libraries needed saving, books needed rescuing and repair and protection. Kings such as Ebrosion of Alfordia were fighting a losing battle to instill literacy, because too many other kings or lower-level nobles under them found it much easier to control people's thoughts and beliefs if they didn't know how to read. Spiritual leaders found it much easier to control their flocks and lead them astray, for their own profit, if no one had the ability to check A'theosius's holy books for themselves.

Filby's couriers were part of the small but determined war band fighting to stop the depredations that depended on ignorance and silence between kingdoms. She confided in Ash, as the girl prepared to leave Kuper's station house, that she and some of her most experienced couriers were considering starting a campaign of searching for libraries and collegiums to rescue books.

"It might be wiser to search for the scavengers," Ash offered. "Cecil told me horror stories of how he obtained some of his books. He has a number of travelers who specifically search for books in odd places, where you wouldn't expect them to be. He had an entire bookshelf, floor to ceiling, of partially dismembered books. People were tearing the pages out to wrap food for travel, or to make twists to light pipes and lanterns."

"I have met enough books in my time that were old enough, full of enough wisdom, to become alive," Filby murmured, her gaze going distant, as if she saw something other than Ash's face in the magic mirror in front of her. "The thought of such spirits being shredded by ignorant fools who never had the chance to learn the treasures preserved in paper and ink ... What is our world coming to?"

Ash thought about that conversation when she set out early the next morning. She imagined exploring forests reputed to be haunted, seeking out abandoned castles, raiding the treasure hordes of ogres and dragons, rescuing books and bringing them out into the light of day so people could read them again. She thought about arrogant kings like Ruprick snatching up every book they could get their hands on, to control learning and gain power over the ignorant and uninformed. Or how books of magic would be misused, their magic twisted to provide him power. She thought about the library at the enchanted castle. Wouldn't the world be better off if all the magic books and books of magic were taken there for shelter, to keep them out of the wrong hands, and allow old books to rest in safety, where they would be dry and dust-free and safe from bright light that would fade them?

She wrote down her thoughts when she stopped to camp in a wayhouse that night, and the next night, and relished the solitude to think. Wayhouses were small shelters, hidden behind a light screen of magic, kept stocked with fuel and blankets and spare clothes and food, for couriers traveling routes that didn't see enough traffic to warrant a station house. She left a message packet with her idea at the next station house, to be sent to Filby.

Two days after that, Ash rode up to Cecil's village on the leading edge of a snowstorm. She skirted the edges of the village, sure no one noticed her through snow blowing almost horizontal as they raced to fasten shutters and close up shops and settle into their homes. She considered stopping at Osward the blacksmith's shop to stable Garan, because Cecil didn't have a stable, not even a shed to store tools or a cart. However, the walk from the blacksmith's stable to Cecil's cottage was a good twenty minutes in nice weather. In this storm, Ash feared the trip would take twice or three times as long, with a good chance of getting lost. While she knew a few spells with her flute to ward off the wind and snow and help her find her way, the wailing of the wind could negate the magic by drowning out the tune.

A reddish glow through the swirling gray and white acted as a beacon, guiding her between buildings. A man called out. Ash could barely see him, standing with the wide doors propped open so the fire from the forge spilled out heat and light. She squinted against snow blowing straight into her face. Was he beckoning for her? Perhaps it would be wiser to take shelter here, and go to Cecil when the storm ended? She tugged on the reins and Garan picked up his pace, likely even more eager for heat and shelter than she was.

A humming surged through her leg, transmitted by the saddle. Fang thumped hard against his basket, jolting into her back. Ash reached back without thinking, knowing already the vibration came from the crown. Kuper had advised her that while her bond with the castle would grow stronger the longer she wore the crown, she could also use it to train and discipline her inborn magic. He had advised her that she might be wise to wear the crown during the long stretches of travel in lonely places. Not just for training, but because the crown could warn her of approaching magic or even danger. Much as her stars had done.

Ash had chosen not to wear the crown for that very reason, still feeling some resentment over the stars inflicted on her by her parents' unknown enemy. Now, feeling her saddlebag hum under her gloved hand, she wished she had listened to Kuper.

"Ready, Fang?" she said, and didn't bother to keep her voice down. She would have to yell for the blacksmith, or whoever was standing in Osward's doorway, to hear her.

The bunny chirped. Ash released the reins, letting the horse move forward again.

"Get in here, ye daft fool!" the man shouted, gesturing for her to hurry. A heavy gust yanked on the door, nearly pulling him off his feet. He reached for the reins. Garan snorted and tossed his head. Ash slid from the saddle, holding the reins and neatly tugging them out of the man's reach. She kept the horse between him and herself as she hurried into the shelter of the forge.

Heat surrounded her. Ash nearly closed her eyes and sagged to the floor in painfully ecstatic relief. She looked back as the man pulled the door closed. She had never seen the wide doors of the smithy pulled into place in all the time she had spent in the village that past summer. Osward had worked in the open air, sheltered by the peaked roof that took away the smoke of the forge. It was a sensible design, and there was plenty of room for her and the horse and the man, who was definitely not Osward.

"And who might you be?" The man stepped around the horse and jammed his massive hands into his hips as he looked her up and down. "Ah, so." He nodded when she brushed caked snow off the courier badge on her cloak and pointed to it. "The question is if that's your badge, or you took it off some luckless soul."

"Filby herself pinned this badge on me," Ash said. "Where's Osward?"

"Who wants to know?"

"Someone who lived here long enough to care about the people of this village, and not trust strange faces. Especially if the offer of shelter in a storm is a trap."

The man stared at her a long moment, his expression unreadable behind the furry mask of his beard and windblown hair and bushy eyebrows. He nodded slowly, brows lowering so his eyes were lost in shadows. "Is that a fact, then? And how long was that?"

"Lucinda can vouch for me. And Max. And Cecil."

"And you expect me to just stroll out into that storm and fetch all of them to look at your face and tell me you're safe?" He laughed like he thought it was a joke. His tone was light, but his eyes, now that she could see them again, were sharp with suspicion and alertness.

"Am I safe? Are any of them safe?" Ash reached up to tap on the side of the basket.

He reached out so swiftly she nearly didn't see his hand move, and grabbed hold of her wrist before she touched the basket. The firelight glinted off a ring on his smallest finger. Braided of gold, silver and ebony.

"What do you know?" he growled, when Ash stared at the spirit ring too long.

"Who do you serve?" she growled right back.

The ring flashed, bright green, making the man gasp and curse. He released her and staggered back a few steps, clasping his fingers in his other hand. His pained expression turned confused for a moment.

"Fang," Ash said.

The bunny leaped from the basket, slamming the lid back hard enough it sounded like the clang of a hammer on stone, and landed in front of her. The man stumbled back two steps, then his face creased into a crooked grin.

"You have to be Ash. But I thought …" He shook his head.

"Who do you serve?" She rested her hand on her belt pouch. Ash didn't know if she could whip out her flute and play a tune to restrain him quickly enough to do any good, but she had to try. Either that or depend on Fang to hit the man hard enough to send him staggering back into that pile of ruby and gold coals.

"Not Camwell," a woman's voice said. The ring flared green light again. "We're here to protect Cecil. The Nightflower Alliance liberated several of us from Camwell's service before he was attacked, and we learned enough from our fellow slaves before they were silenced to guess what he would do and what those invading Purple Sky magicians will try to do."

"You're protecting Cecil? From the justiciar or from Lathia?" Ash couldn't let herself relax just yet. This might be an elaborate hoax.

"Probably both," the man said, glaring down at the ring. "Did you have to be so harsh?"

"I had to get your attention," the ring responded. "Girl, you're not wearing—" She made a sound like glass chiming and cracking. "Was he taken from you? Destroyed?"

That cut several cords of tension in Ash's chest. She tugged aside her cloak and reached inside her shirt to pull out the chain where she had hung the ring for safekeeping. Filby had recommended that, and Kuper had given her a chain woven with spells that would prevent it being removed from her body without her permission.

"Silenced," Ash said, and held out her hand with the ring lying on her gloved palm.

The man was Godric, and he admitted with a sheepish grin that he was responsible for the snowstorm currently swirling around the village. He and the ring had set up several layers of wards around the village for more than a mile out, to detect the approach of magic. The threats from Justiciar Camwell and the Purple Sky were real. They were also serious enough that the Nightflower Alliance, a band of enchanters from Inderweil and Nordwell and several other kingdoms, sent Godric and the ring and three other wizards to protect Cecil. They believed both nemeses expected Ash to come back to visit him.

And of course, she had. The presence of the crown and her newly released inborn magic had triggered the warning spells and the defenses. Godric had apprenticed as a blacksmith before his magic awoke, so he had persuaded Osward to let him use the smithy as the center of his spellcasting and defenses for the village. The other wizards were already unraveling the blizzard spell, now that the ring had identified Ash.

"They're well-meaning, but rather clumsy all the same," Cecil confided to Ash less than an hour later. "They thought, wrongly, that coming in secretly would create less panic. I sussed them out in less than a day. All those wards they wove around the village set up such a discord, I couldn't sleep at night." He chuckled and reached across the table to rest both his hands on hers. "It's good to have you back, my dear girl." He sighed, his smile drooping on one side. "For however short a time we're allowed."

Ash didn't argue. She agreed with Godric's team that she needed to move on. Cecil was bait in a trap aimed at her. Godric gave her and Cecil until dawn to talk and plan.

The spirit ring, whom Godric referred to as Twink, short for Twinkletart, a good approximation for her name in the spirit ring language, joined them. She sat on Ash's journal to absorb everything she had copied over from the books about spirit rings in the enchanted castle's library. When Ash had left, Twink would share everything with Cecil, and they would work to find answers. Starting with restoring the ring's voice. Twink declared that the ring's spirit was still attached to the ring, but he was in a deep sleep. A deeper enchantment than she had ever encountered in all her decades of travel.

Ash told Cecil about Filby and the fulfillment of his vision and what she had learned and done in the enchanted castle. Twink agreed with what Hazel had proposed at the start of Ash's journey, that the spirit ring, all the spirit rings, would enjoy settling down in the castle with all the other resting, healing, mending magic that had come to be stored and protected there. The enormous library fascinated her even more. Just like

Ash's spirit ring, Twink enjoyed learning more than anything else. She had been even more disgusted and discouraged than he had been, by the paucity of Justiciar Camwell's library and the limited range of literature and culture available to her when he took her out of his treasure room.

Twink asked for permission to study the crown. She went silent for a considerable length of time after Ash set her on the table inside the circle of the crown. Ash and Cecil worked on creating a map of the enchanted forest. He was fascinated by the warping that surrounded the castle, how it compressed and bent everything to make room for the castle without disturbing the actual ground and trees of the forest. Ash laughed quietly when she recognized eagerness in herself to go back to the castle. Yes, it could be considered a trap, yet Ash considered the risk worthwhile if the secrets of the enchanted forest could be plumbed and the sequence of portals opening and closing could be charted and put to good use. And there were all those books. Dusty books and neglected books were just as cranky and dangerous as books filled with warped and twisted and malicious magic. A librarian's presence would be good for the library, and maybe for the entire castle.

"I can feel threads of magic reaching for the crown, and the crown sending out threads to find them," Twink announced after they had made a rough draft of the map. "I found that portal we theorized, Cecil. Those book-stealing thugs came through in the Tayanny Cliffs."

"That could be dangerous," Cecil murmured. "How did they keep from tumbling over the heights when they emerged? The cliffs look like honeycombs, full of holes," he hurried on, "but none of those holes in the rock are any closer than fifty feet above the ground."

"I would wager that's one of those portals that are only visible when they're open, and bad timing can prove deadly," the ring said. "Come through at the wrong time, and you can get trapped inside solid rock."

Ash winced, imagining that final moment of life as she found herself becoming part of a mass of stone. No wonder Ruprick's men had been in something of a hurry to get out of the village with their stolen books. They understood enough of the timing of the forest to fear being unable to leave the same way they came. She wondered how long they had waited in the enchanted forest before they could go back home. Or did they understand the portals well enough to go out another way, closer to Rathelshiffen and travel overland the rest of the way?

Keeping bullies and thugs and arrogant thieves like Ruprick from taking advantage of the forest's pathways to harm others was another good reason to return to the forest and the castle.

Twink declared she needed more time to study the crown because it wasn't very cooperative. Most of its purpose was bound up in serving the needs of the castle. It would protect Ash, but only to ensure she returned to the castle. Twink theorized the crown had the power to open portals at need, out of the proper timing, if Ash was in danger. She didn't know if the crown would do that for anyone who wore it, or if it had bonded strongly enough with Ash that it would only serve her now.

"I sincerely hope that is not true, because if the crown is becoming part of you then it can also influence you," the ring added.

"Like when I ate the cherries the castle put in my satchel, and I forgot why I was in the library." Ash shuddered. "Am I protected at all, since I'm warned? Since I know what it will try to do, turning me into a princess? And what kind of princess does it want?"

"From all you've told me, it makes no sense for the castle to want a princess from legends, unable to think very often for yourself," Cecil said, his tone sour. "I agree, there is twisted magic influencing it. Consider how it's sneaking into your mind, rather than just asking politely. I daresay you are exactly the kind of princess the castle needs, but until the magic is healed, it won't let you be the princess who is best for it. And I fear the books are doing the same thing to you, just from a different angle."

"Oh, but the books need ..." Ash's protest died away and her face warmed. A dropping sensation pushed her down more heavily on the bench. "Oh. Yes. I see that now."

"The castle needs you, and that gives it an unfair advantage," Twink said. "Part of you senses this, and wants to serve. Be careful, girl. Put as much distance as you can between you and the crown. Yes, you need to take it back. You didn't take it on purpose, but you didn't ask permission. Magical things that are determined to get their way can be very tricky, twisting the laws of good manners and common sense to suit them. Wrap it up as thickly as you can, avoid touching it with your bare skin, when you return it."

"If I'm not wearing the crown when I return to the castle, the armor will just chase me everywhere with more crowns for me to wear. At least this one is comfortable," Ash said with a sigh. All the precautions felt like a heavy weight and made her feel somehow guilty. "You should see the gaudy, ostentatious, fluttery, glittery, useless concoctions they were offering me. This one lets me get work done. The others would immediately turn me into fluff and feathers the moment I put them on."

CHAPTER NINETEEN

"And that is likely what saved you," Cecil said. "If you gave in to vanity and greed and took a big, flashy crown, the castle would have acted on that flaw in you. Instead, it adapted its tactics to suit the person you proved to be. And honestly, if you think about it, you're a much better choice as princess of the castle. I would never advise you to step into that trap, yet consider how much good the enchanted castle could do the entire world, if someone sensible and not swayed by riches and power were in charge there."

"How long would I stay sensible and grounded if I let it turn me into a princess? As you said, the magic is sick, broken right now. The castle wants fluff, someone to pamper and cosset and treat like a pet, not someone to take care of it and put things right. How long can I resist such tricks, once I start giving in?" Ash sighed. "I need to talk to Filby. I need to visit her library again."

Cecil agreed with her, and expressed some regret that he couldn't go with her. Ash remembered how she and the ring had enjoyed their time in the time pool library, all the information the ring had absorbed, and different things they had discussed sharing with Cecil when they saw him again. She hoped the ring would remember those things when he was finally restored. She hoped she could come back soon and spend more time with Cecil. For now, though, she had to move on. Godric's team had felt some tendrils of testing, seeking magic more than two weeks before Ash showed up. Chances were good either Justiciar Camwell's people had been looking for her, and would come back regularly to check, or Lathia's magicians were seeking her. It was best for everyone if she moved on quickly and made her way to Willemsport and Filby.

Ash left at night, with Fang bounding ahead of her, glowing in the moonlight and appearing to float above the treetops for minutes at a time. Her head felt jammed full of all the things she had learned from Twink and discussed with Cecil, and she couldn't resist chewing on her resentment at having to leave so soon. She had hoped to spend the entire winter with Cecil. So much had been disrupted by her unplanned stay in the enchanted forest. She even resented her commitment to become a courier for Filby, and that was ridiculous. Had her stay in the castle stolen some of her common sense and practicality?

"Maybe it put some of that fluff and feathers into me, and I can't get it out," she muttered to Garan and the quiet, snowy road ahead of her.

The horse's ears flicked and the moonlit open countryside didn't answer. Ash decided she preferred it that way. Although she wouldn't have minded if the ring suddenly awoke and started speaking to her again, even if it lectured her on all the mistakes she had made since he went silent.

At the crossroads, midway between midnight and dawn, the crown buzzed through the padding around it and against Ash's thigh. She resisted the temptation to swat it like an annoying fly. The bag that held it twitched, jerking in the direction of the road to her right. According to Cecil's map, that road would take her halfway to the Tayanny Cliffs. To head to Willemsport, she needed to keep going straight, heading south. Shaking her head, she resisted the urge to tell the crown to shut up, she wasn't going to go anywhere near the portal in the Tayanny Cliffs.

The smart move was to keep going forward, but she couldn't. The sporadic, deep marks of Fang bounding through the fresh snow showed he had taken the road to the left. He had always warned her of trouble lying in wait, so Ash chose to wait for Fang to come back, rather than forging ahead and making him catch up with her. There had to be a reason why he had gone down that road. Maybe some of his bunny magic had warned him not to continue down the highway they had been traveling.

Or he was just hungry and needed to stop and hunt down a snack.

Or he felt dawn approaching, even if several hours away, and he wanted to find a place to settle in for a good day's sleep, rather than riding in the basket behind her saddle.

Sometimes Fang was rather hard to predict.

Ash decided to count her heartbeats until she reached one hundred. If she didn't see or hear signs of Fang by then, she would continue forward. A long wait meant he was hunting. Any other activity would allow him to return to her much sooner.

She reached forty-two when a chattering and squealing erupted from the trees maybe two hundred yards down the left-hand road. Before she could turn to look, expecting to see Fang leaping from the shadows, a flicker of movement on the road ahead of her caught her attention. A dusty, purplish cloud billowed up from the snowy road and spread to swirl up snow from the ditches on either side. Lightning crackled in the center of the cloud. Fang let out that roar she had heard only one time before. She yanked on her horse's reins and turned to see Fang emerging from the trees with another purple cloud following him.

The crown bag thumped against her thigh, swinging out and pointing directly to the right.

Ash took two heartbeats to decide. Twink had said the crown would protect her. Trust the magic she was coming to know? Or the magic churning up the countryside from two directions, aiming toward her? The magic nasty enough, terrifying enough to make Fang flee, with his eyes burning red?

Before she could dig her heels into Garan, her mount fled, stretching out into a gallop fleet enough to make the wind scream in her ears. Ash bent low over the horse's neck and held on tight. She raised her arm to look under it and back, to check on Fang. He was catching up.

More important, was that cloud catching up?

Why purple? Logic said the Purple Sky was so called because its magic created a purple light. There was something seriously wrong with a band of magic users who were so ostentatious. It felt like a waste of energy.

Fang caught up and bounded alongside her, great low, long, distance-eating leaps. Ash reached out to pull him up into the saddle. Her arm bounced wildly in the resistance of the air and Garan's leaping strides. Fang bared his fangs at her, then leaped forward, faster. In a few heartbeats he was a length ahead of her. Then two. Then three. Ash tried to laugh at the idiocy of thinking he needed help.

Over the scream of the wind in her ears and the drumbeat of hooves against the snow-streaked road, she heard a churning, roaring sound. Was the cloud getting closer, catching up with her? Was that the sound of the cloud, or something cloaked inside it? Ash refused to look back.

The crown bag thudded against her leg, out of rhythm with the horse's stride. What did the wretched thing want?

Ahead the road branched in three directions. She searched for signs of Fang's footprints in the snow. The moonlight was fading. Garan turned down the left-branching road before she could decide. She silently pleaded with A'theosius, her thoughts keeping pace with the clatter of hoofbeats. The road plunged downward, between massive, black trees that created a canopy overhead where their ancient branches interwove. Water sparkled ahead of her. Then the horse was splashing through, hooves rattling on rocks. She braced for that jarring moment when Garan stepped into a hole in the riverbed, but moments later they were up on the opposite bank.

For a moment, she wished the old fables were true, and evil magic couldn't cross running water. Ash pushed that thought aside, scolding herself for getting distracted. Was that what fear did? Stole common sense, stole the attention and energy she needed to keep herself alive and free?

The road angled upward again, leading to massive walls of rock that stretched up to the sky, blocking her path.

The Tayanny Cliffs.

Ash yanked on the reins, intending to turn around, with a half-formed notion she would find the purple clouds wasn't there anymore. It was just an illusion. A nasty trick of the crown to force her through the portal and back to the enchanted forest.

Shrieking, whipping bits of ice and pebbles and grit and bark, twin purple whirlwinds raced up the bank from the stream. Ash froze, blinking, trying to understand what she saw but her brain didn't want to recognize.

Were those faces inside the clouds? She turned and slapped Garan's flank hard. Morris the vampire's head had elongated like that just before he bit Fang.

The crown flopped against her leg. Ash snatched at the bag, yanking hard enough to snap the leather thong that held it to her saddle. She clutched it against her chest with one arm and clung to Garan's neck with the other.

"All right, you're supposed to protect me," she snarled. "Do your job!"

Light erupted through the leather of the bag and the cloth padding the crown. The growling scream of the whirlwinds behind her went up two octaves, then seemed to break with a clattering sound and died. Fang leaped out of a passageway that opened up to her right, bounced over her, and headed down another passageway through the rock. The cliffs were a fractured series of impossibly narrow canyons where veins of softer rock had been worn down by wind and water over the centuries. They formed a natural maze. Legends claimed that people had gotten lost among the tall, winding, crooked passageways, never to emerge.

The light from the bag faded as Garan slowed to deal with the rubble filling the passageway. Ash looked back. No sign of the whirlwinds. How long would that last? She knew better than to hope the burst of light had wiped them out in one blow. Nothing was ever that easy.

The crown buzzed and hummed through the padding and bag. Ash knew what it wanted. Could she trust it?

Fang bounced over her head, ricocheted off the sheer sides of the passageway four times, and came back to rest a few yards in front of her. He breathed heavily, loudly, and the angry red manic gleam had faded from his eyes. His ears drooped with exhaustion.

That decided her. Ash yanked the bag open, snapping the leather drawstring. She tossed the bag aside and the blanket padding the crown a moment later, pulled her hood down, and took a deep breath before slapping the crown on her head.

"Help me lose them," she said, her voice breaking with the effort not to snarl. Cecil had emphasized that politeness, asking instead of demanding, always helped when dealing with magical things on the verge of becoming aware. "Please."

The passageway wasn't wide enough to turn her horse around

without tricky maneuvering that would waste time. She might have to dismount. Ash urged the horse forward. She held out her hand and Fang leaped up into her arms. He clutched at her and she fought a sob at the rapid flutter of his pulse, the bellows heaving of his breath. Something rattled and whispered behind them. She refused to look back. The crown was silent and still. She hoped that was a good sign.

Light angled into the passage they followed, showing an intersecting crevice through the rock. Ash silently commanded the crown to tell her which way to go. It remained quiet. She let Garan choose. They kept going. After a dozen paces, the passageway widened. They could turn around here and go back the way they had come. If it was safe. A whiff of something foul drifted to her on the flutter of breeze coming from behind them.

Ash nudged the horse to move faster. He didn't fight her. Fang shifted on her lap and twisted to look around her.

"Are they coming?" she whispered. He tightened his hold on her, his claws digging through the tough material of her trousers and jacket.

That was answer enough. Ash nudged Garan. Again, he obeyed, moving faster, at a trot just strong enough to make her jolt a little in the saddle.

The passageway curved to the right and a few steps later opened into a bowl that took them down a gradual incline. Everything was shadows and snow and mud and stone. Ash turned her head, looking in all directions, trying to spot another split in the bowl where another passageway led out.

An angry rebuke caught in her throat as she inhaled and caught the scent of ripening apples and cherries. She followed her nose as a warm breeze wrapped around her like a gentle hand.

Perhaps a third of the way around the bowl, to her right, green light flickered and danced, like sunlight through thick branches tossed by an afternoon breeze. Ash whispered her thanks, to A'theosius and the crown, and tugged the reins to get Garan moving. She needn't have bothered. He sniffed loudly and his ears perked up and he trotted straight toward the light.

Behind them, a clattering and scraping and wailing spilled out into the bowl. Ash looked back and saw the purple whirlwinds spill out. She choked on laughter as they stumbled and slid down the slope of the bowl, toward the pile of debris in the center. The two purple clouds collided and bounced off each other. Ash nudged Garan faster, an image in her head of those clouds bouncing straight across the center of the bowl, to cut off her escape.

Maybe twenty steps until they reached that green light. Ash bit her lip and refused to look back. A sound like a strangled, breathless cry echoed around the bowl, then that scraping sound returned.

Halfway there. The slope turned upward, and Ash had a brief, frightening image of Garan's hooves sliding on that water- and wind-scoured smooth stone. Five steps. Fang chirped. She looked back just as the horse's nose went into the light.

"Go, go, go!" she yelped, and dug her heels in as the battling clouds of purple suddenly grew huge, filling up the space behind her. "Close. Please close! Don't let them through," she ordered the crown.

They stumbled out into warm air and sunshine and burst through a wall of trees at the top of a slope down into a river plain.

Ash held onto Fang with one arm and the reins with the other, when she wanted to clutch at the crown, afraid it would bounce off her head as Garan jolted down the slope. She glimpsed twists and turns in the river ahead of them, places where it turned entirely around and created a handful of small islands, before plunging through rapids, then down a short drop that cast up spray in all directions.

That had to be the Snarl River ahead of her, if Cecil's map and the lore he used to build it were correct.

Kispies nested in those clusters of trees on either side of the falls. Common sense said to steer wide around them, if even a third of the stories about kispies were true.

Shrieks of outrage erupted behind her. Ash looked back in time to see a man tumble down the slope after her, leaving a trail of purple sparks. A purple cloud burst through a slit in the air between the trees, and a moment later shattered into more sparks, spewing out a second man, who followed the first.

Fang chuckled and chirped and wriggled against Ash's arm around him. The manic gleam returned to his eyes. He wanted to fight.

"Are you sure?" She had her doubts. After all, why would only two magicians come after her unless they were strong enough not to need greater numbers?

The world turned upside down. Purple sparks filled the air around her, biting and buzzing. Garan reared, shrieking pain, lashing out with his forelegs. Ash went flying, grappling for the reins. Fang bounced off her chest, snarling and chattering, aiming for the two staggering magicians.

Stars filled Ash's eyes. Then she felt the impact, first the side of her head, then her back. She rolled, the breath knocked out of her, flipping and rolling, lopsided, until her forehead slammed into something hard. More stars. She smelled blood. Tasted it.

Through the muffled thudding of her heart, the rasping of her breath, she heard Fang scream and roar. Then further away, the furious shrieks of the two magicians. The scrabbling of feet on moss and stones. All fading away.

Panic had her struggling upward through the blackness trying to suck her down. Ash opened her eyes. The light hurt, like broken glass jabbing straight through her eyes into her brain. Nausea surged and her entire body shrieked pain as she spasmed, trying to heave. She clasped her head, trying to keep it from shattering like a melon dropped from a tower window. The cool silver braid of the crown hummed against her fingers. Hot wet slicked one hand.

"Fang," she whispered. She couldn't get the breath to yell.

Yet what could he do to help her?

Garan huffed and hooves clopped on the ground nearby, then warmth and damp prodded her side. She got one eye open, to see the horse standing over her. Ash blinked, unable to comprehend for a few seconds why he was still with her. Other than warhorses, most horses fled at the smell of blood. Courier horses were well-trained. Garan huffed again and moved up her side. His loose reins brushed against her arm. Ash took a few breaths, each one deeper than the last, bracing herself, trying to convince herself she wouldn't shatter if she tried to sit up. She grasped the reins. One hand was slippery with blood. She needed a few seconds to figure out what to do, then wiped the wet away on her jacket. With a firmer grip, she pulled herself upright, holding onto the reins. Garan backed up. She swallowed down a whimper and the surging of her stomach when that simple, slow movement made the world tip and spin around her again.

Clutching the reins, Ash waited until the world and her stomach and sense of balance settled again, then reached higher on the bridle. Garan raised his head, and she nearly wept with gratitude that he understood what she needed. Her legs dragged on the ground for what felt like hours before she got them steady under herself. She pressed her face against his head and gasped for breath and refused with all her force of will to collapse or heave or let go.

Fang still had not returned by the time she gingerly shuffled down the horse's side and clawed her way up into the saddle. Ash blinked blood and sweat out of her eyes and turned Garan around enough to see up the slope. What had happened to Fang? Had the magicians killed him? Or were they still running, with the furious bunny shrieking and gnashing on their heels? If the magicians had won, they would be down here right now, finishing her off. Her eyes ached, the daylight too bright to stand. Maybe Fang had to find a shadowed place to hide until the light dimmed enough he could safely emerge.

A few thoughts came through the throbbing and fearing the bones of her skull would shift and let everything fall out. She needed to find a safe place to hide. Her camp, close to the portal that would take her to Cammerlang. She needed to make a fire and brew a potion to soothe the agony in her head. She especially needed to get away from the river before the smell of her blood drew the kispies. They weren't exactly faerie-kin, but they were tiny and warlike, brandishing a dozen tiny, razor-sharp weapons each, looking something like furry insects.

"Please, Fang… find me," she whispered, and even that effort at speaking hurt. Maybe she had broken her jaw, along with half a dozen spots in her skull. Tugging gingerly at the reins, Ash turned Garan and headed down the river valley. The crown hummed against her skin. She reached up to remove it, but stopped, the effort making her arms ache so she wanted to weep. Even crying hurt.

The crown hummed, softer, settling into a soothing pattern. She allowed her breathing to echo it, and nearly wept again when the aching faded. Slowly. Far too slowly. The world around her grew dim. Ash gave up the fight to keep her eyes open. She fumbled the tongue clicks that told the horse to return to a familiar place. Garan was smart. Could he understand that the signal to go home meant go through the portal? Would A'theosius be kind, and the portal to Cammerlang would be open when they found it?

Through the gray filling her head, the hum became the lullaby Granny Phlox crooned over the twelve orphans when they were all together in her cottage. Ash smiled, gladly slipping into a dream that she had come home. She was small again. Small enough for Granny Phlox to cradle her with one arm and stomp up the narrow stairs to the cottage attic full of bunks and cribs, to put her to bed. The dream grew real enough, she tasted the warm milk heavy with honey to cover the bitter taste of healing herbs, felt it sliding thick and soothing down her throat. Real enough, Ash feared when that warmth hit her tender stomach, so she nearly jerked herself awake.

Cool hands stroked the sides of her face, soothing, and the eruption never came. She pressed her face against a cool, smooth surface and gladly slid downward, into hazy gray flowing sleep, and the touch of satin on her skin, and thick pillows cradling her tender head.

CHAPTER TWENTY

Several times Ash rose up through the dream, finding it changed to the suite of rooms she recognized ... but couldn't remember where. Dark arms held her up, and cool, whispering touches bathed her and dark, cool hands supported her head and put cups and then spoons to her lips, trickling soothing, thick and cool substances into her mouth. She swallowed, dreaming of porridge heavy with crushed berries and honey and rich cream, going down her throat.

When she could finally open her eyes, the dream remained. She lay in a bed with gauzy curtains embroidered in gold and blue and green. Ash stretched cautiously. Then when the throbbing didn't return, because after all this was just another lovely dream, she stretched luxuriously. Her nightgown felt as fine as anything she had helped to bring in from the drying yard for Lady Charlotte and Lady Beatrice. Pillows scented with lavender and chamomile surrounded her. The light spilling through windows on one side of the room was softened by sheer curtains that matched the bed curtains.

Curiosity had her sitting up enough to look around. Yes, this was exactly like that suite of rooms she had dreamed. Ash sighed, content, and contemplated just lying there, curling up, falling even deeper asleep, until the dream faded. But curiosity made her move. She didn't want to waste the dream.

Ash swung her legs out from under the sheets and fluffy blankets embroidered to match the curtains. The world rose and fell under her for a heartbeat or two, and she braced, waiting for the shattered aching to return. But it didn't. Because of course, this was a dream.

Doors to the left, opposite the windows, swung softly open and clothes swirled into the room. Stockings and slippers, petticoats and smock, breastband and a gauzy dress all in swirls of blue and silver, ribbons and necklace, earrings and bracelets. Another door opened in the wall facing the foot of her bed, revealing a bathing room and a tub with steam rising off it. The clothes settled on the bed and a cool breeze wrapped around Ash, guiding her to stand. Of course, a housekeeping breeze. Another housekeeping breeze yanked a wardrobe open and brought out slippers, sliding them under Ash's feet just before they touched the floor. The breezes guided her to the bath, smelling of apples and cinnamon.

Breakfast arrived, boiled eggs and fresh bread and spicy herb tea, just as the housekeeping breezes finished helping Ash dress and brushing her hair. She followed the floating tray out through floor-to-ceiling windows, onto a balcony that looked out over the castle's garden. Two suits of armor stood on either side of the pretty little gilded table, all delicate curlicues. They held trays displaying four crowns each, lying on black satin cushions. The pavement rippled slightly under her feet as Ash reached up for her silver braided crown.

It wasn't there. Of course it wasn't. This was a dream.

Then she looked at the suits of armor and past them, to the garden full of statues, men and women and beasts, so many of them in poses that a sculptor wouldn't have chosen. Ash shivered.

No, this had to be a dream.

She had smashed her head when Lathia's magicians attacked. She was curled up somewhere, hiding, wherever Garan had found shelter for her. Just an odd dream. A fever dream. A hallucination that came from the injury to her head.

Her thoughts snagged on a question: If she was hallucinating in her pain, would she know this was a dream?

Yet the food smelled so enticing and what would it hurt, really, if she wore one of those crowns? She could be a princess in her dreams, couldn't she?

The crown she chose was delicate, simple, a wreath of violets woven of silver, with the petals and leaves picked out with slivers of amethysts and emeralds. Not something she would have chosen to wear while working in the library, but perfect for breakfast on her balcony, in solitude, dressed in gauzy clothes. Maybe later in the day she would choose a more serious crown, gold with red satin and rubies, for when she did whatever princesses did in the afternoon.

After breakfast, she wandered through the castle. The housekeeping breezes opened doors for her as she went from one suite of beautifully decorated rooms to another. She had only looked through four rooms when her head started to ache. Just a little. She was in a suite done all in shades of lilac and lavender when the throbbing started to pulse on the side of her head and light ached in her eyes. A housekeeping breeze swooped into the room with a tall goblet of something that smelled of spearmint and chamomile. Ash took the goblet, cool in her hand, almost slick with condensation.

She hesitated. Should dreams have such details? Why would she allow the ache in her head into the dream?

The breeze wrapped around her arm, guiding her hand holding the goblet up to her mouth. Ash drank hesitantly. The moment the first swallow went down her throat, she blinked and wondered what she had been thinking. She gave the goblet back to the breeze and let another lead her out of the suite of rooms, down several corridors, back to her suite. The blankets had been pulled back on the bed, the pillows fluffed, and she gladly lay down to rest.

~~~~~

The third morning she woke in the castle, Ash asked if she could have breakfast somewhere else. She had a craving for change. After all, how many rooms of luxurious carpeting and furniture and draperies and decorations could she explore, how many dresses and shoes and hats could she look at, how many times could she try on beautiful new clothes, before she grew bored? The sense that she needed to be doing something useful settled into her head where the ache had been.

She followed the housekeeping breeze carrying her tray of breakfast down the long corridors, out into the central gallery of the castle. Her gaze flicked to the far side of the gallery and the long panel of glass doors where light spilled through. Then she followed the tray down the stairs, to the second floor, and a lovely little music room with flutes and harps, violins and cellos, a little white and gilt harpsichord, and all sorts of brass instruments. Ash settled at the table that was twin to the one on her balcony, and listened with delight as trios and quartets of instruments played for her while she ate.

"Flute," she murmured, as she raised her cup of tea to sip. "I have a flute. Is my flute here?"

No response from the trio of harpsichord and two violins. No response from the housekeeping breeze. Instead of shrugging off the question when she got no answer from her invisible caretakers, Ash gnawed on the idea.

Something was off. She couldn't push through the comfortable haze that surrounded her, but that sense that she should be doing something useful, something important, twined with the question of her flute, and grew a little more solid.

When breakfast was over, she clapped and thanked the instruments. They bowed to her and hopped or floated back to the racks and cases that had held them. The breakfast tray lifted up and the door opened. When Ash followed the tray and the breeze to the central staircase, she went down when the tray went up.

For a heartbeat, she expected a breeze to push against her and stop her. Maybe even that suit of armor on the landing would come to life and block the way. She didn't know why she expected that, but she did.

Skirts whispering on the polished wood and rosy granite of the stairs, she went down to the ground floor. The central set of double doors on the inner wall swung silently open. Ash glimpsed light, filtered and soft. The aroma of old paper and leather and dust wafted out to her.
~~~~~

Crash! The clatter of glass and brass came from overhead. Ash went still, knowing that was the sound of those glass doors on the third floor coming open. Pushed hard. Frowning, she turned from those tantalizing doors in front of her and walked back to the stairway.

Something dirty white chattered and bounced from the third floor to the landing, then turned and bounced down to the second floor landing, then turned again.

Ash staggered, her head throbbing once, and grinned despite the ache. She pressed her fists to her temples and startled at the feel of the heavy band of silver studded with pearls and opals she had chosen this morning, to go with her silvery gray dress edged with peacock patterned ribbons. Why, she wondered as she stared at Fang bouncing down the last flight of stairs, would she ever wear a crown like that? Why would she choose a dress like this, and actually put it on?

Her knees folded and she staggered forward, reaching for the newel post at the foot of the stairs as Fang came to a thudding stop in front of her. He chittered and waved his ears and bounced up and down. The sound made her head ache as it hadn't ached since the attack.

"Stop! It hurts!" She took a step back. "I wish I could understand what you're saying!"

Shouldn't she be able to understand Fang, if this was just a dream?

Fang went silent, tipped his head to one side, and studied her. Then he hopped a few steps up to her and wrapped his arms around her knees. She was startled to feel him tremble.

"Why haven't you been in my dream until now?" she whispered.

Ash's stomach clenched around her breakfast. Fury throbbed in time with the renewed ache in her head. She reached up to take off the crown. For two heartbeats, it resisted her. She yanked, taking strands of hair with it. She nearly flung it aside, but knew better.

"Fang, where have you been?" She took a deep breath, fighting the need to shout, maybe curse. "How long have I been here?"

Fang's ears snapped and waved and curved, but of course, she couldn't understand him.

"Ring," she whispered, wishing for the spirit ring to translate for her, and the next moment panicking when she didn't know where the ring had gone. What had the castle, the suits of armor and the housekeeping breezes, done with her clothes, her gear, her horse, and the ring?

Ash darted up the stairs. Her head hurt more by the time she reached the landing between the second and third floors. She gritted her teeth and pushed on. When she got to the top, she staggered forward, intending to find her suite of rooms, and tear it apart if she had to, to find the ring. She took five steps, then turned and went back the other way. To the glass doors into the mirror room.

"Eyesallova, what has this place done to me?" she demanded, as she burst through the doors.

"Hello, dear. I've been waiting for you to come," the magic mirror greeted her.

"Where is the ring?"

"Right here. I could at least get that much cooperation. Quite a few residents are upset with me that I helped you escape before." The mirror turned and swiveled downward in her frame, directing Ash's attention to a table a few yards away from the circles of chairs and benches surrounding her.

The ring sat on a wooden tray on a small table. Ash leaped over two benches, seriously hampered by her skirts, and snatched it up. She put it on her thumb and clenched her fist, to keep it from sliding off.

"What happened? How did I get here?"

A housekeeping breeze swirled into the room, carrying a dark green curve of what might have been stone. The size of her thumb, it bobbed in front of Ash's face.

"Take it," Eyesallova said. "You wished for it. It's not at all polite or wise to refuse when the castle provides what you asked for."

"Wished for it?"

Fang hopped up and settled at her feet. He pointed at the green thing with his ears.

"It's an ear cuff. Put in on your ear, so it goes behind the curve. You'll understand what he's saying now," Eyesallova said. "Not word for word. There's too much interference from all the idiots over the years trying to twist the magic to serve them, but you'll understand the meaning."

Ash hesitated, because how could she really trust anything or anyone here in the castle? Her stomach twisted and her face warmed as she thought back over the hazy days of drifting, constantly telling herself she was dreaming. How could she have been so foolish? So trusting?

Fang tapped her knee with his paw and looked up at her, making his eyes big and fluttering his lashes. Ash sputtered laughter that took away the ache throbbing through her temples again. Sighing, she put on the ear cuff. Then she sat down and let Fang and Eyesallova explain what had been happening.

Garan had returned her to her camp by the stream, but she fell off. In her delirium, she kept making the signals to send him home, to bring help. When the tunnel of snow and roses opened, her faithful horse went through. When she lost consciousness, the crown took over, summoning help. The suits of armor and the housekeeping breezes had tended to her injuries and fed and washed her, just as a princess deserved. Eating the food provided by the castle, sleeping in the bed, and wearing the clothes and crowns had tightened the bond between her and the castle, and its claim on her as its princess.

I'm not a princess, Ash told herself repeatedly during the telling. *I never will be. Bad enough the ring kept calling me Lady Ashlyn. I could handle becoming a lady, eventually, but never a princess. Too many curses waiting to trap princesses. Too many magical traditions.*

Fang had chased the Purple Sky magicians back through the portal as it was closing. He couldn't get back through. He had taken more than four months traveling to the only portal he knew, the tunnel of roses and snow, and waited until it opened again. Knowing only a few days had passed for Ash in the enchanted forest was no comfort in his worry.

When he reached the castle, the doors refused to open for him. The statues in the garden had blocked him from getting through to Eyesallova and the mirror room until just that morning.

Eyesallova hadn't been able to help him. She was somewhat on the outs with the rest of the castle, because of her support of Ash freely choosing if she would be a princess or not. The castle took advantage of her injury to ease her into living as a princess, until she was changed enough in her mind and spirit that she would gladly stay.

"Why did the portal we came through close so quickly? Did the magicians do something to it?" Ash asked, after digesting that news.

"You made it open out of its proper time and sequence, dear." Eyesallova sounded rather proud. "Once it did as ordered, it closed again. Granted, it trapped Fang on the other side, but it also kept those Purple Sky fools from coming back through. The crown found the nearest portal and you had enough strength in your inborn magic, as untrained as it is, to force the portal open. You also managed to turn it into a trap for those imbeciles, so you stripped them of much of their magic when they followed you through."

"Not enough to keep them from hitting me hard enough I was knocked lightless." Ash gingerly touched the side of her head where she remembered finding blood. A slight ache responded to her prodding, but not nearly as bad as she had expected. "How long have I been here?"

"Six days." Eyesallova sighed. "Long enough that the castle has made its mark on you. I'm sorry, but the castle will not let you leave. You are its princess."

"If I'm its princess, shouldn't it obey me?"

"Eventually. Yes."

"How long is eventually?"

Eyesallova had no idea. Far too many things had changed since the castle was knocked loose of its anchor and began drifting through the enchanted forest, which in turn knocked the forest loose. More than two-thirds of the portals to the rest of the world had shattered. At one time, the enchanted forest had multiple portals in every kingdom, and the passage of time had been the same on both sides. Eyesallova had lost regular contact with the mirror web. The need for a princess had warped and taken over the purpose of the castle, which had once been open for the use of all who came seeking knowledge, in peace and honesty. The raids through the years to steal magical objects, combined with the castle becoming a magnet and dumping ground for broken and warped and insane magical objects, had merely added to the pressure.

"You are needed here," the mirror told her. "The castle needs a mind and heart to direct it. Someone to give it purpose. Someone to lead in the defenses and bring order." She snorted. "Once it gets straightened out and freed of all those tangled, sticky webs of lore and legend."

"Am I the first girl to come here?"

"No. And I'm sure that a prince would be just as acceptable to the castle, in its desperation and hunger. Many have come here through the years, on quests for cures and help, and for weapons, but the castle chose you. Maybe because of all that untrained magic bursting forth, maybe because you were chosen by fate and prophecy. Who knows?"

"So I should just sit back and submit and let it make me into a princess?"

"What kind of a leader would you be if you did that, dear? Leaders think and choose, they don't let others think and choose for them. The castle would be no better off."

That thought stayed in Ash's head as she and Fang spent the next several hours trying to find some way out of the castle. Every door stayed stubbornly shut. Every shutter refused to be pried open, every pane of glass refused to shatter, no matter how many benches and chairs she slammed against them. Until her head ached and she was dizzy and felt ready to heave again.

That lingering illness and pain made Ash suspect that she had been near death, and the castle had saved her life. Meaning she owed it a debt, no matter how much she refused to comply with its plans for her.

Very well, if she couldn't escape, then she needed to learn enough about the magic of the castle, and her own magic, until she grew strong enough to order the doors to open, or at least find a way out the castle couldn't close against her.

She went to the library. Now that she understood Fang, he became a great help. He couldn't read, but he understood the shapes of the letters, and hopped from one set of bookshelves to another, studying the spines of the books. With his help, she gathered up an idea of how the library was arranged, without having to walk the length and breadth and crawl up ladders to study every shelf.

In essence, the library had little organization. Part of that was a result of the raids over the years. Part of that came from the books being left to look after themselves and choose who they did and didn't want to sit beside on the shelves.

Very well. As Ash searched and read and made notes, she would bring order to the place. First, she needed to become familiar with what the library contained, to have an idea just how to accomplish that. It wouldn't do her much good, after all, if she started out storing all the books relating to the history of one kingdom in one place, and then after she had rearranged half the bookshelves, found a dozen more on the topic, with no room to jam them into the shelves with the other books.

Soon, she and Fang had a routine. She woke at dawn and dressed herself, so the housekeeping breezes couldn't impose their frilly, gauzy, fluttery taste on her. She repeatedly requested breakfast be served on the table in the main entryway outside the library doors, until the castle complied. The library wouldn't allow food inside now, which made no sense, because she had been allowed to eat in there before. Eyesallova couldn't explain the change either, unless the books had been bullied into compliance by the rest of the castle. She had all her meals there in the entryway, though every few days the housekeeping breezes tried to get her to eat in the grand dining room, and even tried to get her to change into formal clothes.

Ash asked repeatedly until the suits of armor brought back the simple crown of braided silver for her. She had to wear a crown, or she would have a suit following her every step as she tried to work, holding out arms strung with crowns for her to wear, and often getting in the way as she climbed ladders and hauled books from one pile to another.

In the evening, she washed away the dust and ink and the glue from repairing books, and she and Fang settled in the mirror room for a long talk with Eyesallova. The magic Ash had brought with her allowed the mirror to contact the outside world again. Granted, it was in fits and spurts, thanks to the time differential, but Eyesallova was often giddy with excitement after catching up with an old friend. She sent messages to the closest mirrors to pass on to Ash's friends, to let them know she was all right. Or rather, as all right as she could be, trapped for the foreseeable future in the castle. And every day that passed in the enchanted castle meant a month had sped by in the outside world.

CHAPTER TWENTY-ONE

Three times, Ash came out of a haze and found herself not hard at work in the library, but curled up in the music room, the next time sitting on the balcony, and the third time, in the sitting room of her suite, embroidering on a tapestry so intricate and huge it would take her three years to finish. Each time, she was dressed as a princess, instead of in sensible, although still elegant trousers and shirt and vest and sturdy boots. The castle had managed to impose its desires on her. Each time, Ash found that something had interfered to keep Fang away from her, so he couldn't knock her over and wake her.

Each time it happened, Eyesallova could only give her the same advice: she needed to learn to impose her will on the castle. Even the smallest detail where she gave in and let it make choices for her could prove to be a weak spot. When she woke from the haze with an embroidery needle in her fingers, doing a masterful job despite never having embroidered before, Ash knew what she had to do.

She spent the rest of that day exploring the castle, especially the wing with the living quarters and guest quarters. She chose a smaller, much simpler suite of rooms, far from the elegant, lavish suites clearly set aside for the royal family. This was a room fit for a lady, not someone of high standing and pure royal blood. Someone who perhaps had duties to earn her place in the castle. Ash then filled the wardrobes and chests in that smaller suite with the clothes she chose to wear. Simple dresses that she could work in and not feel guilty getting dust and glue and ink on them. Sensible shoes. Comfortable trousers and vests and shirts. No jewelry except the ear cuff that let her understand Fang, the quiet spirit ring, and her silver crown.

"These are my rooms," she announced, standing in the doorway once that task was finished. "You will not change them. You will keep them clean. You will not block me or Fang from entering. Or Eyesallova, if she wants to come talk to me," she hurried to add. The magic mirror could walk somewhat on the legs of her frame, it just took her some effort and time to accomplish it. "I will dress as I choose, and eat as I choose, and work as I choose. I am the lady of the castle. Not the princess. The *lady*. I will take care of you and guard you and let you attend to my needs, but on my terms. I am Lady Ashlyn, not Princess Ashlyn, and you will be happy with that. Is that understood?"

She waited, hoping devoutly that the castle did not have a heretofore unrevealed ability to talk to her, and talk back to her.

Fang looked around, ears twitching, waiting for a response. Finally, he tipped his head back and looked up at her, grinning.

We need to celebrate, he said through ear twitches.

"Indeed we do." Ash let some of the tension bowing her shoulders leak away. "Castle, would you please serve us dinner in the mirror room tonight? Bring the biggest, bloodiest side of meat you can find for Fang. And I would be very happy with venison stew and cinnamon butter bread. And lemon fruit ice. If that's not too much trouble?"

After all, Lady Charlotte had impressed on her long ago that politeness and gratitude were the oil in the hinges of life, and the perfume that made every day sweeter.

~~~~~

Naming herself the lady of the castle brought about a change in the castle's attitude toward and treatment of Ash. Until then, Eyesallova had been prevented from showing her views of anything outside the castle, no matter how many different and sideways approaches Ash took to asking about the enchanted forest. Specifically, the portals, where they were located, and what places they opened into in the world outside. It was as if the castle wanted Ash to feel there was nothing outside the castle. Not even the gardens. Enormous creeper vines with even more enormous leaves had grown over the doors onto the balcony from the mirror room the day after Fang broke in and Ash woke up to herself again. Not only couldn't Ash see out, but Fang's fiercest attacks couldn't open the doors.

The morning after Ash named herself Lady Ashlyn, the vines were gone, Eyesallova was delighted to report. Her communication with magic mirrors by going through the portals also became much easier. Her voice took on a growl, when she speculated that the castle had been interfering with her ability to hear and exchange images with the other mirrors. She found that exceedingly rude and high-handed, especially after Ash's exit from the enchanted forest wearing the silver braided crown had punctured a sort of barrier that had blocked hearing other mirrors.

Eyesallova spent the day locating the portals that were open and contacted the magic mirrors closest to them, to catch up with them. She also focused on locating those portals in the enchanted forest. Ash felt it vital to the safety of the castle and the forest's inhabitants to know what kingdoms the portals touched, so they could anticipate who might stumble through. King Ruprick of Rathelshiffen couldn't be the only greedy despot who had figured out some of the enchanted forest's secrets. All the magic concentrated in the enchanted castle gave the forest itself a magnetic sort of quality. Heroes needing to prove themselves found the forest with far greater ease than common sense said they should.
~~~~~

Princesses in danger, innocent maidens fleeing ogres, and worthy-but-poor youths fleeing evil masters fell through the portals without warning. Far too many made foolish mistakes and ran afoul of the magical traps scattered through the forest without ever encountering the castle. And far too many evil enchanters of all different levels used the castle as a dumping ground for their prisoners in dozens of enchanted forms, when they ran out of storage room in their fortresses and lairs. So naturally, when the heroes destined by fate to rescue those victims came looking for them, they were drawn or led to the enchanted forest and the castle.

The traffic through the enchanted forest was rather stunning, when someone actually sat down to think about it.

And frustrating. Ash wondered how long she would have to wait until a hero had penetrated the castle in search of his lady love, or at least a kidnapped princess who would make him king in her father's place, and open the castle door, allowing her to escape. Eyesallova anticipated that question, that idea, almost before it was clear in Ash's mind.

"Sorry, dear," she had said, "but a prince, a miller's son, and a swan princess have already come and gone since you returned. You were in a daze during the first two visits and never realized the men were searching the castle. Plus, the castle cast all sorts of illusions to guide them away from your rooms. The swan princess never got past the large pond in the gardens. The enchanted lilies she was looking for grow there."

All that changed, or at least there was the promise of change, now that Ash had claimed some authority. The day after Eyesallova regained contact with the mirror web, a wall in the library grew a doorway into an entirely new wing of the library. That wing held maps. Ancient kingdoms and current kingdoms, and even a dozen hazy maps where the boundaries rewrote themselves while Ash watched, depending on the current decisions and movements being made in the political and social structure of those kingdoms. Those maps were hung on the wall behind thick layers of what felt like glass, but tingled if she rested her fingers on the surface too long. She supposed it was protective magic, or the spell itself that changed those maps.

The maps that fascinated Ash the most were of the enchanted forest. Past and present. Notations of weather and plant life and geography changed as she watched, listing what lay on each side of the portal. She was fascinated and frustrated by tiny stars that indicated some deep magic was linked with each location, other than the portal anchored there. For instance, a place where an enchanted prince or princess lay sleeping, waiting for rescue, or a faerie king had hidden a treasure, or some deeply magical item waited for the prophesied hero or heroine to find it.

Studying the maps of the enchanted forest threatened to devour large chunks of Ash's time and attention. She feared the books might get jealous and blockade the door to the map room if she let that happen, so she strictly disciplined herself not to go into the map room until midway through the afternoon. She spent the first hour of every morning mending books, sewing pages, gluing covers back together, and creating new covers to replace ones that had worn out entirely. Then an hour listing the contents of several short bookshelves, or one ceiling-scraping bookshelf. When she had the full listing of all the books in the library, which could take her several months, then she would know how to rearrange it. Depending on how many books by each author, or how many books were devoted to one subject, or how many books were produced by a consortium or collegium of scholars or enchanters, that would determine how the books were arranged. She smiled sometimes, remembering how large a chore she thought it had been, arranging Cecil's library for him.

The remainder of her morning, her lunch hour, and until she went into the map room, was for studying. Whenever she found a book that looked interesting while she cleaned and worked on the catalog, she put it on her study table. Soon, the books learned to guess what interested her, and they added themselves to her study piles. When the piles on and around the table grew to the point of being barricades, she took to talking to the books as she made her choices, to try to slow the increase of numbers.

Fang didn't appreciate the silence and the tedium of making lists of book titles and authors and contents, so he spent the mornings exploring the castle, At lunchtime, he joined Ash at her table in the entryway and regaled her with stories of what he had found. There was always at least one magic item that didn't appreciate having its sleep disturbed and got into a fight of some kind with Fang, or threw itself at him to drive him out of the storage room. Ash learned about the warren of storage rooms underneath the castle, and thanks to Fang's reports, drew an ever-expanding map and simple lists of what they contained. The storage rooms needed to be organized just as badly as the library did. She tried not to think of how long she would have to be living in the castle before she finished with the library and started on the storage rooms.

In the evenings, Ash and Fang climbed the stairs to Eyesallova's domain, to have dinner and talk about what they had found and done during the day. The mirror always had a message for Ash from Filby or Cecil or Hazel. Once Eyesallova had regained contact with the mirror web, she had asked that small mirrors be given to the seer and the hedge witch. Since a month went by in the outside world between every nightly visit with the mirror, there was always news of some kind. Ash tried not to grumble and feel resentment that she couldn't speak directly with anyone. Yet as the days turned into weeks and then a month, she couldn't help her irritation. She sometimes felt as if everyone in between them were reading the letters she wrote to Filby, Hazel and Cecil, and they wrote in turn to her.

She found some comfort in learning that the two magicians Fang had chased out through the portal again had suffered a drastic loss of their magic power, and that had affected all the Purple Sky magicians. No attacks had occurred yet against Castle Fairhold. Hazel had sensed no inimical powers pressing against the rings of watchful wards she had erected around the entire territory held by Lord Digory's family.

Justiciar Camwell had ceased his demands that Ash be captured and made to return all the magical items stolen from him. Filby had written to several people who held more authority than the justiciar and presented what she knew as facts. After he was publicly reprimanded, many people who once respected or feared him now ignored him.

Filby and Cecil and Hazel all agreed that the silence from Lathia and her minions should be frightening, not encouraging. The longer she seethed and plotted and her minions worked unseen, the more dangerous and damaging the attack would be when she finally struck. Now, going on three years in the outside world since the attack on his home, Winston had yet to speak. He spent his days sitting in silence, gazing into the distance, growing thinner and paler, and startling at the slightest sound.

Ash didn't feel much of anything, hearing how those two men were suffering their just comeuppance. She didn't feel triumph or vindication, and she certainly didn't pity them, either.

"It's the effect of the castle, dear," Eyesallova said, when Ash put her nebulous feelings into words, and wondered if something were wrong with her. "You're so separated from the outside world, everything out there seems like a fable. Which is ironic and amusing, I suppose, considering that the forest is merely fable to the outside world."

"When will I become a fable, do you think?" Ash asked after several moments of deep thought, while she nibbled on a decadently good dessert full of crushed fruit and pudding and chunks of rich cake.

"People need to know you're here, to tell stories about you. The castle is very good at distracting people who come to the castle, so they don't come inside. If the castle can determine what the heroes are searching for when they reach the forest, it sends the questing items out into the gardens. It makes things so much easier if people find what they're looking for, fulfill the conditions of the quest, and leave, as quickly as possible."

Ash decided to be amused by how the castle made things easier for heroes. The other option was to become depressed and angry at the steps the castle took to keep her hidden. Trying to see from the castle's viewpoint, that it was protecting its lady, didn't help much.

She had to admit she had brought some of this on herself. Hadn't she wished several times that she could spend the rest of her life in the library, exploring and learning? Not just silently, but aloud. Too late, Eyesallova had warned her that speaking wishes in the enchanted castle was a tricky business. Her wish might be granted, but unless she spent a great deal of thought on her phrasing and the details of that wish, the warped and tangled and bubbling cauldron of gathered magic here ensured that wishes were never granted exactly as the wisher wanted. Plus, wishes were often spoken in the heat of the moment, at the breaking point of patience or in frustration. And unwise, unplanned words were often the most dangerous of all.

Ash shared with Eyesallova the concern she had for the lost libraries, the caches of books that had been forgotten when castles and towers and underground lairs were abandoned or their owners died in solitude. Or what was sometimes worse, their owners had been defeated by more powerful nobles or enchanters, and the libraries had been left behind when all the other riches and magical items had been carted away. After all, as Filby had explained, many victors in a battle, whether through arms or magic, considered the weapons or the books of their defeated opponent as useless. They had failed in the crucial moment of defense.

Those books waited and moldered in the darkness. If they were lucky. The unlucky libraries were raided by animals looking for materials for their nests. Insects ate through the paper, rodents chewed on the leather of the covers. Or lightning strikes damaged the library, so it burned or simply lay exposed to the weather. Then there were the human rodents who came in and used the books for fuel. Or like Ruprick's bully soldiers, they hauled away books to add to a hoard that would likely never be used, because the magic-users it was meant to attract disdained to cooperate.

Eyesallova found the whole idea of lost libraries pitiable, and she sympathized. Often, magic mirrors were abandoned and left behind under the same circumstances as the libraries. She included other magic mirrors in the quest to find the libraries. It was a challenge and a game of sorts for them.

Until they found a library and a magic mirror that had been forgotten, left in the darkness and silence for decades. The enchanter who had conquered the very minor, scholarly wizard who owned the small tower was enraged that his conquest efforts had yielded so little return. He had cast a spell around the tower, rendering it silent and invisible. The magic mirror had been unable to call out to anyone until the concerted efforts of nine magic mirrors broke through to her. By this time, she had become a gibbering, pitiable creature who refused to believe the voices speaking to her weren't her own imagination. Until she responded, none of the other mirrors could determine the condition of the tower or the books trapped with the mirror.

"Can't we do anything to help them?" Ash asked, when Eyesallova told her about the mirror that evening.

"None of the mirrors are assigned to a tower or castle. They don't have regular contact with people, so they can't ask their king or wizard or hero to go help. They assist in passing on messages and strengthening lines of communication between points that are too distant for direct linking with the web. That's why they had the energy and the time to spare to find Dewshine and her tower in the first place." Eyesallova sighed. "What is truly despicable about that particular sore loser enchanter is that the spell reached outward, affecting the memories of those who once knew her wizard. They forgot Dewshine existed."

"That is horrible." Ash swallowed down a feeling like she might be sick. "Is that what you went through, cut off from the web?"

"Hmm, something like that. But at least I could see what went on in the forest and speak to the other magical items here in the castle. I wasn't locked up inside myself, in the dark and silence." The mirror's frame rocked from side to side several times, her equivalent of shuddering. "I agree, dear, we need to do something. Dewshine has suffered long enough. What's truly ironic is that idiot who cursed the tower, Schmendragos, had the exact same thing done to him perhaps sixty years ago. He only targeted very minor enchanters who were easy to defeat, so he got very little profit out of absorbing their powers and confiscating their magical artifacts. Too often, he expended far more strength and magical tools than he gained. In the end, he was an easy target when someone finally got irritated enough with his greedy ways to slap him down. They chose his favorite tactic to punish him, wrapping him in a spell of silence and isolation. Perhaps giving Dewshine the news he was finally punished will help her heal."

"Yes, but is anybody going to try to break through the spell and set her free?"

Eyesallova asked, but by the time Ash went up to the mirror room for dinner the next evening, no heroes had been found. Any league or conclave or collegium of magic-users close enough to try a rescue were too busy. Or weren't powerful enough. Or didn't have the right kind of magic specialty to overcome Schmendragos's spells. Any magic-users who had a hope of defeating those spells were too far away, and again, too busy, dealing with rogue wizards or defending their kingdoms against raiders or floods or fires or magical creatures on a rampage.

Ash was all too aware that every day that passed for her was a month more that Dewshine and her books suffered in darkness and silence. Yes, they had been suffering more than a century now, but that didn't make it all right to add another month to their imprisonment.

She spent the next morning in the map room trying to determine what portal would open out closest to Dewshine's hidden tower. She and Eyesallova had come up with a method to identify which portals opened onto what kingdoms and lands. When Ash was in the map room and saw a change occur in the forest on the map, she sent Fang racing up to Eyesallova to tell her. The mirror called out until she made contact with a new mirror in the web. When the mirror identified herself, then Fang brought the names and information to Ash, who added that information to her growing journal cataloging the portals. Eventually, she would have the pattern charted. She would know what kingdoms were accessible and when, and from what points.

Through the minor mirrors in the web, Ash hoped to locate the tower holding Dewshine, and which portal was closest to her. Certainly there were enough magical artifacts in the storage rooms of the castle to help her break down Schmendragos's curse.

"If I promise to come back right away. If I promise not to stay away more than three hours. If the portal is less than a day's ride from Dewshine's tower, will you ask the castle to let me go and rescue her?" she asked Eyesallova as soon as she stepped through the doors into the mirror room that evening.

The mirror was silent so long, Ash wondered if she had done something wrong. Had the castle intervened, cutting off contact with Eyesallova? She pushed that thought aside immediately. The castle was pushy, but it wasn't that cruel, letting her come in and see Eyesallova and talk to her but not let the mirror answer.

"I think that's a lovely idea," the mirror finally said. "I simply don't see how the castle would allow you to leave without ... well, without imposing some dreadfully heavy spell on you. Something to make rather large, drastic changes in your mind and spirit. The kind of changes that could very well make you wonder why you wanted to rescue Dewshine in the first place. And I can't countenance the use of such drastic magic. Especially when I think the castle is being a stubborn brute to begin with. Why can't it just ask you to stay and commit yourself to being our lady, instead of holding you prisoner until you give in?"

CHAPTER TWENTY-TWO

Fang chirped and hopped slow circles around the two of them, until Ash got the understanding of what he was saying. Then she laughed.

In essence, Fang had commented that the castle was like an entire warren of bunnies where the parents had gone away on a war against another warren that had insulted them. They were gone so long, the young bunnies had to take care of themselves. They didn't like it at all. Especially when nasty, meat-eating creatures such as weasels and foxes came sniffing around the doorways to the warren at night and tried to dig down to them. When their parents came home, the young bunnies tried to block as many openings into the warren as they could, to make sure their parents could never go anywhere again. Not even outside to graze. And wasn't that foolish?

"Can the castle hear that?" Ash asked.

Eyesallova chuckled. "Oh, yes. It might not have wanted to listen, or even like being compared to young bunnies, but it heard. We have quite a philosopher in our Fang, don't we?"

They got no answer from the castle that evening. Not that Ash expected to hear actual words, or even writing on a wall or some other method of direct communication. Eyesallova didn't speak directly with the castle but had to rely on impressions and whatever the suits of armor did in reaction to requests made and questions asked.

However, a little more than two hours after Ash went to bed, a suit of armor came into her room and shook her awake. It deposited a small trunk on the floor of her room and walked out. Then the lamps came on. She opened the trunk and found boots, gloves, and a set of sturdy clothes, what she would consider traveling clothes. All of the best materials, of course, as suited the lady of the castle. On one side of the trunk was a mask all in silver and onyx. A wolf's head. She brushed her fingers over it and they tingled with clear evidence of strong magic.

"What does the mask do?" she asked Eyesallova less than twenty minutes later. Enough time to put the clothes on and hurry across the gallery to the mirror room.

"It grants you the strength and the gifts and the senses of the wolf …" Eyesallova sighed. "And it will not come off until you return to the castle."

Ash inhaled to retort that she had already promised to return. Wasn't that good enough? She didn't, because yelling at Eyesallova was pointless. She didn't want to irritate the castle enough that it took back the gift. She had to see it as a gift, a chance to get outside, to do something worthwhile, to rescue books. Grumbling about the conditions attached to the gift would just waste time.

"Then I guess the only question is which portal will bring us out closest to Dewshine," she said after several more minutes, studying the mask, turning it over and over in her hands.

In truth, she had several more questions, but she had learned to deal with the most important ones, and then worry about smaller things later. Such as how to get from the portal to the tower, how to break through the spell isolating Dewshine, and how to transport the books back through the portal before it closed.

A suit of armor strode through the door and touched a small hand mirror to Eyesallova's frame. All her swirls of blue and green and purple magic compressed into a bright spot where the hand mirror touched her surface, and then exploded across the surface of the smaller mirror. The armor then handed the mirror to Ash.

"I'm in here, dear," Eyesallova said. Her voice even sounded smaller. "I'll be talking to my friends the entire time. Hurry. The portal has already been open five hours. We have less than seven to get there, then travel to Dewshine's tower, and get back."

"But how do we break through the spell?" Ash let the suit of armor grip her shoulder and turn her and give her a nudge toward the doors.

The answer was a large battering ram that looked like it was made of glass, or perhaps ice, lying in the bed of a long wagon that sat outside the castle doors. Seven suits of armor, all of them plain matte black, stood around the wagon. There was no horse or any other creature harnessed to the wagon. Ash wouldn't have been surprised if the suits of armor moved into position and grasped the long hitching bar that extended in front of the wagon.

They don't trust you not to run away, Fang commented as he bounced past her and up onto the battering ram. A flash wrung a yelp from him and he leaped crooked, to land with a thud on the seat of the wagon. *That hurts!*

"Imagine what that will do to the barrier spell," Ash murmured. She took a deep breath, looked around, studied the silent suits of armor that stared straight ahead rather than watching her, for a change, then climbed up into the wagon seat.

Nothing happened.

"You need to put the mask on," Eyesallova told her, after she sat there for several moments, waiting for the suits of armor to do something.

Ash hesitated, because other than holes for the eyes, her face would be entirely covered. The mask curved to cup her chin and attach behind her ears. How could she breathe?

The castle was letting her leave to rescue Dewshine. She had to trust it. Even though it obviously didn't trust her to keep her promise.

Well, as Lord Digory had said many times, trust was a treasure that had to be earned over time. If she had to prove herself trustworthy … then maybe she needed to demonstrate some trust in the castle, first.

Taking a deep breath, she closed her eyes and raised the mask to her face. A gasp escaped her when the mask grew warm and softened and bent to clasp her head. For a few seconds, she couldn't breathe.

Then the smells of the forest gushed into her nose and mouth, so potent and yet each scent so individual she shuddered from the impact. Ash opened her eyes. The starlight was as bright as noonday. She looked at the wagon seat where she had put Eyesallova, and the mirror's frame gleamed with shimmers of green and gold magic. The battering ram pulsed in rainbow streaks. Fang glowed a rich gold streaked with red.

"I'm borrowing …" Ash took another deep breath, startled at the huskiness of her voice, with undertones of growls and howls. The scent of the forest called to her, sending streaks of energy through her arms and legs. She wanted to run, and run, and sing to the moon, although there was no moon visible in the enchanted forest. The essence of it, the power of it, was there. Ash smelled the moon hidden in the darkness.

She looked down at herself. Her hands were longer, wider, covered with silver and black-streaked fur. Her nails were long, thick, curved into claws. She reached up to touch her face. She couldn't feel the mask. Her cheekbones were wider, sharper, her face longer, her nose elongated. Ash ran her tongue over her teeth and felt … fangs. Trembling, she ran her hands through her hair. It now fell in a thickly curled mane past her shoulders.

"If it's any comfort, you're lovely. Frightening, but lovely," Eyesallova said. "Would you be more comfortable running alongside the wagon for while, or do you need to sit until you get used to the changes?"

"I'll stay here."

The wagon lurched forward. The long hitching bar rose up so it pointed to the horizon and didn't threaten to catch on anything. The eight suits of armor walked alongside and in front of the wagon. Fang perched on the seat next to Ash, ears swiveling in all directions, on alert. The wagon didn't lurch and thump and bounce through the forest, but found smooth paths that Ash hadn't guessed were there. Perhaps under the thick growth of the forest, there were roads, waiting to be used again. She thought about some of the prophecies she had heard about the castle and the forest, and the warning she had been given about a sword and not falling on it. Could the castle be anchored again, and the forest restored to the normal flow of time? Could people travel through the forest again without fear of losing their lives and loved ones in the space of a few days?

That was a question for some other time. She needed to get used to seeing and smelling and tasting and hearing the world through the wolf senses of the mask.

After half an hour, the restlessness pulsing through her legs grew strong enough she had to leap down from the wagon. She couldn't simply walk, she had to run. The wagon sped up, and the suits of armor kept up without running. Their strides covered more ground with each step. The smells of the forest filled her head. Ash thought she might howl, and that was exhilarating and frightening both at the same time.

What if the mask refused to come off when she returned to the forest?

A new gush of smells caught her nose and Ash put that worry away for later. She followed the aromas of bog and moss and ancient trees.

"We're coming to a portal," she called back to Eyesallova. Ash laughed, the sound low and furry. "I could go through the portal with my eyes closed. This is amazing!"

The portal opening was framed in several massive fallen, moss-garbed oaks that had tangled their upper branches and held each other up. The suit of armor leading the group gestured for Ash to get into the wagon. She obeyed, knowing she had to be perfectly behaved this time out, if the castle would let her go on other rescues in the future.

Moss dripped down from inside the archway of oaks, and Ash ducked, wary of the smell of wet and rot. They emerged into darkness, the wagon wheels suddenly splashing through bog, sticking every few feet in the thick mud under the water. The air grew thick and Ash thought her lungs would fill with wet and mud and moss.

Then they emerged through a curtain of thick moss into bright moonlight.

"Oh … my …" Eyesallova sighed. "What a difference! It's like I've been shouting through twenty layers of curtains against a solid stone wall. Hello! Yes, I hear you! Excuse me, dear, while I get our bearings." Laughter rippled from her and her light grew brighter.

The wagon continued forward. The suits of armor plodded alongside. Fang leaned against Ash and sat up as tall as he could, sniffing, turning his head in all directions.

"What do you smell? What do you hear?" A humming filled her ears and the fur covering them tingled. Her ears twitched. There was far too much to get used to, going in wolf-shape and wolf-mind. Best to stay in the wagon, even though her legs ached to run again.

Eyesallova had good news and bad news. She had made contact with nine mirrors, all eager to help them find their way to Dewshine's hidden tower. However, every one of those mirrors was either living in hiding with their masters, because of the constant magical and political feuding within their country, Nayrdoweil, or they were just as abandoned and lost as Dewshine. They were within twenty minutes of travel of the nearest major road which would take them to within an hour of Dewshine's tower. However, they couldn't remain on that road and risk the countryside panicking if anyone saw Ash as she was now, or eight suits of armor trotting alongside the wagon that moved without any horses to pull it.

Three mirrors monitored the traffic on the roads of Nayrdoweil to assist the king's forces in protecting innocent travelers, and collect tolls for that protection. They volunteered to guide the rescuers down side roads and animal trails that would keep them out of the sight of people. The journey would take slightly less than two days each way.

Two days on the Nayrdoweil side of the portal equaled roughly one and a half hours inside the enchanted forest. They had roughly five hours before the portal shifted to a different location. They had time. If they weren't delayed getting through the magic shielding Dewshine's tower, and further delayed by any defensive spells that might still be intact.

If they were stranded on this side of the portal, would Ash have to keep wearing the mask until the portal opened again to the enchanted forest? Or would the suits of armor let her take it off, so she could deal with people in the daylight? Or would they set off across the landscape and kingdoms until they found the nearest open portal? They didn't respond when she asked. Maybe they didn't know or couldn't decide until the time came.

How long would that take?

Eyesallova was busy catching up with all her friends in the mirror web and the suits of armor didn't talk. Ash was grateful for the ear cuff and the mask that let her speak with Fang more clearly. He seemed to be having great fun teaching her to open her wolf senses, how to interpret what she smelled and heard and tasted on the wind and felt vibrating through the ground when she trotted alongside the wagon.

Fang taught her to hunt. Mostly, she terrified animals so they blundered in their flight and ran into him. She and Fang needed to eat along the way, after all, and nobody thought of provisions when they rushed to get out of the castle and through the portal. Ash hesitated over the first kill, a forest-dwelling antelope. How long would it take to build a fire and butcher the hindquarters of the antelope and cook strips of meat?

The wagon and the suits of armor continued moving away from them. They hadn't stopped when Fang led Ash on the hunt. She only felt safe to leap out of the wagon and go hunting with him because Fang kept track of the wagon. Ash considered settling down right there and testing the armor's patience, to see if they would come back for her. Maybe get angry enough to pick her up and carry her to the wagon? She didn't like the mental image of being slung over the shoulder of any of those suits of armor, bouncing against it until they reached the wagon. Sighing, she slung the antelope across her shoulders and loped after the wagon. When she caught up with it, she tossed the carcass into the back and crouched next to the battering ram and ripped chunks out of the carcass with her claws.

Only later, when she leaped out of the wagon to splash through a nearby stream and wash the blood off her hands and muzzle, did it strike her how easily she had done that. Carrying that heavy weight, catching up with the wagon, and then ripping apart her food. She didn't let herself linger too long on the question of whether she had enjoyed it or not. She was just happy she hadn't gotten violently ill at the first taste of bloody, warm meat, the feel of it going down her throat.

Maybe there were some benefits to being partially transformed into a beast?

That thought struck her as funny. Fang demanded to know what made her laugh. He laughed when she told him. Then they fell into a strangely philosophical discussion, comparing her partial transformation to wolf with his partial transformation to vampire.

Going in partial wolf shape made it easier to curl up on the seat of the wagon and sleep. Ash didn't need a blanket or pillow to get comfortable. She had a few odd dreams where she had a tail and it flicked around, tickling her nose, startling her awake several times. She found it slightly odd at first to be awake at night, trotting alongside the wagon, while she slept during the day.

They reached Dewshine's hidden tower several hours sooner than anticipated, just past midnight on their second day of travel. Ash saw nothing but devastation spreading around them as they followed the overgrown trail down into a shallow valley. All the toppled trees and pools that reflected the moonlight made the landscape look as if a flood had come through here and torn everything up by the roots. However, the sour smell lingering in the air, sometimes biting at her extra-sensitive wolf nose, wasn't the smell of standing water and rotting wood.

That's the smell of angry magic, Fang told her, after she had sniffed and sneezed half a dozen times, repelled by the stink that grew stronger with each step. He chirped laughter. *That's also the smell of fury that he wound so much of his magic into keeping the spell going, he crippled himself when he was attacked in turn.*

"Serves him right." Ash flinched when the wagon stopped for the first time since leaving the castle. "We're here?"

"We're here," Eyesallova confirmed, from her spot on the wagon seat where Ash had propped her up so she could see ahead of them. "This shouldn't take long. Stand back, dear."

Ash moved away from the side of the wagon. Four suits of armor climbed up into the wagon bed, picked up the battering ram, and slid it out into the waiting arms of the other four suits. Then they tromped out into the widest of the ponds. Their feet didn't splash and they didn't sink down into the water. Ash held her breath, fascinated, as the suits adjusted their hold on the battering ram. Their arms pivoted at angles that were impossible if they had had people inside them. They swung the ram backward, then slammed it forward.

A clanging, off-pitch ringing echoed through the valley. Ash caught a flash of light where the fist-shaped front of the ram hit something in mid-air. Back it swung, then forward, with even more force. Dark green streaks of magic raced up and down the length of the ram and swirled around the fist. Sparks shot out when it hit the invisible barrier. The ringing fractured, going even more off-key, into different octaves. A third slam. A fourth.

On the fifth impact, fracture lines radiated through the air, hissing and sparkling in black and red and a dirty shade of purple.

On the sixth strike, those fracture lines shrieked and rose to a crescendo of multiple chords that abruptly harmonized, just before the entire valley fractured and flashed bright green and pinky-purple. The toppled trees and pools and moss vanished, turning into a devastated valley full of rubble, burned and broken blocks scattered outward from the shattered trunk of a tower.

When Ash's eyes adjusted from the brief blinding dazzle, the suits of armor were already tearing at the remains of the double doors at the base of the tower. The battering ram was nowhere in sight. Eyesallova later explained that the ram had been solidified magic, and it had evaporated, all its strength used up in the effort of breaking through the spell.

Ash snatched Eyesallova from her perch on the wagon seat and followed the armor into the tower. They went downward. Eyesallova generated a soft golden light to illuminate the way. Ash and Fang could see in the dark, but Eyesallova needed the light to find Dewshine.

The mirror was small enough to sit on a bookshelf, jammed between two enormous volumes that looked as if they had been soaked, then set on fire, then soaked again, then trampled by a herd of angry bulls before being put on the shelf again. Ash had dealt with enough books already that had gotten muddy and rumpled, she could imagine how furious their condition made those magic books. She didn't look forward to having to deal with them when they got back to the castle. No matter how much knowledge they contained, some books had the least common sense when it came to necessary procedures to repair them. Some had tried to bite her while she was removing mud ground into their pages or sewing them back into the binding.

Ash and Eyesallova had planned what they would do when they reached the captive mirror. She picked up Dewshine, an oval in a quartz frame just slightly taller than the hand mirror containing Eyesallova. She pressed the two mirrors face-to-face, then hurried them up out of the underground chamber, into the moonlight, and set them on the bench seat of the wagon. Now everything rested on Eyesallova to reach the poor mirror, so wounded in its mind and spirit it refused to believe that rescue had come.

Ash got to work helping the suits of armor haul the captive books out. She was both relieved and disappointed that she only had to make three trips with her arms full of burned, torn, waterlogged books. The load of books barely reached the top of the wagon sides when the last volume had been hauled out. She cringed in anticipation of all the work to repair and restore them and grumbled silently over the effort that yielded perhaps one hundred books.

The moment she deposited her last armload, the wagon turned around and started the return journey. Ash perched on the wagon seat for less than half an hour. Her wolf senses allowed her to hear Eyesallova talking with Dewshine, and the mirror's whimpers made her ears itch. She trotted alongside the wagon, sometimes racing ahead with Fang to scout the way. She worked off her jumbled feelings by chasing night creatures into panic.

When daylight came and the wagon got off the road, Ash crouched in the back of the wagon bed and tried to sort through the books, creating some kind of order to save herself time when they reached the castle. Some of the ruts the wagon bounced through made that task difficult, knocking over the piles she had just made.

CHAPTER TWENTY-THREE

They reached the boggy area hiding the portal by early afternoon on the second day of their return trip. Fang and Ash scouted ahead, finding paths without people on them. The wagon kept moving, traveling on the open road because at this point it was the only solid ground. Bog stretched out for a dozen yards on either side of the road. Ash spotted the archway made of fallen trees, then the sound of men shouting in excitement made her turn around and race back to the wagon.

A dozen men raced alongside the wagon, struggling to climb up into it as it picked up speed. Their shouts were mixed fury and pain when the suits of armor plucked them off the sides of the wagon as easily as men would remove ticks from their horse's hides. Each man's shout ended in a yelp and a splash, as they landed in the bog. They pulled themselves out of the mire and splashed through the mud, back onto the road, and tried again to climb onto the wagon. They outnumbered the suits of armor, so there was always someone on the point of success. Ash howled her fury at the sight of a muddy man swinging a dripping, muddy leg over the side of the wagon, about to step down onto the books.

The man stopped and pointed at her, his eyes round in astonishment. He stammered a few times before shrieking, "What is that?"

Then Fang bounced past Ash and slammed into a man who had climbed up on the wagon seat and picked up Eyesallova and Dewshine. The mirrors flew up into the air. Ash howled again, envisioning the mirrors hitting the stone paving of the road and shattering. She leaped without thinking, snatched the mirrors out of the air, and cradled them against her chest before she hit the road. She rolled, slamming up hard against the stones that marked the side of the road and kept wagons from going off into the bog.

"Go away!" she roared and leaped to her feet.

One man leaped from the wagon before a suit of armor could grab him. Several others cowered away.

"What are you?" the first man called, while several others gathered around to try to knock Fang off the man he bounced on with vicious, red-eyed delight.

"That doesn't matter," Ash growled. "You're too stupid to understand."

Several men shouted protest, clearly insulted.

"How many times do you have to be pulled off the wagon before it sinks into those rocks you call your heads that you can't have these books?" She stalked toward the men, and nearly choked on her glee when as a single body, they backed away from her, matching her step for step.

"But there wasn't nobody driving," a man bleated. "Nobody to claim nothin'. We don't care about no books, we want the wagon!"

"These books and the wagon belong to the enchanted castle, you idiot. This is a magic wagon, or didn't you notice there's nothing pulling it? Didn't you notice the suits of armor?" Ash fought hard not to laugh. She couldn't believe the stupidity of these men. If all the men of Nayrdoweil were like them, no wonder this kingdom was wracked with constant turmoil. "How can you say there was nobody here? Idiots!" She bared her teeth and the men stumbled back three steps.

Some of them turned and fled at that point.

"Dear, I know you're having fun, and these fools need to have a lesson taught them they'll never forget," Eyesallova said. "But we are running out of time. The portal is starting to pulse, preparing to change."

"Right." Ash turned to the wagon. While she had been snarling and shouting at the men, the wagon had kept going. With no one to battle, the suits of armor had resumed their places alongside the wagon. "Fang, keep them busy?"

She turned and ran, clutching the mirrors to her chest. Behind her, men shrieked and Fang snarled and chattered. The smell of dust and sweat and terror billowed down the road to follow Ash.

Fang caught up with the wagon just as it dipped down into the deepest part of the bog and entered the archway of fallen trees. He chirped and his ears flicked and twisted. Ash perched on the wagon seat, holding the mirrors cradled with one arm, and wrapped her other arm around him. She held her breath until they had passed through the portal, into the enchanted forest.

Dawn was just starting to streak the sky with peach and gold. Ash jumped out of the wagon, needing to run off the energy pulsing through her. The wolf senses granted by the mask led her to the castle, and it came to meet her. It followed her trail, guided by the crown she wore. Just as Eyesallova had told her it would do. Ash had never felt grateful for the possessiveness of the castle until that moment. She took Eyesallova and Dewshine to the mirror room, returned Eyesallova to her own mirror body, and put Dewshine on a cushioned bench directly in front of the mirror.

She was exhausted by the time she reached her suite of rooms. The housekeeping breezes had a bath ready and waiting. She had to pass the mirror in her dressing room to reach the bathing room. Ash stopped, stunned at the sight of herself in wolf-shape. There was something compelling about the sleek, muscled form before her. Half her clothes had transformed to silver and black-streaked fur. Her claws glinted in the light as if they were real silver. She bared her teeth, fascinated by her fangs, and nearly giggled in delight at the amazing mane of thick, curly hair swept up off her forehead from a widow's peak and falling halfway down her back. The creature looking back at her was both frightening and beautiful.

Would the mask come off?

Did she want it to?

She studied her claws, and laughed, when she thought of trying to repair books and read books with such hands. Her claws were made for tearing, not for handling delicate, ancient paper.

Ash peeled out of her clothes as she stumbled to the bathing room. She pressed her hands against her face, willing herself to feel the mask and not her own flesh. The mask came off with a sucking sound, as if it had been partially glued to her face. She set it carefully down on the little table next to her deep tub full of lavender-scented bubbles, and gratefully sank down until her ears filled with water.

Lavender dominated her senses, soothing, and she yielded to the haze that partially numbed mind and body. The breeze rubbed her with lavender oil and brushed her hair dry and wrapped her in a nightgown like thistledown. Clouds of blankets buried her as sleep swallowed her down in one long, luxurious draught.

~~~~~

Her clothes were lavender gauze and silk and netting, dotted with amethyst chips, and her hair was a thick mass of curls, shimmering with a lavender haze. A frothy sort of crown, all delicate wires studded with amethysts and diamonds, hugged her brow and twinkled with every move she made. Ash came to herself after what felt like hours, standing in front of a mirror and turning her head this way and that, amused and entertained by the shimmer and sparkle of the jewels.

No, not again …

She took several deep breaths to bolster herself before turning and looking around to orient herself. She didn't recognize the mirror or the dainty lavender-themed sitting room.

"Where is my silver crown?" she asked, raising her voice to be heard. She had had enough evidence that the castle was always listening, but it was always smart to leave no room for doubt that she wanted to be heard. "This is a princess crown, and I am a lady. Not a princess. Where is my lady crown?"

Then, two more deep breaths, and she turned to stride to the nearest door. Not glide. Not float. Not dance. Stride. As a lady with heavy responsibilities would walk. Not as a frothy, decorative, useless spun sugar princess.
~~~~~

A black suit of armor met her, holding out her braided silver crown, when she reached the gallery. Ash had to restrain herself not to snatch it. She removed the amethyst crown and handed it to him. The armor nodded to her.

Did it … respect her?

Ash turned and found the hallway to her suite of rooms. The housekeeping breeze deposited her favorite trousers and light house boots on her bed just as she walked through the door. Ash restrained a growl. She had no way of knowing which housekeeping breeze had taken advantage of the daze she had been in and dressed her so frothy and sparkly, and imposed the princess image on her. For all she knew, dozens of housekeeping breezes served the castle. She could only hope that some of them supported her, and maybe respected her, like that suit of armor did.

"Please help me change my clothes?" she said, and for punctuation raked her hands through her mass of thick, stiff curls. Lavendar dust crinkled and sparkled and dropped from her hair. Well, that was some comfort. Her hair wasn't naturally glowing with magic.

When she left her suite again, Fang came bounding up the stairs. He didn't throw himself at her to hug her legs, but stopped several steps away and looked up at her. His eyes didn't gleam red or with manic energy.

"Fang?"

He flipped his ears at her and chirped, but she didn't understand him.

"They took my ear cuff, didn't they?" Ash fought down another growl. She skirted the stairs and crossed the gallery to the doors to the mirror room. Fang hopped along behind her. She knew something horrid had happened when he didn't pass her, but let her go into the mirror room ahead of him.

"Eyesallova, what happened while I was … was … while my brain was asleep?" She turned to see Fang looking through the doorway. "What did I do to Fang?"

"It's all right, Fang. She back." Eyesallova leaned forward, gesturing at the long padded bench facing her. "Sit down, dear. You're still exhausted. That mask took far too much out of you."

"How long have I been gone?"

"Just half a day."

"Long enough to do something stupid?" A soft touch on her knee startled her. Ash looked down to see Fang looking up at her, his eyes big and pleading and sad. "Fang, whatever I did, that wasn't me!" She bent down and scooped up the bunny, then settled on the bench and cuddled him. "Eyesallova—"

"You shrieked at him to go away, that he was disgusting and bloody and he would ruin your clothes."

"I would never—"

"And then you kicked him down the stairs."

"No!" Ash held Fang out at arm's length, staring in horror at him. He nodded. "I'm sorry. That wasn't me. I swear!"

Fang studied her while she held her breath, waiting. Then he leaned in until his nose was almost touching hers and patted her cheek.

"I'm never going to wear that mask again."

"Well, maybe not that mask, but the castle isn't going to let you leave again unless you wear a beast mask. You'll need to draw on your inborn magic and your strength of will to resist the influence of the mask. And then resist when the castle takes advantage of your exhaustion to press you into that useless, fluttery mold again."

Ash opened her mouth to retort that if that was the case, then she would never go on another rescue mission again. Her skin tightened, feeling magic pooling in the air around her. She carefully closed her mouth and took several deep breaths, fighting the surge of anger that wanted to shove foolish words out between her lips. The magic was listening and would enforce whatever she said.

"Then I need to find some books to teach me tricks of discipline and resistance, don't I?" she said after several moments.

"Indeed you do, dear." Eyesallova sighed. "Well done. You're learning."

Fang chirped and flung his arms as far around her as far as he could reach.

~~~~~

That evening, when Ash tottered up the stairs after hours of repairing books and convincing the rescued books that they wouldn't be thrown out and burned, Eyesallova had news. The mirrors in Nayrdoweil were humming with the gossip and excitement that had been sweeping through the kingdom in the wake of the scuffle on the bog road. The mirrors knew the truth and found great delight in keeping it to themselves. None of their masters had the sense to ask the right questions, which the mirrors would have been compelled to answer.

A Beastly Beauty, who came snarling out of the night to best fifty stout warriors and steal books to give in tribute to the enchanted castle, was already the stuff of legend. Kingdom officials had sent investigators to find out the truth, and there was talk in various council chambers of a reward for the capture of the creature. Rumors were filtering in from other kingdoms of princes and nobles seeking the Beastly Beauty, believing she had control over the portals into the enchanted forest.

Ash laughed at the assertion that a great beauty lay hidden under the beastly shape. How could those idiots who had fought the armor on the
~~~~~

road be sure? She had faced them for maybe two minutes at the most. What had they seen? They were too busy fighting armor and then running away from Fang to have gotten a good look at her.

"It's not funny," Eyesallova scolded her. She was tired and frustrated from a day of trying to convince Dewshine she was free and safe. "The more those fools focus on wanting to find you, and find the castle, the easier it will be for them to stumble through a portal. That's the nature of magic, especially tricky magic, or nasty magic. The more you think or talk about it, the more energy you generate, and you draw it to you."

Ash thought over that bit of information for several minutes. "Will the castle let them in if they're looking for me?"

"Eventually. But with lots of tricks and traps, and a dozen tasks to fulfill. Eventually, one of them will turn out to be a prince with the right magic and the right heart and soul to rescue you."

"Not if I don't want to be rescued."

Eyesallova was silent so long after that response, Ash worried. Was she busy with Dewshine? Or was this some frightening or depressing or simply worrisome bit of news the mirror wanted to shield her from?

"You could be right, dear. I hope you're right. Just remember that just like every castle needs a princess, especially enchanted castles, every prince needs a princess. Not always for the same reasons, and sometimes with great resentment."

"I'm not a princess. I'm Lady Ashlyn, not Princess Ashlyn. I don't have to accept a prince if I don't want one." She sighed. "I suppose that's another one of those flaws and negative points in being a princess that the ring was warning me about."

"You are too right." The mirror chuckled softly. "We'll find a way to keep you safe, don't you worry. But you need to be careful. You've made headway in holding your own against the castle, putting yourself in charge and resisting the spells that try to press you into a mold. That's very good. The castle needs a leader, a caretaker, not a figurehead. But the more you set down roots and resist the forces that might try to take you away, especially the good-hearted, well-intentioned ones that want to rescue you ... well, as I said, you set down roots. Some roots cannot be torn up and replanted. You can become part of the castle by your own choice, without realizing you are making that choice."

Ash paused, with the words, "Would that really be so bad?" poised on her tongue. She understood Eyesallova's meaning just in time. Making a comment like that would certainly be seen by the castle as acceptance of her fate. A fate designed by outside forces. Ash wasn't ready to succumb. She had struggled too far and too long, and had too many questions yet to answer, to let the castle take over her life.

Besides, she had the awful feeling that if she relaxed and settled in, eventually the castle would win in the struggle to make her into something glittery and fluffy and feathery and twinkly sweet. A figurehead princess, something out of the oldest fables. Not the princess it really needed. What would happen if it changed her before the warped and sick magic was healed, and the castle essentially came to its senses?

Would she stay the useless, fluttery figurehead? Nothing like herself. Nothing like the woman she would have been if her parents hadn't died in the battle at Tippessee. She had magic she had yet to understand and tame. She could be an enchantress, with enough studying and practice behind her. Enchantresses didn't let themselves be pushed into molds, turned into spun sugar princesses who didn't do anything except inspire quests.

"We have a lot of work yet to do," she said instead. "There are more books and mirrors to rescue, and I still have to find a way to wake up the ring and free him. Years have gone by, and Lathia is still a threat. We need to figure out how to protect against her schemes. I'll deal with the castle's need for a princess later."

~~~~~

The Purple Sky magicians struck that evening. Fang came bouncing into Ash's bedroom, glowing with excitement, and carrying the wolf mask. She hesitated to put it on, but the more Fang jabbered about the call for help and the mess the magicians were making, the more Ash liked the idea of not only snatching their newest victims from underneath them, but giving them a metaphorical black eye.

"Not that real black eyes would disappoint me," she muttered as she raced down the hallways and then the stairs. Fang leaped the entire depth of the staircase in one bound and the scents of the forest poured in through the open doorway.

This time, twelve suits of armor had come out for the mission, and they rode in two wagons. They carried weapons, and when Ash put on the wolf mask, she saw the streaks of magic pulsing and darting up and down the pikes and swords and maces and spears. Every suit of armor had a shield sitting propped up between its knees, and the largest suit of armor, sitting at the front of the second wagon, handed Ash a long, triangular shield. Clearly, she was expected to use it.

"They're nasty and determined and growing desperate," Eyesallova reported, when Ash climbed onto the bench seat of the first wagon. The hand mirror sat in a padded box clamped to the seat.

The wagons sped away from the castle gates with a jolt that nearly sent Ash tumbling off the bench and down among the seated armor.

The mirror in danger this time was named Glint. He and the books and cache of enchanted rings and bracelets under attack hadn't been abandoned. Their master, Andros, had sealed up his tower while he took
~~~~~

his wife across the ocean to Paraxia to help her sisters. They were dealing with the fallout from the curse that he had broken to rescue her. There were nine sisters left of fifteen who had been imprisoned separately, scattered across the entire continent. Andros expected to be gone at least three years on the mission. His mistake had been telling some of his friends, all fellow students in a school for enchanters that had only lasted six years.

"One of many reasons why enchanters at all levels of talent and strength should take on one student at a time, and not mix magics in large quantities," Eyesallova said. "There's always a sneak and a bully and an arrogant snot who thinks he knows better in every group. Without the intimate connection between master and apprentice, those flaws don't get ground out of them and mended."

One of Andros's old classmates had several weaknesses, including a weakness for strong spirits and not knowing how to keep his mouth shut. The worst was a passion for gambling. And he was a bad gambler. Most of his magical energies were spent trying to rig the dice or cards or enchant the racing pony to help him win. He failed miserably, because his magic wasn't sensitive enough, thanks to his constant drinking, to detect spells to prevent cheating. He couldn't seem to learn his lesson, despite massive fines weighed against him.

Andros had asked a few friends to check on his tower and make sure people who came to him for help were attended to. The Purple Sky magicians had found his old school chum in a moment of drunken weakness, talking to himself, trying to remember the keyhole spell so he could borrow the magic mirror and some jewels until he got his feet under himself again.

Glint picked all this up by listening to the magicians arguing over whether information from such a fool could be trusted. Or whether Andros really had any worthwhile magic, because what kind of decent enchanter would be friends with such an idiot? And even worse, trust him with the keyhole spell to his tower?

CHAPTER TWENTY-FOUR

The Purple Sky were a talkative, argumentative bunch who couldn't work together. Glint found it amusing, in an ironic way, to listen to them argue and get into fistfights when their spells didn't work. They were clearly desperate and frustrated. They were focused on confiscating all the magical artifacts they could find, to siphon off the power and add it to their own, before they could complete their mission. The defensive spells around previous targets had drained them. Several of those spells had attached to them, creating a leak in their power stores.

"According to Glint," Eyesallova said, and shuddered inside her padded box, "they're all dressed like that inexplicably popular sect that has unfortunately crossed over the ocean. The Prosperittians."

"I never heard of them. What do they believe?"

Ash flinched the moment the words left her lips. She had the awful feeling she really didn't want to know. Then again, it was best to know everything possible about her enemies before she faced them.

"It's a new wording for an old foolishness," the mirror said, punctuated by a long sigh. "They insist that A'theosius never wanted his followers to enjoy anything in life. They have to earn their way into his presence and reward. Why in the world would anyone come up with such a contrarian idea? Look at the incredible world A'theosius made for us, all the color and variety and beauty. Why wouldn't the Maker want us to enjoy what he made? And besides, any fool who can read or at least listen to someone reading the Holy Writ knows it's impossible to earn their way through the judging door. A'theosius states it flat out in sixty-three places in just the books of Banipal the seer, not to mention the hundred and five other visionaries and prophets who compiled the scrolls of the Holy Writ."

She made a sound like she wished she could spit and get a foul taste out of her mouth. Unfortunately, magic mirrors didn't have mouths. While yes, they could take on faces if they wished, to make their masters or the people who consulted them more comfortable, those mouths didn't take in breath or food and certainly couldn't spit. Or bite. Eyesallova had admitted to Ash during one long night of hilarious, ridiculous stories that she had wished she could take a bite out of a large number of imbeciles who thought a magic mirror could solve all their problems. Not a one of them could comprehend that they had to ask the right question before she could give them the right answer. Not a small number of them had tried to smash her when she failed to read their teeny tiny minds and unravel what they couldn't decipher for themselves.

"That certainly sounds like someone who would accept every lying word Lathia said and throw themselves wholeheartedly into punishing people who said no to her," Ash said. She thought perhaps she was still partly asleep, because she wanted to laugh.

Then they reached the portal. This one was less than an hour from the castle. It was an overgrown arch of brambles. Clusters of dried berries clung to the brambles, which had lost all their leaves, an indication of the weather in the land ahead of them.

Signs of harvest were everywhere on the other side of the portal, spread across a rolling plain, golden with sheaves of wheat, clusters of corn stalks bundled together, piles of hay, all sitting on scalped fields, ringed with towering trees brilliant with gold and scarlet leaves. Ash inhaled deeply, catching that tangy fall scent of ground tilled for the planting of winter wheat, bonfires, and the perfume of smokehouses full of freshly butchered hogs and deer.

Andros's tower stuck up from the rolling plains dotted with small farmhouses and tall barns, visible for miles in every direction. It was at least six stories tall, and Ash's legs ached for a moment, considering how many times someone had to climb all those stairs in the course of a day. Lady Charlotte's study had been on the third floor of the tallest tower in Castle Fairhold, and that was considered quite a climb for an elderly lady. She always laughed and claimed that the exercise kept her strong and alert, and helped to keep away pesky folk who could stand to learn some moderation in their drinking and eating.

They emerged through the portal at the beginning of sunset. Fang snarled and ducked under the bench seat. He slapped Ash's leg, and she bent down to look at him. He held out the shirt she had modified what felt like a lifetime ago, to protect him from sunlight. The effects of the wolf mask made her much more limber and flexible, and she had no trouble sliding down to kneel in the space in front of the bench and reach under to help him scramble into the shirt.

"We need to find you something better, more protective and worthy of your dignity," she told him. She refrained from adding that the Beastly Beauty, because she rather liked the title, had some dignity to uphold as well. She wouldn't be taken seriously and feared properly if she was accompanied by an oversized bunny hopping around swathed in a ragged old shirt, with sleeves on his ears.

Fang chattered about colors and materials as he leaped from the wagon and darted ahead of them, to scout out the situation around the tower. The wagon had gone perhaps another mile and reached a low point in the landscape with a wide, shallow river cutting through it, when he returned. He smelled of brimstone and scorch marks streaked his shirt. The sleeve protecting his left ear was missing, and he had his ear folded flat inside the hood. The Purple Sky magicians were lobbing buckets of tar at the tower doors and windows and then firing crossbow bolts, coated in brimstone and set on fire.

Andros's defensive spells created a gap between the tower itself and the shield, so the tar slid down to the ground. The tower sat on a small hillock, mostly rock, and the tar spilled downhill toward the magicians. They were too busy scorching their fingers and stamping out the fires on their crossbows to notice the streaks and fingers and puddles of tar surrounding them until someone caught their robes on fire and stumbled into a puddle, which immediately erupted in flames. Tar usually didn't catch fire that easily, with a whoosh and a gush of hot wind, but apparently the tar was enchanted to burn far more rapidly than normal. Fang had bounced into the chaos that resulted. Some of the magicians tried to put out their burning companions. They set themselves on fire when they spattered tar all over themselves. When others burst out laughing, several magicians leaped in with fists flying to defend their burning friends' honor. Fang got spattered with tar. Several magicians shot fire from their fingertips against their companions, and he got singed in the crossfire.

"Why didn't they just shoot fire from their fingers, instead of fussing with the crossbows?" Ash wanted to know.

"They strike me as a bunch who want to look far more elegant and crafty than they really are," Eyesallova said. "Someone read the wrong books, all about heroes and adventure, when they should have been studying their spellcraft."

Ash laughed, because she had a good idea what books the mirror referred to. She had devoured such books, back at Castle Fairhold. She had set out on her quest with a handful of wrong ideas about foraging, sleeping on the ground, building fires, hunting for food, and finding shelter. Fortunately, the ring had been there to correct her and give her better advice.

The heroes of some of those adventures advocated for a certain "look" when conducting a siege. Some heroes were clearly more concerned with heroic stances and speeches than using common sense and accomplishing the rescue or attack as quickly as possible.

Eyesallova excused herself, saying Glint had contacted her. Ash helped Fang get out of the much more bedraggled shirt. Sunset had progressed enough for sufficient shadows to shield him. By this time, the wagons had crossed the shallow river and were traveling up the slight incline, with Andros's tower less than a mile ahead of them.

"I have good news and bad news," Eyesallova announced, her swirls of blue and green and purple brightening. "Glint finally got hold of Andros. He had to go through five nodes in the mirror web. The mirror in the castle Andros and Serena are currently cleansing of several generations of foul magic has been out of communication for nearly that long. She's constantly needing to be updated on protocols, and half the time thinks she's hallucinating when someone talks to her."

Ash winced for the mirror's sake. The situation reminded her too much of Dewshine. That poor mirror might never regain her sanity.

"Anyway, Andros has given permission for us to go into the tower, with all the keyhole spells, and several master spells to re-set the shields, and raise up some emergency shields. He didn't want to put them up when he left because the spells are so strong, Glint wouldn't be able to communicate with anyone."

"How much longer will Andros and Serena be gone?" Ash asked.

"Oh, they've barely begun rescuing her sisters. Two who don't need rescuing have gone entirely bad and they're teaming up with the sorceresses who initiated the curse four generations ago, to interfere with the rescue operation."

"But what about Glint? How long can he go, entirely cut off from everyone?"

"He won't be." Eyesallova chuckled. "That's the good news. Andros has asked us to remove all the magical artifacts, all his books, anything that he and Serena truly value, which isn't much, actually. We're to leave behind quite a lot of furniture and dishes and decorations and an entire castle's worth of ugly tapestries. All wedding gifts from royals they didn't dare insult and enchanters who were just trying to empty out their castles so they could redecorate. Let those idiots laying siege have them, if they ever get through the defensive spells. We're to haul everything back to the castle, and Andros will come retrieve their goods when they've taken care of the curse. And don't worry, we have plenty of room. He had the foresight to put everything they valued into several locked chests and bags of accommodation before they left.

"It seems he didn't quite trust several of his old school chums not to dig around and borrow things without permission. Some of them have quite sensitive feelings, and if he gave the keyhole spell to some but not the rest, there would just be too much fussing and sniping and trying to turn different members of the group against each other. The school reunions would be utter misery. Better to take some extra precautions and salve the touchy ones' feelings by including them."

"Are magicians and wizards and such always so troublesome to deal with?" Ash asked without thinking. "Maybe dealing with magic does something to the mind?"

"More like all that power does something nasty and corrosive to the heart and soul, dear."

A quarter mile from Andros's tower now, and the stink of brimstone and scorched rock and burning tar reached them. Ash wished the senses that came with the wolf mask weren't quite so sharp. She thought she might be sick, and breathing through her mouth didn't reduce the pungent strength of the smell.

The largest suit of armor raised its arm. The wagons stopped and the armor climbed out, brandishing their weapons, the magic filling them flaring brighter for a few heartbeats. Then they all turned to her.

"They want instructions," Eyesallova told her. "You're Lady Ashlyn, after all."

Fang hopped up on the bench seat and gestured wildly with ears and forelegs, chattering eagerly. Ash took a moment to understand. What he said made sense, mostly because it went against the grand heroic warfare taught in those books the Purple Sky magicians had probably read when they should have been studying their spellcraft.

"Fang, we need to find a spell so the books will read themselves to you, so you can study warfare. You have a great future ahead of you as a warrior. The kind who goes around rescuing others," she hurried to add, when the bunny's face wrinkled up in perplexity and a flicker of suspicion.

He thought for a few moments more, then his face shifted to that manic expression she missed. He bounced out of the wagon, landed in front of the largest suit of armor and beckoned toward the tower with his ears.

None of the armor moved. They clearly didn't understand bunny. Or, more likely, they were waiting for instructions from Ash.

"I have to learn to be more careful what I say inside the castle," she muttered as she climbed out of the wagon. She had proclaimed herself Lady Ashlyn, leader of the castle, hadn't she? The armor was taking her at her word.

"Here's what we're going to do," she said, as she reached back into the wagon and brought out that shield. How had the armor known she would need it? And how much good would a shield, even a magically endowed shield, be against those Purple Sky magicians?

The best situation was that she would never need to learn. Fang's plan was brilliantly simple. The armor would attack and distract the magicians while Ash and Eyesallova reached the tower door and used the keyhole spells. When the armor had driven away the magicians, they would bring the wagons up, load them, and get out of there before the magicians returned. The plan meant keeping them from realizing the tower had been emptied of everything that would make their efforts worthwhile.

Andros had even told Eyesallova he hoped the magicians were so infuriated when they finally got into his tower, they would destroy everything. Then he and Serena could finally redecorate the place to suit themselves, instead of bowing to everyone else's taste to avoid offending anyone.

Ash carried her shield on her right arm. The largest suit of armor ran ahead of her, around the left side of the cluster of magicians who were still arguing and lobbing fireballs at each other. Meanwhile, the other suits of armor attacked from the right, distracting the magicians so they wouldn't see her get through the defenses.

Fang added to the chaos, bouncing off heads and chests, his eyes glowing red. He gnashed his teeth and screamed what Ash later learned was bunny epic poetry, in between proclaiming himself the lord of the vampires.

The magicians fled screaming. Those who weren't still punching and pulling each other's hair. Four suits of armor picked them up bodily and raced away with them. Ash looked back, just before she closed the tower door. The landscape surrounding the tower was a smoking wreck of puddles of tar and the smoldering remains of the magicians' wagons and tents.

"Glint? We're here," Eyesallova called out, her greeting punctuated by Ash slamming the door, and all the spells clicking into place again.

"Welcome, welcome, ladies!" Glint called, his voice echoing down the spiral stairs tucked in the back corner of the octagonal tower. He had an amazingly deep, booming baritone voice, for such a long, skinny mirror. Ash reckoned she would have to stand sideways to the mirror to see herself fully in him. "I haven't had such fun in a long time. You really must introduce me to the bunny. Are they truly as magical as I've heard?"

"You'll have plenty of time to chat with Fang on the way back," she said. "Let's get you loaded and get us out of here as swiftly as possible. We don't want those imbeciles following us back through the portal."

Far faster than Ash had dared to hope, they had the trunks and bags of accommodation floating on a handy levitation spell Glint had pulled out of an old book Andros had been intending to repair. The wagons pulled up to the littered yard in front of the tower just moments before Eyesallova triggered the spells to open the door. The suits of armor were nowhere to be seen. Ash hoped they were busy chasing the magicians all over the countryside, and hadn't been shattered, maybe their magic drained away. The wagons started rolling back down the road as soon as she climbed into the front wagon.

Glint was propped up against the footboards of the driver's bench, so he could see the countryside as they passed. Fang crouched on the bench seat next to him, with Eyesallova back in her box. The shimmering, chiming language of the mirrors spilled through the night as they traveled. Either the sound or the heavy scent of magic in the air kept away all the animals and maybe even the people they would have encountered on the way. Ash couldn't understand the mirrors, but clearly Fang did. She grew drowsy, having nothing to do but ride. She didn't want to fall asleep. She had the awful feeling that if she did, she would wake up days later, once again dressed in flouncy, fluttery, glittery clothes.

The third time she felt herself sliding forward and jerked awake, she jumped down off the wagon and ran alongside it. The fresh air rushing past her, the intoxicating soup of scents, the music of the life of the countryside, made her heart race and sent a howl bubbling up in her throat. She didn't let it out, though keeping it back made her throat ache a few times.

They were less than a mile from the portal when the suits of armor caught up with them.

And someone else.

Glint called out, "Oh, no," and Fang yelped and leaped off the wagon.

A flash of yellow-tinged light shot down in front of the leaning sheaves of wheat that framed the portal. For half a second, Ash thought they would burst into flame. The light expanded into a sheet, shimmering and crackling with angry energy, blocking the portal.

The wagons slid to a stop. The suits of armor spread out from the two parallel lines they had been running in, with the largest suit at their head, and surrounded the wagons. Or more accurately, Ash realized, they surrounded her.

I am the lady of the castle, after all, she admitted, and wasn't sure if that made her feel better, or more apprehensive.

"What do you want?" she called out and followed her nose to the scent of stronger magic, tingling in the air, an almost visible cord of energy connecting it with the sheet blocking the portal.

"Thieves don't get to ask questions," a man called in a mellow tenor.

"They're not thieves, Brandyweiss," Glint called. "You really should stop listening to Santiss. Especially when he's had more than two cups of wine." He chuckled and added in a softer tone, "Which is all the time, even when he's asleep."

"Glint? What threats are they holding over you?" A line of yellow light shot down to land between the blocked portal and the suits of armor. It expanded to another sheet of light. Ash wondered just how few tricks this magician had at his disposal. Or maybe he just didn't care about variety and impressing people with showmanship. That would be a refreshing change, after what she had learned about magicians and enchanters and such folk. A man, most likely this Brandyweiss, stepped through the sheet of light. He was dressed in browns and golds and yellows. Ash supposed that was his signature color. If that was something he learned in the enchanters school, she agreed with Eyesallova that the concept wasn't a very good idea.

"No threats at all, and if you had come to help me when those intruders first set up their attack, we wouldn't be here," the mirror boomed back. "These folk have rescued me and all Andros's treasures. Before you start shouting about evil magic suborning my free will, talk to him yourself."

There was a pause. Ash glanced back to see a young man with caramel-toned skin and red-gold hair peering out of Glint, over the side of the wagon.

"Some help here, please?" he said.

Ash climbed up into the wagon, just because she didn't think the suits of armor were going to let Brandyweiss get past them. She turned Glint around and propped him up on the bench seat so Andros could look out through him and talk to his friend.

"Hah! You caught them. Lovely!" a slurred sort of voice caroled. A splash of greenish-yellowish light hit the road behind the circle of armor, and a saggy-baggy man with a large bald patch, straggly, dirty hair, and pockmarked skin staggered out of it. He held a skin of wine in one hand and raised it in salute, then brought his empty hand up to start to pour. He caught himself and stared at his hand, clearly expecting a cup to be there.

"Someone take Santiss home and put a sober-up spell on him?" Andros said. "Bran, I swear, I asked these kind folk to take my things away to protect them."

"Folk?" Brandyweiss gestured at Ash. "What sort of curse are you under? Who do you serve?" he demanded.

"You'll not talk to Lady Ashlyn, lady of the enchanted castle, in such tones," Eyesallova called out. Her tones were chilly enough Ash thought she saw circles and whorls of frost gather on the metal parts of the wagon.

Fang chirped and snarled and bounced up and down, viciously enough Brandyweiss took two steps back.

CHAPTER TWENTY-FIVE

"Indeed, the vampire speaks the truth. The Beastly Beauty led her forces out to rescue me and defend Andros's property that Santiss put in danger," Glint said.

Some of Brandyweiss' irritation and stiffness visibly melted away. "Why do I find that far too easy to believe?"

"Why do you always blame me?" Santiss whined.

"Because you always are!" Andros and Brandyweiss said nearly in unison.

"Excuse me," Eyesallova said, "but we're running out of time. We have less than an hour until the portal closes. Glint, give the node address for the mirror where Brandyweiss can reach Andros. You two can finish this discussion through another mirror. We need to get home."

"Indeed we do," Glint boomed, ending on a chuckle.

"Beastly Beauty, eh?" Brandyweiss said. "Are you looking for a prince to kiss you and break the curse, lady of the enchanted castle?"

Ash choked, caught between shouting "no thank you!" and laughing outright. She settled for shaking her head. Why did men always think that women needed rescuing? Did it never occur to them that without men interfering and complicating things, women were more likely to rescue themselves, with far less fuss?

She delegated the leader of the armor to pick up Glint and hold him while Andros and Brandyweiss talked, and Santiss sulked. Ash led the wagons through the portal. She flinched when the swirls of magic around the edges of the portal twitched and flickered a few times. She considered darting back through again, to hurry up the farewells. She had an image in her head of the armor being cut off from the magic of the castle if the portal closed, and collapsing, maybe falling on Glint hard enough to break even a magic mirror.

Just in time, the armor came through. Glint was chuckling. Ash took that as a good sign.

"You have quite an admirer," he told her, once he was settled back in the front of the wagon. "Several, actually. Santiss is just liquefied enough to declare he is in love with you and he will find the magic to free you. Brandyweiss ... well, he's always up for a challenge, and he has a much larger romantic streak in him than he is comfortable admitting."

Ash thought about that for several minutes as the wagons skimmed down the road. She bit back several responses, some of which could be considered rude or insulting. These men, however competent they were or weren't, were trained magicians. Of one sort or another.

"Thank you. Please tell them thank you but no thank you," she said, after trying to imagine what Lady Charlotte or Lady Beatrice would say in similar circumstances. Not that either lady would ever come close to the circumstances Ash was in right now. "You will have communication with them? Or at least ask Andros to tell them?"

Glint assured her he would have regular communication with his master. Although the time differential between the outside world and the enchanted forest did complicate things.

"Tell them I am very happy as I am. And besides, this," she gestured at her wolfish face, "is temporary. I'm not allowed out of the castle without the mask. It gives me skills I need to deal with trouble like those magicians."

"And ties you more strongly to the castle each time you put it on, if you don't mind me saying so," Glint offered, all humor fading from his voice.

"I know. It's a price I'm willing to pay."

For now, she added silently.

"Lady Ashlyn is precious to the castle," Eyesallova said. "She is doing great and good things, when she leaves the forest and risks being stranded in the outside world. You would still be under siege from those idiots, if she weren't willing to come out with the resources of the castle to rescue books and mirrors."

"True," Glint said after a thoughtful moment. "I am in your debt, Lady Ashlyn."

They trundled on in silence, and Ash felt that drowsiness creeping up on her again. She considered getting out of the wagon to run again, but they were close enough to the castle she saw the lights in the towers and along the battlements. Then Glint chuckled.

"If I might offer some advice? Let me show them your true face and explain about the mask. That might be sufficient to disappoint them and discourage them from pursuing you. There's a certain cachet and bragging rights that come from breaking nasty beastifying spells."

Eyesallova laughed, so Ash agreed. Then she excused herself and jumped out of the wagon and ran the rest of the way to the castle. The idea of courtship, especially misguided courtship, made her itchy. First Morris the vampire, now these magicians. She was far too busy to put up with the fuss and waste of time that accompanied courtship. Yes, Eyesallova had warned her that eventually, when the castle relaxed its defensiveness toward her, princes and heroes would get through and actually see her, maybe even meet her face-to-face. An idiotic number of them would want to rescue her, and if she wasn't careful she would be forced to marry one of them, even if she didn't truly need rescuing.

"Not need rescuing?" she muttered when she had finally reached her room. She nearly wept aloud at the sight of her bathing tub full of apple-and-cinnamon-scented bubbles. "Who says I don't need rescuing? But I think I can rescue myself, thanks very much." Her hands shook a little as she peeled out of her clothes, her claws tangling in some of the strings. "What idiots came up with the idea that just because a man rescues you from some problem you can't solve because you don't have the right kind of magic or you aren't strong enough to swing a sword, that you are therefore forced to spend the rest of your lives together? That's just as bad as the nonsense about true love's kiss being the first kiss. Yes, a kiss coming from purity does have the power to break curses, but ..." She sighed, ending on a groan, as she kicked aside her hosen and stepped into the tub.

Ash didn't realize until much later that she had gone into the tub still wearing the wolf mask. And went to bed wearing the wolf mask. When she woke, the castle dressed her in severely elegant, rich clothes as befitted a wolf queen. She came to herself roaming the battlements, looking out over the thickly tangled forest surrounding the castle, thinking of how she would defend it against all comers.

Common sense told her that the castle, as it had proven far too clearly, could defend itself.

That made her stand back and look around and start asking questions. Those questions helped her break free of the haze that made her quite happy to stalk around, thinking defensively, wolfishly, regally.

Ash pulled the mask off and took a few deep breaths to fight the urge to toss it over the battlements. That wouldn't solve anything. A suit of armor would probably rush out and catch it before it hit the ground outside. She didn't want to anger the castle, and honestly, she liked going in wolf-guise.

Just not all the time, without her permission.

She stomped back into the castle and down the flights of stairs from the battlements to the main entryway, where the lean, elegant, dull silver suit of armor she had designated the seneschal stood at the foot of the stairs.

"Please put this away where it belongs," she said, and held out the mask.

The suit of armor reached out to take the wolf mask and bowed to her. Then she hurried up the stairs again, snarling at the heavy weight of her skirts. Honestly, did they have armor woven into them? In her room, she peeled out of her wolf queen robes and left them in a pile on the floor.

"I don't want to see these clothes again unless the castle is under siege and I need armor, do you understand?" she told the room, and the castle in general. Then she dressed in her simplest shirt and vest and trousers and went in her stocking feet down to the library to work. No repairs today. No lingering over the map room and daydreaming. She needed to find a spell that would bring back the ring. She needed his guidance, his advice, and his help to break free of the castle's slowly growing influence.

~~~~~

"Apologies, dear," Eyesallova called, when Ash came into the mirror room much later than usual that evening.

She and Fang had a late dinner in the entryway, rather than eating with Eyesallova. She wanted to talk with him about the new details she had learned about spirit rings.

"For what, exactly?" she said, rather than accepting the apology. She was too tired and headachy, her head full of half-formed ideas, to spare the energy to be gracious.

"The castle is quite grateful. You rescued all those items, all that magic, that might have been suborned or drained away by those Purple Sky nincompoops," Glint said.

He stood in a corner where he could look out through the glass doors at the garden. Ash supposed he would enjoy that after being locked up who knew how long in the tower, guarding Andros's possessions.

"I didn't do it alone. There was Fang and Eyesallova and all the armor."

"Yes, but without you, the castle is unable to act. Especially not act outside its domain or reach through the portals. The castle needs a princess because the princess is the focal point of its power, the guide for its magic. Without you, the armor wouldn't move, the wagons wouldn't roll."

"It knows you're unhappy, feeling rather betrayed," Eyesallova said. "It has spent so many years fighting off greedy fools who would abuse the magic and destroy the potential for good, it has been trained, essentially, not to trust anyone. It's first reaction in all situations is to impose its will, its standards, on whoever comes within its clutches."

"It doesn't have to be so heavy-handed with me," she muttered.

"Yes, well, decades of defensive thinking is hard to put aside. You're exactly the sort of mind and heart the castle has longed for. And to be completely honest ... well, you're resisting it enough to be a challenge. The castle hasn't had so much fun in years."

"I'm sorry, but I don't find it fun when something bigger and more powerful than me imposes its will on me. I may be just an orphan, a servant—"

"You are neither of those things," Eyesallova cried, accompanied by chirps and squeals and snarls from Fang that pretty much said the same
~~~~~

thing, but laced heavily with bunny profanity.

"I don't know what I am!" Ash turned around, arms spread, as if presenting herself to the mirrors, the room, the entire castle. "I have magic in me I haven't even begun to explore. Who knows what A'theosius made me to be, what he gave me to do? Stop pushing me. I'm scared half to death you'll try to mold me into something that is utterly wrong and I'll … I'll … I'll just break. I'll warp. I'll go bad." She dropped down on the nearest cushioned bench. "Do you hear me, castle? I don't want to go the wrong way!"

Ash could almost have laughed at the sudden release of pressure in her chest that she hadn't even realized was there until it escaped. The servant she had been certainly wouldn't have thought to resist when a more powerful force gave her orders. She hadn't struck back until injustice slapped her. She wouldn't have ever thought to resist if Lady Charlotte and Lord Digory hadn't made it clear that even servants, even orphans without names, had a right to dignity and fair treatment, and not to be made toys for the warped amusement of spoiled brats.

Now, with so much potential, so many unanswered questions, so many possibilities in front of her, the person she struggled to become and understand shrieked in fury at every effort to force her into choices she didn't like. Essentially, taking away the ability to choose.

"You're quite right, dear," Eyesallova said.

In the silence, Fang bounced softly over to her and wrapped his forelegs around her knees. Ash choked on something that might have been laughter or tears, or maybe both. She scratched between his ears and down his back.

The door onto the balcony opened with a click that sounded loud and seemed to echo off the glass ceiling. Ash sat still, her hand resting on Fang's head. Was another suit of armor, or maybe one of those slowly prowling statues in the garden going to come inside? She waited until the silence rang softly.

"Am I allowed in the garden now?" She was exhausted, as if putting the struggle deep inside into words had been a draining effort.

Ash knew better than to hope the balcony door opening meant she could come and go as she pleased. That would only happen when the castle gates opened, and no mask waited to tether her to the castle.

"It's quite a large garden," Eyesallova offered. "A lot to see and enjoy. And relatively free of dangerous magic."

"Relatively?" A bubble of wry laughter escaped her tight throat.

"Well, some of the statues have rather bad tempers. They've missed enough chances at rescue that they've gotten somewhat rude and pushy when heroes show up, which just sends them running even faster. But you don't have to worry about that. The nicer statues will protect you."

"Thank you." She tipped her head back, taking in the entire castle. "Thank you."

Ash got up slowly, her limbs heavy. Fang settled down on his haunches and watched her go. She was grateful because she honestly did want to be as alone as she could manage.

She walked down the curving stairs into the moonlit garden and took the graveled path to the right. Every time the path split, she took the right branch. Ash didn't care where she was going, and half the time, she didn't even look around herself. She just walked and let the sounds of the garden at night seep into her mind. The cool of the night soothed the place she had rubbed raw with her outburst.

Eventually she came to a little summer house, a confection of white marble latticework, frothy and airy, despite the flowering vines wound in and out, nearly making the walls solid. The air was thick with a refreshing perfume. Ash stepped through the wide doorway. A bubbling little spring sat in the center of the tiled floor. It was a mosaic of sea creatures, all swimming and frolicking, and looking rather benignly silly with big smiles on their otherwise frightening faces. Ash settled on one of the deep benches that lined the shelter and put her head back against the thick tangle of vines and flowers and closed her eyes. She wondered what would happen if she fell asleep here. Would she be allowed to spend the night, or would the castle send a suit of armor to pick her up and bring her inside?

A soft scraping sound came from the deep shadows in the corner. Ash opened her eyes but otherwise didn't move. More scraping, stone on stone. A statue moved out of the shadows. It was a girl in a long, flowing dress with draping sleeves, a style from maybe two generations ago, Ash guessed. A princess, judging by the simple coronet resting among the soft curls covering her head, under a veil that seemed sheer enough to see her hair. Ash wondered for a moment how a sculptor could give the impression that something was sheer, then scolded herself that she was tired and should go to bed. This wasn't just a statue, this girl was under an enchantment. No sculptor had made her because she certainly hadn't started out as stone.

"I'm sorry," she said, bracing to get to her feet. "I've intruded."

The girl shook her head. How did she do that without shattering the stone? She smiled, just the slightest upward quirking of her lips, and gestured at the bench. Ash guessed that meant she wanted her to stay.

The girl sat down on the bench facing her, folded her hands, smiled again, then tipped her head back against the wall and closed her eyes. Ash wished for the ring. Could he speak to the statue for her? Would the statue be able to hear? She hoped she wasn't misreading, putting intentions to what the girl statue meant. Ash sat still, listening, letting the quiet seep in, until she copied the girl's pose and closed her eyes.

~~~~~

When Ash asked about the girl the next evening, Eyesallova could give her no help. There were so many statues in the castle. Most were in the gardens, but there were dozens that had been deposited in the many underground corridors and storerooms as well. She had tried to keep watch on who came and went and what they brought over the years, because after all what was a magic mirror to do when she couldn't talk to other mirrors? Unfortunately, there were nasty blocking spells scattered through the underground levels of the castle, casting darkness and silence where even a magic mirror couldn't see and keep watch. Many hadn't been cast by thieves or enchanters who didn't want others to know what magical mistakes they hid in the castle. Some warped magic had a tendency to combine with other magic and expand, twist in new directions, and in a sense birth new spells. Eyesallova had given up trying to keep a tally and remember what statue or enchanted chest or weapon or jewelry belonged to whom. When thieves and heroes seeking magical help or to break an enchantment came to the castle, keeping count of what had been taken away or destroyed was just as difficult.

Ash spent an hour with the girl statue that next evening, sitting with her. The company seemed to please her, and she literally glowed when Ash attempted to make conversation. She responded with hand gestures and smiles and nods and shakes of her head. She couldn't give Ash any clue to her name, and tears appeared on her cheeks, little dots of stone that gradually faded away, when Ash asked if she would mind having a name.

"People have names. I know you had one once … do you remember your name, where you came from?" Ash inhaled sharply, as soon as the words left her lips. "I'm sorry. That's probably very hurtful. I didn't mean—"

The girl reached out in that slow, gliding way she had of moving, and rested her hand on Ash's on the bench between them. She smiled, shaking her head.

"If you don't mind, may I give you a name? It just seems rude to think of you as the stone princess."

The girl nodded, still smiling.

The next day, Ash searched for lists of princesses who had been stolen by enchantments. She found several books, three of which had blank pages at the back. The ink seemed to be newer on the last several pages. The books each covered a different continent. Eyesallova confirmed her suspicion that the books had been created and spelled to keep an updated tally of lost princesses, princes, and poor-but-deserving maidens and lads who had been unfairly enchanted or suffered a curse on someone else's behalf. And were still waiting for rescue.
~~~~~

"Could we do the same here?" she mused, studying the books she had piled in front of Eyesallova. "Find some enchantment to write a list of all the statues, all the enchanted people in whatever form they have now, here in the castle?"

"That would certainly make things easier for the heroes who come seeking a specific person to rescue," the mirror said with a chuckle.

Ash considered that, and she found it a little amusing too. She decided not to ask if the castle would let her talk to those people. She didn't want to know if the answer was no.

When she carried several of the books out to the summer house that evening, the stone girl looked startled. She froze for so long, Ash feared maybe the magic that wrote the books interfered with the spell that had partially reanimated the girl. Then the statue held out her hands for the books. Ash gave two to her. They were large, and the statue girl was a head shorter than her and dainty. With more stone tears slowly trickling down her cheeks, the girl sat and held one book on her lap and opened the other on top of it, and slowly leafed through the pages.

Ash nearly slapped her own forehead at a realization that struck her and made her feel rather foolish.

"You can read?" she finally asked when she couldn't think of any other way to ask the question without feeling stupid. The girl nodded and kept reading. "Do you like to read?" Another nod. "What do you like to read? I can bring you books, if you want. At least, I think the library will let me bring you books."

The girl looked up at her, eyes wide, her stone lips trembling into a smile.

Then Ash had another thought. "Do you remember your name? If I gave you pen and paper, could you write it down for me?"

A quick nod had her racing back into the castle, up to the mirror room and down the stairs to the library. She brought several sheets of paper, and four pens, just in case the girl's stone fingers weren't kind to pens.

CHAPTER TWENTY-SIX

The girl's name was Dulcibella. She preferred to be called Bella, because her older brothers and stepbrothers insisted on calling her Dulci, emphasizing "dull." She couldn't remember much beyond that, and a terrible argument her mother and stepfather had with a team of enchanters. She woke up in the garden when some ragged, maniac apprentice enchanter shattered several spells and tried to weave them together. She didn't remember the name of her kingdom and had no idea how long she had been in the garden. She liked histories and fables and studying botany. She invited Ash to visit the corner of the garden she had taken over and tamed, since being awakened. She knew there was a castle, but no matter how many times she walked around the gardens, she couldn't see anything but blank stone walls. No doors or windows or stairs up to the mirror room balcony. And no gates to get out.

Ash came outside when she stopped for lunch the next day, and brought a handcart full of books, stacks of paper, pens, and ink. Other statues gathered around as she and Bella agreed on where to put the cart. Several ladies with elegantly slanted eyebrows and pointed ears wept as they picked up books and immediately sat down to read. One rather large man with furry arms and small horns at his temples tried to hug Ash, shaking with silent tears. Bella stopped him. Ash held still, grateful for the intervention, terrified of hurting anyone's feelings, but even more terrified of being crushed by those massive stone arms.

"Can you talk to each other? In your minds?" she asked, when she and Bella were alone again. Her friend had three books spread open on the cart, looking at the illustrations with delight that threatened to crack her face.

Bella nodded. Then she grinned and picked up a pen. *We can hear. A little. It is very slow. Many don't even try anymore. The big statues, like the centaurs and ogres, are busy keeping the cruel statues, the insane ones, from coming into this part of the garden. Will you leave the books for them to read, when they are off guard duty?*

"And I'll bring more. Every day. And pens and ink and paper. Are you very bored?"

Bella grinned, then reverently brushed her hand over the text she had been devouring with her eyes.

"Now you see," Eyesallova said, when Ash climbed up to the mirror room a short time later and told her what had happened. "This is why this castle needs a princess. Too many undeserving prisoners suffer, without anyone to think about how to help them. I'm proud of you, dear. Your ring will be proud of you, too, when he learns what you've done."

Ash nodded and quickly excused herself to go back to her studies. Too many thoughts and questions and unsettled feelings churned through her. She had to get away before she said anything rude or awkward or embarrassing. She had the awful feeling she might cry in another moment.

She threw herself into her research, with renewed determination. More than ever, she needed to give the ring back his voice, free him from whatever prison Justiciar Camwell had thrown him into. Or, the prison Lathia had imposed on him, in her efforts to be free of her own spirit ring.

It wouldn't do to consider the idea that the Purple Sky magicians had found a way to not just silence the spirit ring, but destroy him utterly.

~~~~~

The next morning, as Ash settled down for breakfast, her mind full of ideas for that day's research and how to make it easier, Fang appeared. The bunny held two hand mirrors and a traveler's satchel that had two pouches just the right size for the mirrors to go into. He handed them to Ash, his ears gesturing wildly as he gave her the tangled details of their next rescue mission. She wanted to grumble about rescues coming so close together but held her tongue. After all, what was only a day or two for her were months since the last time a mirror or library had called for help.

Fang brought two mirrors because both Glint and Eyesallova wanted to come on this mission. The mirror calling for help was a friend of them both. They had been cast in the same enchanted glassworks. They had been catching up now that Eyesallova could call out to other mirrors and Argent had awakened from a decades-long nap. Her mistress was a frostfire sorceress who had fallen in love and changed her very nature to help her prince rescue his father's kingdom from greedy, murdering relatives. Frostfire sorceresses by their very nature required solitude. The sorceress fully intended to return to her lair once she had made sure that her grandsons got along and wouldn't fight over her son's throne when he died. Frostfire sorceresses rarely had daughters, and the power and longevity only ran in the female side of the line.

Argent had called for help because the lair, safely hidden away under nearly a mile of ice and snow, faced a thaw. There had never been a thaw in all the time the sorceress had been in residence, and there shouldn't be a thaw for another hundred years or so. A weather enchanter had predicted the thaw. The sorceress had the approximate date recorded in her journal and was prepared to deal with the problem when it arose. She wasn't ready for this thaw taking place now and was busy dealing with the birth of twin grandsons. She had it on good authority that several neighboring faerie godmothers were preparing to weave together a
~~~~~

complicated curse on the twins at their christening. They held to the tough love philosophy of forcing anyone of royal blood into being heroes by throwing all sorts of dire destinies on them. The sorceress refused to let them cast those curses when there were no prophets or seers available to verify the curses would do any good in shaping the twins' characters. Naturally, the faerie godmothers refused to listen to reason, which made the sorceress too busy to rescue her books and Argent.

Besides, there were warning signs to indicate the thaw was deliberately initiated. Most likely bait in a trap, to bring her back to her lair and drain her of her magic while she was distracted and uncomfortable. She hated getting wet, and thaws were always very wet.

Before Ash could ask, the seneschal suit of armor appeared with a new mask for her to wear. This one was a polar bear. Only two suits of armor and one wagon accompanied Ash, Fang, and the mirrors on this rescue. The sorceress's lair and library were both relatively small. The suits of armor stood guard. They didn't go with her to haul the books. Ash agreed that suits of armor would have some difficulty swimming, but couldn't they walk along the bottom of the inland sea that surrounded the lair? The problem was that it hadn't been an inland sea two days ago, and the silt near the bottom was thick, almost to the consistency of clay. The armor would have had a struggle and taken ten times longer than it took for Ash to swim, in bear shape, to and from the lair four times. The castle provided her with a large waterproof sack that she filled four times and hauled with her.

While Ash rescued the books and Argent, the mirrors prepared to deal with any magical interference that might arise, once the enemy realized that someone other than the sorceress had come to deal with the flooding. Fang and the mirrors were disappointed that no attack came. Ash thought they were rather reckless, especially since she ended up doing all the work. Her irritation grew when they returned to the castle and the minor mirrors keeping watch over the castle reported what had happened.

The entire rescue operation, from the time Ash hurried out to the wagon without her breakfast to when she returned, her temporary fur still dripping ice, was less than two hours in enchanted forest time. In that time, the castle suffered an invasion. The mirrors keeping watch did nothing but keep watch. They weren't alert and awake, like Eyesallova, Argent, Glint, and poor suffering Dewshine.

"Highly suspicious," Eyesallova announced, after she had studied the images recorded by the sentinel mirrors. "It's too convenient that he found the best route through the castle to hide his actions from the mirrors. It's like he knew the mirrors were there, and he kept ducking into the cover of the blocking spells."

"Do you think he knew we were gone?" Ash flinched, blushing a little, because she had spoken with her mouth full and spat out a few crumbs of scrambled eggs.

The problem with taking on one of the masks and the accompanying animal form was that along with being drained, and risking spending a day or two as a spun sugar princess, she also inherited the appetite of the beast. In this case, the polar bear's hunger after coming out of hibernation.

"There's no telling if anyone knows you're in residence, or that there are alert souls and minds in the castle, keeping watch," the mirror announced after several long moments, considering Ash's question. "I'm more inclined to think this is one of those evil princes with the incredible good luck that is always incredible bad luck for everyone and everything they encounter. That poor princess who is so clearly in love with him is case in point."

"He rescued a princess?" Ash found that a little hard to believe. Evil princes didn't rescue anyone. Unless it profited them enormously, of course.

"No, he brought her with him," Glint said, when Ash spoke those thoughts. "I agree. Poor deluded princess. She was constantly asking him if he was sure the box of beauty would make her beautiful enough for their wedding. What an idiot. Actually, he's the cruel idiot and she's the deluded one. Every bride is beautiful. If love is true. Even if it's just on her part and not his. If what she feels is true, then she becomes beautiful and enchants him. Hopefully long enough to capture his heart tight and strong and ensure they have a happily every after. If they both work at it, of course. But ..." He sighed loudly. "I don't trust him to even have enough heart to be enchanted. What's wrong with the girl? She's not bad looking at all. Granted, she doesn't have hair like sunshine and her eyes are muddy hazel instead of sapphires or emeralds, and her nose is a little long, but her voice is lovely. When it isn't pleading for his approval. She'll age with great dignity."

"I've identified her," Argent announced. "She looks so much like Prince Dazron, I'm willing to bet my frame on it."

"Dazron?" Eyesallova sighed. "Now that's a sad story. He and his wife, Esperiana, both inherited several nasty, unfair curses. The kind where someone powerful is so disgusted with a despot or evil stepmother, they cast a curse on them and all their descendants for six or seven generations. Or even worse, the curse skips every other generation. I suppose sometimes that's useful, because one generation learns from the mistakes of their parents, but then their children are snots like the grandparents and need to learn a harsh lesson to keep them on the straight and narrow ... but with Dazron and Esperiana, they had the bad luck to both be the cursed generation. Usually such people manage to marry someone with enough blessings and good luck and magical gifts to counter the curse."

"What happened to them?" Ash interrupted. She had listened to Eyesallova's lectures enough by now to sense when the mirror was about to launch into a philosophical rant that could last hours.

"They both made foolish promises, in the hopes of warding off the curses, and ended up getting themselves whisked away at their daughter's christening. As far as I know, they're still waiting to be rescued. For all I know, whatever things or animals they were turned into are right here at the castle. Hmm, that's an idea. Maybe the prince came here with the girl — what was her name again? Oh, that's right. Plicity. Awful name. Probably hoping to inflict some good character on the child from birth. Maybe he brought her here to rescue her parents and prove himself worthy to inherit the throne as her husband. That's how far too many heroes become kings, entirely sidestepping a girl who might just have the brains and good character to be a good ruler in her own right." A long sigh followed.

"If they broke any enchantments while they were here," Glint said, "there would have been some residue to alert us when we returned. I sensed nothing."

"No. Me neither," Eyesallova admitted. "I have to wonder why the counselors who have been running the kingdom since Dazron's disappearance would allow her to take a risky journey and come here with her prince. Unless there was a very great reward at the end."

"What did they take?" Ash held up a hand to stop them responding. "I know. There's no inventory, and he probably took something from within those blank areas where the sentinel mirrors can't see. We really do need some system of inventory, so we know what we have, what's dangerous, what should be sealed behind a dozen locked and spelled doors, and maybe even who brought it here. Just so we can give warning to the kingdoms where they get taken if we can't stop thieves and heroes and whoever comes here from taking things in the first place."

The recorded images caught the prince rolling his eyes and grimacing quite often behind Princess Plicity's back. They also caught him picking up a number of smaller magical items. Goblets of plenty, a few enchanted daggers that never missed their mark, coins that always returned to their purse. Minor magics that wouldn't have any impact beyond the city or the small kingdom around them. Ash pitied the merchants who would sell their wares to the prince in good faith and then lose that money. That wasn't fair, was it? And what about those daggers? Yes, they were useful for bodyguards, but what about in the hands of assassins, or just someone with a nasty temper, who threw knives at anyone and anything without thinking?

Eyesallova tried to contact the magic mirror in Plicity's castle, but she had vanished. From the castle and from the mirror web. Neither Argent nor Glint had any idea if she had been broken or silenced. They hadn't had any reason to contact the mirror, and she hadn't contacted them, because the nobles entrusted with running the kingdom until Plicity grew up were honorable, intelligent men who didn't need help.

"Perhaps we need a listing of all the mirrors in the web, too," Ash commented, just before a yawn broke in. She was so tired, she ached all over. That worried her, because she hadn't spent entire days wearing the polar bear mask, as she had with the wolf mask.

She had hoped to avoid the long sleep, and the risk of waking up in a frilly dress in whatever color scheme the castle favored now. That hope was dashed. She resigned herself to not getting any studying done that afternoon. Hopefully the castle would listen this time when she asked it, politely, not to change her clothes. Just to be sure, she checked the set of the silver crown in her hair. It was secure. While it had made her somewhat vulnerable to the castle's interference, now Ash considered the plain, sensible crown a defensive measure.

"A listing would be very helpful," Eyesallova agreed. So did Argent and Glint. "We need to keep in contact and watch out for each other. Too many times, a mirror that has fallen silent ends up being melted or warped to serve a truly evil master. That's a very good, responsible idea, dear. You just keep proving why the castle needs a princess."

"It seems to me we need more than one person. Even with all of you advising me. This castle is huge, and you've even admitted that it has tripled in size to accommodate all the magic stored here. I need to recruit more people to help. Maybe you can ask Filby to ask Friar Ipswich to come here? Not just to chart all the portals but take inventory. We need to warn people before some petty thief makes himself an evil enchanter king with something he took from here, and we didn't know what it was until it was too late."

"We." Eyesallova chuckled. "What a lovely word. See? You're making changes already."

Ash held her tongue. She was fairly certain she was so tired, she would say things better left unsaid. And she had an awful tendency to make wishes when she was tired or upset. Making wishes, as Eyesallova had warned her, was especially tricky in the enchanted castle, if not the enchanted forest in general.

"I don't know about bringing in people to help you. Is this Friar Ipswich a member of some holy order of enchanters? It's chancy if anyone without magic in their blood can stay here very long without becoming … well, let's just say, affected."

"Afflicted," Glint offered with a grunt for punctuation.

"Insane, from some stories I've heard," Argent added.

"Unfortunately, yes. Anyone who lingers here too long gets greedy and angry and wants what they can't have, if they don't have magic in their blood. It's sad, because I've seen too many otherwise worthy folk go bad, or run away for fear of their souls. It's like there is a song playing throughout the castle, just below the level of hearing with your ears. Yet you can hear it all the same. And if you can't sing along at some point ... well ... I just don't know." If Eyesallova could have shrugged, Ash thought she would have.

That wasn't much help. She hoped she would feel better about the questions and the answers she got once she had had a good long sleep. Thinking of that just made her even more achy tired. She excused herself to go to bed.

Eyesallova's advice whispered through her thoughts as she crossed the upper gallery to the residence wing of the castle: *Think carefully, phrase your thoughts even more carefully, and then ask A'theosius for guidance.*

~~~~~

The next day, Ash took her lunch break to relax with Bella and several of her statue friends. She read to them so they could all enjoy the book at the same time instead of having to wait and take turns to read the book. Fang shrieked from the balcony of the mirror room and Ash came running.

"Sorry, dear," Eyesallova said as Ash skidded into the room.

"It's that rotter, Ruprick," Glint said. He quickly explained while Fang hopped over to the mirrors with the hand mirrors they used for travelling.

A frantic call came through the mirror web from a reclusive community of magic scholars and mirror-makers. They had existed for several centuries now, hidden in the walls of a narrow canyon on the edge of a vast sea of the purest silver sand, imbued with magic and perfect for mirrors. The community had very few defenses because hardly anyone knew they were there. Or so they believed.

"Most of their books deal with making magic mirrors, all the guidelines related to that specific grade of sand, the melting process ..." Glint let out a gusty sigh.

"Their library is small. Most of what isn't related to mirror making and the journals of their predecessors are poetry." Eyesallova took over as Glint transferred from his long, thin frame to the hand mirror. "I don't know what it is about scorching winds and sandy wastes that makes men wax poetic ... You might need to fight this time. I'm sorry. The castle insists." Then Fang was putting the hand mirror up to her surface and all her sparkles and swirls of magic transferred over.

The seneschal suit of armor met Ash at the castle doors with a lion
~~~~~

mask. A male mask, because it had a mane that covered her head with long, flexible strips of gold and topaz chips. Ash shuddered once as she took the mask and stared into the empty eyes. She thought of what a lion could do if it had to. Did she despise Ruprick and his bully-boys enough to rake them with her claws, bite and hit hard enough to break bones, maybe even kill, for the sake of books?

"We must hurry," Eyesallova called. Fang had already put her and Glint in the padded traveling box in the wagon. Argent was staying to oversee the castle since the sentinel mirrors had proven somewhat useless. "The defenses are weak. They've never needed defenses except against the winter flooding or the summer sandstorms. Ruprick has brute force and wizards just as greedy and arrogant as he is."

Before Ash could answer, the seneschal armor caught hold of her wrists and raised her hands to slide the mask over her head. She caught her breath as heat and the scent of blood washed over her. Ash went to her knees, shuddering as short bristles of fur erupted all over her skin. Her clothes turned to leather in multiple shades of sand and gold. Her arms were bare, except for gold bands, two each above and below her elbows. Her hands ached as they grew longer, wider, and wickedly curved talons erupted at her fingertips. Ash fell forward and lunged out through the doors on all fours.

She led the way, exulting in the rush of the air ramming scents down her nose and throat. Every detail in the forest around her was clear, though she ran at a speed she had never known before. She reached the portal, an archway of red-tinted stone, and leaped through in one bound. Fang let out a warbling shriek, a bunny war cry that made even her lion-shaped heart skip a beat.

The sour tang of magic slamming against magic caught in her nose. The scent guided her. The anger and frustration in the air made her slow. She went on all fours up a rugged incline of wind-carved sandstone, to come out on a plateau, looking down into the narrow, zig-zagging canyon. Red-tinted light flashed as men in scruffy, threadbare red robes flung their arms forward, throwing bolts of energy at the opening of the canyon. When the energy hit, the shield flared into visibility. It crackled, and Ash's nose twitched at the scent of burning.

She laughed, knowing most of that burning came from the cut-rate wizards Ruprick had brought to tear down the magical defenses. Their magic was twisting back on them, scorching them, punishing them for pushing beyond their strength and skill. Still, the defenses were starting to crack.

CHAPTER TWENTY-SEVEN

"We need to settle this quickly," Eyesallova called from behind her.

Ash looked back to see the seneschal suit carrying the two hand mirrors. Fang crouched on the plateau where she lay, looking down into the canyon. He grinned at her, eyes glowing red with battle lust. She thought about letting him go down there and terrorize Ruprick's bully soldiers until they either collapsed in fear or exhaustion or ran away.

No, that won't be any fun.

"Found it," Glint announced. He sounded rather breathless from effort.

"We need to stop that attack. Just long enough to slip the new shields into place, and establish the anchor for the dimensional slide," Eyesallova said. "I hate to ask this of you, dear, especially with the effect ..." She sighed. "Just don't get too close to the canyon entrance. And for A'theosius's sake, don't enjoy yourself too much."

"Distract them?" Ash laughed, a low rumble that vibrated through her whole body. "Sounds like fun. Ready, Fang?"

He chortled. He leaped, but Ash was a heartbeat faster, launching with powerful thrusts of her legs, up over the edge of the plateau and then down. At the back of her mind, she knew she should be terrified of the steep path down the side of the plateau, but the lion at the front of her mind roared exultation. She landed with hands and feet, pumping hard, pouncing and leaping and racing toward those men in all their smelly, sour metal and boiled leather armor, who still hadn't turned around to face them.

Ash raced through them. Fang bounced off the soldiers. Several men shouted and immediately dropped their weapons and fled. Likely they had been among those soldiers who had come to Cecil's village, and they recognized Fang. Ash ignored the chaos erupting behind her, focused on the two wizards. They didn't even glance over their shoulders at the noise but kept their arms raised, pushing hard, draining themselves dry.

A man cursed off to her left. Ash didn't look, but she smelled him, heard him, felt him with all the triply alert nerves in her fur. She leaped, hitting both wizards, raking at their arms with her claws. She spun herself in mid-air, using their shoulders as pivots, and swept her body across them, knocking them both over while she rode them to the ground. Claws ripped into their robes. They gasped, stinking instantly of terror. Both raised their hands, the color of magic sparkling on their fingers changing to a greeny-yellow that filled her mouth with a taste like the stench of their fear. Ash laughed and caught the collars of their robes in each hand. She yanked them halfway to their feet as she stood, then slammed them down to the ground. Their heads made thuds like too-ripe melons. The magic died out in fizzles and sparks.

"Well, and what do we have here?" that man said from behind her. She smelled the tang of forged metal and the sweet-spicy aroma of magic coating his weapons. "The Beastly Beauty, in the flesh." He snorted as she turned to face him. "Idiots don't know the difference between a wolf and a lion."

"I am all beasts to meet all needs," Ash purred. "Ruprick, king of thieves?"

He stood up taller, bristling at the sneer in her voice. "I am King Ruprick of—"

"I know what you are! You'll not be taking what belongs to others. A'theosius denies your claims and I am here to bring—"

Dark green and gold magic flared in the canyon opening and a cold wind slammed into Ash's back, knocking her forward onto hands and knees. Her furious speech, borrowed from a book about heroes she had considered rather overblown and dramatic, until now, died on her lips.

She slid several yards, laughing as Ruprick tumbled backward, knocked out of his heroic pose. Sword and spear went flying, clattering and clanging. He turned a somersault, landing on his face. Ash got to her feet, staggering a little, dizzy from the force of the magical blow. She looked back over her shoulder and skidded to a stop.

Where there had been canyon walls and a zig-zagging passageway leading to the community of mirror-makers, there was now nothing but a vast, undulating sea of sand. Dust devils swirled up halfway to the sky, far in the distance. The horizon vanished in a haze of heat waves.

"No!" Ruprick shrieked, a good two octaves higher than his speaking voice. He struggled to get to his hands and knees.

Fang hit him, slamming him hard onto the sandy rock, making him bite his tongue.

Go! Go! Go! Fang bounced twice on Ruprick, squeezing out a few bleats. *Time. No time! Trap!*

"Ash, now!" Eyesallova called from the plateau above them.

"Get her," Ruprick whispered, spitting blood and looking at her cross-eyed.

Movement to the right. Several men stepped forward, aiming crossbows at her. Their bolts sparked with orange-tinted magic.

The lion wanted to leap at those men and slash them, knock them flat, take their crossbows in her jaws and splinter them. The girl behind the mask screamed for her to run. Fang had said trap—a trap for her? A magic trap?

Movement from the corner of her eye turned into three bolts streaking toward her, faster than thought. She leaped, snarling, two stories high. An exultant roar burst out of her as her hands and claws caught the edge of the plateau.

Fire bit into her hip, her thigh, her calf, making her shriek and gasp.

Icy jagged teeth dug into her flesh. A force pulled from behind those teeth. Her claws dragged on the stone, giving off sparks. Ash felt, she smelled, the magic chains attached to those crossbow bolts in her leg, pulling on her.

Sharp heat erupted from her chest as she roared and swung herself sideways, up onto the plateau. Again, the magic chains pulled, yanking her sideways and backward as she struggled to her feet. Ash swiped at the chains as Fang chattered and snarled behind her and men shrieked and bodies slammed loudly against the rock. That same sharpness and heat traveled from her chest, down her arm, slicing at the chains. Freeing her.

She staggered to her feet and lurched down the slope, toward the archway of the portal. The seneschal suit was setting the two hand mirrors in their padded box.

Another yank. The magic chains had reattached. Ash let out a furious sob and twisted sideways. Off balance, she threw herself forward, reaching for the wagon.

The bolt in her thigh tore loose, its barbed head taking a chunk of flesh as wide as her thumb with it. Ash gasped at the shock. She slapped her hand over the hole gushing blood and staggered forward.

Cold metal hands enclosed her arms. She snarled and struggled to free herself, to claw and punch. Her vision blurred and she blinked away hot tears and the haze of pain shock to see the helmet of the seneschal armor looming over her. Understanding, she went limp. She gasped for breath as the armor carried her the last few steps to the wagon. He tossed her in and climbed in beside her. He held onto her as the chains tried again to pull her back, out of the wagon. Into Ruprick's clutches.

The dozen yards to reach the archway of the portal felt like a dozen miles. Ash clutched at the armor's arms, bracing for the next yank.

It never came, though the crossbow bolts burned cold into her flesh. She held her breath as the wagon rolled through the portal. Fang bounced into the wagon, snarling, and dug his claws into the front of her shirt. Ash tried to weep, but the lion in the mask blocked tears.

The cold burn of magic halted with an abruptness as shocking and painful as when the crossbow bolts dug into her flesh. Ash shuddered. Fang's snarls turned to croons. He held onto her.

"Don't!" Eyesallova cried, as Ash reached up trembling hands to remove the mask. "You need it to start healing you. I'm sorry, dear, but you're bleeding something dreadful. Leave the mask on until we can get you home and bandaged. And we can pull those awful things out without hurting you worse."

Ash closed her eyes and focused on the beats of her heart and willed the pain to go away.

~~~~~

Ash dreamed. She knew she dreamed because she would never act so feather-headed while she was awake. Not even to save her life.

She giggled and skipped down long hallways and twirled around, watching her gossamer skirts sparkle in the lantern light. She fell back on thick couches and kicked her legs up so she could admire the glitter of light on the crystal beads on her dancing shoes. She skipped through a maze of roses and plucked petals off as she went, tossing them up in the air to shower down on herself. She sang silly songs full of "tra la las" and "deedle do dos," and other words that made absolutely no sense.

She sat on a high perch and giggled and tossed daisies down at men in armor who called up to her, pleading, flattering her, promising her sweets and jewels and asking her questions she didn't understand. From time to time, she ran away to a room full of crowns, some so ostentatious they were too heavy for her to lift from their shelves, others glittery and delicate, and she dithered over the crowns for what felt like hours before choosing a new one. Then she would giggle and dance and twirl down the halls again, until she came out onto her high perch. The men were still there, calling up to her, asking her to let them in, begging her to be a good girl and tell them how they could free her.

Free her? From what?

Dizziness wrapped around her, made her legs buckle. Maybe she was sitting too high? She waved goodbye to the men, generating shouts of dismay and more pleading for her to come back, talk to them, be a good girl and go down and open the door. What door? She didn't know where the door was. Then she went back to the crown room and chose another. The one she was wearing now made her head ache.

Fang caught her in the corridor. Ash laughed in delight at seeing him. She held out her arms. He leaped, hitting her square in the chest, knocking her against the wall.

Gasping, stunned, she slid down to the floor. Fang landed in her lap and reached up and yanked on her crown.

"No! Don't! Don't take my pretty away!" She wailed as he succeeded.

He bounced on her chest for good measure, knocking the air and the wail out of her.

Wake up, you stupid girl! You can't let them in.
~~~~~

"Let who in?" Ash winced, her head throbbing abominably.

Ruprick's men.

"Why would I let them in?" She opened one eye to find Fang leaning down so his nose almost touched hers.

Are you back now? I've been trying for three days to pull you loose from the castle. Are you yourself?

"Myself?" Ash straightened her arms and pushed herself upright. She felt prickly and slick material under her hands and got her eyes open again.

Gossamer material dusted with jewels covered her in a massive mound and puddled all around her on the floor. All in shades of pink. She hated pink. Wincing, she stretched out her leg, dreading what she would find. The movement sent a hot ache up her leg, but she forgot that as she glimpsed pink sparkly dancing slippers peeking out of the mounds of petticoats and silky skirts.

"It did it to me again. You did it to me again!" she shouted, then broke down coughing. She rested her head in her hands. Her face felt hot. Wet with sweat. Had she been feverish?

Ash caught her breath, wanting to spew at the realization that the dream hadn't been a dream. What had she been doing? Had Fang said three days?

"I'm back." She raked her fingers through her sweaty hair, which smelled of gardenia. She hated gardenia.

She didn't recognize the decorations on the walls or the color of the rugs on the floor. Where was she? Most likely the guest wing.

Getting to her feet, the throbbing in her leg brought back memories of facing down Ruprick. The arrogant thief had shot her! What kind of magic was in those crossbow bolts?

"Fang, help me get out of here?"

He hopped sedately beside her as she leaned on the wall and limped down the corridor. Ash felt somewhat dizzy when they finally came out onto the gallery. She sat down on a padded bench and caught her breath. Three days now, and she still hurt? What had gone wrong? Or were her injuries worse than she thought?

A clanking of metal on stone jolted her out of a drifting daze. Ash braced herself and rubbed her face. The seneschal armor approached. Furious at this latest interference from the castle, she blamed him. He kept trying to change her crowns, didn't he?

"Take me to Eyesallova." She didn't say please.

The armor bent and held out his arms without hesitating. She ached too much to enjoy that little bit of triumph properly.

"Did Fang succeed?" Eyesallova cried, as the armor carried Ash into the mirror room, and all the way to the padded bench directly in front of the mirror.

"Please, please, tell me I haven't been flirting with Ruprick's men," Ash said, once she had caught her breath. "Or worse, Ruprick." Amazing how exhausting pain could be. "How did they even follow us?"

"That rotter had tracking spells embedded in the crossbow bolts," Glint said.

"And backed them up with a spell that held the portal open once you passed through," Argent added.

"It appears the stories of the Beastly Beauty who rescues books have spread farther than we expected," Eyesallova said. "You were quite sick, dear. We didn't realize how sick, until you got out of bed and went out to taunt those men from the gate tower. It's quite embarrassing. You were most definitely not yourself. Such silliness and giggling and blowing them kisses and..." She made a high-pitched, disgusted sound.

"Please tell me I didn't invite them in?" Ash hid her face in her hands.

No. Stopped you. Castle helped. Fang chortled. *Kept making you change your crowns. Shouldn't have made you all fluttery and silly.*

Ash muffled a groan.

"I don't suppose we can just sit here and wait for them to get tired and run out of food and go away?" She swallowed hard and braced herself for more bad news. "Did Ruprick come with them?"

"Thank A'theosius, no," Eyesallova said. "But his men have strict orders to defeat the Beastly Beauty and drag her home to his menagerie, and rescue—bah! Rescue? We're the rescuers, not him! As I was saying, rescue the library and bring it to him. You've been so sparkly and silly, they haven't figured out that you and the Beastly Beauty are the same girl. Some of them are quite enamored of the fluffy little princess. We've been spying on them. They've decided they're going to rescue the princess and bring her to Ruprick to marry, and then he'll have full rights to the castle and all its contents."

"Will he?" she asked quietly.

"I don't think so," Glint sneered. "However, several prophecies make them think if their king can marry you, that will anchor the castle and bring it out into the real world again. And then Ruprick can annex the enchanted forest to Rathelshiffen and become the greatest king in the entire world."

"Not if I can help it."

"Well, yes, that's the general plan, dear," Eyesallova said.

"It's not that simple," Argent said. "I've been going through everything I can find in the library relating to the castle and the forest. There are too many prophecies, many of them contradictory. Meaning there are many possible futures, many different cures and means to anchor the castle again. The only consistent detail is that the forest will rejoin the standard flow of time."

"More important," Glint said, "we need to get those men out of the forest and through another portal before Ruprick's cut-rate magicians latch onto them and force the portal open. We managed to slide the magic wedges free and get the portal to close after the first dozen men got through. We don't want to risk Ruprick and his entire army coming in."

"So we have to get rid of them." Ash sighed and pushed herself upright. She had been starting to tilt to the right. "I have to get rid of them."

Us, Fang said, and thumped on her good thigh. *After you change your clothes.*

The first part of the plan was to have Fang go from one portal to another, using the partially charted map of the enchanted forest Ash had been compiling. He needed to determine which ones were open, which ones had been open the longest, meaning which ones were closest to closing.

The second part of the plan was for Ash to put on a mask, mostly for the healing properties of the animal's nature to finish mending her injuries. She would leave the castle and show herself to Ruprick's men and lead them on a merry chase, straight to the portal due to close the soonest. The tricky part was to get them to follow her through the portal without realizing it was a portal. Then she would come back through just before it closed, leaving them trapped in a foreign kingdom. Preferably so far away from Rathelshiffen it would take them months of travel to return to Ruprick.

Fang went out, carrying Argent transferred to a hand mirror. Argent had the map Ash had assembled, displayed on his larger body still sitting in the mirror room. As he and Fang went from portal to portal, he would mark the place and the strength of magic, and sense of time passing, on the map. When Fang returned, they would calculate Ash's route for the chase.

Meanwhile, Ash took a long soothing bath thick with healing herbs, packed her wounds with salve, bandaged them tight, and went to the mask room to pick the animal she would become to lead Ruprick's men on the chase. It had to be something fierce and swift, yet not so strong they would be frightened away, and not so easy to overcome that some would stay back at the castle and hope for another sighting of the flighty princess. She shuddered at the sight of the lion mask. She didn't want to go into that bloodthirsty mindset ever again.

The bear was too big, and lumbering. She knew she could be faster than the wind on ice, but how would she run through the forest, uphill and down?

That thought had her looking for a horse mask. No such creature.

Which might just be a good thing, because while unicorns were swift and fierce fighters with those horns, they were also somewhat flighty and fickle, easily captured by virgins. Not that any of Ruprick's men would be a trap for her, in that aspect.

A leopard? An eagle? Ash considered how hard it might be to learn to fly. How big would her wings have to be to let her fly? How easily could those bully boys of Ruprick's shoot her down?

She found another mask that was rather fierce and bird-like and wondered what it was, until she touched the red-tinted feathers trailing down its long neck. She pulled her hand away, her fingertips singed. A hot mask?

"Firebird," she whispered. "Or worse, a phoenix. I do not relish going up in flames if I'm injured or ..." She shook her head.

The wolf? She had felt most comfortable, the most like herself, the most fully alive while wearing the wolf mask. Granted, she had run into trouble when she fell asleep in the bath wearing the mask, but she could ask Fang to make sure she took it off. Maybe yank it off her, if she did fall asleep again while wearing it.

Yes, she could be a wolf again. She took the wolf mask with her when she returned to the mirror room. By that time, Fang had found four open portals. One had begun shifting and changing to the next portal while he was still there. Glint and Eyesallova were doing the calculations of which portal would close next, the sequence for closing all the portals, and the best choice for where to lead Ruprick's men. Close enough she wouldn't exhaust herself or lose any of them, but not so close, with so much time that the portal would stay open and allow them to return, once they realized what had happened.

CHAPTER TWENTY-EIGHT

Filby would enjoy hearing about this adventure. Thinking of Filby brought her up with a jolt. How long had she been here in the castle? How many years had passed, out in the real world? What did her friends think of her? Were they worried about the long silence from her, on their side of the portals?

Instead of taking the long nap she needed, Ash composed letters, just in case she failed in this mission. To Lady Charlotte. Filby. Cecil. Dunstan. Hazel. She thought about giving Dunstan instructions how to find the portal of roses and snow. More than a year had gone by back at Castle Fairhold, and he was out on his adventure. Wouldn't exploring the enchanted forest be the greatest adventure she could give him?

Then she remembered Eyesallova's cautions about people without magic in their blood, being harmed, affected by the forest and the castle.

If she was his friend, she couldn't do that to Dunstan. A fortnight here in the forest was more than a year of absence and silence back home in Alfordia. A decent adventure would require at least a month, maybe two. She couldn't do that to Lord Digory and Lady Beatrice, who had been good to her.

She amused herself with dreaming up a letter to Lathia, impressing on the arrogant twit that all the harm she had hoped to inflict had turned into great good fortune. Yes, Lathia would be a queen someday. If her husband's people didn't rise up in disgust and revolt. With Lathia's undeserved luck, she would turn out to be just the kind of queen those people wanted, and she would be much beloved. Ash wanted Lathia to know she had lost. That the nameless servant she thought to abuse for her amusement had been born with the potential for great power, a worthy custodian for all the secrets of the enchanted castle.

"Worthy," Ash whispered, as she ran the words through her mind. Was she proving herself worthy? Had she been formed for this destiny from the moment of conception? Friar Ipswich had certainly believed that was so for everyone, no matter how lowly or exalted their station, no matter how many or how few identifiable talents they possessed: everyone had a destiny, a task A'theosius had chosen specifically for them, and them for the task.

Had the castle used such heavy-handed methods to keep her here and form her into a princess because she resisted, instead of seeing this as great good fortune? Because she wanted to get away rather than prove herself worthy?

"I'm too tired. Maybe I'm so tired I'm wobbly philosophical," she whispered, and sighed laughter. Tired or not, the thought was in her head and she doubted she could avoid considering the idea again.

First, she had to lead Ruprick's men away from the castle, get them lost, and get them out of the forest before those magicians forced a portal open. If they figured out how to keep it open, Ruprick would have constant, uncontrolled access to the forest. If he managed that, how long would it take until he gathered enough magicians together to overcome the castle?

"A'theosius ... help me succeed. And if I don't succeed ... don't let the forest and castle suffer because of me?" she whispered.

She left her letters on the bench next to Eyesallova, without telling her what they were, and went out into the garden. Bella came to sit with her. She pressed her hands together against the side of her face, gesturing for Ash to go to sleep, then leaned back against the wall of the summer house and closed her eyes. Ash fell asleep to the whisper of the breeze through the vines and flowers, and the soft bubbling music of the spring.

Fang came for her, waking her by putting the wolf mask in her lap. Ash woke instantly, without startling. Bella was gone. Silently, she put on the mask. Her body changed more swiftly and easily than before, all her senses expanding, as she walked through the garden to the stairs to the balcony. Before she put her foot on the bottom step, the garden gates creaked open.

Was that a gift from the castle? She had considered how she would leave the castle without opening the gates and risking the soldiers getting in.

"Thank you," she said, and broke into a lope. Fang kept up with her, racing silently through the gates, around the castle. She came to the edge of the land surrounding the castle and leaped over the moat in one graceful bound.

In moments, she reached the camp of Ruprick's men. Such as it was, with just bedrolls and two fires and their horses picketed in the shade of the trees. The dozen men lounged about on the grass and moss on either side of the pebble pathway leading up to the moat and the drawbridge.

"Beauty! Princess beautiful," a man called in a singsong tone that indicated he had been calling so long he no longer cared what he was saying. "Please, beautiful maiden, come talk to us. Let us into the castle. Let us rescue you. Don't you want to be a queen?"

"No, she doesn't," Ash called.

When that didn't get their attention, she tipped her head back and howled. They all turned and gaped at her long enough Ash wondered if their brains had frozen in their pleading phase.

"Beast!" the tallest and widest of the men shouted. "Let the princess go! King Ruprick commands it!"

"He's not my king, and she's not a princess. Go back to that lying thief and tell him to stay away until he learns how to read the books he's been stealing." She turned her back on them and sauntered away, adding a wiggle to her backside that would have had her gagging in disgust just a year before.

If Ash had a tail, she would have flipped it at them. Maybe if she wore the wolf mask long enough, she would grow a tail?

Frightening thought. And somehow amusing.

The men shouted behind her. Some ordered her to come back and surrender to them.

Ash glanced over her shoulder. Several men had left the group, halfheartedly following her. That wouldn't do. She needed all of them.

She tried to remember all the rude gestures she had seen the servant boys making behind the backs of self-important fools like Camwell and Winston. That got some more shouts, a few more men moving toward her. Still, not enough.

They need a prize, Fang chirped from the shadows where he waited.

"A prize? This isn't a game …" Ash's eyes narrowed, and the wolf in the mask howled delight. Images of wolf games of chase and hunt and tumble flashed through her mind. Yes, she could use the wolf mind, the wolf idea of play.

"You bore me!" she called, and walked backward, watching the men. "Let's play a game. If you're man enough to try."

"What kind of game?" the leader shouted back.

"A wolf game. A beast game. The one who captures me wins the castle. All the magic stored in it. All the riches." Ash laughed as several men leaped forward, drawing swords, reaching for the spears propped against the trees by their horses. "Think of it. King of the enchanted forest, lord of the enchanted castle. More powerful than Ruprick." Another laugh. "And you can give him the silly, stupid girl."

Two men leaped at their fellows, knocking them down before dashing after her. The others scrambled to give chase. Ash howled and ran. Her injured leg throbbed once, threatening to fold. She pushed the pain away, and then she was part of the wind.

In moments, she had lost them, the sounds of their shouts and scuffling muted among the trees. That would not do. Ash curved back around. The portal closing the soonest was perhaps a mile away. She could run that in mere minutes. It would start closing in twenty, according to Fang. Better to lead the men farther away, make sure they were all following her, get them lost, get them frustrated. Give them time to think about what she offered them, stir them up and put their greed over their loyalty to and fear of Ruprick.

She came back around, approaching the castle from the other direction, and nearly ran into four men on horseback. So, they were smarter than she thought. She darted back into the trees and waited until they passed. She growled under her breath. The horses snorted and their ears flicked and they tossed their heads. They understood even if their riders were oblivious dolts.

When they passed her, Ash waited to be sure there weren't others behind them. She stepped out of the trees. Counted to five. Then she howled. The horses shrieked and two reared. Ash laughed and made sure the men saw her. Then she fled with the wind.

She doubled back, looking for the others, and changed the choice of portal again, until she had all the men following her, all on horseback. All cursing, some mocking the others, ordering her to give up, promising brutal punishment if she didn't obey. Ash burst out of the trees, to cross a meadow where Eyesallova had showed her deer dancing in the moonlight.

Unimpeded by trees and underbrush, the horses began to catch up with her. Ash waited until she felt the thunder of the hooves in the ground and the hot breath of the horses. Then, laughing, she doubled her pace, stretching her legs out with an ease that made her want to leap and dance.

Later. She would wait until later to dance.

More shouts and cursing rang out behind her. She reached the shelter of the trees on the other side of the meadow, ran a dozen steps, then leaped up into the branches. Ash perched on a high branch, shielded by the leaves, and caught her breath as the horses raced by underneath her. She counted until all of them had gone past. Then with a howl, she leaped down and stood, arms and legs spread, waiting until one head, then another, then another turned and the men saw her and fought to turn their horses and race after her.

The portal she wanted now stood on the edge of the bank of the Snarl River. Above the falls. Near the trees where the kispies nested. It was a risky choice. The kispies could decide she was the enemy just as much as the soldiers. But what fun if she evaded their notice and they tormented Ruprick's men with their tiny, sharp weapons. If they didn't drive the intruders through the portal, then perhaps they would send them over the falls?

Ash faltered for two steps at the thought of killing anyone, even if from several steps back. She shook her head. *Think about the moral conundrums later.*

What mattered now was staying ahead of these men, staying in their sight, keeping them chasing her, and most important of all, finding the portal. Timing wouldn't be worth anything if she couldn't find it at the proper moment to lead the soldiers through it. Fang had reported that this current portal opening led out onto another riverbank. They wouldn't realize the change from enchanted forest to outside world until it was too late.

If she worked this right.

This first attempt had to succeed. She couldn't keep running all day. There were limits even to the wolf strength and endurance and fleetness, and she didn't want to discover what it was at the most inconvenient time.

She led her pursuers down a shallow slope into a narrow valley that ran between two hills that eventually grew into cliffs, then spilled out onto the plain beside the Snarl River. They had finally given up shouting after her, ordering her to stop, taunting her with punishment, and even mocking each other for their hopes of capturing her.

Ahead was the river. On the other side, among those scraggly pines, lay the portal. Were Ruprick's soldiers alert enough to look ahead and notice the difference in landscape on the other side of the trees? More important, would she find it in time, to avoid racing up and down the bank, searching?

Ash studied the riverbank as she ran, and nearly stepped into a rabbit hole. She snarled at her obliviousness and leaped forward faster. Get to the riverbank, cross it, then look around. She didn't need to fall, maybe break a bone, and be captured. Ash didn't want to find out that she was already so much the lady of the castle, yes, one of these bully brutes would win it from her, simply because she said so.

And hadn't Cecil and Friar Ipswich both told her that gambling and games of chance were fools' toys and traps?

"A'theosius … Please. Just … please," Ash gasped out, and picked up the pace, stretching her legs out even farther, as she approached the riverbank.

She leaped, gathering her legs under herself, reaching forward with her arms, willing herself to fly. She hit the riverbank with her hands and somersaulted, twice, going crooked and spinning around but somehow managing to land on her feet. She staggered back, gasping, laughing, and turned to look for the soldiers.

Two leaped the bank. Their horses' hind feet landed in the river. Three more leaped, stumbling but landing on solid ground. Another horse mis-stepped and went down into the water halfway across. Ash backed away, keeping her gaze on the men as they regathered. From the way they looked around, they had lost her among the pines. She wouldn't gamble on how much time she had.

A glimmer of pale blue light caught her attention. Her fingertips tingled, at the roots of her claws. She felt that tingle when she handled books that were exceptionally heavy with magic. The portal was near. Ash stretched out her hand, letting the tingle guide her. The glimmer of blue light deepened, and through two tall pines, where their branches intersected, she saw deepening shadows. On the riverbank behind her, the coming of night painted the sky orange and crimson and gold and purple. There was no sun to set. Through those trees, she saw a crescent of sun just above the horizon.

"Got you!" a man shouted, lunging off his horse. His hand snagged on the shoulder of her sleeveless leather shirt. Ash snarled and turned her head to bite. He shrieked and she leaped away, heart racing too hard to let her laugh.

More footsteps and shouts. She ran out into the brighter daylight, ready to dodge and duck. Hooves nearly raced up her back. She rolled, under the legs of the horse, and pulled herself up on its stirrup. The rider shouted and swung a sword at her. Ash caught his wrist and swung herself up into the saddle behind him. He shrieked agony as she twisted his arm behind his back. His hand spasmed, releasing the sword. She snagged it before it fell and clubbed him across the back of the head with the hilt. Clutching him, she grabbed the reins and dug her heels into the horse's side and turned it to the portal.

Men shouted. Hoofbeats pounded. Ash held her breath as the horse leaped through the portal. She kept it running, counting twenty steps before she leaped off, kicking hard at the man so he fell, unconscious, from the saddle. On this side of the portal, everything was twilight. She melted into the shadows. A second horse came through. A third. A fourth. Then a long pause, when no more came in.

Crouching low, she crept back to the portal and stepped through. She gasped, trying to muffle the sound. The effort to get back through startled her. So, the theory of tides in the portals was true. Traveling one direction was easy, like breathing, but try to cross back through too soon and she could drown. Would that resistance be enough to stop the men, once they were all through?

How much time until the portal closed altogether?

The other men were busy getting their fellows out of the water where their horses hadn't been able to make the leap. All of them were on this side of the river. Now, to get their attention and get them all to go through.

Ash stepped out into the full daylight and crouched, making herself as small as possible, waiting, watching. How to make them think she was trying to hide from them, so they wouldn't realize she led them through the portal until it was too late?

The wolf wanted to race out and leap on them, take the men down, off their horses' backs, one by one.

A new throbbing crept into her awareness. Tingling magic. She turned her head, just enough to see the slight pulse in the blue magic edging the portal. Brighter, then dimmer. Slow, but enough to catch the change.

Time was running out.

Fun. Fun. Fun. Fang hopped down next to her, nearly startling a yelp out of her. He crouched low, ears twitching with excitement, eyes bright. *My turn now?*

"Doing what?" she asked. "We're running out of time. The portal is going to close. I don't know how soon."

Chase! He leaped up, bouncing high enough he nearly hit several branches of the trees around them. Shrieking, he bounced out to meet the mounted men.

Bounced past them. Got behind them. Leaped at them, bouncing off their backs and their horses' rumps. Made the horses shriek and bolt.

Fang wasn't getting them to chase him—he was chasing them.

Straight toward Ash. She held still, waiting, as time seemed to slow.

The front horse was maybe ten galloping steps away from her. She leaped to her feet as if frightened and raced into the trees. Men shouted. Several horses collided but kept running. Ash ran for the portal. The pulsing was faster. The dimness deeper in the low spots. Resistance slapped her so she faltered, just for a heartbeat, as she flung herself into the portal. She caught her breath.

Then she was through.

And slammed face-first into a horse's flank. Hands scrabbled at her, tangling in her thick curls. Ash snarled and bit and dug her claws into the horse. It reared. The man fell but didn't let go until he had almost pulled her down on top of him.

The other horses and men coming through the portal nearly trampled them. Ash rolled and staggered to her feet. A horse careened toward her. She rolled under its belly, out between its leg, and darted aside as another nearly knocked her aside. Men shouted and horses screamed and swords swung. The scent of blood streaked the air. Men cursed and swung at each other, searching for the one who sliced them. Ash scrambled backward, fighting the need to curl up, into herself, and cover her head and pray none of them saw her.

The wolf snarled to flee, but she had to linger. Long enough to ensure all the soldiers were through the portal.

But how long was too long?

The pulsing of magic slowed. The pauses longer, so for a few heartbeats Ash thought they had stopped altogether and she was trapped.

Fang screamed from the other side. *Come! Come! Come!*

Were all the soldiers through?

What did it matter if she got trapped here with them?

Ash ran. A man shouted. The magic around the portal lit up, so faint she wouldn't have seen it without shadows around it. Ash screamed in her heart for A'theosius and leaped. The air was thick around her, resisting, trying for a moment to push her back out.

Then she was through, rolling on the riverbank. Fire slammed into her shoulder and she rolled again, shrieking as the shaft of the arrow snapped, and landing pushed the arrowhead deeper into her flesh. Gasping, fighting not to gag from the shock, Ash pushed herself onto her face. She lay still, afraid to move, knowing she might need to run at any moment.

Hurt. Fang crooned and nudged her temple with his nose. *Go. Kispies heard. Lots of blood spilled. They like blood.*

Holding her breath, fighting not to sob, she levered her good arm under herself and pushed upright, sideways.

Odd. She didn't smell blood. Ash braced for that first jolt of pain and reached with her good hand to touch the wound in her shoulder. It was dry. There was a tear in the leather of her shirt. No blood. Her claw snagged on something, an indentation in her skin. She probed a little deeper, waiting for that pain, that gush of blood.

Wait. Where was the arrow shaft? She had felt it snap and break off. Ash probed tenderly at the indentation, catching on something … hard? She looked around and saw charred bits of stick. A charred portion of fletching. Had the arrow burned?

"Fang? What do you see?" She gestured at her shoulder.

Burned. Something in you. Burned.

"What's on the other side of the portal?"

Fang hopped away to look. He came back quickly, nose quivering, eyes bright with pleasure. *Snow!*

"We're safe." She relaxed, and felt the something in her shoulder catch, but it didn't exactly hurt. Not as if it was a fresh wound. If the arrow had burned, maybe from passing through the portal as it closed, then maybe the arrowhead had burned and sealed the wound before she could bleed?

Ash wanted to curl up right there and sleep. Maybe cry a little. When the wolf mask was off.

She knew better. The kispies would come soon, attracted by the blood the soldiers had spilled as they chased her and fought each other over which one would capture the Beastly Beauty. She got to her feet and walked up the riverbank, away from the trees and the falls, to a place she knew on the map where a pretty little arched bridge of stones would let her cross without needing to leap or strain or get her feet wet. Walking made her arm hurt, reminding her with every gentle swing that she had an arrowhead, however burned down, in her shoulder. Trying to stop the movement just made it worse.

When the enchanted castle appeared in front of her, pushing through the narrow valley and warping it to make room, Ash nearly went to her knees, tears in her eyes. And laughing. Why did anything the castle did still surprise her?

Still, this proof that it followed her made her want to laugh and cry.

She stepped through the gates and the armor met her with a tray of salve and bandages, clean clothes, and an enormous bucket of hot water. One picked her up, cradling her like a baby. They carried her up to the mirror room, and stood at attention, perhaps like an honor guard, as the seneschal dug the burned arrowhead out of her shoulder and treated her wound. Then Ash took the mask off. She gasped, all the aches in her body shouting loudly enough to bring tears. She was tempted to just go headfirst into that bucket of hot water. She stood behind a screen painted with a cluster of dragons twining around each other, washed and changed her clothes, and discussed the chase and hunt with the mirrors. They were proud of her but scolded her for worrying them. Eyesallova scolded her for leaving letters to be delivered to her friends if anything happened to her. Ash was too tired to be irritated or to laugh. She ate her dinner and curled up to sleep in a makeshift bed of cushioned benches pushed together. Some time during the night, the housekeeping breezes brought pillows and blankets and adjusted the bed around her, and she never woke.

When she woke, she was still on the bench bed. Still in the clothes she had worn to sleep. The castle hadn't interfered.

"Now we're learning to get along," she murmured. "All right now, what should we do to make sure something like yesterday never happens again?"

THE END

About the Author

On the road to publication, Michelle fell into fandom in college and has 40+ stories in various SF and fantasy universes. She has a bunch of useless degrees in theater, English, film/communication, and writing. Even worse, she has over 100 books and novellas with multiple small presses, in science fiction and fantasy, YA, suspense, women's fiction, and sub-genres of romance.

Her official launch into publishing came with winning first place in the Writers of the Future contest in 1990. She was a finalist in the EPIC Awards competition multiple times, winning with *Lorien* in 2006 and *The Meruk Episodes, I-V,* in 2010, and was a finalist in the Realm Awards competition, in conjunction with the Realm Makers convention.

Her training includes the Institute for Children's Literature; proofreading at an advertising agency; and working at a community newspaper. She is a tea snob and freelance edits for a living (MichelleLevigne@gmail.com for info/rates), but only enough to give her time to write. Her newest crime against the literary world is to be co-managing editor at Mt. Zion Ridge Press and launching the publishing co-op, Ye Olde Dragon Books. Be afraid … be very afraid.

And please check out her newest venture: Ye Olde Dragon's Library, the storytelling podcast. Interspersed between the chapters will be interviews with authors of fantastical fiction. Listen to the podcast on your favorite podcast app or listen on the website: www.YeOldeDragonBooks.com, and click on the Ye Olde Dragon's Library link. Then go to her blog to interact: www.MichelleLevigne.blogspot.com

www.Mlevigne.com
www.MichelleLevigne.blogspot.com
www.YeOldeDragonBooks.com
www.MtZionRidgePress.com

NEWSLETTER:

Want to learn about upcoming books, book launch parties, inside
information, and cover reveals?
Go to Michelle's website or blog to sign up.

Thanks for reading!
**If you enjoyed this book, would you help Michelle by posting a
review on Goodreads?**

**Are you a member of Book Bub? If so, please follow Michelle on Book
Bub, and you'll get alerts when new books are coming out.**

**As a way of saying thanks, Michelle invites you to the Goodies page
on her website. It will change regularly, offering you a free short story,
a sample audiobook chapter, sneak peeks at new cover art, inside
information on discounts and new release dates, etc.**

Please go to: Mlevigne.com/good-stuff.html

Also by Michelle L. Levigne

Guardians of the Time Stream: 4-book Steampunk series
The Match Girls: Humorous inspirational romance series starting with **A
Match (Not) Made in Heaven**
Sarai's Journey: A 2-book biblical fiction series
Tabor Heights: 18-book inspirational small town romance series.
Quarry Hall: 11-book women's fiction/suspense series
For Sale: Wedding Dress. Never Used: inspirational romance
Crooked Creek: Fun Fables About Critters and Kids: Children's short
stories.
Do Yourself a Favor: Tips and Quips on the Writing Life. A book of
writing advice.
To Eternity (and beyond): *Writing Spec Fic Good for Your Soul.* A book
defending speculative fiction.
Killing His Alter-Ego: contemporary romance/suspense, taking place in
fandom.
The Commonwealth Universe: SF series, 25 books and growing
The Hunt: 5-book YA fantasy series
Faxinor: Fantasy series, 4 books and growing
Wildvine: Fantasy series, 14 books when all released
Neighborlee: Humorous fantasy series
Zygradon: 5-book Arthurian fantasy series
AFV Defender: SF adventure series

Young Defenders: Middle Grade SF series, spin-off of *AFV Defender*
Magic to Spare: Fantasy series
Book & Mug Mysteries: cozy mystery series
Quest for the Crescent Moon: fantasy series
Steward's World: fantasy series reboot and expansion
The Enchanted Castle Archives: fantasy series